P9-DKF-618

PRAISE FOR
ANNE GRACIE AND HER NOVELS

"[A] confection that brims with kindness and heartfelt sincerity. . . . You can't do much better than Anne Gracie, who offers her share of daring escapes, stolen kisses and heartfelt romance in a tale that carries the effervescent charm of the best Disney fairy tales."   —*Entertainment Weekly*

"I never miss an Anne Gracie book."
—*New York Times* bestselling author Julia Quinn

"For fabulous Regency flavor, witty and addictive, you can't go past Anne Gracie."
——*New York Times* bestselling author Stephanie Laurens

"With her signature superbly nuanced characters, subtle sense of wit and richly emotional writing, Gracie puts her distinctive stamp on a classic Regency plot."
—*Chicago Tribune*

"Will keep readers entranced. . . . A totally delightful read!"
—RT Book Reviews

"The always terrific Anne Gracie outdoes herself with *Bride by Mistake*. . . . Gracie created two great characters, a high-tension relationship and a wonderfully satisfying ending. Not to be missed!"
—*New York Times* bestselling author Mary Jo Putney

"A fascinating twist on the girl-in-disguise plot. . . . With its wildly romantic last chapter, this novel is a great antidote to the end of summer."
—*New York Times* bestselling author Eloisa James

"Anne Gracie's writing dances that thin line between always familiar and fresh. . . . *The Accidental Wedding* is warm and sweet, tempered with bursts of piquancy and a dash or three of spice."   —New York Journal of Books

"Threaded with charm and humor. . . . [An] action-rich, emotionally compelling story. . . . It is sure to entice readers."
—*Library Journal* (starred review)

"Another [of] Ms. Gracie's character-rich, fiery tales filled with emotion and passion leavened by charm and wit."
—Romance Reviews Today

"The main characters are vibrant and complex. . . . The author's skill as a storyteller makes this well worth reading."
—*Kirkus Reviews*

"A well-plotted, richly emotional and delightful read, this Regency novel brims with wonderful characters and romance."
—Shelf Awareness

Marry
in
Scarlet

ANNE GRACIE

JOVE
New York

A JOVE BOOK
Published by Berkley
An imprint of Penguin Random House LLC
penguinrandomhouse.com

Copyright © 2020 by Anne Gracie
Penguin Random House supports copyright. Copyright fuels creativity, encourages
diverse voices, promotes free speech, and creates a vibrant culture. Thank you for buying
an authorized edition of this book and for complying with copyright laws by not
reproducing, scanning, or distributing any part of it in any form without permission.
You are supporting writers and allowing Penguin Random House to continue to
publish books for every reader.

A JOVE BOOK, BERKLEY, and the BERKLEY & B colophon
are registered trademarks of Penguin Random House LLC.

ISBN: 9781984802064

First Edition: May 2020

Printed in the United States of America
3   5   7   9   10   8   6   4   2

Cover art by Judy York
Cover design by Sarah Oberrender
Book design by Kristin del Rosario

This is a work of fiction. Names, characters, places, and incidents either are the product
of the author's imagination or are used fictitiously, and any resemblance to actual persons,
living or dead, business establishments, events, or locales is entirely coincidental.

If you purchased this book without a cover, you should be aware that this book is stolen
property. It was reported as "unsold and destroyed" to the publisher, and neither the author
nor the publisher has received any payment for this "stripped book."

*To the Word Wenches—Mary Jo Putney, Patricia Rice,
Nicola Cornick, Andrea Penrose, Joanna Bourne,
Susan King and Susanna Kearsley—with whom I blog
each fortnight, and who provide ongoing friendship,
support and encouragement. Thank you.*

Chapter One

❧

It is a truth universally acknowledged, that a single man in possession of a good fortune, must be in want of a wife.
—JANE AUSTEN, *PRIDE AND PREJUDICE*

AGATHA, LADY SALTER, TAPPED HER FOOT IMPATIENTLY AND glanced at the ormolu clock on the mantelpiece. Twenty-six—no, twenty-seven minutes he had kept her waiting. So far.

Young people nowadays. No manners at all.

But she would not allow the duke's rag-mannered behavior to distract her from her purpose. What was that line again? *It is a fact, widely understood* . . . No, that wasn't it. *It is a truth*—yes, that was it, a *truth*.

It is a truth universally acknowledged, that a single duke in possession of a large fortune, must be in want of a bride. That was the line. A very sensible observation to commence a very silly book.

Young gels deciding for themselves who they would marry or not. Ridiculous!

Had it not been for the commonsensical actions of an aunt, that foolish, stubborn Elizabeth would have whistled an excellent marriage down the wind. But her aunt had saved the day when she'd taken the gel to visit the young fellow's estate. That had made the foolish gel sit up and take notice.

Lady Salter glanced at the clock again. Twenty-nine

minutes. Disgraceful. She'd expected he might be reluctant to see her. But that was no excuse for tardiness.

He'd been more or less jilted at the altar—a little pique was understandable. Young men had their pride. But it had not been, after all, a love match. It was an arranged marriage between her beautiful niece Lady Rose Rutherford and the Duke of Everingham, the catch of the season. The *match* of the season.

Weeks of careful strategy on her part to get the two together. And when the betrothal was announced, she had basked in universal admiration. While it lasted.

Rose had let her down badly. A secret marriage! And to the veriest nobody. A scarecrow returned from the dead, ragged and dirty, in the middle of the ceremony! An absolute disgrace. It didn't bear thinking about.

But she would not admit defeat.

The door to the sitting room opened. The duke stood in the doorway. Finally!

Lady Salter looked up and inclined her head graciously. "Good afternoon, Redmond." She'd known him since he was in short coats. The use of "Redmond" rather than his title was to remind him of the fact.

Redmond Jasper Hartley, the fifth Duke of Everingham, strolled into the room. He'd kept her waiting a good half hour but he made no apology. He bowed over her hand and said in a bored voice, "Lady Salter, how do you do?" His cold gray gaze was indifferent.

Lady Salter came straight to the point. "I understand my niece has apologized for her disgraceful behavior."

He raised a dark brow. "Niece?" As if he had no idea to whom she was referring.

Her lips thinned. So he was still angry. Coldly furious, under the indifferent-seeming facade, if she was not mistaken. Pride was one thing, incivility to his elders quite another. Besides, she was as much a victim of Rose's carelessness as he.

"I refer to Lady Rose Rutherford, as you very well know. She came here last week, I believe, to apologize."

The duke strolled to the window and stood looking out,

his back to her. After a moment he said in a tight voice, "Is there a purpose to this visit, Lady Salter?"

"You are still in want of a bride."

He stilled, then turned slowly to face her and in an arctic voice said, "And if I am, madam, what business is it of yours?"

Lady Salter lifted her chin and said what she had come here to say. "I have another niece."

He didn't move. His expression was carved in ice.

She continued, "She is also, of course, the daughter of an earl, though her mother was of the yeoman class. Georgiana herself is young, attractive, healthy and—"

"Ambitious."

She blinked. "Not in the least—quite the contrary, in fact. She has—"

"All her teeth too, I'm sure. A picture of perfection, no doubt, but I'm not interested."

She glared at him.

His lip curled and he continued with silken insolence, "We are not at Tattersalls, Lady Salter. There is no need to act the coper and enumerate your niece's various qualities. I am not interested in furthering either her ambitions or yours."

She bristled. Likening her to a horse coper indeed! "You forget yourself, young man—duke or not. Your mother would be appalled." His mother was her goddaughter, as well as a friend.

He glanced pointedly at the clock.

His indifference was infuriating, as was his assumption that she was ambitious for her niece. She was, of course— Georgiana had no sense at all of where her duty lay—but the duke could not know that. He and Georgiana had barely even met. She doubted they'd exchanged a dozen words. It was yet another situation where an aunt was needed to step in and take control.

"Your mother and I—"

"—will, in future, kindly keep your noses out of my business. I've had enough of your interference." In two paces he crossed the room and yanked on the bellpull. "Good day to you, madam."

Interference? Madam? She almost choked on her indignation. Such ingratitude toward one who'd worked tirelessly—selflessly!—to arrange a suitable marriage for him.

The butler appeared in the doorway. The duke said, "Lady Salter is leaving, Fleming."

Lady Salter rose and with great dignity stalked toward the door. As she reached it her temper got the better of her. She turned and in an icy voice said, "I was mistaken in thinking you and Georgiana would suit, Redmond. Far from being ambitious to marry you"—she gave a scornful huff—"the truth is, Georgiana did her level best to dissuade Rose from marrying you—"

"Wanted me for herself, no doubt."

"Your arrogance is misplaced, sirrah! Far from wanting you, she was quite vocal in her dislike of you—and I see now she has a point. In any case the ridiculous child has declared far and wide that she would rather live with dogs and horses than marry."

That silenced him, she could see. She added, with crisp satisfaction, "I had thought, your grace, that marriage to a young woman of good family, an independently minded young woman who would not hang off your sleeve, a girl who wants nothing more than to retire to a country estate and be left to breed horses, dogs—and possibly children—would be exactly what you required. A wife who would keep out of your way and give you no trouble." She paused to let that sink in. It was exactly the kind of wife he'd described back when Rose was the bride being considered.

She made an airily dismissive gesture. "Even so, it would have taken all my considerable powers of persuasion to coax Georgiana to wed you."

His eyes grew flintier, and she added with barely concealed relish, "I would not be surprised if we'd had to *drag* her to the altar in the end. My niece is a headstrong gel who disdains the advice of her elders and betters. You, sir, are equally stubborn. Almost, I think, you deserve each other, but since you both lack a proper attitude to marriage—and to *me!*—I wash my hands of you." She sailed from the room in high dudgeon.

"I'M NOT AT HOME," HART TOLD HIS BUTLER AFTER LADY Salter had left. "Not to anyone."

The news of his aborted wedding had spread like wildfire through the ton. His doorbell had been jangling constantly ever since, with women—ladies of the ton—eager to soothe his injured feelings and shove him straight back into the marital noose, if not with themselves, then with their daughter or niece or granddaughter.

To hell with them all. He'd had it with women—no, not with women, with *ladies.*

He tried to resume his correspondence, but the annoyance lingered. What the devil business of anyone else's was it whether he married or not? He knew he needed to get an heir, but what was the hurry? He wasn't yet thirty. And just because he'd been brought up to the mark once didn't mean he was ready to do it again, dammit.

Because look how well that had ended.

A few days before, his erstwhile bride had called on him, supposedly to apologize, but then she had the cheek to invite him to the ball that had been planned to celebrate his wedding. Its purpose now was to celebrate her husband's return from the dead, blast him. Hart had nothing against the fellow, but why the devil hadn't he come back from the dead a week or two earlier and saved them all a lot of fuss and botheration?

He narrowed his eyes. Now he came to think of it, he had met the girl Lady Salter had just tried to foist on him. Lady Georgiana Rutherford had accompanied Rose on that little errand. A long-legged, dark-haired wench, with more than a dash of impudence.

She'd pulled her skirts up to warm her legs at the fire. Dropped them, cool as you please, when he'd entered the room, not embarrassed in the least. A hoyden, if not a light-skirt.

Damned fine ankles, as he recalled.
She would rather live with dogs and horses.
He snorted. She was welcome to them.

"*WHAT?*" LADY GEORGIANA RUTHERFORD COULD HARDLY believe her ears. "You offered *me* to that . . . that . . . *duke?* Like a . . . a cake on a plate? Without even consulting me?"

George was taking afternoon tea in the drawing room with her uncle, Cal; his wife, Emm; and her two great-aunts: the sweet one and the sour one. The sweet one, Aunt Dottie, was knitting haphazardly in between poring over a dish of jam tarts and sipping her tea. Her sister, Aunt Agatha, sat like an offended poker, looking down her nose at them all, disdaining the offerings before her.

Cal, lounging on the settee beside his wife, chuckled. "Like a cake on a plate, George? More like a hedgehog in a bag." He bit into an almond biscuit.

George ignored him. She glared at Aunt Agatha. "How dare you go behind my back and make such a . . . such an offer?"

Aunt Agatha made a dismissive gesture. "Well, *someone* must make a push to find you a husband, and Emmaline is otherwise occupied breeding The Heir. Besides, since Rose's disgraceful behavior left the duke embarrassed at the altar, this family owes him reparation."

"Possibly, but we don't owe him *me!*"

The old lady set down her teacup with a snap. "If a duke is going spare, my gel, it doesn't do to dally!"

"But I don't *want* a duke! I don't want a husband *at all!* I've said so repeatedly. And even if I did, Everingham would be the last man I'd consider!" George didn't know what it was about the Duke of Everingham, but he . . . he irritated her with his cold, hard gaze, so indifferent and superior and I-rule-the-world. She longed to take him down a peg.

"Nonsense! Every gel needs a husband. And, all appearances to the contrary, you *are* the daughter of an earl and need to marry and be a credit to your family."

The flat dismissal of her views infuriated George. "Not me. I don't want a husband, I don't need one and I won't have you or anyone else arranging one for me."

"Don't be ridiculous, child."

"It's not ridiculous and I'm not a child. I'm almost twenty and—"

"And well past the age you were married and off your aunt's and uncle's hands. Ashendon and Emmaline are starting their own family." Aunt Agatha gestured to Emm's swollen belly, then trained her lorgnette on her rebellious great-niece.

George put up her chin and glared back. She wasn't sure whether the old lady actually needed the eyeglass to see with, or whether it was just her chosen weapon of intimidation. Whatever the reason, George would not be intimidated.

Aunt Agatha continued, "Ashendon's sisters are now married—in however scrambled a fashion—and their future is taken care of. There is only yourself remaining—an ill-mannered, unfeminine, ignorant, tomboyish hoyden with no idea of ladylike or even polite behavior—and worse!— no interest in acquiring it. You should be grateful that I'm taking an interest in your future."

"*Grateful?* For unwarranted and unasked-for interference?" George was ready to explode. The insults stung; there was no denying there was some truth in them, but she would never let Aunt Agatha get the better of her.

"You cannot expect your uncle and his wife to care indefinitely for his late brother's unwanted and unacknowledged offspring—especially a gel who's more trouble than she's worth. A charitable gesture is one thing, an embarrassing millstone quite another."

Emm sat up angrily. "George is *not* a millstone, Aunt Agatha! Nor is she an embarrassment. She's a dear sweet girl and a beloved member of our family and as far as I am concerned she can live with us until . . . until she's a hundred years old!" She reached out a hand to Cal and he took it, a silent gesture of support.

Aunt Agatha gave a dismissive wave. "That is your condition speaking, Emmaline. Breeding women are notoriously hysterical." She turned to Cal. "You see? Yet again Georgiana is causing your wife distress. And endangering The Heir."

"I'm not the one upsetting people," George muttered.

"Now look here, Aunt Agatha," Cal began.

"Oh, don't worry, Cal," George said. "I know better than to mind the spiteful outpourings of an interfering, officious, presumptuous old b—"

"George," Emm said in a warning tone. George glanced at her and bit off the remainder of the insults she had stored away. She would cross swords with Aunt Agatha any day, but upsetting Emm was another matter.

Aunt Agatha drew herself up, an outraged silver-haired praying mantis. "Abominable gel! Never in my life have I been subjected to such disgraceful incivility from a chit not yet in her majority. And from a member of my own family!"

"If the cap fits, wear it," George said sweetly. "In any case, I won't be on Cal and Emm's hands forever. The minute I turn twenty-five and get my inheritance, I'll be out of here and nobody need bother about me at all."

Aunt Agatha primmed her lips. "More than five years to wait, then. A young married couple should not have to endure the company of—"

"I've asked and asked Cal to arrange for an allowance to be paid to me, an advance on my inheritance. He always refuses, but if I had it, I'd be gone and out of their hair in an instant."

"Precisely why I won't do it," Cal said firmly. "There's no question of enduring anything or anyone, Aunt Agatha. Emm and I are very fond of George and, as Emm said, she's welcome to live with us as long as she likes."

"Exactly! We love you, George, and there's no question of your being in the way," Emm said. "Now, please, let us all enjoy our tea and stop squabbling."

At the word *tea* George's dog, Finn, rose and sat down beside Cal, fixing the half-eaten biscuit in Cal's hand with a mournful gaze.

George frowned and said in a low voice, "I do cause you trouble. You can't deny it, Cal."

Cal exchanged a glance with his wife and smiled a slow smile. "Let us say, rather, that you enliven an otherwise relatively humdrum existence." Then as Finn nudged him, he added, "You and your enormous hound, I meant. And, no, Finn, this is *my* biscuit and is not for dogs." He finished it in two crunches. Finn slid to the floor with a dejected sigh.

Emm nodded. "The house is going to feel so empty with both Lily and Rose gone. We couldn't do without you, George."

George glanced at the mound of Emm's belly. The house wouldn't be empty for long. Or dull. The baby would take up all Emm's time and attention then. "I *will* leave when I'm twenty-five."

"We'll talk about that when the time comes," Cal said. "Nobody is going to force you into matrimony, George, but I don't want you living alone."

"Why not? I did for most of my life." Except for her faithful Martha.

"A situation I deeply regret," Cal said grimly. "Henry should have been shot for his lack of care for you. And for keeping your existence a secret from us all for so long. But you are part of this family now, and so you will remain."

"I can never decide which I like better, the plum tarts or the strawberry ones," Aunt Dottie said into the silence that followed. "Of course the marmalade ones are very nice, but I always think red jam is such a happy flavor, don't you agree?"

The tense atmosphere eased.

Aunt Agatha set down her teacup with a clatter. "Pshaw! If that's your attitude, I wash my hands of you."

"But the red jam *is* the sweetest, Aggie dear. There's no need to get upset about it," Aunt Dottie said. She winked at George.

"I'm not talking about the jam, as you very well know, Dorothea. Marriage is the only option for a gel of our order." She trained her lorgnette on her sister. "We've already got one failure in the family, we don't need another."

"Aunt Dottie is not a failure—" Emm and George began at the same time.

Aunt Dottie chuckled. "Don't worry, my dears, Aggie always takes a swipe at someone when she's thwarted or put out in any way. It doesn't bother me in the least." She offered her sister the plate of tarts. "Try one of these, Aggie; they really are very good. They might even sweeten your tongue."

Aunt Agatha waved them away. "You eat too many of those things. No wonder you're so fat!"

"She's not fat," George said hotly. Aunt Dottie was plump and cuddly and George couldn't imagine her any other way. Wouldn't *want* her any other way.

"See?" Aunt Dottie twinkled at George. "She's annoyed, so she takes it out on the nearest person, usually me. Just like a wasp, poor thing. It's been like that ever since we were children in the nursery. I take no notice of her crotchets and you shouldn't either." She pored over a small dish of sweet-meats and selected one carefully. "Life is to be enjoyed, Aggie, and I enjoy every bit of mine. Do you?" She popped the sweet in her mouth and placidly resumed knitting.

There was a short silence, broken only by the sound of teaspoons clinking against teacups and the sound of crunching from behind the sofa. Emm raised her brow at George, who shook her head and looked at Cal, who tried to look innocent.

Avoiding his wife's eye, he said, "Well, Aunt Agatha, don't keep us in suspense—how did the duke respond to your proposal?"

George swallowed, feeling suddenly hollow. He couldn't possibly have agreed to it—could he? She hadn't given any thought to the duke's reaction—she was only thinking of her aunt's interference.

"He refused, of course, in no uncertain terms. No gentleman," she added with thinly disguised satisfaction, "would want an ill-trained, boyish, impertinent hoyden for a wife."

"Did he say that?" George flashed indignantly. "In so many words?"

Aunt Agatha arched a sardonic eyebrow. "What did you expect? That he wouldn't notice your many inadequacies? I did my best, but . . ." She shook out her skirt, took hold of her ebony cane and rose. "I have other calls to make. Good day to you all. Ashendon . . ."

Cal rose and escorted his aunt from the room.

An ill-trained, boyish, impertinent hoyden. "How dare he! How dare she!" George jumped up and began to pace around the room. She didn't know who she was angriest with—Aunt Agatha or the Duke of Everingham. She could happily shoot them both.

The knowledge that Aunt Agatha had offered her to him—and that he'd rejected her—even though she emphatically didn't want him!—made her squirm with humiliation.

"It's not for him to reject me! It's for me to reject him." The thought that she hadn't had the chance to, that he had rejected her, unasked, was both mortifying and infuriating.

"He's rather handsome, though, isn't he?" Aunt Dottie had only seen him at the church, at his aborted wedding to Rose. "I do rather like a tall, dark, moody-looking man."

"Handsome, perhaps," George said. "And moody is right. He's also cold, haughty, rude and arrogant. He looks down that long, aristocratic nose of his as if we're all worms, beneath his notice."

She'd only met him a handful of times, while his marriage to Rose was being arranged—and what a lucky escape for Rose that had been!—but she'd disliked him on sight.

"His friends—and he doesn't seem to have many of them—call him Hart—his surname is Hartley—but he's known in the ton as Heartless, and doesn't that tell you something? Rose made a lucky escape, and I'm dam—" She broke off and glanced at Emm. "I'm blowed if I'll be the sacrificial lamb in her place." She clenched her fists. "Aunt Agatha had no right!"

"No, she didn't," Emm agreed. "And nobody will force you into marriage, dear, if you don't want it."

"No. But Aggie means well," Aunt Dottie said, and at George's look of surprise, she added, "Oh, I know she's

bossy and interfering and thinks she knows better than anyone what needs to be done and that we're all sheep who
need to be herded. But she does mean it for the best."

George's jaw dropped. "How can you say that?"

"To Aggie, marriage is the be-all and end-all. And she
thinks it is for everyone. But . . ." Aunt Dottie sighed. "She
made three marriages and not one of them brought her happiness. Wealth, yes, but happiness?" She shook her head.

Emm touched her belly. "You mean because she never
had children?"

Again Aunt Dottie shook her head. "Children are a
blessing, of course, but happiness is another matter entirely.
I never married and never had children, but my life has
been—and still is—a happy one. The trick, George dear, is
to know your own heart and decide accordingly. I made my
own choices in life, and have no regrets."

And seeing her tranquil face and serene smile, George
could believe it.

But she wasn't Aunt Dottie and didn't have her gentle,
accepting temperament. Aunt Agatha's interference made
George want to scream. Or to hit someone—preferably
the duke who'd so smugly rejected her—when she'd never
wanted him in the first place! She was as tense as an over-
wound clock. She needed to get out, to escape from this
smothering attention and breathe.

But the afternoon's obligations stretched ahead of her.
Morning calls, endless and unbearable, with coy questions
about male attentions, and about Rose's husband's incredible
return from the dead—that seven-day scandal still wasn't
over—and delicate and less-than-delicate inquiries about
how the poor duke was taking it. A duke, pipped at the altar
by some scruffy nobody—so scandalously delicious.

And then there were the gentlemen pursuing George . . .
Cal dealt with the obvious fortune hunters pretty swiftly, but
still, there were several gentlemen who, like Aunt Agatha,
refused to believe she was serious about not marrying.

At the best of times George found morning calls difficult. Today they would be unbearable.

"I need to go out," she said abruptly. "I want to take Sultan for a ride." To get away.

"You already rode this morning," Cal said, reentering the room.

"I need a longer ride." She glanced at Emm. "As long as you don't need me for anything, Emm."

"No, you go and ride the tension away, George dear. Everything's under control here; the last responses to the invitations are dribbling in, Burton has all the arrangements for the ball under control—he's in his element, I suspect—and Rose is fully occupied getting the new house ready to move into—"

"Harrying hapless workmen," Cal said with lazy amusement.

"And Lily's off with her husband, I know not where," Emm concluded. "You are free to do whatever you want."

"As long as Kirk goes with you," Cal added, naming the dour Scottish groom he employed to keep an eye on the girls when they rode out.

"Yes," Emm said. "Because Cal is about to accompany me on a short walk in the sunshine, while it lasts."

Cal blinked. "I am?"

"Yes, across the park to Gunter's." She dimpled. "The baby desires some more of that delicious pistachio ice cream they make."

"Oh, the *baby* does, does it? Well, in that case . . ." Cal rose and helped his wife to her feet.

At the door, Emm turned back to George. "And after my walk I plan to have a nap, so go on, my dear, escape the irritations of polite society, take your dog and your horse—"

"And Kirk," Cal reminded her.

"And run wild for a time," Emm finished. Dear Emm. She always understood.

"But not too wild," Cal added.

Chapter Two

❧

He was not an ill-disposed young man, unless to be rather
coldhearted, and rather selfish, is to be ill-disposed…
—JANE AUSTEN, *SENSE AND SENSIBILITY*

"OF COURSE THE OLD HARRIDAN WAS TRYING TO PLAY
me—she's my mother's godmother, and I wouldn't put anything past the two of them. Expecting me to believe that the
girl has no interest in marriage." Hart snorted. Would need
to be *dragged to the altar* indeed! He hadn't included that
bit when he'd told his friend Sinc the story. It was all rubbish, of course, and Sinc was a good fellow, but his tongue
tended to be rather loose, especially after a few drinks. Hart
wasn't going to have that little morsel spread around the ton.

His friend Sinc—Johnny Sinclair—had called in shortly
after Lady Salter's departure, on his way to Jackson's boxing saloon, and had stayed for a spot of lunch instead.
"Lady George, eh? Splendid girl. The sort of girl a fellow
can feel comfortable with."

"*Comfortable?*" The ice in his voice took Hart by surprise.

Sinc was oblivious. "Yes, no pretense about her at all.
Says exactly what she thinks, so a fellow knows exactly
where he stands. Not on the hunt for a husband. Makes no
secret of it. Plans never to marry. Wants to live in the coun-

try and raise horses and dogs—well, can't argue with that, can you?"

Hart could, actually. "So she's an eccentric."

Sinc shook his head. "Wouldn't go that far. She's marriage shy, that's all. According to m'sister, who knows her family quite well, her father abandoned her and her mother when she was a baby. Mother died, Lady George left to grow up alone and in poverty. Disgraceful business— daughter of an earl and she didn't even know it! Left to starve in a cottage." He drained his glass and held it out for a refill. "Didn't even know she had any living family until Ashendon discovered her and brought her to London and launched her along with his half sisters."

"Very affecting tale," Hart said dryly. He didn't believe a word of it.

"It is, it is." Sinc nodded. "No wonder the gel's wary of the bit and bridle. Still, it makes a pleasant change to dance with a pretty young thing and know she's not secretly plotting how to hook you."

Hart shifted impatiently. "Don't be naive, Sinc, of course she is. Her tactics are a little more subtle than usual, that's all."

"So speaks the eternal cynic. Well, if she's so keen to hook a husband, why has she knocked back half a dozen fellows that I know of?"

Hart frowned. "Half a dozen?"

"At least. There's Porter, Yeovil, Trent"—he counted them off on his fingers—"Towsett, Belmore and who else? Oh, yes, Morcombe—and they're just the ones I know of."

"*Towsett?* You mean the earl of?" They'd been to school with Towsett. The dullest boy he'd ever met had grown into the most pompous man.

Sinc nodded. "The same. He's mad for her by all account. Won't take no for an answer. Been refused several times, but determined to wear the girl down." He chuckled. "It's the joke of the clubs—such a stuffed shirt full of self-consequence, utterly desperate for such a lively, unconventional filly."

Hart swirled his wine thoughtfully. Towsett was a more

than eligible match for any girl in the ton: titled, wealthy and . . . solid—if you liked that kind of thing.

"My money's on Lady George."

Hart looked up sharply. "You're *betting* on her?"

Sinc grinned. "Lord, yes, the odds are irresistible. Most of them are backing Towsett—well, you have to admit he's very eligible. All the matchmaking mamas are in hot pursuit—any one of their daughters would snap him up in a heartbeat—but he won't look at anyone except Lady George. But the others don't know her like I do. She's not like those other girls—she's an original. Prefers her independence."

"So you hope."

Sinc grinned and raised his glass. "Oh, I'll win, all right. She doesn't want a bar of him—of marriage at all—and there's the joke, you see. Hardly anyone believes her, least of all Towsett. He can't imagine anyone turning him down, let alone a girl like Lady George."

Hart shrugged. "There's your answer then—she's aiming higher." For a dukedom, apparently.

"Cynic. Well, time will prove which of us is correct. Now, tomorrow night—what do you think about dropping into the opera? Dine at the club beforehand, of course."

Hart raised a brow. "The *opera*?" It was the last place he would have imagined Sinc. "Whatever for?"

"Monty has his eye on one of the dancers, and the little minx has been leading him a right merry dance. She hinted that she'd give him her answer tomorrow night, so a few of us are going along with him in case the poor fellow needs consolation. Monty's mama has a box. So, are you coming or not? Should be quite entertaining—not the caterwauling, of course, but watching Monty trying to corral the little filly."

Hart shrugged. "I'll dine with you at the club, but that's all." He was not fond of the opera, and was indifferent to Monty's success or otherwise with the opera dancer. He knew it would be a purely financial transaction—if Monty offered the girl enough, she'd accept his attentions; if not she'd be looking for another protector.

Opera dancers and young ladies of the ton—in his experience they were all the same under the skin. It all depended on the offer.

GEORGE'S HORSE, SULTAN, PICKED HIS WAY FASTIDIOUSLY through the crowded London streets, superbly disdainful of all the activity—the dogs, the urchins, the barrows, carts and carriages. Oh, he didn't like them—George could tell by the way his ears went back and swiveled and the way he tensed up from time to time, but months in London had taught Sultan that at the end of these tediously unpleasant streets lay a glorious run.

It was too late in the day to ride again in Hyde Park, unless one wanted to walk placidly along, bowing to acquaintances, and every now and then to break out wildly with a staid trot for five minutes. Neither of them, nor Finn for that matter, would enjoy that, so they were making for the wide-open spaces of Hampstead Heath. Of course it took much longer to get there, but it was worth it, and Emm had said she had the afternoon free.

And freedom was what George craved.

She rode ahead, Finn trotting along at her side, magnificently indifferent to the yapping street curs. Kirk followed close behind. His eyes were watchful, on the lookout for trouble, but his expression was dour as usual. He'd made this excursion with her many times before and generally enjoyed himself—though it was hard to tell with Kirk—but today he radiated grim disapproval.

It had started when she'd met him in the stable yard, mounted and ready. He usually fetched the horses and brought them to the house, and he'd taken one look at her and frowned.

"Does his lordship know ye're going out in public like that?"

George grinned. "It's Hampstead Heath. I want a proper ride."

"It's no' fitting, Lady Georgiana, ye know that."

"It's a split skirt, see." She flipped up one of the panels of cloth that just barely covered her breeches.

He snorted. "It's a man's saddle."

"No, really?" she said sounding amazed. "And yet here I am, mounted and ready."

He'd opened his mouth to argue, but she'd cut him off. "Oh, don't be stuffy, Kirk. You know perfectly well I've ridden astride dozens of times—even when Cal's been with me."

"Aye, at dawn," he said. "When there's no' a soul about. But it's broad daylight and we'll be riding through the streets. Ye'll cause a scandal, Lady Georgiana."

"Pooh, nobody will recognize me." She pulled out a man's cap and crammed it on her head, tucking in her hair, which was short anyway. She tugged the bill down, almost over her eyes. "See? Now come on." She put an end to the argument by trotting out into the street.

He pursed his lips but followed, looking gloomier than ever.

"Have you ever ridden with a sidesaddle, Kirk?"

He didn't bother answering, just gave her an expressive look.

"No, of course not. And why is that? For all that men tell us that sidesaddles are soooo much better for ladies and are as safe as houses, you won't get a man on one—and why? Because they're silly, that's why. And it takes more skill to ride with them, not less, because sidesaddle you only have the reins and your crop and your balance, whereas astride you can control your mount with your thighs as well—"

"*Lady Georgiana!*" Kirk said in a pained voice.

George hid a grin. She'd forgotten; ladies didn't have thighs, or if they did they weren't to be mentioned.

"So if I want a really good ride, it has to be astride," she finished. There was nothing better than to ride at a fast gallop, bent low over her horse's neck, the wind in her face, and the feeling of being at one with the powerful animal beneath her. Bareback was even better—it was how she'd first learned to ride—but she wasn't even going to try for that. Not in London. But one day, when she was free . . .

It wasn't as if she disliked her current life. Not really.

She didn't much like London, with hundreds—thousands—of people living almost on top of her—or so it felt. And she didn't like the dirt and smells. Why was it that London dirt seemed so much worse than country dirt?

And London noise never stopped. Even at night there were rumbling wheels, shouts, bangs and arguments, and though the country was also full of noise at night—the scream of a vixen, the hooting of an owl, the far-off barking of a dog—they were peaceful noises.

But there were things she liked about this life. Cal had initially dragged her into the family, kicking and fighting—she'd never had a family and was sure she didn't need one—but to her amazement, she liked it, liked the feeling of belonging, liked the companionship of her aunts Lily and Rose, who were more like sisters. And her aunt by marriage, Emm, who was sister, friend and mother all rolled into one—Emm was a blessing. She'd even come to like Cal, bossy-boots that he was.

The great-aunts—well, Aunt Dottie was a darling, but she could do without Aunt Agatha. How *dare* she offer her up to that cold, snooty duke?

The farther they got away from London, the more George's mood lifted. The traffic thinned; the noise and dirt and chaos of the city fell behind them. Browns and grays gave way to a thousand shades of green, and the air felt cleaner and fresher. She took great deep breaths of it and felt lighter and more energized.

Sultan too felt the difference and started to dance a little with anticipation. She felt the leashed power rippling through him and gathered her reins.

"Careful now, Lady George," Kirk murmured. "He's verra fresh still." Lady George, not Lady Georgiana—she was forgiven her breeches, then.

Kirk, the silly old dear, was certain Sultan was too strong, too spirited, too male for a lady, and had said so repeatedly. She'd lost count of other men who'd told her the same thing, in various ways.

But she'd bred Sultan, had been there when he was born, had raised him from a colt and trained him. They understood each other.

Besides, George, titled or not, was barely a lady.

An ill-trained, boyish, impertinent hoyden . . . She pushed the thought aside. She didn't care what the duke said about her.

The heath stretched before them. There was not a soul in sight. She tugged down her cap. "Come on, Kirk, race you to that big old oak on the edge of the forest." And without waiting, she took off. Her dog, Finn, streaked after her.

"Now, isn't this better than spending the afternoon at Jackson's?" Hart gestured to the scene in front of them, an endless sward of green, fringed by a tangled, shadowy forest.

"I thought you meant Hyde Park, not out in the dashed wilderness."

Hart snorted. "Hyde Park? At the fashionable hour?" He couldn't imagine anything worse.

"*I* don't mind doing the pretty, catching up on gossip with all the lovely ladies." Sinc pulled his collar up. "Better than being in the middle of nowhere getting blown to bits in a freezing gale."

Hart laughed. "Stop complaining. It's a brisk breeze, nothing more. Besides, it'll blow the cobwebs away."

"Cobwebs? On *me*? Don't be ridiculous. My valet would have a fit. What am I saying? *I* would have a fit!"

"Come on, let's ride to the top of the hill. You'll feel better when you can see for miles." He headed off at a leisurely canter.

Sinc followed, grumbling. He'd planned to spend his afternoon drinking blue ruin with his cronies at Jackson's Boxing Saloon; Sinc was more interested in the convivial side of the sport than the energetic aspects. But it hadn't been hard to entice him out for a ride instead. Of course he'd insisted on going home to change into more appropriate attire—Sinc was never less than nattily dressed—but now Hart realized his friend had gone to an extra degree of trouble because he'd expected to be flirting in Hyde Park, not cantering across the heath high above the city.

Hart reined his horse in at the crest of the hill, and stood gazing out at the silhouette of London in the distance. He could just make out the dome of St. Paul's. He was trying to pick out other buildings when the sound of galloping hooves caused him to turn his head.

About fifty yards away, a gleaming black stallion thundered across the turf, a magnificent creature moving like the wind, all speed and power and grace. A thoroughbred, with clear Arab ancestry.

A boy—a youth—clung to his back, crouched low over the stallion's neck, like a jockey in a race. He rode as if he were born on the back of a horse. No gentleman he, not with that cloth cap, slightly too big for his head, and those worn breeches and boots. An apprentice, perhaps. Or a young groom. Who was the fool who paid a youth to exercise a glorious animal like that?

Behind the lad loped a lanky gray dog. At some distance behind, came a thickset man—another groom, perhaps? It wasn't clear whether he was with the black stallion or not.

As he watched the movement of stallion and rider, something pinged in Hart's mind, a flash of memory, a fleeting impression, as if he'd seen this horse, this rider some other time . . .

But then Sinc arrived. "Brrr. It's even colder up here. Can't we go home yet?" And the thought was lost.

Hart couldn't take his eyes off the stallion. "What a magnificent beast."

"Hmm? Oh, yes. Very nice," Sinc said as stallion and rider flashed past. He hadn't much interest in horseflesh.

"Dammit, I'm going to buy that horse." Without further explanation, Hart urged his horse forward and was riding in pursuit. Sinc shouted something, but his words were taken by the breeze, and in any case, Hart was entirely focused on catching up with the stallion.

He slowly gained on the rider and his mount. The boy glanced back over his shoulder, a flash of light eyes and a black scowl.

"Hey, there, I want to ask you something," Hart called.

The boy ignored him. The stallion picked up speed.

Hart urged his horse faster. "Wait! I want to buy your horse," he yelled as he drew nearer. "Who is the owner?"

Horse and boy took a sharp turn to the left and plunged down a steep slope. Hart followed. They splashed through a soggy patch, green and weedy.

Mud from the stallion's hooves splashed in Hart's face. He didn't bother to wipe it off. The boy's determination to avoid him was annoying, but the chase itself was exhilarating.

They headed back up a hill. The stallion pulled steadily away and made for a densely forested area. He was stronger and faster than Hart's mount, and with the lighter weight of the boy, Hart didn't have a chance.

"Stop, damn you! I only want to talk," Hart yelled in frustration.

At the edge of the trees, the boy looked back. Hart caught a flash of white teeth as the lad gave what might have been a cheeky wave or—Hart narrowed his gaze—a rude gesture. As the boy and horse disappeared from sight, a light laugh floated back to him on the breeze.

Swearing to himself, Hart rode slowly back to where Sinc was waiting, hunched gloomily on his horse.

"Have fun, did you? I'm just about frozen solid. Though naturally, being your oldest friend, I'm only too delighted to become an ice block in your service."

Hart ignored the sarcasm. "Little mongrel refused to stop. All I wanted was the name of the owner."

"Is that all? Well, you could have asked me. Would have saved you all that gallivanting about. And me from turning into an icicle. You do know your face is spattered with mud, I suppose. As for your boots . . ." Sinc shuddered.

"*What?* You know who owns that horse? Who is it?"

"Forgotten your handkerchief?" Sinc scrutinized his

friend's face. "I have a spare if you need to use it. Can't be seen with mud on your face."

Frustrated, Hart pulled out a handkerchief and scrubbed at his face. "There! Now, who owns that damned horse?"

"You missed a bit. Just here," Sinc said, gesturing to his own face.

Hart rubbed at the spot indicated. "Now, before I strangle you, tell me who owns that blasted stallion."

"Oh, she won't sell," Sinc said.

"*She?* You mean the owner is *a woman*?" Fool woman, to entrust such a valuable and spirited animal to a mere youth. Though he had to admit the boy could ride. Superbly, as it happened. When he bought the stallion, he might even offer the lad a job.

"Yes, of course. Didn't you know?"

"How would I know?" He blinked. "Are you suggesting that I'm acquainted with the owner? Who is she? Where might I find her?"

Sinc gave him an odd, amused look, then jerked his chin to where the stallion and his rider had disappeared. "You just saw her."

Hart looked, but he could see no woman. "Where?"

"On the horse's back. Leading you a right merry chase by the looks of it."

Hart stared. The rider was *female*? Gad, but she could ride. In fact . . . His eyes narrowed . . . There had been something familiar . . .

"Who—?" he began.

"If you ever bothered to ride in Hyde Park, you would have met both horse and owner together. She and her family ride there most mornings—early. Practically crack of dawn," Sinc added with a theatrical shudder.

Hart raised a skeptical brow. "Then how is it that you've seen them? You rarely rise before noon."

"Coming home, of course. Often witness the grisly hours of dawn on the way home from a night out."

"And who is this family that rides out so intrepidly at such an hour?"

Sinc grinned. "The family you almost married into."

There was a short silence as Hart took it in.

Sinc chuckled. "Yes, that was Lady George Rutherford you chased all over the heath just now. Told you she was an original."

Chapter Three

In his library he had been always sure of leisure and
tranquility; and though prepared . . . to meet with folly and
conceit in every other room in the house, he was used to be
free of them there.

—JANE AUSTEN, *PRIDE AND PREJUDICE*

IT WAS A HOT AFTERNOON. GEORGE, AUNT DOTTIE AND
Emm were crossing Berkeley Square on a quest to Gunter's
for ices, when they heard a series of shrieks and yaps. Human shrieks, canine yaps.

An elegantly dressed older lady was jumping up and
down, appalled, flapping her hands and shrieking at a pack
of dogs that were swirling and snapping and shoving at one
another in a noisy canine whirlpool several feet away.

"It's Milly Prescott," Aunt Dottie exclaimed.

"FooFoo!" Mrs. Prescott cried. "Oh, stop it, you brutes!
My poor little FooFoo!"

George saw what the problem was. In the middle of the
pack of dogs was a small, dainty Pekingese, pink satin ribbons in her hair, receiving the eager attentions of a dozen
scruffy mongrels.

"Sit and stay!" George ordered Finn, who was showing
considerable interest in the proceedings. Reluctantly he lowered his behind, almost to the ground. George waded into
the swirling pack, snatched up the little dog and handed it

to the lady. Then she roundly dispersed the other dogs, who retreated a few yards away and waited hopefully.

One brave, enamored beast broke through and leapt up eagerly at FooFoo. Mrs. Prescott screeched, George roared at the would-be swain, and Finn jumped forward with a snarl. All the dogs retreated another few feet.

"Oh, you brave, brave girl, Lady Georgiana! I wonder you weren't bitten—such a heroine you are! Thank you, thank you," Mrs. Prescott exclaimed. "Oh dear, I'm all of a flutter! Those terrible brutes just appeared from nowhere and started attacking my poor little baby."

George glanced at Emm and Aunt Dottie, who were trying not to smile.

"Um, they weren't attacking her," George said.

"They were, they were, didn't you see? Oh, my poor little FooFoo, are you all right, my darling?" She examined the little dog anxiously, straightening her ribbons and murmuring, "Mummy's here now, precious. Those nasty dogs won't bother you again."

"Actually they will," George said. "Unless you keep FooFoo locked up for the next few weeks." The dogs had retreated but were waiting, all eyes on little FooFoo, who wriggled and squirmed to get down.

"Locked up? Why ever should I do that? FooFoo loves her walkies in the park."

"Yes, but she's in season at the moment," George explained. And when the lady didn't seem to understand, she added, "She's in heat. Those dogs know it. They can smell her."

Mrs. Prescott pulled a horrified face. "*Smell* her? But she was bathed this morning with my own special soap. And why would that make them attack her? They didn't attack me and I use the same soap."

George couldn't think how else to explain. Not in any polite way. She cast an appealing look at Emm, who stepped forward. "What my niece means, Mrs. Prescott, is that your dog has entered her breeding season." Emm patted her own burgeoning belly in gentle emphasis.

Mrs. Prescott blinked at Emm's belly, then gasped in

understanding. "No, it cannot be! My little FooFoo is far too young for that! She's still a puppy."

"She's not a puppy anymore, and those dogs know it," George said bluntly. "So keep her away from all other dogs for the next few weeks."

"I will, oh, I will. Thank you so much, dear, brave Lady Georgiana. Good day to you, Lady Ashendon, Lady Dorothea." Mrs. Prescott hurried away, little FooFoo clamped firmly to her bosom, gazing wistfully back at her admirers, her feathery tail gently wagging.

"She was widowed last year," Aunt Dottie explained. "She's childless, and her husband was a cold, hard man who never let her keep a pet. FooFoo is her first."

"The way those dogs were going at it," George said frankly, "FooFoo might just present her with some more."

Emm burst out laughing. "George, darling, you are such a breath of fresh air. Don't ever change."

"I agree," Aunt Dottie said. "And now, ices."

THE FOLLOWING AFTERNOON THE DUKE'S FRONT DOOR-bell rang again. It had rung on and off all day—to no avail. Hart made a grimace of satisfaction and bent over his correspondence. The gossip-seeking vultures would get no joy here. Fleming had his instructions.

He stared down at the note he was trying to compose. It was more difficult than he imagined. The previous evening he'd sent a note around to the Earl of Ashendon, offering to buy the black stallion. He didn't mention that he'd seen the horse being ridden by the earl's niece, let alone that the young hoyden had been riding astride. He was sure Sinc was wrong, saying the horse belonged to the girl.

But a brief note had arrived this morning in which the earl informed him that the stallion belonged to Lady Georgiana and that he doubted she'd sell it. However, if Everingham was interested in breeding the stallion to one of his mares, she might consider that. Everingham should apply directly to her.

It was ridiculous. Ashendon had always seemed like a levelheaded fellow, but allowing his niece to be directly involved in the breeding of a valuable, blood stallion . . . A young, unmarried girl shouldn't even know about the breeding of horses, let alone arrange it.

He finished the note, making her a generous offer for the horse—he would not even consider discussing stud arrangements with a lady—addressed and sealed it, then returned to his business correspondence. Much less complicated.

A short time later voices in the hall, one of them female, caused him to look up. *What the devil?*

His butler knocked discreetly and looked in. "Your grace, forgive the interruption but—"

"What part of *I am not at home* did you fail to understand, Fleming?"

"I'm sorry, your grace, but—" the butler began.

"Oh, what nonsense, as if my son meant you to deny *me*," said a soft voice from the doorway.

His butler gave him an agonized look of apology. Hart waved him away. He might be irritated, but he understood. Most men were helpless before his mother.

The Duchess of Everingham brushed past the butler, all slender, helpless frailty and fluttering draperies. Pretty and still quite youthful looking—she did not admit to forty, although since he was eight-and-twenty she could hardly deny it—she cultivated an air of delicacy and fragility that brought out the protective instincts of a certain type of man.

Hart was not one of them.

"The *library*, Redmond?" she said plaintively. "You receive your mother in the library?"

He gestured to the papers spread out on the desk before him. "I'm working."

His mother pouted, then tottered across the room, sank gracefully into the most comfortable chair and gave an exhausted sigh. Hard on her heels came her most recent companion, a colorless woman clad in a depressing shade between gray and purple, clutching a large, lumpy reticule.

He nodded to her. She was some kind of distant cousin.

Harriet? Henrietta? He couldn't remember her name. His mother changed her companions so often it was hard to keep up. They all started off devoted, but after a few months, they became "impossible" and Hart was instructed to pension them off.

The companion produced a number of little bottles and vials and arranged them on a small table next to his mother's chair. Smelling salts, hartshorn, feathers for burning, and various potions guaranteed to revive the feeblest invalid: Mother's battery of armaments.

Not that his mother was an invalid. The Duchess of Everingham was said by some to enjoy ill health. Hart would have said that far from enjoying it, his mother positively relished it. As far as he was concerned, she was as strong as a horse.

The medicines were there purely as a silent warning that any opposition to his mother's wishes would have dire, possibly fatal consequences. He'd learned that lesson young.

The companion pulled a shawl from the seemingly bottomless reticule and arranged it around his mother's knees. Her grace had a horror of drafts.

"Oh, stop *fussing*, Hester." His mother kicked impatiently at the shawl. "Go. Leave us. I wish to talk to my son."

Handing a dainty crystal vial—probably smelling salts—to his mother, Hester turned to Hart and said in an undervoice, "Try not to upset her, your grace. She's feeling very poorly today."

When was she not? Particularly when she wanted something. But he didn't say it aloud. He glanced at the doorway where his butler still hovered. "Tea and cakes, Fleming."

"Oh, no, I couldn't possibly," his mother said. "Just a little barley water. With honey and a slice of lemon. And perhaps a rusk. I need to keep up my strength, such as it is."

Fleming bowed and left, taking the companion with him. Silence fell. Hart turned back to his correspondence. His mother sighed. He kept writing.

"I miss this house so much."

Hart ignored her. All his life his mother had complained

about the inconvenience and old-fashioned furniture of
Everingham House, saying it was too big, too grim and too
cold. His late father had spent a fortune trying to please her,
but nothing ever did.

Papa had never learned that lesson. Hart had.

Several years ago he'd finally given in to her complaints
and bought her a pretty house just around the corner that
was smaller, lighter, warmer and more modern. She'd had
it entirely redecorated, and happily moved in, all the while
confiding sadly to her friends that her son had callously
thrust his mother from her family home.

He himself had been living in bachelor apartments at the
time and had shut Everingham House up. But last year,
when he'd decided to take a bride, he'd reopened it, had it
redecorated and some parts of it modernized—the kitchens
and the plumbing in particular—and moved back in.

Naturally his mother had conceived a desperate yearn-
ing to live there again.

She sighed again, and when he showed no sign of putting aside his correspondence, she said in a plaintive voice,
"It utterly exhausts me to venture out into the world, you
know."

"Then why bother?"

"Because I am in despair, Redmond, utter despair!"

He kept writing.

"Despair about you and your situation, Redmond!"
Seeming to realize the waspish tenor of her speech, she
added, "Dearest."

He didn't look up. "Don't worry your head about me,
Mother. There's no need."

"But there *is* need, my son. That frightful aborted ceremony, the gossip, the scandal, the disgrace! The horrid *slur*
on our family name! I am nigh on prostrated with mortification." She shuddered, unstoppered the tiny vial and took
a restorative sniff.

Hart said nothing. There was no point. They'd had this
conversation numerous times. Yes, there was gossip, but

gossip never lasted. And if she didn't go to so many parties—forcing herself, naturally—she wouldn't have to hear it.

"Do not fret yourself, my son, I shall *try* to weather the storm," his mother said, rallying bravely. "It's *you* I worry about, my dearest. I thought that you were all settled at last, and that *finally* I could go in peace." She sank back feebly in her chair and closed her eyes.

"Go where, Mother? Off to Bath again, are you?" He blotted the ink of his letter, folded it and reached for his seal. "Or perhaps a sea-bathing treatment this time? I've heard that a bracing dip in the cold salt sea does people a power of good."

She shuddered and clutched her vial feebly to her bosom. "Such a thing would kill me."

"Only if you drowned, and I believe there are muscular females at the dipping sites whose job it is to prevent that. It's perfectly safe."

She sat up and glared at him. "Don't be so obtuse, Redmond—my darling boy. You must know that the only thing that keeps me alive—the *only* thing, dearest—is the desire to see you settled. Married."

"Then I shall postpone my nuptials indefinitely and provide you with a long life."

"No! No—oh, but I see you are teasing me, and you really must not." She waved the smelling salts feebly but with delicate emphasis. "Dr. Bentink says my constitution is extremely fragile and any shock, even a small one, could carry me off."

Hart didn't bother responding. Dr. Bentink knew which side of his bread was buttered.

Fleming entered then, followed by a footman carrying a tea tray, containing a teapot, two cups, a glass of barley water, a dish containing several almond rusks and a plate of luscious-looking cream cakes.

The duchess waved them away. "Oh, how pretty, but I couldn't, I couldn't eat a thing."

"You must keep your strength up, your grace," Fleming murmured. He produced a small table and placed it on the other side of the duchess. He poured out the tea, added milk and two lumps of sugar, stirred it well and placed it, the glass of barley water, the dish of rusks and a plate containing two small pink cakes oozing with cream on the duchess's table. Then he poured black and sugarless tea for Hart and set it pointedly next to the chair opposite the duchess.

"I'll just finish this." Hart blotted, sealed and addressed the letter. When he looked up there were still two cakes on his mother's plate, but there were now several fewer on the larger plate. As always, Fleming had calculated his mother's tastes exactly.

Hart left his desk and sat down opposite his mother. He sipped his tea.

"I couldn't eat a morsel, Redmond, I am in such distress."

Hart drank his tea.

"Perhaps a rusk. One must force oneself for the sake of one's loved ones." She picked up a rusk and toyed with it. "Dear Lady Salter—"

"Came the other day and delivered your latest suggestion for a bride. I sent her off with a flea in her ear."

His mother gasped. "Don't tell me you were uncivil to her, Redmond! Apart from being my godmother, she is one of my dearest friends."

"I was blunt rather than uncivil, and I'll tell you what I told her. Stop meddling in my life, Mother, or—" He broke off, as his mother fluttered back in her chair, gasping in apparent distress. He waited.

After a few moments she registered his indifference and stopped gasping. "Or what?"

"Or one of these days I'll return the favor."

She narrowed her eyes. "What do you mean?"

"Perhaps I'll give my consent to one of those puppies you encourage to hang around you. They're always pestering me for your hand."

She sat up. "You wouldn't!"

Hart shrugged. "Jeavons has approached me three times already."

She patted her hair complacently. "The dear sweet boy, but of course it would never do."

Jeavons was several years younger than himself, an impressionable puppy.

"I should think not. He's barely out of leading strings."

She sniffed. "Hardly."

"No, Bullstrode would be far more suitable."

She stiffened. "Bullstrode! That arrogant bully! He's an oaf! A ruffian! He's, he's . . . vulgar. Ungentlemanly!"

"He adores you, Mother. He has several times importuned me for your hand."

"Then you must refuse! What am I saying? *I* refuse!"

"Ah, but Bullstrode is the kind of man who would take your refusal as a kind of flirting from an indecisive female. I'm sure you've heard his views on the inability of females to know what is good for them."

"I've heard! And I'm not indecisive. I *loathe* the man!" There was nothing helpless or fluttery about his mother now.

In a thoughtful voice he said, "I wouldn't be surprised if Bullstrode decided to kidnap you and force a marriage—if he thought he had my blessing, that is."

She shuddered again, this time genuinely. "Redmond! No! He doesn't have your blessing . . . Does he?"

Hart pondered the contents of his teacup as if considering it.

She crumbled the rusk between her fingers. "You wouldn't, would you? Dearest?"

He looked up. "I might—if you and that skinny godmother of yours don't stop pestering me."

A huff of laughter escaped her. "Skinny? Lady Salter? Oh, you are wicked. But Bullstrode, Redmond. You would never—"

"Are we finished here, Mother? Because I have work to do." He gestured to the pile of papers on his desk.

She pouted. "Never any time for your nearest and dearest. Your father left all that sort of thing to his secretary."

"I am not my father." He rose and rang for his butler.

She hesitated, and fiddled with a handkerchief. "Do you go to the opera this evening, Redmond, dear?"

"No."

"Oh." She considered that. "What about next Thursday?"

"No." He looked at her with narrowed eyes. "Is this another attempt to foist an eligible female on me?"

She gave an indignant little huff. "Of course not. You've made yourself perfectly clear. Though you must admit that the last girl we found for you—dear Lady Rose—was perfect."

"And look how well that turned out."

"Well, how were we to know the silly gel had contracted a secret marriage?"

"Good-bye, Mother and remember what I said. A word from me and Bullstrode will be yours."

His mother applied a wisp of lace to her eye. "So harsh, so cruel to treat your poor mama so. I don't know where you get it from. Your father was always so sweet to me."

Hart's father had lived a dog's life, wrapped as he was around his wife's little finger and driven to distraction by her imaginary ailments. Hart had no intention of going down that path.

The door opened and his butler appeared. "Her grace is leaving, Fleming. And have this delivered, will you?" He handed the butler his note to the Rutherford girl. "Good-bye, Mother."

His mother sighed. "Unfeeling, unnatural boy. I'm not surprised some people in the ton call you Heartless." She floated tragically from the room, a martyred exit overlaying a barely suppressed flounce.

Hart kept a straight face. He had no intention of encouraging Bullstrode, of course—he was a bully and a braggart and Hart would rather shoot the man than have him as a stepfather—but if the threat kept his mother from her eternal meddling, it was worth it.

He returned to his correspondence. He had a man of affairs, but not a private secretary. Some things he preferred to do himself. He administered a number of estates, his own and three for which he had recently become a trustee. These last three, which had belonged to a late cousin, took up most of his time; Arthur Wooldridge had not only left his young son and heir to Hart's wardship, he'd left his affairs in a mess and his estate in debt.

Fortunately, Hart enjoyed a challenge.

TWO HOURS LATER HE RECEIVED AN ANSWER TO HIS NOTE.

My horse is not for sale, to you or anyone.
                                        G. Rutherford.

Chapter Four

❧

I have not the pleasure of understanding you.
—JANE AUSTEN, *PRIDE AND PREJUDICE*

THE LAST THING GEORGE HAD EXPECTED TO ENJOY WHEN she'd first been thrust into the life of the ton was the opera. But to everyone's surprise—including hers—she did. The first time, she'd attended it reluctantly with Rose and Aunt Agatha, knowing it was just some excuse for Aunt Agatha to introduce Rose to the duke.

Except he hadn't turned up.

For Aunt Agatha the evening had been a waste of time; for George, it had been a revelation. The music, the drama, the story, the costumes—she'd been entranced.

She'd always liked music, always enjoyed a song or two, but she'd had no musical education. According to Martha, Mama had a very sweet voice—she'd played the pianoforte and sung—but she'd died when George was a baby. The music in church was always her favorite part of Sundays, and she'd loved to listen to the villagers playing their fiddles and other instruments whenever there was a wedding or some other celebration. Several times she'd even sneaked into the grounds of some of the grander local houses and eavesdropped on their balls and parties.

But opera was something else again. She couldn't understand most of the words—she spoke no Italian or German;
no other language except English, in fact—but Emm, who
knew about opera, usually told her the story before she went,
so she could follow along. Often the story seemed a bit silly,
and the characters a little on the ridiculous side, but then a
voice would begin to soar and she would be transported out
of the theater, away from London, into a realm she'd never
known existed.

It didn't always happen, but with some singers, and some
pieces, the opening notes would send a prickle down her
spine, across her skin, and she'd lean forward toward the
stage and let the music soak into her. And be transported.

Aunt Dottie also shared her love of music. She didn't often come up to London—she preferred her home in Bath—
but she'd come up for Rose's wedding, and was staying on for
Rose's ball next week, so she'd come with George and Aunt
Agatha tonight.

A burst of masculine laughter came from the box next
door—nothing to do with anything happening onstage. The
box had been empty for most of the opera, but now, more
than halfway through, a group of young men had entered
noisily, talking and laughing, indifferent to what was happening onstage or whom they might be disturbing.

Lots of people talked through the opera. It drove George
mad. Why did they come if they had no intention of listening to the music? She knew the answer, of course—because
it was fashionable. To see and be seen, to show off their
clothes and jewels. And meet friends and gossip.

Most of them showed little interest in the music. She'd
even seen people play cards right through a performance,
their backs to the stage. At least cards were relatively quiet.
These young men weren't.

Two of them were leaning over the balcony. "There she
is, the little one third from the left," said one, pointing. He
was making no attempt to lower his voice or be discreet in
any way.

"The one with yellow hair? In pink?" asked another.

"Yes, that's her."

"Pretty—oh, look, she's seen us." They leaned forward, waving.

George refused to look. She knew what the men were talking about. Picking out opera dancers—they had a reputation as notorious light-skirts—as if they were going shopping. She didn't care what the men did, she just wished they would do it silently. Preferably somewhere else.

Beside her, Aunt Dottie sighed and shifted restlessly. The men's conversation was disturbing her too.

George tried to fix her eyes and ears on the stage and the glorious music coming from the singers and musicians, but the men's discussion—loud and annoying—continued until she was almost at screaming point. She turned to face the men over the low wall that divided the boxes. "Hush!" she said in a low, vehement voice. "Some of us want to listen to the music!"

"Well, who's stopping you?" one man said. He'd clearly been drinking. "That fat woman is loud enough to wake the dead. Can't hear myself think."

"You and your friends are ruining our evening with your inane conversation," she hissed. "So be quiet or leave."

"Inane? Well, I like that. I'll have you know that—"

"Leave? This box belongs to my mother."

"Georgiana," Aunt Agatha said in a quelling tone.

George didn't bother to answer. It would only be some kind of reprimand, something like *Young ladies don't talk to gentlemen in the next box*, or *Young ladies don't tell gentlemen to be quiet*. She snorted. Gentlemen indeed. *Young ladies should only insult gentlemen to whom they have been introduced.*

Besides, she never answered to Geor*giana*. She turned back to the stage. The aria began, and, oh, it was glorious. For about half a minute.

"Oh, I say, it's Lady George." It was one of the men in the next box. A different one. "Evenin', Lady George."

She refused to look. The aria had started.

"Lady George," the voice continued, louder. Another one who'd drunk too much. "Doncha remember me?"

"Shush!" she hissed.

"But we danced together last week, at the—dash it all—forgotten which ball it was."

George clenched her fist around her fan, wishing it were a pistol. Or a club.

"Sinc, do you recall whose ball we went to last week? It was the one where—ouch!" He blinked at George in shock and rubbed his shoulder. "You *hit* me. With your fan." He glanced down, where the fan had fallen onto the floor in his box. "Broke it too. Pity. Looks like a pretty thing."

"I'll break something else if you and your friends don't shut your mouths!"

"Georg*iana*!" Aunt Agatha snapped.

George sat down again, but Aunt Agatha persisted. "Georgiana, I'm speaking to you."

George gritted her teeth, waited pointedly until the soprano had finished and then turned to her great-aunt. "Yes, Great-aunt Agatha?" Aunt Agatha hated being called Great-aunt Agatha, especially in public. Great-aunt was the correct form of address for George to use, but it was oh, so aging.

Aunt Agatha glared through her lorgnette, her lips thinned almost to invisibility, then jerked her head in a subtle sideways direction. George frowned, unsure of what she was signaling. Aunt Agatha rolled her eyes, then with a palpable effort, she forced them into a smile, turned and bowed graciously in the direction of the next box. "Good evening, your grace."

George followed her gaze. A dark shadow leaned forward, picked up her fan from the floor and stepped forward into the light.

She stiffened and swore under her breath. The Duke of blasted Everingham. She hadn't noticed him, lurking there in the background. He was dressed, as usual, in severe black evening clothes, the only gleam of color about him an emerald tie pin. The candlelight threw half his face into shadow and gilded the rest: the proud nose, the chiseled lips, the stubborn jaw. He stood there, all born-to-command and superior, looking down his nose at her.

His eyes glinted, dark and unreadable tonight, but she'd noticed them before, when he was betrothed to Rose, and she thought them the coldest eyes she'd ever seen.

"Georg*iana*," Aunt Agatha prompted.

George knew she wouldn't stop, so she gave the duke a reluctant nod.

He inclined his head at her. His lips twitched slightly as if he found something amusing. Found *her* amusing.

No doubt he was amused by the little provincial's insistence on an audience actually listening. Not to mention her inappropriate behavior in addressing people in the next box—*gentlemen* in the next box.

Or perhaps the amusement came from Aunt Agatha's offer of George as a potential bride. And his rejection of her. *An ill-trained, boyish, impertinent hoyden.*

She put up her chin. She didn't care what he thought.

Well, actually she did—she wanted him to know she wasn't the slightest bit interested in him, never had been, and that the idea of offering her to him as a potential bride was nothing to do with her and wholly Aunt Agatha's preposterous and insane idea. Made entirely without George's knowledge or permission.

But she couldn't exactly explain that, not here, not now, especially in this company. She crossed her arms and eyed him coldly, fuming at the thought that he might assume she was angry with him because he'd refused her. She was *not* a woman scorned! *He* was a man scorned—only he didn't know it.

So infuriating.

"Good evening, Lady Salter, Lady Dorothea, Lady Georgiana," Hart said smoothly. "Enjoying the evening, I hope?"

He'd decided to accompany Sinc and his friends at the last minute. His mother's less-than-subtle queries the day before had convinced him that Lady Georgiana would be attending the opera tonight, and though he had no interest either in the opera or in courting her, he was very interested in obtaining her horse.

Her note of curt refusal had annoyed him, but he'd taken it as the opening salvo of a negotiation, female-style. Or some kind of blasted flirtation.

Lord, but he was fed up with women and their tricks. From his mother, to his first and subsequent mistresses—even the first girl he thought he might love—it had been nothing but deception, lies and devious female stratagems.

He'd planned to step into her box at the next interval, bringing champagne for the ladies, and then sit down and discuss the sale of her horse. Monty and his friends had probably spoiled any chance of a civilized conversation tonight, at least, but Hart might be able to salvage something from the evening.

He'd watched her from his shadowed corner and been intrigued by her rapt expression as she gazed down at the stage. Had she been feigning interest in order to attract some musical gentleman?

Women did that, he knew. He'd lost track of the various interests females he'd known had claimed, only to learn that they were almost invariably false. One young lady who'd declared she had a passion for hunting—because he was known to be a bruising rider to hounds—hadn't even been able to ride. Unless to bounce along on the back of a horse like a sack of potatoes was to ride.

But he hadn't been able to spot whoever Lady Georgiana was aiming to impress at the opera this evening. He'd observed with fascination the various expressions that crossed her vivid little face as she watched the stage, following the story, seemingly as open as a child in her responses. She gave every indication of being wholly enraptured by the opera.

Her profile was limned by the light from the lantern behind her, a golden halo, outlining a firm little nose, a determined chin and the soft curve of her cheek. She was dressed in pale amber, the scooped neckline subtly enhancing the shadow between her breasts.

The more he'd watched her, the less he understood. *This* was the "boy" who'd taken him on a wild, exhilarating chase? The boy who rode as well as any jockey? This seemingly demure young lady watching the opera with her two elderly aunts?

And then she'd turned on Monty and his friends and ripped into them like an angry little governess, seeming not to care in the slightest what anyone thought. A slender, entrancing firebrand.

She glared at him now, her lips pursed. Her skin was smooth, like rich cream or satin, not pale like most of the women he knew, but warm and faintly sun-kissed. Or was that the effect of the theater lights?

Her face had a slight elfin suggestion, with high cheekbones and a delicately pointed chin, but her nose was small and straight and imperious. And her mouth—oh, lord, her mouth—plump and lush and altogether enticing. Hart stared at her mouth and swallowed.

Soft, plump, satiny-looking lips, dark against the purity of her skin. They didn't seem to go with the rest of her, all lissome and leggy and . . . well, he wasn't able to think of her as boyish, not dressed like this in an amber gown that clung to her slender curves and subtly enhanced them.

Short, glossy dark locks clustered and curled around her face. In this light he couldn't quite make out the color of her eyes—something light, possibly blue or gray. He would have to see her in daylight to be sure. Fringed with long dark lashes, they were beautiful, even when narrowed at him as they were now.

He tried to put this Lady Georgiana with that other one: mud-spattered and dressed as a boy—in breeches and boots, no less!—in the middle of nowhere, riding a magnificent stallion that was—that should have been—far too strong for a lady.

She glared at him and folded her arms beneath her bosom. He tried not to drop his gaze to take in the gentle curves, and failed.

However had he imagined that the rider he'd pursued across the heath was a boy? There was nothing boyish about her. It was more than a little disturbing. Why had he never noticed her before?

He'd met her, what—half a dozen times? Exchanged no more than perfunctory greetings with her. He vaguely recalled a couple of comments she'd made—erring on the cheeky side as he recalled—but certainly there had been no actual conversation.

But he'd never really looked at her, not really. His attention had always been elsewhere, on the other people in the room. Or the church. And who noticed other women when you were betrothed and in the process of being jilted? Still . . .

Blind. He'd been utterly blind. But now . . . now he *saw* her.

"Enjoying the evening?" Lady Georgiana repeated. She glanced pointedly at his companions. "Trying to—and failing."

"Ah," Hart said, adding with deliberate provocation, "so, you have no interest in fat men and women caterwauling in public?"

She gasped and her slight bosom swelled with indignation. "How dare you!"

He ostentatiously fingered her broken fan—two of the ivory ribs had snapped. It was no mere flirtatious tap she'd given to Monty's friend—and raised a brow. "How dare *I*?"

Her eyes sparked. She flushed but held out her hand in an imperious gesture. Keeping his gaze locked with hers, he slipped the fan into his pocket.

She lifted her chin. "Thieving now?"

"I say, miss," one of Monty's friends interjected. "Don't you know who this is?"

"Of course she does, lackwit," Sinc said in a low voice. "Lady George was one of the bridesmaids at his wedd—the canceled er—the Unfortunate Event." His words carried across to the other box.

His friend sniffed. "Gel lacks respect."

Her eyes flashed. "*Respect?* What have you—any of you—ever done to deserve respect? Nothing except be born into a life where you've been pampered and petted until you think you are tremendously important." Hart had no illusions about who her little speech was addressed to; she might have waved a scornful hand at all of them, but she hadn't taken her eyes off him.

Sinc, Monty and friends were shocked to silence.

"Georg*iana*!" Lady Salter hissed something else Hart couldn't catch.

"And am I not?" Hart said, all ice and silk. Women rarely challenged him. Not like this—head-on. He wasn't sure whether he was aroused or annoyed. Perhaps a little of both.

"No, like your friends, you're an arrogant, ignorant boor." Ignoring the gasps all around her, she gestured angrily toward the stage. "These people have *talent*, serious God-given talent, and they've devoted their *lives* to honing it. And when they make music, people should listen and be grateful that they're alive and privileged to hear it. Not blunder in with their drunken friends, responding to . . . to *glory* with crass jokes and mindless, mocking, suggestive bibble-babble."

"Georg*iana*!" her aunt snapped. Lady Georgiana lifted her chin, but otherwise ignored her.

Hart raised his brow. "I see." Was she serious? Taking him to task in public? *An arrogant, ignorant boor*, was he? He was no longer intrigued. He was seriously annoyed.

She snorted. "I doubt it. I doubt whether you—"

"Georg*iana*! That's *quite* enough!" Lady Salter said with freezing authority. "Come, Georgiana, Dorothea, we're leaving." She rose and, gripping the girl by the arm, turned to Hart. "I apologize for my niece's outrageous incivility, your grace—"

"I don't," the niece interjected. "I meant every word."

"Hush, you appalling gel!" Her aunt hustled her out. Plump little Lady Dorothea, gathering up shawls and various bits and pieces, lingered a moment and threw him a mischievous smile over the division between the boxes.

"Will we see you at our ball, your grace? Next Wednesday, Berkeley Square?"

Cheek must run in the family. She was old enough to be his grandmother. As if he would honor the blasted Rutherfords by attending their blasted ball.

"Doro*thea*!" Lady Salter snapped from the door. The little aunt winked at him and hurried out. The door closed behind her. The box was empty.

Monty and his friends eyed Hart surreptitiously as he resumed his seat without comment. Aghast, outraged and secretly thrilled by the exchange that had taken place, they discussed it nonstop in ironically low voices until the final act was drawing to a close and Monty was recalled to the purpose of the evening: his opera dancer.

Hart sat brooding. He did not look at the stage. He did not participate in the discussion. The music and the talk passed over him unnoticed. And when Sinc and his friends went to the stage door to meet Monty's opera dancer, Hart made his excuses and went home.

It was a fine night and he decided to walk. He had his sword stick with him, and frankly, if he encountered any robbers, he would welcome the exercise.

But no robbers obliged him.

No one had *ever* spoken to him like that.

Certainly no female ever had. Was she hoping to pique his interest by acting the opposite of almost every female he'd ever met? Throwing insults instead of gushing with compliments? Risky tactics, if so.

But they had worked, dammit. To a degree.

Arrogant? He was well aware of it. Nothing wrong with arrogance, as long as it was well placed—and in his case it was. Was he to creep around feigning humility? Pretending to be less than he was? Such disingenuousness was beneath him.

He marched on, brooding.

Ignorant? Of opera perhaps—he'd never cared much for music. As a boy he'd been dragged to the opera by his mother, supposedly for his education, but it hadn't taken him long to realize her true purpose was otherwise. The presence of her young son was intended to keep the behavior of her various escorts in check. Mama craved masculine admiration, but didn't care to follow through on the expectations she aroused in the breasts of her ardent admirers. Mama liked to keep men dangling.

Just as she did her son; the maternal tenderness she lavished on him in public was never in evidence at home or in private. Unless she was playacting for the sake of one of her schemes. They worked on Papa, but by the time he was fourteen, Hart knew better.

Lady Georgiana though . . . He'd watched her from the shadows, her face well lit by the chandeliers overhead. She'd shown no interest in the young men in the next box, nor in the rest of the glittering, overdressed audience. Her attention had been wholly given to the music—until Sinc's friends had distracted her with their drunken comments.

Her anger seemed genuine.

Then again, she was a woman, and in his experience, women had a tendency to playact and fake things.

Her aunt had offered her to him as a bride. But if that little tirade was meant as some kind of enticement . . . He thought about it. No. She wasn't flirting. She'd meant every word.

Who was she, really? Boyish equestrienne? Demure opera lover. Bold virago?

And why had he never noticed her before?

Her broken fan was in his pocket. He wasn't sure why he'd picked it up, nor why he'd kept it. A completely useless item.

He reached Mayfair, and turned in to Brook Street.

A boor, was he? Daisies poked through some railings, spilling onto the footpath, bright in the gaslight. He slashed their heads off with his stick and strode on.

Dammit, he never let a woman have the last word.

He hadn't even had the chance to talk about buying her blasted horse.

And somehow, infuriatingly, he was aroused.

* * *

"Never in all my life have I been so mortified by a young gel's behavior, Georgiana, especially one in my charge! And in such a public place!"

George sat in the carriage and let Aunt Agatha's tirade roll over her. She had no regrets for what she'd said . . . well, perhaps a few. She really hadn't meant to upbraid the duke in quite such a manner. All she'd really wanted was for people to be quiet so she could listen to the music.

But the way he'd emerged from the shadowy corner of his box, that look in his eye—dripping with superiority. Standing there, looking down his long nose at her, so arrogant with that *I-rule-the-world* expression. It had annoyed her from the very first time she'd met him, when he'd become betrothed to Rose.

Thank God that hadn't worked out. She might have been related to him by now.

As soon as he'd stepped forward she realized that he'd been watching her for some time. She'd felt a prickle of awareness, but had told herself that of course somebody would be looking at her, that at the opera everybody looked at everyone else. But the faint, disturbing prickle hadn't gone away.

She was a little bit embarrassed that she'd broken her fan on that other man, but he'd kept talking on and on loudly after she'd asked them several times to be quiet. And the fan was a delicate one, easily broken, so it hadn't actually hurt him. Just made him realize she was serious.

But when the duke had picked it up, his long fingers playing with the broken ribs as he eyed her in that knowing way . . . And then when he'd refused to give it back to her, sliding it into his pocket as though he had every right to keep it—and what would he want with a lady's fan, let alone a broken one?—it was a move calculated to spark her temper. And then, to insult the performers . . .

When her temper rose, her tongue loosened. Perhaps she had gone a bit far, speaking like that to a man she barely knew, and in public, but it was true—men like the duke did assume the world was theirs to rule, that nobody else mattered. But other people *did* matter.

That faint, mocking smile, that knowing glint in his eye, that ironic lift of his eyebrow—just one brow—she couldn't say why it was all so annoying, only that it was. And to call the glorious singing caterwauling . . .

He'd deserved it.

"Oh, Aggie, stop ranting at the gel," Aunt Dottie interjected. "What's done is done, and if you want my opinion, it won't hurt those boys to have heard a few home truths."

"Those boys? We're talking about the duke, not those other ones—though she shouldn't speak like that to any gentleman. And as for home truths—she mortally insulted him, or did you not hear it?"

"I heard every word. But that duke—handsome, brooding devil that he is. I do like a bit of arrogance when it's deserved, and I suspect in his case it is. The man has potential, but it won't hurt him to be taken down a peg or two."

"Potential? He's *a duke*!"

"Yes, dear, I noticed, but he's also just a man, and a man, as dear George pointed out, who has no doubt been indulged and spoiled and pampered all his life. I've never had any time for that silly mother of his."

"The duchess is a friend of mine," Aunt Agatha said stiffly.

"Yes, I know, strange as it is. Can't think what you see in her, Aggie—and, yes, I know she's your goddaughter but you needn't be friends with a goddaughter—but of course, she's a duchess, so of course you're friends."

Aunt Agatha made an offended huffing noise and stared out the window for a minute or two. Aunt Dottie glanced at George and winked. George grinned back at her.

Aunt Agatha thought of another grievance. "And that reminds me, Dorothea. What did you say to the duke as we were leaving?"

Aunt Dottie smiled. "I reminded him about our ball, of course—Rose did give him an invitation, didn't she, George?"

"Yes," George said. "In person." He hadn't exactly received it with pleasure. His response at the time had been scathing. She'd added her own mite: *If you came, you could demonstrate to the ton your supreme indifference. You'd like that, wouldn't you?* He'd ignored her, acted as if she wasn't even in the room.

"Of all the foolish things," Aunt Agatha snapped. "Of course he won't come to the ball. Why would he court humiliation? Attend a ball that was to have been his own wedding ball and is now to celebrate Rose's hole-in-the-corner marriage to a nobody? Ridiculous!"

"That boy will surprise you," Aunt Dottie said tranquilly.

"Which one?" George asked.

"Both of them, I hope. Rose's husband is a dark horse, and the duke is a dark horse of a different color." She clapped her hands. "All these lovely handsome young men. I'm so looking forward to the ball."

Aunt Agatha snorted.

Chapter Five

❦

Surprises are foolish things. The pleasure is not
enhanced, and the inconvenience is often considerable.
—JANE AUSTEN, *EMMA*

SEVERAL EVENINGS LATER, SINC CALLED IN AT EVERING-
ham House to collect Hart for a card night out with friends.

"Won't be a minute," Hart told him, shuffling through a
pile of invitation cards. "Just need to get this off. Help yourself to a drink if you want one."

Sinc sauntered over to the bottles and decanters set out
on a side table and with comfortable familiarity helped
himself. "What is it?"

"Just need to respond to an invitation."

Sinc's jaw dropped. "Respond? But you never respond to
invitations. Famous for it."

"Nonsense."

"You are, you know. So what's this extraordinary acceptance for, then?" He swirled the wine in his glass, sniffed
deeply, then drank.

"A ball."

Sinc choked. "What ball?"

Hart didn't respond. He'd found the invitation he was
looking for and had begun to scrawl an acceptance.

Sinc drained his glass, refilled it, then said in an airily

casual tone, "Which ball is it again?" It was so unlike him that Hart looked up with a frown.

"What is it to you?"

"Might be going too. Could go together. Company, y'know." Sinc made an expansive gesture. "Depends on the ball, of course. It wouldn't be the Rutherford ball, I suppose?"

Hart snorted. "The Peplowe ball, though why it matters to you, I can't fathom."

"Doesn't matter a bit, old fellow. Not a bit, not a jot. Just being friendly, makin' conversation, don't you know."

Hart eyed him thoughtfully. "You're babbling, Sinc. Now why would that be?"

"Babbling? Me? Not a bit of it. What's the world coming to when a chap can't inquire about the plans of another chap without being accused of babbling." Avoiding Hart's eye, he turned to refill his glass.

"You've bet on me, haven't you?"

"Me? Bet?" Sinc said with a feeble attempt at indignation.

"On whether or not I'll attend the Rutherford ball."

"*Pfft!* Bet on you? My oldest friend? As if I would. Good heavens, what an impertinence that would be." He darted a glance at Hart. "You're not going, are you?"

"Of course not."

"Damn."

"Problem?" Hart asked dryly. Of course Sinc had bet on him. Sinc bet on everything.

"Dropped some wine on my breeches." Sinc scrubbed energetically at an invisible stain.

Hart returned to his note.

"So . . . the Peplowe ball tomorrow night," Sinc said. "What brought that on? I thought you hated balls."

Hart gave a lazy shrug.

"But you never attend balls—only for that short time when you were engaged to Rose Rutherford. And you can't be pining after Lady Rose because that was the most cold-blooded arrangement I've ever—" Sinc's eyes brightened. "Oho, so that's it."

"What is?" Hart signed the note with a flourish.

"Everyone knows the Rutherfords and the Peplowes are practically joined at the hip. You're hoping to meet up with Lady George, aren't you? I told you she was a charmin' gal—oh." His eyes narrowed. "You're not planning to punish her for that little contretemps at the opera the other night, are you, Hart? Because if you were . . . well, it wouldn't be gentlemanly."

Hart raised a brow. "Contretemps? I have no idea what you're talking about. I merely wish to purchase her horse."

"Her horse?" Sinc gave a crack of laughter. "Naturally, you're going to a ball for a horse."

"I think you've had quite enough wine."

"Not nearly enough, if you're going to a ball to see a girl about a horse. A horse." He chortled. "Of course you are. Nothing to do with a bright-eyed girl who just happened to set you on your ear the other night."

"She did not set me on my ear," Hart lied. He hadn't been able to get her out of his mind.

"No? I could feel the undercurrent between you. Positively crackling, it was."

"You are imagining things," Hart said coldly. "There was no undercurrent. I am only interested in her horse." He folded the note, addressed and sealed it.

"Yes, yes," Sinc said in a soothing tone. "Of course, her *horse* is the attraction." He paused a moment, then added, "So why not simply make her an offer? To buy the horse, I mean. Not make her any *other* kind of offer."

Sinc had definitely drunk too much, Hart decided. "I did make her an offer for the animal. She refused."

"Told you she would."

"It was an opening gambit. She'll sell. That stallion is far too strong for a lady."

Sinc pulled a doubtful face. "You didn't think it too strong for her the other day when you thought she was a youth."

Hart stood abruptly. "It's time we left."

Sinc drained his glass and set it on the side table. "I always knew it took wild horses to drag you to a society ball, but this is a new one on me. Going to a ball to buy a horse indeed. Most of us just toddle down to Tattersall's and make a bid . . ."

GEORGE STEPPED OUT INTO THE GARDEN FOR A LITTLE fresh air. It was a warm night and Lady Peplowe's ball was "a frightful squeeze" which meant it was a tremendous success. Why people didn't just say that was beyond her.

It wasn't just fresh air she was seeking, though. She'd spotted Lord Towsett weaving his way toward her with that look on his face—again. Would the man never listen?

She'd immediately headed toward the conservatory—it had been locked but she knew where the key was—resolving to have it out with him once and for all. She had a plan.

She'd refused him three times so far, and from the determined expression on his face tonight, he was planning to make it four. She already knew his long-winded declaration speech by heart—it didn't vary much. Of all the charming young ladies in the ton this season, she was, according to Lord Towsett, the fortunate one who met all his requirements.

Requirements indeed!

Pudgy, pompous and supremely smug, Lord Towsett expected her to be overwhelmingly flattered by his offer. He'd blinked when she refused him the first time—quite pleasantly and politely—then laughed and said he understood what she really meant, and what a naughty puss she was to keep him dangling. He knew what ladies were like, he'd said, saying one thing and meaning another.

"No, I mean it," George had insisted. "Thank you for your offer, Lord Towsett, but I decline."

The second time he'd proposed to her, she had been less pleasant and more firm. "I won't marry you, Lord Towsett, not now, not tomorrow, nor any time in the future. I said no last time, and I meant no."

In answer to which he'd chuckled knowingly and called her a naughty puss again. It was infuriating.

The third time he'd proposed, she'd been curt, there was

no other word for it. "Lord Towsett, stop pestering me! I have no interest in marrying you and I never will. So just go away and leave me alone."

But the man was as stubborn as a pig. Once more he'd shaken his head in an infuriatingly understanding manner and told her he would never give up hope.

"Give it up," she'd told him. "There is no hope. I will never change my mind. Find some other girl to annoy."

And here he was again. And here she was, slipping into the conservatory to lurk amid the ferns and the palms.

It was all Emm's fault, of course. The last time Lord Towsett had proposed, she'd told Emm in a fit of temper that if he had the gall to propose to her again, she would have no alternative but to punch him on his very prominent nose.

Of course Emm had been horrified, and before George left for the ball this evening, she'd had to promise that she would neither hit nor slap nor smack nor kick Lord Towsett, nor tip wine or ratafia or hot tea or cream trifle with jelly and custard over him. Or in any way make a public scene.

Unfair tactics. She knew George never broke a promise.

"Just avoid him," Emm had finished airily. Never having had to deal with the man and his impenetrable ego.

It was Penny Peplowe's birthday ball and both Penny and Lady Peplowe were particular friends of the Rutherfords. Lady Peplowe had gone out of her way to befriend Emm and the girls when they'd first come to London and knew nobody. And Penny was a dear, jolly girl and George wouldn't upset her for the world.

Besides, she'd been looking forward to Penny's ball for ages.

Emm was no longer up to attending balls, and given the state of affairs between George and Aunt Agatha, she'd asked Aunt Dottie to play chaperone. Living in Bath as she did, Dottie rarely got to attend large and fashionable London balls and had been looking forward all week to donning a pretty new ball dress and catching up with old friends. There was also a certain perceptible glee in her demeanor at being asked to play chaperone instead of her older sister.

George wasn't going to break her word to Emm—not technically, anyway—nor ruin Aunt Dottie's night. Nor Penny's birthday, or Lady Peplowe's ball. But she sure as anything planned to ruin Lord Towsett's evening.

She'd come up with a Plan.

She would teach him that when she said no she meant it. She wouldn't hit or kick him, and though there would certainly be a scene, inside the dark conservatory it would be perfectly, beautifully private.

She glanced down at the bucket of fishy-smelling sludgy liquid that Lord Peplowe kept for fertilizing his beloved plants. Her promise to Emm had made no mention of accidents with smelly buckets . . .

If Lord Towsett called her a naughty little puss one more time—and he would, oh, yes, he would . . .

She grinned to herself. She had a short, scathing speech of her own to deliver, to be punctuated with the contents of the bucket. Afterward she would show him to the back gate where he could make a discreet, reeking, squelching exit.

He'd never bother her again.

Fanning herself gently with a fern frond, she waited. It was a warm night; the air inside the conservatory was humid and the smell of the bucket . . . She wrinkled her nose. Covering the bucket with a large shallow saucer, she moved it onto a shelf closer to the doorway. It was better there, more conveniently to hand.

She moved back to where the smell wasn't so bad. And waited. What was taking him so long? She was sure he'd seen her come in.

The conservatory door opened. Aha! George peered through the shadowy tangle of greenery. Was that him? He was just a dark silhouette, outlined against the bright globes of lantern light that illuminated the garden outside where Lady Peplowe's servants had hung dozens of pretty Japanese-style lanterns.

The silhouette moved and she cursed under her breath.

It wasn't Lord Towsett after all. This man was taller, leaner, broader shouldered.

She edged farther back into the shadows. She didn't want to be caught lurking in here by some stranger.

Slow, heavy footsteps came toward her, crunching over the crushed limestone that covered the conservatory floor.

George held her breath.

She jumped as the door burst open, and three ladies tumbled in, laughing. One called out, "Such a delightful tease you are, Hart."

Hart? George stiffened. She only knew one person called Hart. The Duke of blasted Everingham. What on earth was he doing here? He never attended society balls. And what was he doing sneaking into the conservatory? She cursed under her breath.

She recognized one of the ladies—Mrs. Threadgood, a married lady with something of a reputation—her long-suffering husband was no doubt inside in the card room. She was with another lady of about her own age. The third was much younger, the other lady's daughter, perhaps.

Mrs. Threadgood laughed coyly. "Naughty boy, you wanted us to follow you, didn't you?"

The ferns rustled beside her. George stiffened. The duke had retreated into her dark corner. Over the rich, fecund scents of the conservatory—and the faint reek of the bucket— a crisp, masculine cologne teased her senses. He was close enough to touch. She was trapped.

Did he know she was there? She stood frozen, barely breathing. Curse him, curse him, curse him!

Two of the ladies had seized lanterns from the garden and were approaching down separate pathways between the plants, chanting, "Come out, come out, wherever you are." The lights bobbed and swayed as they came closer.

Any minute now she'd be discovered, hiding in the dark conservatory, alone with the duke.

"Get rid of them," the duke murmured.

George jumped. He did know she was here. "They're

your ladies, you get rid of them," she whispered. She didn't want to be found here at all.

"You want them to find us both here alone, together in the dark?" He sounded amused. Of course, no one would blame *him*. It was always the women who were at fault in these things.

The ladies with their bobbing lanterns were getting closer. Curse them. Curse him.

George took a breath, then stepped out into the lamplight, saying coolly, "Were you looking for me, Mrs. Threadgood?"

The ladies stopped dead. One held her lantern higher. "Good heavens, Lady George, is that you?"

George inclined her head. "Yes, I'm having a little rest. It was so hot inside. I felt a headache coming on but didn't want to spoil the evening for my aunt. It's so cool and refreshing in here." She paused, then added, "Were you looking for someone?"

"Oh, no, no, no. Just a little game we ladies were playing," Mrs. Threadgood said hastily. "And getting some fresh air, just like you. Er, you didn't see a gentleman come in here, did you?"

"Yes, though I didn't catch his face. He was tall, but was only here for a moment. He went out that door." Peering intently at the floor around their feet, she gestured vaguely toward a side entrance.

One of the ladies tried the side door. "It's locked," she said with a suspicious glance at George.

George shrugged indifferently. "Mmm, is it? Must have latched it behind him." She continued scrutinizing the floor around their skirts.

The ladies followed her gaze. "What are you looking at?"

"Oh, nothing. I just thought—oh, yes, there it is! Don't move, you'll frighten it."

"Frighten what?" Mrs. Threadgood glanced nervously around.

"The rat. I'm trying to catch it—" Whatever else she

meant to say was drowned by shrieks and squeals of horror as the ladies shoved each other through the door in their panic to escape. "It's for my dog," she called after them. "He loves rats."

The door slammed behind them.

"Such a peculiar gel," one of the ladies exclaimed. "Chasing rats! At a ball!"

George couldn't help it, she gurgled with laughter. It was joined by a deep chuckle from the duke. "You realize it will be all over the ton by morning that you hunt rats in your ball gown. The lady ratcatcher."

She shrugged.

"Don't you care what people think of you?"

"Not much. Not people like them, anyway." Or people like him, for that matter. Only insofar as it affected her family.

There was a short silence, then he said, "Well, that's my headache gone. Who's yours?"

George had no intention of explaining. "Don't you mean how's yours?"

He snorted. "No one with a grain of sense would bring a headache into this humid atmosphere—not to mention the frightful stink coming from over there." He gestured toward her bucket. "You're hiding, lurking amid the ferns and palms—"

"I'm not hiding!" She actually was lurking, but she wouldn't admit it.

"Ah, then I am interrupting a romantic rendezvous."

"Nothing of the sort. I only came here—" She broke off as the conservatory door opened again.

"Lady Georgiana, Lady Georgiana Rutherford, are you in there?" It was Lord Towsett—finally. George shrank back into the shadows. Curse it, it was all going wrong. She did not want an audience for her encounter with Lord Towsett.

"Your noble swain arrives," the duke murmured.

"He's not my swain!" she hissed back. More of a swine, really.

"I'm told there's a vicious rat in here," Lord Towsett

called. "Are you there, Lady Georgiana? Don't worry, I will save you."

George groaned.

The duke moved forward. "No women in here, Towsett. No rats, either."

"That's a matter of opinion," George murmured in a voice only the duke could hear.

"Eh? What? Who's that?" Lord Towsett called, peering into the gloom.

The duke stepped into a better light. "Everingham. And as I said, there are no females here, for which I thank providence. Now push off before you attract the ladies' attention, there's a good fellow. I'm trying to grab a few moments to myself, away from the hurly-burly."

Lord Towsett held the lantern higher. "You sure there's no one else here, Everingham? Mrs. Threadgood told me Lady Georgiana was in here, with a rat."

She was, George thought. With two rats.

"Lady Georgiana *with a rat*?" the duke repeated incredulously. He shook his head. "Mrs. Threadgood has clearly drunk too much champagne. There's only me here. And now you."

There was a short silence. "Have you seen Lady Georgiana Rutherford at all? I've been trying to catch a word with her all evening."

The duke snorted. "Dammit, Towsett, do you imagine I, of all people, would be keeping tabs on a Rutherford female?"

"No, no, no, of course not. Though Lady Georgiana isn't like—no. Well, then, I'll be off. Evening, Everingham." He left, shutting the door carefully behind him.

The duke turned back to George. "Your ardent suitor, I collect."

She didn't answer.

"Heard you've refused him several times."

Again she said nothing. It was none of his business.

"Surprises me that you feel you have to hide from him. Thought you had more backbone than that. He's not exactly fearsome, Towsett. Persistent, but not a brute."

"I wasn't *hiding*! I'm not the least bit frightened of Lord Towsett," she flashed. "If you must know, I came here because—" She broke off. It was none of his business.

"Because?" He prompted, but she said nothing.

"No need to be embarrassed, Lady Georgiana," he almost purred. "I'm all ears."

She gritted her teeth. He was enjoying this. "If you must know, I'd promised my aunt I wouldn't make a scene. Anyway, I wasn't the only one who was hiding."

"Would you rather they spied the two of us together?" Even though it was dark, she knew he'd arched that eyebrow of his in that annoying manner he had.

"We weren't 'together'!" she said indignantly. It was his fault those wretched women had come in. She knew what they'd think, what they'd say.

"Truth doesn't matter to gossips like La Threadgood. Appearance is all they care about." And now she could feel his shrug, even though he was several feet away from her.

"They were after you, not me."

"Is it my fault that females chase me?" There was smugness beneath the disdain. The arrogance of the man was something to behold. "Wherever I go, they pop up, like fleas on a dog. It's always been annoying, but since your sister jilted me—"

"Rose did *not* jilt you! It was . . . there were circumstances beyond her control. And she's my aunt, not my sister."

He dismissed Rose with a careless wave. "You have too many aunts to keep track of. Since I *failed to get married*, then, it's become incessant. They call, they write, they try to bribe my servants. One even tried to climb through my window one night. The married ones are irritating enough, but the unmarried ones—what do you imagine those three females wanted just now?"

She shrugged, then realized it was pointless in the dark. "No idea."

"To be compromised. One virgin angling for the appearance of seduction—or at least to be compromised—and two married witnesses." He added thoughtfully, "It might be different if they were all married."

George was disgusted. "Well, I don't want to be compromised, and I have no interest in marrying you, so I'll thank you to take yourself off—discreetly!—before anyone else comes in."

He didn't move. "I'm not finished with you yet."

"What do you mean?" She eyed him suspiciously. "Is this about what I said at the opera the other night?"

He snorted. "Hardly. But I did come to this ball specifically to talk to you. So when I saw you enter the conservatory, I followed you."

"Why?" She backed away. "I don't want to talk to you."

"It's about your horse."

"My *horse*?" It was the last thing she'd imagined.

"The black stallion. What's your price?"

She stared at him a moment. "He doesn't have a price."

"Well, think of one," he said impatiently. "I wish to buy him."

"Well, you can't. Didn't you get my note? He's not for sale."

"Nonsense." He named a price that made her blink.

The very assurance of him, the arrogant way he just assumed that her horse was his for the taking, that all he had to do was name a price infuriated her. "You're as bad as Lord Towsett."

"I am *nothing* like Lord Towsett." His indignation was balm to her ears.

"Yes, you are—you're exactly the same. Each of you is so puffed up in your own consequence that you can't possibly conceive of anyone refusing you anything. I'm fed up with men who can't take no for an answer. So listen here, duke—I don't care if you offer me a million trillion pounds, Sultan is not for sale. He's mine and he's staying mine. Now go away."

There was a short silence.

"I said, go away."

"I'll leave," he said eventually, "but this conversation is not over."

"Oh, yes, it is."

George heard the crunch of gravel under his feet as he made his way to the door. He opened it and paused, a stark silhouette against the bright party lights outside. "I always get what I want in the end."

"*Worse* than Lord Towsett," George called after him, but the door had already closed.

Chapter Six

❧

She attracted him more than he liked.

—JANE AUSTEN, *PRIDE AND PREJUDICE*

HART SLAMMED THE CONSERVATORY DOOR BEHIND HIM.
Worse than Lord Towsett indeed!

The whole point of coming to this ball had been to
discuss—in a civilized manner—the sale of her horse. Instead he'd had to put up with impertinent queries, blatant
invitations and suggestive remarks—and that was before
he'd even spoken to Lady Georgiana.

He'd noticed her surreptitious entry of the conservatory
and been simultaneously annoyed and intrigued. It was no
business of his with whom she chose to have assignations—
but it irritated him that she'd turned out to be yet another
light-skirt. It shouldn't have surprised him, but it did.

He'd waited a few moments and when nobody seemed
to have followed her in, he did. If her lover was already
there, serve them right for being indiscreet.

Instead he'd found her alone, hiding in a dark corner of
the conservatory, and that had surprised him. She hadn't
struck him as either shy or timid.

And then he'd realized that she was hiding from Lord

Towsett, avoiding yet another proposal from the self-important little tick, because she'd promised her aunt that she wouldn't make a scene—and that he could believe.

Breathing in the fresh, cool air of the night, so welcome after the humid mustiness of the conservatory, he glanced up and saw Towsett leaning on the balustrade of the balcony that led from the ballroom to the garden and the conservatory. He was sipping champagne, and glancing back and forth between the ballroom and the garden. Towsett noticed Hart, raised his glass in greeting, then returned to his surveillance.

Each of you is so puffed up in your own consequence that you can't possibly conceive of anyone refusing you anything. I'm fed up with men who can't take no for an answer.

The sight of Lord Towsett standing so smug and self-assured, drinking champagne while Lady Georgiana lurked in a fern-filled conservatory instead of dancing with her friends, kicked Hart's mood from irritation into anger. He marched across the garden and mounted the steps to the balcony.

Towsett greeted him with a broad smile. "Ah, Everingham, old man, don't suppose you've seen that little filly of mine. She's provin' demmed elusive this evenin'." The cheery man-to-man greeting darkened Hart's mood further.

"A word with you, Towsett." Without waiting for a reply, he seized Towsett's elbow in a hard grip and steered him through the ballroom, ignoring the various greetings and salutations as he passed.

Towsett trotted along beside him, trying to wriggle out of Hart's grip, while at the same time trying to hide that he was being unceremoniously marched from the room. "I say, Everingham—what the devil— Ouch! You're hurting me. What the—? Where are you taking—? Ow!"

Hart took no notice. He wasn't quite sure what he was doing; all he knew was that he was furiously angry. He marched the man through a series of hallways and anterooms until he found an empty room. He thrust Towsett from his grasp.

The man staggered back and tried to smooth his rumpled coat. "You're being very mysterious, Everingham," he joked in the way that a man did when he was nervous and didn't want to appear so. "Not planning to murder me, are you—ha ha."

"Not tonight."

Towsett took a step back. "Now look here—"

"You're leaving the ball," Hart told him. "Immediately."

"But I haven't—"

Hart cut him off. "You will take leave of your hostess, explaining you have a headache."

"But I don't—"

Hart took a step toward him. "You will not talk to another soul. You will go straight home."

"Now look here, Everingham, I don't know what you're playing at, but I don't have any intention of—oof!" Hart shoved him back against the wall.

"I'm not finished. You will go straight home and you will write a letter."

"A letter?"

"To Lady Georgiana Rutherford, in which you will apologize for pestering her—"

"Pestering? I have never pest—"

Hart seized him by the shirtfront and banged him against the wall, holding him just above the point where his feet could touch the floor. In a soft, savage voice he said, "In this letter you will apologize for pestering the lady. You will also withdraw your suit—unconditionally and forever. Do you understand me?"

Towsett scrabbled to escape his grip. "But Lady George—"

"Is not interested."

"I love her."

"Tough!" Hart banged him against the wall, harder. "For God's sake, Towsett, how many times have you proposed to the girl?"

"Three."

"And how many times has she refused you?" He'd wager she made it perfectly clear too. He'd only met her a handful of times, but she struck him as a girl who spoke her mind.

Towsett looked away sulkily. "Women say no when they really mean yes, everyone knows that."

"Not everyone! Three refusals definitely means no!" Hart shook him hard. "Do. You. Understand?"

"All right, all right, there's no need to be brutal," Towsett muttered, trying to wriggle free.

When Hart thought of the way the girl had hidden herself in the conservatory, just to escape the attentions of this self-important little weed, he wanted to strangle the man. "Go home and write that letter. And if you bother Lady Georgiana again, you'll have me to deal with, do you understand?" He gave the man a last shake and released him.

Towsett straightened his clothing and gave Hart an aggrieved look. "I suppose you want her for yourself."

"Don't be ridiculous. I barely know the girl."

"Then I don't understand why you would—"

Hart took a menacing step forward. "Go home, Towsett. Now."

Towsett scuttled away.

"WELL, HOW DID IT GO LAST NIGHT?" ROSE DREW HER horse up level with George's. It was not long after dawn, and Hyde Park was deserted, except for Lily and Rose and their husbands and Kirk, the groom employed to attend them. It was a regular Rutherford family ritual, to ride out together first thing in the morning, and then eat breakfast at Ashendon House, regardless of who was married now and where they lived.

This morning the men rode in one group, while Lily and Rose rode either side of George, catching up on the gossip. "Did you finally get through to the pushy little squirt?"

"I didn't get the chance," George said. "But—"

"I saw him arrive," Lily interjected, "and he made a beeline, straight for George—who promptly dived into the ladies' withdrawing room."

"Oh dear." Rose tried not to laugh. "Were you stuck there for long?"

George pulled a face. "Long enough to pin up six hems."

Rose laughed. "And did all six have to be repinned?"

"What do you think? I've never been any good at that stuff."

"So what happened with Lord Towsett?" Rose asked. "I thought the plan was to get him alone and have it out with him once and for all."

"It was. I slipped into the conservatory, and I had a bucket of Lord Peplowe's stinkiest fertilizer all ready to tip—accidentally of course—all over Lord Towsett." The others laughed.

"But—I can feel there's a *but* coming," Lily said.

"Yes. I know he saw me—he was up on the balcony, keeping a lookout for me, and I saw him give a start, then hurry toward the steps."

"But he didn't come?" Rose prompted.

"Oh, he came, but he wasn't the only one." George slipped a sideways glance at Rose. "The duke got there first."

"Which duke—?" Rose broke off and turned her head sharply. "No! You don't mean Everingham, do you?"

"The very one."

"Good heavens. He practically never attends balls. And he followed you into the conservatory? What on earth did he want?"

"To buy Sultan."

Lily gasped. "You're selling Sultan?"

"No, of course not, and I'd already told him so—but his grace the duke of arrogance thinks he can have anything he wants. I told him again that I wasn't selling. I said he could offer me a million trillion pounds and it would make no difference."

Rose chuckled. "He won't like that."

"He didn't," George said with satisfaction. "He stormed off in a huff."

"But what happened with Lord Towsett?" Lily persisted. "I thought getting him alone and giving him a piece of your mind was the plan."

"It was." George so regretted that bucket of fertilizer. She had pictured his face as she dumped it on his smug head. "The duke sent him away. Towsett didn't even realize I was there."

"So you'll have to endure another unwanted proposal? Oh—and his next opportunity will be at my ball tomorrow night!" Rose exclaimed. "Oh dear, and I did so want everything to go smoothly. We don't even have a conservatory. Oh, I could shoot Lord Towsett."

"That's the strange thing," George said slowly. "You won't have to. I received a letter from him this morning—it arrived during the night, hand delivered." She pulled it out of a pocket in her riding habit. "Here, read it."

Rose took it and read it aloud, then stared at George in amazement. "He apologized? And has withdrawn all claims to your hand and will never bother you again? That's wonderful."

"But how? I mean, if you didn't even talk to him last night . . ." Lily began.

"Exactly."

"And Cal wasn't at the ball, so he couldn't have confronted the horrid beast on your behalf," Rose added.

"Cal doesn't even know Lord Towsett has been pestering me," George said. "I swore Emm to secrecy. I wanted to deal with Towsett myself."

"Then what do you think happened?"

George shook her head. "I don't know. It's a mystery." There was a second, smaller mystery that she didn't mention: A footman had come to the conservatory with a message that Lord Towsett had left the ball. And when she'd asked him who sent the message, he refused to say, which made George think he'd been bribed.

She could think of only one person who might have done such a thing, who even knew she was in the conservatory—

but why would the duke care enough to send her a message? It couldn't possibly be him. She'd seen him briefly when she returned to the ballroom, but he'd given her an icy glance, made no attempt to talk to her and left immediately afterward.

So, no, she wasn't going to mention that little incident. It would only stir up speculation, and she wanted to forget all about it.

But for the rest of the evening, free of Lord Towsett's presence and the duke's, she'd had a lovely time. Danced until the wee small hours.

They rode on, and the strangeness of Lord Towsett's unexpected about-face was soon forgotten as talk turned to the ball to be held on the following night, when Rose's husband, Thomas, would be presented to the ton for the first time.

HART SCOWLED. WHAT THE DEVIL WAS HE DOING? HE'D had no intention of attending this wretched affair. It would cause the kind of gossip and speculation he loathed.

And yet his feet kept on moving.

He turned the corner into Berkeley Square, saw the crowd outside Ashendon House and the many carriages lined up, dropping people off. The sight of them alone should have given him pause—he hated crowds—but his feet kept moving.

"Hart! Dear fellow, don't tell me—you are, you are!" Sinc almost fell on him, chortling with delight. "You're going to the Rutherford ball, after all! Oh, that's splendid!"

"Whatever makes you think that?" Hart said dryly. They were almost at the steps leading up to Ashendon House.

Sinc's face fell. "But you're wearing formal duds, enough black for a funeral, except it's nighttime, so—oh, you're bamming me, you rat." He grinned in relief and slapped Hart on the back. "I'm delighted to see you, old fellow, simply delighted."

Hart eyed his friend thoughtfully. "You are showing an unwonted joy at the prospect of my company, Sinclair. Another bet, I suppose."

"*Moi?* Bet on you? My dear old friend?" Sinc tried to look hurt. It failed—smiles kept popping out—so then he tried for humble sincerity. "I am simply pleased to have your company for the evening, my dear fellow."

Hart wasn't fooled for a minute. "You bet on me to attend." They were inside the house now and had joined the crowd of magnificently dressed guests moving slowly up the stairs leading to the ballroom.

Sinc's smile tried desperately to achieve ruefulness, but glee won. "The odds were irresistible."

Hart laughed. "You're a disgrace."

"I know, but I'm a very much richer disgrace than I was ten minutes ago—or I will be as soon as you step through that ballroom door." He pushed Hart up several more stairs, then turned to wave to some of his cronies, standing below them, staring up at them with jaws agape. "Losers," he explained to Hart. "Bet that you wouldn't come." He rubbed his hands in glee. "But I knew better."

Hart frowned. "How? I had no intention of coming." Until half an hour ago, after several hours spent pacing and fuming and being ridiculously indecisive—which wasn't at all like him.

"Ah, yes, but I've known you a devilish long time—ever since we were seven-year-olds, trembling with fright outside the headmaster's office, abandoned by our nearest and dearest and facing the prospect of living with hundreds of young savages dressed in civilized sheep's clothing—and all bigger than us. Ghastly. Remember?"

"Yes, but what does the first day of school have to do with betting I would attend this wretched ball?" They climbed another few stairs.

Sinc grinned. "It doesn't. But I know you. The moment that girl refused to sell you—no, before that—the moment she ripped strips off you at the opera, I knew."

"Knew what?" Hart said irritably. It was more than he knew.

Sinc shot him a knowing look. "No one *ever* refuses you. I knew you couldn't let it rest. And then, when I heard the *on-dit* that Towsett had apologized to Lady George *and* withdrawn his suit, well—the money was practically in the bag. And now you're here, it is, it is! My bag!"

Hart frowned. "How could you possibly connect me with—"

"Towsett's withdrawal?" Sinc chuckled. "So that wasn't you marching him across the floor as if to a court-martial?"

"Oh." He'd been so angry he hadn't thought about witnesses.

"But who cares about Towsett? I collected on that too, and the minute you step into that ballroom, I'll be so delightfully plump in the pocket I won't know what to do with myself—the odds against you coming tonight were stupendous!" He danced up the last couple of steps and practically shoved Hart through the wide double doors leading into the ballroom.

The ball was well underway and the receiving line had disbanded. A dance was in progress. The Rutherfords' butler announced them in a ringing voice: "The Duke of Everingham! The Honorable John Sinclair."

At the announcement there was an audible hush. Heads turned in their direction. Hart ignored them. Then the Countess of Ashendon, lush with child and draped in a green dress that seemed to emphasize rather than disguise the fact, moved serenely across the room to greet them. At the same time, Lady Salter, thin and elegant in shades of smoky gray, cut across toward them from the other side of the ballroom, a thin smile of triumph on her face.

The buzz of conversation resumed, louder than before.

Lady Georgiana was dancing with an elegant young sprig and laughing as if she hadn't a care in the world. Hart knew she'd heard him announced, for she'd turned her head in surprise. As their eyes met, her smile faded to a scowl.

So be it. He bowed over Lady Ashendon's hand.

* * *

"WHAT'S *HE* DOING HERE?" GEORGE MUTTERED TO LILY, indicating the duke. He stood looking around the ballroom as if he owned it, darkly elegant in black, those cold eyes of his half closed as if he were bored to death already.

"But it's a *good* thing he came," Lily said. "Isn't that why Rose invited him? To show everyone that there were no hard feelings?"

"Yes." But there were hard feelings, George knew. He just hid them under a veneer of boredom and ice. And superiority.

Curse him. She'd anticipated a night of unalloyed pleasure, enhanced by the last-minute apology sent by Lord Towsett to Emm, claiming something had come up preventing him from attending. Which was an unexpected joy and a relief.

But now the duke was here, and she knew, she just knew that he was going to spoil everything.

That look in his eye as he met her gaze . . . She didn't trust it. He'd come to make trouble.

Her partner arrived for the next dance and George tried to forget the duke and to enjoy the ball. All her friends were here, and now that nobody was pestering her to marry him, she could relax and simply have fun.

Except that she could feel the duke's gaze, like a cold and sinister weight on the back of her neck, following her around the room.

He had a score to settle with her—the opera, no matter what he'd claimed before, her words had to have rankled. And as for what she'd said to him in the conservatory—he hadn't liked that at all.

Too bad. She'd meant every word. But if he tried to spoil Rose and Thomas's ball, the one that Emm and everyone had worked so hard to organize, when really, all Emm should be thinking about was the coming baby—well, George would make the duke sorry he ever crossed her path.

She mightn't have been part of this family for long, but

she was devoted to each and every member. And would protect them with her life.

Oh, stop being melodramatic, she told herself. Yes, he was focused on George for some reason—every time she looked at him, he was watching her—but he was probably only getting ready to pester her again about selling Sultan. These men who thought they only had to snap their fingers and everyone would rush to please them . . .

The next time she glanced at the duke—for some reason she felt impelled to keep an eye on him—Emm glided across the floor to welcome him, and a moment later Rose joined her. George tensed, bracing herself to hurry across the dance floor and intervene if necessary. Though what she would do, she wasn't quite sure.

She watched anxiously, but the conversation between them seemed a little stiff but quite civilized. At the end of a short exchange, the duke bowed, and then he and his friend strolled toward the card room.

George breathed again. Perhaps it would be all right after all. Maybe the duke was not planning to revenge himself on Rose and Thomas.

Her own partner arrived and they joined a set made up of friends, jolly and young and carefree. One of the young men decided to play the fool, pretending to have forgotten the steps, and there was much laughter and silliness as they steered him through the movements of the dance.

When George had first come to London she hadn't expected to enjoy any of the social whirl, tied down as it was by endless rules, spoken and unspoken—very few dos and hundreds of do nots. She hated most of the do nots.

As well, she'd never danced in her life and had dreaded having to perform in public, fearing to make a complete fool of herself. Rose and Lily and Emm and Cal had taught her, as well as a little Frenchman who made his living teaching the latest dances to all the best people.

To her surprise, once she stopped feeling like a clumsy oaf, George loved to dance and was even quite good at it, if her partners' compliments were to be believed.

After the dance, still smiling with remembered laughter, George sat sipping a lemonade her partner had fetched for her. Next up was the supper dance. She was looking forward to that—and to the supper afterward; she was starving, and glorious scents had been coming from the kitchen all day. She looked around for her partner but saw instead Aunt Agatha sailing toward her like the ship of doom, grim purpose in her eye.

"Georgiana, come with me." Aunt Agatha didn't ask, she commanded.

"But it's the supper dance, and Sir Matthew Carmichael has—"

"Sir Matthew has found another partner. Come." Seizing George by the wrist Aunt Agatha tugged at her to move. On the other side of the ballroom George could see her erstwhile partner, Sir Matthew, bowing over the hand of another young lady. He caught George's eye, grimaced a rueful apology and led the young lady onto the floor.

How odd. Sir Matthew had been so keen to dance with her that he had reserved this dance several days earlier. What had changed his mind?

Bemused, George allowed herself to be towed. Until she saw where they were headed. "Oh, no. Not him." She tried to pull away, but her aunt's bony fingers gripped like death.

"He is an honored guest and you will not make a fuss," Aunt Agatha snapped. Short of wrestling with her elderly aunt in public, George's only alternative was to allow herself be led up to the Duke of Everingham. Those cold graygreen eyes bored into her as she approached. Lichen on stone. Frosted ice on a pond.

Would it hurt the man to smile?

"Your grace, may I present my niece, Lady Georgiana, as a desirable partner for this dance." Aunt Agatha's voice oozed with satisfaction.

The duke's heavy-lidded eyes showed nothing, not pleasure nor anger nor any kind of human emotion at all. Except boredom. Such fun to be him.

There were any number of ladies here who would swoon

with delight to be presented to the duke—why did it have to be her? The family sacrifice on the altar of reconciliation and politeness.

He bowed slightly and offered his arm. "Lady Georgiana, may I have the pleasure of the next dance?" Said without the slightest hint of pleasure or enthusiasm. Or even interest.

George ached to refuse him, but she was committed to making this ball a success, and common politeness forced her to allow the duke to lead her out onto the dance floor with every appearance of willingness.

She didn't smile at him, though. If he wanted to act as though she were a dreary duty, she wouldn't bother to pretend His Frozen Grace was a desirable partner.

"Do you always get old ladies to kidnap dance partners for you, duke?" she said as he led her toward a set that was forming.

"Lady Salter offered," he said smoothly, adding, "I expect she thought you needed help finding a suitable partner."

"I *had* a suitable partner. He engaged himself to dance with me several days ago." How had he convinced Sir Matthew to give up this dance? Bribery? Intimidation? Or had Aunt Agatha done it?

The music started, they bowed and moved into the dance. "Most men I know find their own partners—" They separated to twirl briefly around with another partner. When they came back together, George continued. "Dukes are different I suppose—" She broke off to twirl with another partner. "Silver spoon and all that. I expect all your needs are provided by others."

The gray eyes glinted as he took one of her hands in his and set the other at her waist. "Not all of them."

At her first-ever ball, when she was still quite nervous of dancing in public and getting her steps mixed up, George had discovered that the right partner made an enormous difference. The revelation happened during a progressive dance, where a couple would perform a set figure of steps and then the lady would be twirled on to be received by the next partner. She'd gone from having to concentrate hard, to dancing effortlessly and gracefully, not missing a beat. She'd thought she'd mastered the dance and was enjoying herself hugely—until she was passed on to her next partner, an earnest, clumsy young man, who took them both back to beginner status.

The duke was, she had to admit, an excellent dancer, though it was a mystery how he'd achieved that level of skill when he rarely attended balls. The way he guided her through the steps was both deft and masterful—and a little unsettling.

It wasn't that he behaved in any inappropriate way; indeed he was perfectly cool, distant and conventional. It was just that whenever his hands touched her—and it was only in the various required movements of the dance, nothing untoward—she . . . she *felt* it. The warmth, the strength of his hands—even though they were both wearing gloves.

Shivers ran through her, though she wasn't at all cold.

To be twirled and turned and steered this way and that effortlessly and confidently by his big warm hands . . . She felt like a leaf caught up by an irresistible tide. She didn't like it, the feeling of helplessness. But, she told herself, it was just a dance, a perfectly ordinary dance. She could stop, or step out of it any time she chose. And he was just a man, one she didn't like very much.

His scent disturbed her too, a combination of clean pressed linen, soap and a faint hint of cologne—citrus and spice, something crisp and masculine. It took her instantly back to those moments when they'd stood, almost touching, in the darkness of the conservatory. It felt . . . too . . . too intimate.

It felt as though every eye in the ballroom was on them.

She couldn't wait for the dance to be over.

"I suppose you're used to it, all this attention," she commented as they came together in a movement. It was polite, after all, to make conversation. Not that he was bothering.

His shoulder moved in the barest hint of an indifferent shrug.

"So disheartening," she said, "seeing that after all these

years of civilization, and for all our so-called sophistication, most people are still no better than the ancient Romans, gawking at a spectacle, hoping for blood—or scandal."

A dark eyebrow rose. "Lions and Christians?" he said when they came together again.

"Yes."

His eyes glinted. "And which would you class me as— lion or Christian?"

"Oh, neither." The dance separated them then, and when the steps reunited them, his brow rose in a silent prompt.

"You'd be the emperor, above it all, looking down your long nose at the struggles of the mere mortals, untouched. Uncaring. Indifferent."

His eyes narrowed, but he said nothing.

They danced on. A dance had never felt so endless.

Finally it was suppertime. But George found there was no way for her to wriggle out of supper with the duke. She tried, asking to be excused because she had a headache and needed to lie down.

To which he replied callously, "Nonsense. You'll feel better with some food in you. And if the headache persists, we'll find you a nice humid conservatory to cool off in." Proving he had no belief in her purported—and imaginary— headache.

He escorted her into the supper room and, to her surprise, steered her away from the top table, toward a table that was already filling. Aunt Agatha and her tame escort hesitated, then made for the top table where Emm and Cal and Rose and Thomas were already sitting.

The duke seated her and took the chair beside her. There was a mild scuffle as two ladies dived to get the seat on the other side of him, much to the discomposure of their partners. The duke appeared not to notice any of them; his attention was all on George.

As George removed her gloves and tucked them into her reticule, Aunt Agatha leaned forward and, from across the room, eyed George in a minatory be-nice-to-the-duke fashion. George bared her teeth in not quite a smile.

The duke proved to be a solicitous supper partner and presented George with a variety of dishes, all very much to her taste. She accepted a portion from every one. She really was very hungry, and the spread was magnificent. The memory of hunger, going several days without food, was not all that far in her past, and it simply wasn't in her to refuse food when it was offered.

Nor could she waste good food by toying with it in a ladylike manner and leaving most of it on her plate. She allowed her plate to be filled and ate the lot. She ignored the sideways looks from the ladies close by. What she did was none of their business.

The lady beside the duke kept trying to engage him in conversation. As far as George was concerned she was welcome to him, but the duke merely responded to the woman's gushing efforts with bored-sounding monosyllables, then returned his attention to George. It was very annoying. He ought to have better manners.

What was he playing at? If his purpose in coming here tonight was to indicate to the ton that there were no hard feelings between him and the Rutherford family—Rose in particular—he could have left after his dance with Rose.

This very particular attention to George—so uncharacteristic and public—was drawing unwelcome attention from some of the ladies. Speculative attention. Unfriendly speculation at that, she could tell.

She tried to engage the gentleman on the other side of her in conversation, old General Fairfax, a former commander of Cal's, but the general was deaf and extremely focused on his supper. For each of her efforts he gave a smile and a nod and returned to shoveling in food, as if at any moment someone would come to snatch his plate away.

As a distraction the general was useless.

The duke plied her with food and drink and gave her his full attention. Taking her cue from the general, George gave supper her full attention.

She felt like a mouse feeding under the gaze of a cat. Or a hawk. A lady mouse with an unladylike appetite. She did her best to throw off her self-consciousness. If he didn't like her eating so much, he shouldn't have served her all this delicious food.

Besides which, eating prevented conversation, and that suited George. Every time she'd spoken to this duke she'd managed to offend him. Crab patties were safer than opinions, when one was trying to be good.

"The crab patties are very good, don't you think?" the duke murmured as he signaled for her glass to be refilled with champagne.

She almost choked. Had he been counting? Was his comment sarcastic, an oblique accusation of gluttony? She gulped down some champagne and muttered, "Cook has done a splendid job."

Around the tables there was a buzz of conversation, something about Rose's husband and an earl. She couldn't quite make it out. She glanced across to where her family was sitting on the other side of the room. They all looked happy enough.

The duke followed her gaze. "Lady Rose's husband looks rather better than the previous time I saw him."

"Yes, well, he would. He'd had a difficult time of things." And then before he could make any critical comment about the man who'd supplanted him, she added firmly, "We are all very fond of Thomas."

"Lady Salter spoke of him earlier—she didn't seem very fond of him," the duke observed.

"No, well, Aunt Agatha doesn't like anyone very much."

"She likes me."

She slid him a sideways glance. "Exactly."

The winter-gray eyes glinted, but whether with amusement or irritation she couldn't tell.

Her plate was empty. "What will you have next?" the duke asked. "Fruit tartlets? A cream horn? Lemon curd cake? Brandied custard? Jellies, frosted grapes, ice cream? All of the above?"

"Just some ice cream and grapes, thank you." She couldn't resist ice cream, and the frosted grapes, dipped in beaten egg white and coated with finely pounded sugar—she'd watched them being made in the kitchen—looked cool and delicious.

He filled a bowl for her, then served himself. She watched with reluctant amusement as he filled his own plate. He'd eaten sparingly from the earlier dishes—that hadn't surprised her; he was very lean and hard looking—but it seemed the duke had a sweet tooth. It almost made him seem human.

Almost.

"I noticed the other day on the heath that you are a very fine rider, Lady Georgiana."

George tensed. Here it came, the purpose behind all this attention—his next offer to buy Sultan. Would the dratted man never give up?

She clenched her jaw and waited, but instead he said, "I presume you enjoy hunting."

"You presume wrong," she said curtly and turned her attention to the last of her ice cream.

He raised a brow. "You don't ride to hounds? Then you're missing—"

"Foxhunting is despicable. It's cruel and uncivilized and—"

"Nonsense! It's a fine sport."

"*Sport?*" Her temper rose and she put down her spoon with a clatter. "You think it's *sporting*? Dozens of men on horseback and a baying pack of hounds, all chasing one small fox?" Despite her vehemence, she managed somehow to keep her voice low. "And when the poor little thing is finally exhausted and cornered, you watch as the hounds rip it apart! It's utterly barbaric!"

"Foxes are vermin and their numbers need to be kept down." His voice was cold.

"They are God's creatures and have as much right as any of us to exist. As for controlling their numbers, how does that explain why when someone attends their first hunt—their first kill—and most of the time it's a child—you cut off the fox's brush and wipe its blood on the child's cheek

and call it an *honor*! Blooding a *child*! If that's not barbaric, I don't know what is."

There was a short silence. She bit off a grape and
crunched through the hard, sugary coating, then added in
case he didn't get the point, "I despise foxhunting and all
who participate in it."

His face was carved from granite, his expression unreadable, his eyes cold and flinty. She turned her face away
and became aware that people were leaving the supper
room. Thank goodness. This ordeal was over. She set her
napkin aside.

He immediately rose and politely moved her chair out of
her way. "A moment more of your time, if I may, Lady
Georgiana."

He'd taken up quite enough of her evening. "I'm sorry, I
have an engagement for the next dance."

"Your partner won't mind. This won't take a moment."

"He won't mind? I suppose you've fixed it so that he has
relinquished his dance, too? How many more of my partners have you suborned?"

"Don't be melodramatic. A quiet word in his ear was all
that was required. The fellow went quite willingly." He
gave an infinitesimal shrug. "To the victor go the spoils."

"I am not anyone's *spoils*."

His gaze moved over her in a leisurely sweep. "No,
you're not, are you?"

What did he mean by that? She didn't know but she
didn't like his tone, or the way he looked at her, like a cat
surveying his next dish of cream.

"How splendid to be you and have everyone fall in with
your wishes," she said sarcastically.

"It is, rather," he agreed. "Now, show me where the library is."

What did he want with the library? she wondered. But if
that was what it took to get rid of him . . . "It's along there."
She pointed.

He took her elbow in a light grip. "Show me."

She glanced across at her family. Cal was helping Emm

up from her chair, so tender and solicitous of his wife it caused a lump to rise in her throat. Rose was smiling up at Thomas, who looked stunned and a little preoccupied. Lily was already leaving the room, arm in arm with her Edward, oblivious of the fashion that husbands and wives should not live in each other's pockets. Aunt Dottie was still happily eating and talking animatedly to her escort, a handsome, elderly gentleman.

Aunt Agatha was eyeing George through her lorgnette. She indicated with a jerk of her head that she should go with the duke. So she was in on this, whatever "this" was. All for the duke, was Aunt Agatha.

For a second it occurred to her that perhaps Aunt Agatha had lied the other day when she said the duke had rejected George as a possible bride. However he wasn't acting the slightest bit suitorlike. And he must know from his friends that she had no interest in marriage. No, he probably only intended to make her another offer for Sultan.

"Lady Georgiana?" he reminded her. "The library."

George gave him a long cool look. "Very well." She would show the duke to the library and then, finally, she would escape.

Chapter Seven

❧

Heaven forbid!—*That* would be the greatest misfortune of all!—To find a man agreeable whom one is determined to hate!—Do not wish me such an evil.
—JANE AUSTEN, *PRIDE AND PREJUDICE*

HART OPENED THE DOOR TO THE LIBRARY—IT WAS EMPTY—and held the door for her. "Just a quick word," he said. She gave him a narrow, suspicious look, but stepped inside. He followed her in and closed the door.

Her smooth complexion was delicately flushed—temper, he assumed. She hadn't liked being given no choice about going with him. Just as she hadn't liked being forced to dance with him, and going in to supper with him.

He didn't think it was an act either. At the opera he'd wondered whether her outrageous comments were designed to attract his attention—he was inured to the things women would do to make him notice them. But she'd made no attempt to follow them up or to engage his interest at any future point.

His friends seemed to think that was just how Lady George was—unconventional and outspoken. But they liked her anyway. No doubt because they'd all swallowed the nonsense about her planning never to marry and felt perfectly safe with her.

Hart wasn't convinced. Of course she might have an aversion to men as a gender, and if that were the case, he had no use for her. But he didn't think that was so.

At the opera, and in the conservatory he'd been aware of an undercurrent of sexual attraction between them. He'd certainly felt it, and he didn't think it was one-sided.

His mouth dried each time he watched her cross the room, with that coltish yet oddly graceful, long-legged gait of hers. And her gaiety as she'd danced with her friends, sprightly and slender, laughing unselfconsciously—it was quite . . . appealing.

Just one question remained in his mind.

"So, what do you want?" she demanded. A few tiny crystals of sugar glittered at the corner of her mouth. Hart couldn't take his eyes off them.

"Is it about what I said to you at the opera? Because if so, I'll have you know—"

"It's not about the opera."

She folded her arms beneath her breasts. "So it's about my horse, then? I told you, Sultan is—"

"Not for sale. I know."

She frowned. "Then what's it about?"

"This." He drew her toward him.

She leaned away from him, pushing at his shoulders but not hard enough to break his hold. "What are you—?"

He cupped her chin. "You have sugar on your mouth, just here." She blinked, and before she could react, he bent and licked it away, tasting the sweetness and crunch of the sugar along with a hint of her own female sweetness. The swift streak of heat startled him.

He drew his head back and stared at her. He hadn't expected this. Sweetness, heat. Hunger.

Her eyes, wide and dark, scanned his face. She looked bewildered, troubled, surprised. And wary, like a vixen scenting a trap.

She'd felt that heat too, he was sure, and didn't know what to think of it. Her lips were parted. Her breathing hitched—and he knew why it did, because his own pulse was pounding.

She pressed her palms against his waistcoat, holding him off, though not quite pushing him away. "What do you—*mmph*!"

He bent and kissed her again, softly at first. Her mouth was lush and soft. He eased her lips apart and deepened the kiss, hungry for more of her. Lord, but the taste of her swept through him like wildfire, hotter than before, as if he were already addicted.

She raised her fists—he half expected her to beat him off—but instead they wavered, and after a moment of hesitation she gripped his lapels and clung hard, angling her mouth to fit herself better to him. And pressing her body against his.

She tasted of sweet, hot honey, unexpectedly luscious and somehow wild. And there was anger and surprise and hunger, deep hunger.

By the time he released her he was breathing heavily. Stunned, he stared down at her. He'd thought her attractive, but this . . . His head was spinning. And his body was afire, hard and aching.

She blinked and after a few seconds managed to muster a glare. "H . . . how dare you." But it was a feeble, half-hearted objection and they both knew it. She tried again. "What do you think you were . . . ?" She faltered, realizing where her question was leading, and that it was to nowhere that would do her any good.

His little termagant was delightfully flustered. He was damnably shaken himself, but determined not to let her see it.

She suddenly noticed where her hands were and released his coat abruptly, then staggered.

He caught her by the waist and steadied her.

"Stop that! Let go of me!" She pushed at his hands. He released her instantly and she stumbled back, and she bumped into an armchair. She grabbed the back of it and steadied herself.

Her cheeks were flushed wild rose, her lips were plump and damp. Those extraordinary smoky eyes of hers were wide and dark and glittered with emotion.

A woman aroused. By one little kiss. Well, two. Barely.

"Well now, you're full of surprises, aren't you?" he murmured and was pleased to hear he sounded quite cool. Quite the opposite of what he felt.

She dashed the back of her hand across her mouth as if to wipe his taste away. "I don't know what you mean. Get out."

He didn't move. "I was curious. I wished to see whether you have an antipathy to men, as is rumored." And how wrong rumor was. It took all his considerable powers of control not to snatch her back into his arms and finish what he'd started, but this was neither the time nor the place. He needed to get away, to think. To plan.

"I do have an antipathy to men—especially to you!"

He gave her a slow smile. "No, you don't."

"I do. I cannot bear you! I loathe the very sight of— *mmph*." He kissed her again.

This time when the duke released her, George's knees simply gave way. She collapsed into the chair. She sat with eyes closed a minute, dazed, trying to think of something scathing—really, really scathing—to say to the duke. But her heart was pounding and her brain was in turmoil and nothing, not a single word, scathing or otherwise, came to mind.

And when she opened her eyes, he was gone.

She stared at the open door, then touched her fingers to her mouth. It wasn't sore, but it felt swollen. She wanted to scrub her whole mouth out to remove the taste of him—it felt almost as though he had branded her. She needed something to wash his taste away.

A tray sat on the sideboard with glasses and several decanters. Someone had been in here tonight, drinking. She rose to pour herself a glass—lord, but her legs were as wobbly and uncertain as a newborn foal's. What had that wretched man done to her?

She poured herself a large brandy, drank a mouthful, choked—it was horrid stuff—and drank again. Medicinal use. She waited. The liquor burned deep within her, warming and smooth.

But it didn't banish the duke's taste. Instead it was as if it had blended with his essence, so that forever after the taste of brandy would evoke the Duke of Everingham.

No loss, George decided. She'd never liked brandy anyway. But it had poured strength back into her legs. She would return to the ballroom and act as though nothing had happened.

Because nothing had. She would put it—him—the kiss—entirely from her mind.

HART WALKED HOME, TURNING OVER THE EVENTS OF THE evening in his mind. He hadn't planned to kiss her. Oh, who was he fooling, of course he had. Just to test his theory.

He hadn't planned on . . . that.

Fire and innocence and rebellion and . . . he didn't know what else. Surprise.

What a mass of contradictions she was.

Graceful dancer, passionate music lover, outspoken animal defender—outspoken everything—and loyal to her family. He hadn't missed how swiftly she'd leapt to the defense of Lady Rose's husband, who she'd only known a short time.

Lady Salter's words came back to him. *I had thought, your grace, that marriage to a young woman of good family, an independently minded young woman who would not hang off your sleeve, a girl who wants nothing more than to retire to a country estate and be left to breed horses, dogs—and possibly children—would be exactly what you required. A wife who would keep out of your way and give you no trouble.*

The last—no trouble—was clearly nonsense, but at least she wouldn't bore him. She wasn't the least bit intimidated by him—not by his title, not by his manner. And *obedient* was probably the last adjective one would apply to her. That would have to change, of course, but from everything he'd learned about Lady Georgiana Rutherford so far, the rest was true.

His main reason for marriage was to get an heir. Did it really matter what his wife did after that? Especially if she wanted to live in the country, raising her horses and dogs and children. Leaving him to get on with his life. It would be better than having a wife cuckolding him in London, as many married men had.

There was about her the air of a free spirit. Could she be tamed? Would he want her tamed, or was that part of what currently appealed to him?

He thought of how she appeared on horseback. A magnificent horsewoman, a veritable young Amazon—born for the hunt, of course, though she didn't believe it. And yet, what she'd said about hunting—it wasn't the usual sentimental claptrap some ladies bleated on about. There was passion and fury beneath her convictions. Mistaken as they were.

She didn't know what she was talking about. Get her out on that stallion of hers one crisp winter's morning, with the hounds baying and the excitement of the chase alive in the air. He could just see her—

Hart stopped dead in the street, staring blankly into the shadows between two gaslights.

He *had* seen her. Dammit, it was some years ago, but now he'd made the connection, it was all coming back to him.

No wonder the sight of her galloping over the heath on that black horse of hers had nudged at the edge of his memory. It had puzzled him, that faint sense of recognition, because he knew very few youths, and the only jockeys he knew were his own. But that horse . . .

Now he remembered. He had seen her, met her—so to speak—one winter morning, three or four years ago.

He'd been avoiding Christmas, as usual. After his father

died, Christmas had become more unbearable than ever. Not because his mother was grieving—although of course she put on a fine show of it—but because his own grief was real and deep. And private.

Then, once he turned twenty-one, she'd started throwing eligible young ladies at him. Inviting them to house parties at Everingham Abbey. And enacting him tragedies when he showed no interest.

It was easier to stay away, so when Stretton, an old schoolfellow, had invited him to visit, promising some good hunting, Hart, of course, had accepted, taking the invitation at face value.

More fool he. It turned out that Stretton's two unmarried sisters were the quarry he was expected to hunt. Hart had gravely disappointed them.

On New Year's Day, an actual foxhunt was arranged, and that was when he'd first come across Lady Georgiana Rutherford. Not that he knew her name, or that she was a lady. He hadn't even realized she was female.

The hunt had started well. It was a crisp, icy, glorious morning, and it hadn't taken the hounds long to catch the scent of reynard. The chase was on.

Over hedges, across ditches, mud flying, cold air scouring his lungs, the baying of the hounds, the sound of the horn—this is what he lived for, why he adored hunting. His horse's hooves shattered the thin layer of ice from the previous night's frost, tossing up mud and the scent of the earth, a distant hint of summer hay, long dead but still sweet.

Utter exhilaration.

Then without warning . . . it all fell apart. The hounds stopped, scattered, distracted, the fox seemingly forgotten.

The master swore and threw down his whip in disgust. "One of these days I'll murder that hell-born brat!" He'd shaken his fist in the direction of a boy sitting bareback on a young black stallion watching them from the crest of a hill. Relaxed, gleeful—his very pose expressed contempt.

Other men joined in. "I'd like to strangle the little wretch."

"Needs a damn good thrashing!"

Stretton came puffing up to join Hart. "Oh, I say, not again. Bad show that."

"What's going on?" Hart asked him. The sudden cessation of the hunt had left him feeling hollow, yet keyed up, disappointed and frustrated.

"Local pest." Stretton indicated the boy on the hill. "Makes a point of ruining every hunt possible." He indicated the confusion of hounds. "Scatters food around, destroys the scent with smoked herring heads, even been known to blow false horn calls that confuse the hounds." He shook his head in disgust. "Blasted fox will be well away now, dammit."

"Why does nobody do anything to stop him?" Hart demanded, gazing at the bold figure on the hill. "Teach him a lesson in interfering with a gentleman's pleasures."

Stretton eyed him. "Why don't you?"

"Dammit, I will." And Hart urged his horse after a different quarry, an insolent boy riding a black horse, bareback.

He recalled the fury that drove him that day, his determination to catch the little wretch and give him a good hiding. The lad rode brilliantly, his horse was young and fleet, but like the boy, not quite into his full growth.

Hart's horse was bigger and stronger and Hart gradually gained on him, the thrill of the chase firing his blood again.

He'd drawn alongside the lad and reached out to haul him from his mount. There was a struggle and they'd both come crashing down onto the muddy ground. The boy didn't move and for a moment, Hart feared that he'd killed him.

But he'd only knocked the breath from his body, and when he took a great, gasping breath, and opened those dazzling smoke-colored eyes, fringed with thick dark lashes, Hart had realized what he'd done. Dragged a young girl off her horse and hurled her roughly to the ground.

He hadn't known what to say. He was shocked. Appalled. Had no words to explain. He'd never laid a finger on any female, not in violence.

"I'm sorry. I—I didn't know," he stammered. "Are you all right?"

She'd given him a long hard look as she gasped to recover her breath. She'd opened her mouth and he'd sat back, waiting to hear what she'd say. Then without warning she kneed him in the balls, scrambled out from under him, swung lithely onto her horse and galloped away, leaving Hart curled in agony on the ground.

Lady Georgiana Rutherford. Not that he knew that back then. The men of the hunt *knew* she was female—damn them! They'd deliberately misled him—but as far as they knew she was just some rich man's by-blow. Not that that was any excuse.

Stretton had sent Hart, in his ignorance, to give a young girl a thrashing.

Hart had confronted Stretton immediately. "Did you know you were sending me after a young girl?"

Stretton had snorted. "Of course. The little bitch needed a lesson. I hope it hurt when you knocked her off her horse. Pity she didn't break her neck."

Thoroughly disgusted, he'd slammed a fist hard into Stretton's face and left the district immediately. He'd never spoken to him again.

He'd put the whole shameful incident out of his mind. Until now.

Hart glanced around him in faint surprise. Somehow he'd gotten himself home. He was in his library, sitting in his favorite leather chair. He had no memory of walking home, none of opening his front door. He could have been attacked by footpads—he'd taken absolutely no notice of his surroundings. He'd even poured himself a brandy. He sipped it now, enjoying the smooth burn as it slipped down his throat.

Lady Georgiana Rutherford. Elusive, rebellious, untamable.

He always did enjoy a hunt.

TRY AS SHE MIGHT, GEORGE COULD NOT GET THE THOUGHT of that kiss—those kisses really, because there were at least two, and there might have been more except she wasn't quite sure when one kiss had started and another ended. All she knew is that they were extremely . . . disconcerting.

And not just because of the effect they had had on her.

Never in her life had her knees turned to jelly, and she didn't trust any man who had the power to do that. To her knees or any other part of her.

Why had he kissed her? It wasn't as if he liked her. It wasn't as if she liked him either. So what had been his purpose?

He'd claimed he wanted to discover whether she had an antipathy to men—and she'd told him she had, especially to him. Surely that was clearer than any kiss. Kisses.

So why?

Was it some kind of payback for what she'd said to him at the opera? Or in the conservatory? Or was he still angry that she'd refused to sell him Sultan?

She'd heard people refer to a "punishing kiss." Was that it? Though it didn't feel very punishy. More disturbing.

She decided to ask Lily and Rose about kissing. Just in a general, nonspecific, casual way. No one must know that the duke had kissed her. If they did there would be a fuss, and she hated fusses.

She asked them after breakfast the following morning, when they were upstairs. Rose was getting ready to leave for her new home with Thomas.

"Have you ever heard of people's knees buckling after a kiss?" George asked casually.

"George!" Rose whirled around from the mirror where she'd been tidying her hair. "You've finally been kissed!"

"No, it was just—I heard some girls talking and I wondered—"

"Who was it?" Lily asked. "It must have been a good kiss if your knees buckled."

"Was it at the ball?" Rose asked. "I was so distracted by what was happening with Thomas that I didn't notice who you were with."

"She was with the duke for a good part of the night. Two dances and supper," Lily said.

"No! So it *was* the duke." Rose turned to her, her eyes wide. "The *duke* kissed you?"

"No, of course he didn't. I dislike him intensely. Why would I let him kiss me?"

But Rose took no notice. "The duke, how strange. Throughout our short courtship he only ever kissed me once, and it was as chaste as chaste can be. Nothing to turn legs wobbly."

"He must have kissed her verrrry thoroughly if her knees went away," Lily said, grinning.

"Stop it," George said, flustered. "Nobody kissed me. It was just—I heard someone saying their knees buckled, as if they'd turned to jelly, and it seemed so unlikely, that's all."

Rose laughed. "George Rutherford, if nobody kissed you last night, explain to us now why your cheeks are on fire."

George pressed her hands to her cheeks. They felt very hot. "All right, somebody did—but I'm not saying who, but—"

"It was the duke," Lily said. "I'm sure of it."

"It wasn't the duke, it was just . . . some . . . man."

"What man? Who?"

"I didn't catch his name."

"A man with no name? Intriguing—if unbelievable."

"But he did have a mouth." Lily giggled. "And possibly a tongue."

"Definitely a tongue if he turned her knees to jelly."

"Oh, stop it. You're both being ridiculous. I don't want to talk about this anymore." It had been a foolish idea to ask them about it. Both Lily and Rose were madly, giddily in love with their husbands, and of course they wanted her to be in love as well—which was never going to happen. She'd never get a sensible word out of them.

Besides, her cheeks were about to burst into flames. George turned her back on them and made a dignified exit. Or it would have been if their giggles hadn't followed her all the way down the stairs.

In any case their knowledge was of no use to her, she decided. Both Lily and Rose were in love. To them kissing was all about love and the effects were an expression of that love.

George didn't love the duke; truth to tell, she disliked him intensely. It was just that his kisses disturbed her.

IN THE DAYS FOLLOWING THE NIGHT OF THE BALL—George couldn't help but think of it as the night of the kiss, even though several momentous things had taken place that evening—she was braced to run into the duke at other society events. She had mentally prepared for it. Had armed herself for it. Was ready and waiting.

She was sure he would come to Lady Pentwhistle's rout. Everyone who was anyone had been invited; it was expected to be the most tremendous squeeze. The duke would arrive, looking sardonic and intimidating—if one allowed it, which she would not. She would ignore him completely—unless he asked her for the first dance, giving her no choice but to accept him, unless she wanted to sit out the night on the wallflower benches, because if she refused him, the conventions of the polite world obliged her to refuse all other gentlemen who asked her that night.

Which of course he would know. Little did he know George was prepared for the sacrifice. An evening of being a wallflower was nothing compared to the look she'd see in his eye when she blithely refused him. Because nobody ever refused the duke.

The duke didn't come to Lady Pentwhistle's rout.

He didn't attend the Heatherton ball, either, or the betrothal party for Charlotte Sandford, or Lady Marclay's Venetian breakfast or any of the other engagements to which she'd been invited.

It was as if the duke had simply disappeared off the face of the earth. Or else returned to his previously unsociable existence.

It was a good thing, George told herself. It was better not

to expect to see him anywhere, though she would quite like to encounter him one more time—she'd now thought of several beautifully scathing things to say to him.

Eventually it became clear that the duke wasn't going to appear at any of the events she attended. Despite that, she couldn't help looking for him.

And every time she looked, there he wasn't.

His disappearance was a very good thing, she told herself. The sooner he was removed from her consciousness the better. Then perhaps she'd stop having those hot and sweaty dreams, where she woke up during the night, gasping, her nightdress all twisted up, her body sticky and overheated. Reliving that kiss. Those kisses.

She tried to get on with her life. She tried to exercise him away. She rode at dawn, in the daytime and at dusk, riding herself and Sultan—and poor Kirk—almost to exhaustion. But all it did was fill her dreams with that glorious chase out on Hampstead Heath. Which in her dreams ended with a kiss—and how wrong—and ridiculous—was that!

She suspected she knew what the matter with her was, and she was fairly sure the problem would pass in a few weeks. All she had to do was to endure the discomfort and the irritation. And wait.

Patience had never been one of her virtues.

The duke continued to stay away, but the dreams didn't. Which was very annoying.

George's life fell back into her usual routine: riding at dawn, morning calls and shopping, walking in the park with Aunt Dottie in the afternoons and then in the evening some party or other.

Rose and Lily had gone to the country, Emm was so near her time she stayed home most days, and George was bored—bored and frustrated. Life had become flat and uninteresting.

Hyde Park at the fashionable hour, could anything be more dreary? Aunt Dottie loved the gentle exercise and the gossip. George loved Aunt Dottie but she hated gossip and found the fashionable hour more tiring than a ride to Hampstead Heath and back.

Three steps along, stop, bow. "Lady So-and-So, how do you do?" Stand for five minutes making boring small talk. Three more steps. "Lady Whoever, what a beautiful hat. Wherever did you get it?" Another few paces. "Did you hear what happened at Lady Somebody's ball the other night? I know! Shocking, isn't it? Do you think . . . ?"

Sometimes the ladies noticed Finn, and the conversation was marginally more interesting. But all too often it was, "No, he doesn't bite. Yes, he is big . . . His name is Finn. A wolfhound . . . Yes, he does eat a lot . . . Yes, he is a dear doggie." That last said through gritted teeth. Dear doggie indeed. As if her noble Finn was some kind of pampered lapdog.

There were times she wanted to scream and run off with her dog into the wilderness. Only there was no proper wilderness, not in London. Only slums and dark alleys and endless hard, unfriendly streets, and she didn't want to run into them at all.

"There's Mrs. Prescott," Aunt Dottie said one day, and when George looked blank, she added, "The lady whose dog you rescued that time."

Mrs. Prescott came bustling up. "Where's FooFoo?" George asked after they'd exchanged greetings and small talk.

"I sent her to the country. She'll be back as soon as her"—Mrs. Prescott glanced around and lowered her voice discreetly—"condition has passed."

"Condition? You mean she's breeding?"

"No, no, of course not. At least I hope not!" Mrs. Prescott said. "I am haunted by the thought that one of those nasty beasts—no! It's unthinkable. Not my dear little FooFoo."

"Let's hope not," George said in a bracing voice. They walked on. Poor little FooFoo, she was at the mercy of her animal nature. George knew just how she felt.

"I bet her precious FooFoo *is* breeding," Aunt Dottie

said. "And to the ugliest brute in the pack." She chuckled. "Mind you, the ugliest ones are often the most attractive. It's not all about looks, you know." She stopped, her gaze across the park, and said with frank appreciation, "Though one must admit that a handsome man is a thing of beauty, particularly on horseback."

George followed her gaze. There, mounted on a magnificent bay gelding, was the duke. He was a picture of masculine perfection. His coat was exquisitely cut to show off his lean, powerful build; his buckskin breeches clung to long, hard, muscular thighs. His horse gleamed, his boots gleamed, his tack was immaculate. Hard gray eyes glinted as he met her gaze and inclined his head slightly.

Then without a word, he rode on.

He'd barely acknowledged her. Or Aunt Dottie.

So arrogant.

Hart saw the moment she'd noticed him; he'd been watching her for the last few minutes, strolling along with her aunt, trying not to look as though she was bored to pieces and chafing at the bit. And despite that hat she was wearing, he could see her reactions quite clearly—she really did have an expressive face. Surprise, relief, expectation and then annoyance, in quick succession.

Excellent. His trip to the country had had the effect he'd hoped, even though his reasons for going had nothing to do with her. His late cousin's estate was in more of a mess than he'd first thought, and a trip to go over the main properties again with his new manager was essential. All kinds of mismanagement had been discovered after Arthur Wooldridge had passed on.

Some of Hart's friends loathed that aspect of being a landowner, considering too close an interest in business to be a sign of ill breeding, perilously close to resembling a cit, but Hart enjoyed it. He found it satisfying to look at a problem, analyze the causes, consider the solutions, select the best option and implement the chosen strategy. And observe the results. And, to be frank, he enjoyed being rich and liked the fact that if he was clever and diligent, he could be even richer.

In this case, his efforts were all for his late cousin's young son, Phillip, only seven years old and already facing a lifetime of debt, thanks to his father and grandfather's improvidence. Not that the boy knew anything about that. Bad enough that he was newly orphaned.

It was a shame that the boy couldn't be sent off to school, but when he'd made the suggestion, his tutor had written back, insisting that the boy was too delicate and high-strung yet for the boisterous environment of a boarding school. Perhaps next year . . .

It was a mess now, but Hart was determined that by the time young Phillip Wooldridge reached his majority, he would inherit a prosperous, well-run estate.

So now Hart was back in London, and the next stage of the hunt had begun. He wanted to waste as little time as possible on arranging his marriage, and his strategy was in place.

He'd pondered the prospect of Lady Georgiana Rutherford a good deal while he was away, applying much the same kind of consideration to her as he did to any business matter. He needed a wife to get an heir. But he didn't want the kind of wife who'd hang off his sleeve and be endlessly demanding. And emotional.

He'd seen what that had done to his father.

Her aunt had claimed Lady Georgiana wished to live in the country, and raise dogs and horses—and children. That would suit Hart perfectly. He didn't need a duchess for ceremonial or political purposes. He had no ambitions in that direction. He didn't need a grand hostess, or anyone to run his various houses—what were butlers and housekeepers and estate managers for, after all?

Lady Georgiana seemed as independent as her aunt had suggested. She was a little volatile, but at least she'd never bore him. That the volatility was partly the effect of unexpected lust—he was sure she was a virgin, unawakened to the pleasures of the flesh—and she didn't quite know how to handle it—pleased him. What pleased him even more was the sensuality that burned beneath that deceptively boyish exterior.

That had really taken him by surprise. Lord, but that kiss in the library still haunted him. It would be no hardship to plant an heir in her.

But lust was ephemeral, and once the fire between them had burned out, he could imagine them settling quite happily—her in one of his country houses, raising her children and animals, him living as he always had, in London, doing what he wished when he wished with whomever he wished.

Lady Georgiana Rutherford was, in short, perfect to his requirements.

As for her apparent determination never to marry—not that he believed it; it was his experience that all women wanted to marry—it didn't bother him at all. He had the solution to that little piece of nonsense well in hand.

Chapter Eight

Her resentment of such behaviour, her indignation at
having been its dupe, for a short time made her feel only
for herself.

—JANE AUSTEN, *SENSE AND SENSIBILITY*

EVERYONE KNEW OLD MRS. GASTONBURY'S *SOIRÉES MUSI-cale* were more to be endured than enjoyed, particularly when her beloved granddaughter was to perform, which she invariably was. Cicely Gastonbury was as enthusiastic as she was tone-deaf.

But old Mrs. Gastonbury was popular, and Cicely was a nice girl. More to the point, Mrs. Gastonbury's cook was excellent and the suppers at the *soirées musicale* were famously superb, so the evenings were always sufficiently well attended and people did their best to smile instead of wince as Mozart, Hayden and Beethoven were routinely murdered.

George sat in the audience between Aunt Dottie and Aunt Agatha, wondering how she could escape. She'd heard that the music would be bad, but hadn't realized quite how bad nor how often Cicely would perform.

"And now before we break for supper, Cicely will enter-tain us with a trio of Scottish ballads . . ."

George closed her eyes and wished she could somehow close her poor lacerated ears. She had to get out.

As Cicely and her accompanist arranged themselves, a footman appeared, bent and murmured in George's ear, "Someone wishing to speak to you outside, Lady Georgiana."

Aunt Agatha, overhearing, frowned. "Who is it?" The footman didn't appear to hear her. At any rate he didn't respond.

Aunt Agatha leaned toward George and said in a low voice, "This is most improper. You cannot walk out on Cicely's performance. Whoever it is, they can wait until supper, when you can speak to this person in the presence of myself or your aunt Dorothea."

But Cicely hadn't yet begun, and George didn't think she could bear one more lustily delivered off-key song. "I won't be a moment," she whispered. "Besides, I need the ladies' withdrawing room." Before Aunt Agatha could respond George gave a silent grimace of apology to Cicely, hurried toward the door and closed it thankfully behind her as the first off-key strains of "The Braes of Yarrow" began.

"Who was it—?" she began, but there was no sign of the footman. Instead, leaning idly against the wall was the Duke of Everingham. "You!" she said. "What are you doing here?"

He straightened and strolled toward her in a leisurely manner that nevertheless had something of a stalking-cat feel about it. "Enjoying the music?"

George backed away. "You know very well I'm not."

"Indeed? I seem to recall that you're fond of music."

"I clearly recall that you're not. In any case"—she gestured toward the door—"I wouldn't call that music." She turned back to him and found he was suddenly much closer than before.

She tried to edge around him and found she was trapped between the wall, the bannister, and the duke.

He was close enough for her to see the fine-grained texture of dark bristles in the skin of his well-shaven jaw, close enough for her to smell his scent—now too disturbingly familiar to her—essence of arrogance.

He knew he had her trapped. He looked disgustingly smug.

Annoyed, she stiffened her spine. She refused to be intimidated. "Was it you who sent that footman?"

He didn't respond. He was looking her over with a slow, lazy gaze that left warm prickles in its wake. She *knew* the neckline of this dress was too low—girls like her who weren't at all bounteous in the bosom department ought to face facts and keep what little they had well hidden. Miss Chance, her outspoken dressmaker, had disagreed.

"Don't worry—it won't be too revealing. We'll just nicely frame your bosom," she'd told George as she'd measured her up. And when the dress was finished, George had felt perfectly satisfied with the neckline.

But now, with the duke's gaze heavy on her, she suddenly felt uncomfortably exposed. She shoved at his chest. "Move back. I don't like you standing so close."

"Yes, you do." He didn't move.

"I don't," she lied. She wanted to lean forward and just inhale him—how could he smell so . . . delicious? But she refused to feel like that. She knew what was happening to her and she would not give in to it. "I find you . . . irritating."

He didn't respond. His compelling gray gaze rested on her mouth, arousing sensations she did not want to have. Heat rose in her as she recalled that other kiss, sparked by tiny sugar crystals . . .

She ran her tongue across her lips. His eyes darkened and, taking no risks, she vigorously scrubbed the back of her hand across her mouth.

There was a glint of something amused and devilish in his eyes as he met her gaze. "You missed me, didn't you?"

"Missed you?" She hoped she sounded incredulous. "When would I have missed you?" Just because she'd noticed his absence didn't mean she'd *missed* him.

"When I was away."

"You've been away?" she said vaguely. "I didn't even notice." If only he'd stayed away another couple of weeks, she would have been back to normal. He'd returned too soon; the heat within her was rising. Just standing so close to him brought about a kind of breathless excitement—it was anger, she told herself. It had to be.

His smile was lazy. "You noticed. And I think you missed me. Certainly your expression when we met in the park yesterday seemed to indicate it."

"We didn't 'meet in the park.' You rode past me as if I weren't even— Oh, were you in the park?" But it was too late to retrieve the slip and his smug expression showed it.

"Your eyes lit up when you saw me."

She feigned indifference. "I was admiring your horse."

"You were relieved to see me. You'd missed me. You were annoyed with me for not coming over to greet you."

It was infuriating to be so transparent. "You're very sure of yourself, your grace of Arrogance, but you have no idea what I'm thinking."

"I do." And when she arched a disbelieving eyebrow at him, he said, "You're thinking of making a very unladylike attack on my cods."

"Your co—oh," she said as he indicated the area below his waist. "Well, if you don't let me pass, you'll find out, won't you?" And it would serve him right.

He turned, angling his body slightly to protect that area of his anatomy. His hands came up as if to hold her off and he said warningly, "Not again, you don't."

She frowned. "What do you mean 'not again'? I've never—"

"You did it once before, five years ago."

She dismissed that notion with a gesture. "Nonsense. I didn't know you five years ago. It must have been someone else—clearly a woman of discernment."

"It was you. We were in Gloucestershire. You'd just ruined a hunt and I pulled you off your horse—I thought you were a boy."

"Oh, was that you? You deserved it, in that case. In fact, now I come to think of it, I wish I'd hit you harder. Now move aside and let me pass. I want to return to the concert."

His lips twitched with amusement. "No you don't. It's a dreadful concert." He added in a voice that almost purred, "And here's me, thinking you never lied."

The fact that he was right—again—inflamed her temper. George shoved at his shoulder. "Ooh, you are so irritating! Just let me pass, will you?" He didn't move, just stood there being big and powerful and warm and infuriatingly smug. Annoyingly attractive—and worse, knowing it.

"Make me." His smile was a slow, sensual challenge. "You know you want to."

How dare he know what she wanted? Anger, desire and frustration warred within her. She was a spring, wound up too tight. It wasn't as if he hadn't been warned . . .

"In that case . . ." She jerked her knee up, aiming for his genitals, but she was too used to wearing breeches, and the skirt of her dress was too narrow. Her raised knee dragged the skirt against the back of her other knee, which buckled. Cursing the impracticality of dresses, she overbalanced.

Into the arms of the duke.

He pulled her up against him, hard, and his mouth came down on hers, not gently as it had that first time, but firmly, possessively, as if he had every right to kiss her. And while a small thready voice in her mind suggested feebly that he didn't, neither her mouth nor the rest of her body cared.

The taste of him—dark, hot, intense—soaked into her, building, like a fever in her blood. She speared her fingers into his thick hair and pressed her mouth to his. Excitement shivered through her, sending spirals of heat to the very core of her body.

He kissed as if he wanted to devour her. She learned from his every move, giving him back kiss for kiss, caress for caress. Learning passion. Intoxication.

She twisted her body restlessly against him, practically climbing him to get closer, heat and aching need driving her. She knew she was out of control; she didn't care.

He slid his hands down over her hips, caressing her as she thrust herself heedlessly against him. She felt him tugging her skirts up. Cool air caressed her heated limbs, and then his hands cupped her bottom and he lifted her against him, where he was swollen and hot and hard.

"Put your legs around me," he murmured, and without thought she locked her legs around his waist and, oh, that was better. Like riding, she was more in control. Her back was pressed against the wall, his hard swollen masculinity pressed against the notch between her legs and she rubbed herself against him like a cat in heat, kissing and nipping and biting.

He groaned and returned thrust for thrust, all the time, kissing her deep, keeping her head swirling while her body ached and writhed against him.

"*Georgiana Rutherford!*" The outraged voice of Aunt Agatha pierced the swirling mists of George's awareness. Dizzily she pulled back, tried to focus.

"*Georgiana!*"

Reality came back to her in ragged shreds. She was clinging to him, her fingers knotted in his hair, the skirts of her dress were rucked up high around her thighs, and her legs—oh, lord, but her legs were wrapped around his waist. Worse, his warm hand was between them!

For a moment she couldn't remember whether she was even wearing any drawers, and she felt for them surreptitiously and heaved a sigh of relief when she found she was.

Aunt Agatha was of the old school that held that drawers on a female were a scandalous French plot against English womanhood, but George felt much more secure in them. They weren't as good as breeches, but at least she wasn't bare-arse naked under her skirts and open to all sorts of drafts.

"Georgiana Rutherford, you're a dis*grace*! Get down from that man immediately!"

George unlocked her legs, and dropped to the floor, wriggling and tugging her skirts back into some semblance of decency, her hands shaking, her brain reeling as she tried to come to terms with what had just happened.

She'd been completely out of control. Had let him do whatever he wanted to her. Worse—she'd wanted him to do it, and more.

She slowly became aware of a babble of voices, and when she peered past the duke's broad shoulders, oh, lord, it wasn't only Aunt Agatha gaping and gobbling at her like an outraged turkey, it was half the audience at the concert. People had come out for their supper, and found George and the duke locked in each other's arms.

A hundred eyes burned into her, curious, scandalized, shocked, disgusted, avid, eating up her mortification with delight. George wished she could shrivel away on the spot. Could it get any worse?

The duke's arms were still wrapped around her, supporting her firmly against him, which was a good thing, she thought blurrily, because sure as anything her legs weren't.

"Redmond Jasper Hartley, what is the meaning of this?" Aunt Agatha demanded stridently. Not even "your grace."

"I would have thought it was perfectly obvious, Lady Salter," the duke said in a cold, clear voice that cut through the buzzing of scandalized comment. George blinked at his apparent dispassion. He sounded perfectly calm and unruffled, even though she could feel that his heart was pounding as raggedly as hers.

"Lady Georgiana has just agreed to become my wife. We were sealing our betrothal with a kiss."

His words drew a wave of muttered comment. Aunt Agatha's brows snapped together.

Wife? George's brain snapped back into life. *Betrothal?* "No, that's not right—"

"*Betrothal?*" Aunt Agatha cut her off sharply. Pasting a smile on her face, she gushed, "Georgiana, my dearest gel, congratulations. No wonder you are all about with excitement—your head must be spinning."

By now, the concert room had emptied into the hallway. Delicious smells wafted from the supper room but nobody moved. A much more interesting dish was being passed around; Lady Georgiana Rutherford, caught *in flagrante* with her legs wrapped around the waist of the Duke of Everingham—her own aunt's jilted bridegroom!

Aunt Agatha turned to the crowd. "Friends, how wonderful that you are here to witness the romantic betrothal of my niece, Lady Georgiana Rutherford—"

"No! I am *not* betroth—" George tried to make herself heard.

Aunt Agatha's voice rose, sharper and loud enough to fill an opera hall. "—to his grace, the Duke of Everingham. A moment of high romance, I think you would all agree."

After the first gasp of shock, a scattering of applause started and a murmuring that grew to a swell of congratulation. And some surreptitious muttering.

"I am not betr—" George tried again.

And again, Aunt Agatha, oozing self-satisfaction, cut her off. "I promoted the match myself, you know."

"We are *not* betrothed!" George shouted.

"Of course you are," Aunt Agatha said.

The duke pulled her against him. "She's a little overwhelmed," he told the crowd.

"I am *not* overwh—"

But Aunt Agatha and the duke were talking over her so she couldn't get a word in. "Yes, you are, my dear." He sounded cold and relentless.

"Perfectly understandable," Aunt Agatha said. "Excitement does that to some gels," she told the crowd. "She doesn't know whether she's coming or going."

"I do know," George insisted "And I'm *not* betrothed!"

"I'll put the notice in the papers in the morning," the duke said.

George stared at him in stupefaction. "You'll do nothing of the sort."

"For heaven's sake, shut your mouth, gel," Aunt Agatha hissed in her ear. "Leave it for now. Discuss it with the duke later, in the privacy of your own home. Or do you have any more appalling indiscretions you wish the world to witness?"

George rather thought they'd already witnessed quite enough but her aunt had a point. The crowd pressing avidly around them, eating up the gossip and no doubt adding to it, was unnerving. "Very well, talk tomorrow morning?" she said to the duke in a low voice. Though there was nothing to talk about, really. She was not going to marry him. The very idea was ridiculous.

He was just being gallant—or something—because they'd been caught kissing.

And how that had happened she had no idea.

He nodded.

Aunt Agatha gave a briskly approving nod. "Eleven o'clock, Ashendon House." She turned to the crowd. "My niece and I shall depart now. Enjoy your supper and the rest of the concert. Devastated to miss it, Cicely, my dear. Your performance was superb. Wonderful hospitality as always. Mrs. Gastonbury, thank you. Come along, Dorothea. Collect my cloak please. We're leaving." Taking George's arm in a steely grip, she led her toward the front door.

George's legs were still distinctly wobbly, and when Aunt Dottie slipped an arm though hers, she felt obscurely comforted. "Don't worry, my love," Aunt Dottie murmured. "I have one of my *feelings* about this. It will all work out for the best."

George managed a weak smile. Aunt Dottie's "feelings" were legendary in the family. George didn't believe in them herself, but it was nice to have some support.

"I WON'T MARRY HIM!" GEORGE SAID FOR THE UMPTEENTH time. They were traveling back to Ashendon House in the carriage. Aunt Agatha hadn't stopped haranguing George since the carriage door closed. If it hadn't been pouring with rain, George would have jumped from the moving carriage and stormed off.

"Don't be ridiculous, child. You have no choice. You were caught by half the ton with your skirts up around your waist, climbing the duke like a tree. If you didn't want to be compromised, you should never have left my side in the first place."

"But—"

"Do not argue with me, gel! If you hadn't behaved like the veriest trollop—and at a ton event—you wouldn't be in this situation."

George bit her lip. That part was true enough. She didn't understand herself how it had happened. One moment she'd been standing in the hallway, telling the duke to get out of her way, and the next . . .

"But it's too late for regrets. I'm only grateful that the duke behaved like the true gentleman he is and made you an offer—and in such a public manner that neither of you can wriggle out of it." Aunt Agatha's expression reeked of triumph.

"I will wriggle out of it," George insisted. "Besides, he didn't make an offer, he made an announcement—and without my permission."

"You gave him permission when you climbed up his torso like a cat in heat, with your dress hitched—"

"I refuse to marry a man I dislike because of one stupid incident." The image painted by her great-aunt's words was embarrassing in the extreme, but it didn't alter George's determination.

"A man you *dislike*?" Aunt Agatha repeated scornfully. "You chose an odd way of showing this so-called dislike. Besides, regrettable as the incident is, the result is one we all ought to be grateful for—"

"*Grateful!* To be forced—"

"*Forced?* Pah! It's an opportunity, gel, one you don't deserve! The sight of you when I came out from the concert, wrapped around the duke like the worst kind of hussy!" She shuddered dramatically. "I've never been so ashamed in all my life!"

George didn't even try to defend her actions. Truth to tell, she'd shocked herself with her response to the duke's kisses. She hadn't believed herself capable of such a thing. How had it happened? One kiss and everything had spiraled out of control. It wasn't like her. She'd never been interested in men before, not like that.

And she didn't even like the duke.

Her aunt's words, however, had confirmed a suspicion that had been hovering at the edge of her mind for some time. It explained a lot. Why she was acting so out of character. How he'd been able to . . . do what he did.

"Of course you'll marry him—and be grateful for it! If he is willing to marry a gel who has proved herself a strumpet—"

"Piffle!" Aunt Dottie said from the corner seat.

"I beg your pardon." Aunt Agatha turned on her sister with freezing hauteur.

"Granted," Aunt Dottie said loftily. "But only as long as you stop this hypocritical nonsense. We all know you're thrilled to the back teeth, so stop ranting at poor George and pretending to be shocked!"

George blinked. Aunt Dottie, normally so mild mannered, had spoken quite sharply.

"*Poor George? Pretending?* Did you not *see* how the wretched gel behaved?"

"It takes two, Aggie—or are you suggesting that the duke was a helpless innocent seduced against his will?"

"No, of course not, but—"

"The trouble with you, Aggie, is that you've never understood the power of passion. You never have and you never will."

Aunt Agatha's bosom swelled with indignation. "That's rich, coming from the family spinster."

Luckily, before the argument could get any worse, the carriage slowed. Aunt Dottie glanced out the window. "Ah, here we are back at Ashendon House, and look, Burton has waited up for us—see, he's opening the door—and, oh, good, he has two footmen ready with umbrellas. No need to get down, Aggie. You go on home and get to bed. What we all need is a good night's sleep. Everything will look better in the morning."

Her sister snorted. "I doubt it."

HART PUNCHED HIS PILLOW. IT WASN'T EVEN DAWN YET, but he was wide awake, despite having barely slept the night before. He hadn't been able to get her out of his mind. Each time he'd drifted off to sleep, he'd awoken a short time later, restless, erect, taut with arousal.

Georgiana Rutherford . . . The taste of her was still in his mouth—along with the cognac he'd drunk when he got home. She'd fired his blood. The cognac hadn't helped; it only inflamed his memory of the taste of her.

He ached for her.

That explosion of . . . passion, that . . . conflagration. Unfeigned, unforced. Her kisses were eager and untutored, but there was a wildness in her, a deep hunger that awakened something in him that he'd never felt before.

It made him uneasy. The whole situation had gotten perilously close to careering out of control. For a while there he'd quite lost his head. He never lost control. Particularly around women. Never.

He lay in bed, waiting for the dawn chorus in the trees outside, but there wasn't a peep.

Of course it had all worked out as planned . . .

But his own, unplanned reaction still shocked him.

The taste of her mouth, the unique female fragrance of her, the remembered feel of her slender thighs locked around his waist . . . His body throbbed. Frustration. Futile agony. A damnable situation.

Exercise, that's what he needed. Fresh air, fresh thoughts, not this everlasting churning of the same scenes over and over in his mind, reliving that extraordinary scene. Those kisses.

He lay brooding, then in a decisive move threw off his bedclothes and leapt out of bed. Dawn rides. She often went riding at dawn, Sinc said.

Hart washed, and donned his buckskins and boots and in a short time was heading for Hyde Park, just as the first rays of light gilded the spires of the churches.

The streets were already busy with costermongers and barrow-boys setting up; but the park, once he passed through the gates, was largely deserted. He rode for a short while, enjoying the loosening of his tense muscles and the fresh scent of the earth, damp and fragrant from the previous night's downpour. The birds were awake now, and the twittering was deafening.

A movement caught his eye. He turned and there she was, demure and proper in a sage-green habit, riding her glorious black stallion sidesaddle, elegant as the finest lady. Her shaggy hound lolloped along beside her, then veered off on some canine errand.

There was no sign of the groom who'd accompanied her before. Good.

Hart started forward, then, with a muttered curse, reined in, as Cal Rutherford, her uncle and guardian, moved into view, mounted on a fine-looking bay gelding.

Damn. Hart had no intention of speaking to her guardian, not here, not now. His little fish was hooked but was not yet in his net.

She called out something and with a laugh raced away, riding fast and furious with a grace and skill few women had. And giving Cal Rutherford—no mean rider himself—a run for his money.

Lord, but the girl could ride—astride or sidesaddle, she outrode them all.

Hart hung back at a distance, watching her, observing her interaction with her guardian. She usually rode out with all her family, Sinc had said, but Lady Rose had left London with her long-lost husband. Lady Lily too had gone to the country with her husband.

Georgiana had been quite alone when he'd first come across her in Gloucestershire, five years before. Quite frighteningly alone, he'd realized in retrospect, with nobody to care for her or protect her, except for the dubious protection of the local squire who'd told the locals not to interfere with her.

According to Sinc's sister, she hadn't even known she had family.

She had family now.

He watched her racing her uncle, winning the race—lord, but that stallion was fleet—and throwing back her head and laughing at something he said. She seemed to laugh easily, with family, with friends. Though not with him. Never with him.

She and her uncle walked their mounts quietly for a time, seeming to be discussing something serious. Was she telling her uncle about the night before? And if so, what was she saying? He hoped her uncle was backing Lady Salter.

She leaned over and pinched a few leaves off a bush, crushing them between her hands and smelling them as she talked to her uncle. Did she realize how sensual she was or was that a discovery that still lay ahead of her? Of them.

Her zest for life—her enjoyment of small, simple things— fascinated him.

Hart was solitary by nature. He had few friends. He'd learned young that most people wanted to be friends with a duke or the heir of a duke, not so much with Hart himself. Who Hart was, what he thought, what opinions he had were almost immaterial. They wanted the duke, not Hart.

She most emphatically *didn't* want the duke. But last night she'd kissed Hart in a way that had rocked him to his foundations. She'd kissed Hart, not the duke—he could tell the difference.

He sat quietly on his horse, watching her, feeling a little like a voyeur; unable to take his eyes off her, unable to make himself leave.

He would have joined them, except he wasn't yet ready to talk to her guardian. He needed to get everything in place first.

Chapter Nine

It is always incomprehensible to a man that a woman
should ever refuse an offer of marriage. A man always
imagines a woman to be ready for any body who asks her.
—JANE AUSTEN, *EMMA*

THEY WAITED FOR THE DUKE TO CALL. GEORGE HAD GONE
for her usual morning ride with Cal. She missed the company of Lily and Rose, but still, it was good of Cal to
come out.

She'd told him what had happened the previous night. His
lips had thinned, but he hadn't said much to the point. Cal
was often like that. A man of action rather than words. leaving her with no idea what he really thought.

And when they'd arrived home, Aunt Agatha was waiting, a silver dragon lady breathing brimstone and betrothals.
"At least you're not wearing those disgraceful breeches," she
said the moment George walked in the door. "Run upstairs
and change into something pretty, something worthy to receive the addresses of a duke in."

George did think of changing into her oldest breeches,
and went as far as pulling them out of the chest. But then
she thought of the way he would look at her down that long,
superior nose of his, and changed her mind.

She put on a dress—the plainest one she owned. She
would not dress up for him.

She paced around the house, rehearsing in her mind what she was going to say to him. The trouble was, apart from "No, I won't marry you," she didn't know what else she could say.

If he, like Aunt Agatha, pointed out her unseemly behavior, she couldn't deny it. If he wanted an explanation, she had none—none that she cared to speak aloud, that is.

According to Aunt Agatha, he was being extremely gallant in offering for her, and George could see that, by some lights, that might be true. Only she had a deep dark suspicion that he'd engineered the situation. He'd sent that footman in to call her away from the concert.

And wasn't it a very strange coincidence that he'd started kissing her just before the break for supper? Had he known everyone would come out then, and find George wrapped around him?

The flaw in that reasoning was that he couldn't possibly have known that George would react to his kisses the way she had. And if she hadn't, if she had pushed past him and walked away, as she'd intended, nothing would have happened.

No matter how George looked at it, it kept coming back to being her fault.

Aunt Agatha argued that if she didn't agree to the betrothal, the duke would be held to be a scoundrel and a seducer. But Aunt Agatha would make any argument that would achieve her aim. She was determined that a Rutherford girl would marry the duke, and George, unsatisfactory as she was, was the only one left.

Aunt Dottie did suggest—very quietly so her sister couldn't hear—that George could always agree to the betrothal, and later, when the dust had settled, she could call it off. Girls were allowed to break betrothals; only men could not—well, they could, but then they'd be regarded as dishonorable scoundrels whose word of honor could not be trusted.

A man's word of honor was held to be almost sacred, but if a woman gave her word, she wasn't taken seriously. Because only men—only *gentlemen*—had a sense of honor. Apparently.

George hated the hypocrisy of that. If she gave her word, she'd keep it. Her sense of honor was just as reliable as any man's. As any duke's.

The duke was to call at eleven. Time crawled on.

By half past ten George was ready to climb the walls. Or murder Aunt Agatha who didn't let up her lecturing for a moment. They'd all gathered in the drawing room to wait for the duke's arrival.

"Of course you will accept, you stubborn child. You have no choice in the matter."

"I'm sorry, Aunt Agatha, but that's not true," Emm said serenely. "I made a vow when I first married Cal that all the girls would be free to choose their own future, and nothing has changed. Admittedly George is in an awkward situation, but—"

"Awkward? She has caused *a scandal!*"

Cal added his mite. "Seems to me the duke is as much to blame, if not more so. Can't see George instigating a thing like that, myself."

George grimaced. Her behavior had been totally uncharacteristic, she knew. She was only just starting to understand why. It was so frustrating the way nobody talked about these things—not to unmarried girls, anyway. It was infuriating to be kept in ignorance of how one's body worked. At least George had been able to put two and two together because of her years growing up in the country. How did gently reared London girls ever work things out? She supposed they waited until they were married—and then it was too late. They were caught.

The clock in the hall chimed eleven. Cal glanced pointedly around the room. "And if the duke is so keen on this betrothal, where is he?"

Aunt Agatha sniffed. "So he's late. He's notorious for unpunctuality."

"Maybe he's changed his mind," George said brightly.

"No matter what the duke does," Aunt Agatha persisted,

"a scandal has occurred and the family must handle it. And if you won't send the foolish gel down the aisle, what do you intend to do?"

Emm and Cal exchanged glances. "I suppose you could go to the country for a while," Emm suggested. "Wait for the fuss to die down. You could go to Ashendon Court for a few weeks, or go and stay with Lily and Edward. Old Lord Galbraith would be happy to welcome you. And of course there is always your own house at Willowbank Farm. Martha would be delighted."

George considered that possibility. She'd grown used to living in London, but there was no denying she missed the country. She'd often thought of returning to Willowbank Farm, the place where she'd grown up. Martha had begun as George's nursemaid. Later she became cook, housekeeper and the closest thing to a mother—to any kind of a parent—that George had ever had.

And when the money from her father had run out, Martha had stayed with George, working for no wages, sharing the desperate struggle to survive. George loved Martha dearly, and knew Martha would happily welcome her back.

But when Cal had taken George away from the farm—kicking and loudly objecting—Martha had chosen to stay behind, deeming herself unsuited to a fashionable life in the city. Cal, who believed in rewarding loyalty, had then arranged for Martha's recently widowed youngest sister and her five small children to go and live with Martha.

Martha's own opportunities to marry and have children had been set aside when she devoted her life to taking care of George. Now she relished having a houseful of children to help raise. And having been assured that Willowbank Farm would be her home for as long as she wanted—for life—she'd gained confidence as well as security. Martha was no longer merely the cook or the housekeeper—she was the woman of the house, with a generous income and servants and farmhands of her own.

George could visit and be welcomed as a beloved guest, but if she returned to Willowbank Farm for any length of time, she knew what would happen; Martha would revert to being her servant—she wouldn't be able to help herself—and George never wanted to see that happen.

So Willowbank Farm wasn't an option and neither, now she came to think of it, was Ashendon Court or staying with Lily and her husband. Or any other kind of cowardly retreat. "I won't run away. I won't hide out in the country as if I've done something wrong," she declared.

"Brava," Emm said softly.

"But you *have*—" Aunt Agatha began.

"Oh, bite it, Aggie," Aunt Dottie said. "We all know what you want, but it's George's life, and it's her decision."

"I'm staying here," George finished. "As long as it's all right with you, Emm and Cal."

"Of course it is," Cal said. "Society tabbies are always looking for something new to talk about. Scandals might be uncomfortable to weather, but they never last long."

"Besides," Emm added, "if you're going to be the baby's godmother, I'll need you on hand when he or she is born."

"Godmother? Me?" George swallowed, surprised and deeply moved. "Are you sure?"

"Emmaline! How can you say such a shocking thing!" Aunt Agatha snapped before Emm could respond.

They all turned to frown at her. "But George will be perfect—" Emm began.

"It's our decision," Cal said at the same time.

"Will you never stop interfering, Aggie?" Aunt Dottie added. "George will make an excellent godmother."

"Pish tush, I don't care about godmothers—though you could do better. What I do object to," Aunt Agatha said with freezing authority, "is any suggestion that this child might be *a girl*! You are carrying the Rutherford Heir, my gel, and don't you forget it."

For a time they almost forgot their purpose in gathering in the drawing room as thoughts of the imminent baby dominated conversation.

And then the clock in the hall struck twelve.

The last chime faded away. "He's not coming, is he?"

George said. She wasn't sure whether she felt relieved or insulted. Certainly she was frustrated—all keyed up for a confrontation and then . . . nothing.

Was she never to get the chance to say no to the duke?

"DAMN HIS BLASTED CHEEK!" CAL EXCLAIMED AT THE breakfast table the following morning. He slapped down the newspaper he'd been reading.

"What is it?" Emm asked. "Whose cheek?"

"Everingham. He's made the blasted announcement without so much as a by-your-blasted-leave."

George looked up from her kedgeree. "What announcement?" Dread filled her. She knew, she just knew . . .

"Read it yourself." Cal passed her the newspaper. "There." His finger stabbed at a notice surrounded by an elegantly printed border.

As George read it her mouth dried. It was a notice announcing the betrothal of Lady Georgiana Rutherford to the Duke of Everingham. "But he can't do that!"

"He blasted well has," Cal said grimly. "You know, I didn't mind the fellow when he was going to marry Rose. Bit of a cold fish I thought, but no real harm in him. But this"—he jabbed the notice with his finger again—"I'm getting to see a whole new side of him now."

The butler, Burton, quietly entered bearing a folded note on a silver salver. "This note was just delivered, m'lord," he murmured. "A footman is outside, waiting for an answer."

Cal glanced at the seal, broke it open and scanned the note. "Tell him I'll be waiting for his explanation." He glanced at the clock. "Eleven o'clock, on the dot—none of his blasted unpunctuality." He tossed the note aside. Burton glided out.

"The duke?" Emm asked.

Cal grunted. "I'll see what the fellow has to say. And it had better be good." He retrieved his newspaper, shook it out and retreated behind it.

"I won't marry him," George muttered.

"I believe I've noted that, George," came a rumble from behind the newspaper. "I wasn't deaf the first time you said it and the following thirty-eight repetitions have been quite unnecessary."

There was a moment of quiet, broken only by the ticking clock. Then Emm said thoughtfully, "If Cal has seen the notice, Aunt Agatha will have too." She glanced at the clock. "I give it another fifteen minutes before she arrives."

"Oh, lord." Calling Finn to her, George fled.

AT PRECISELY ONE MINUTE TO ELEVEN HART RANG THE Ashendon doorbell. The butler bowed, said his grace was expected and ushered Hart into the library. Cal Rutherford, very much Earl of Ashendon, stood in front of the fireplace, ramrod straight and wearing the famous Rutherford scowl.

It looked better on his niece. Hart gave the earl a curt nod. "Ashendon."

"Everingham."

There was a short silence. It became clear that Ashendon wasn't going to invite him to be seated, but Hart was damned if he would be treated like a naughty schoolboy, so he chose a leather armchair and sank into it with every appearance of casual unconcern.

The Rutherford scowl darkened.

"Stop looking at me like that. You know as well as I do that it had to be done. We were caught *in flagrante*," Hart said after a moment.

"Yes, and how the hell did that happen?" Ashendon growled. "My niece is not that kind of girl."

Hart, who thought she was very much that kind of girl, shrugged. "No use repining over spilled milk. What's done is done."

"Stop hiding behind clichés," Ashendon snapped.

"Clichés exist for a reason. Without wishing to hash over the past, let us agree that having allowed Georgiana to be caught in a compromising position, I am honor bound to marry her."

"And placing that blasted notice in the blasted papers without so much as a by-your-blasted-leave? How do you explain that?"

"An accident," Hart lied smoothly. "I had drafted a notice in anticipation of the event, and an overefficient secretary acted without my knowledge." He spread his hands in a what-can-you-do movement. "Of course, as soon as I saw it in the paper, I contacted you."

There was a long silence. Ashendon eyed him coldly. "You know she doesn't want you."

"She doesn't know what she wants. Yet."

Ashendon snorted. "You don't know her very well, do you?"

Hart shrugged. "That's immaterial. Most couples get to know each other after marriage."

Ashendon's eyes narrowed. "Why are you really pursuing this? You could have any woman in the ton. Why pursue a girl who doesn't want you?"

"I want her." It was risky being so blunt, but they were men of the world, after all.

The gray eyes filmed with ice. "Your wants matter nothing to me, Everingham. The only question I care about is, does my niece want you? And she doesn't."

"I think she does. I think she's just nervous, like a filly being brought to stud for the first time."

"My niece is not *a filly*." Ashendon's voice was icily savage.

"No, she's not," Hart said, soothing ruffled feathers. "It was a clumsy and inappropriate analogy."

There was a short silence, filled only by the rumbling of thunder. A moment later, rain started pelting down.

Hart spoke again. "Look, we can dance around the issue all morning, but let us not waste time. Having compromised your niece—and without resorting to vulgarity, let me just point out that she was not an unwilling participant, no matter what kind of girl you imagine she is—I'm doing the gentlemanly thing and preventing a scandal by making her an honorable offer. You know I'll be generous with the settlements." After all, they had negotiated the financial arrangements for his marriage to the earl's sister Rose only a short time before. Ashendon knew who and what he was dealing with.

Hart stood. He was impatient to get things settled. "So, do we have an agreement?" It wasn't really a question. With his niece compromised and a betrothal notice in the papers, Ashendon had no other choice but to agree. Hart's visit was a mere formality.

To Hart's surprise, a faint note of amusement lightened the flinty gray eyes. "You have a lot to learn about Rutherford women, Everingham. I'm George's uncle, not her keeper. She makes up her own mind. It's not me you have to convince—it's George."

Hart frowned. The marriage was necessary. Surely there was no doubt. "I presume you've explained the situation to her."

"Oh, she knows the situation." Ashendon seemed to be almost enjoying himself now. "But George isn't your average young lady."

Of course she wasn't. Hart would never have contemplated marriage with her otherwise. "May I speak to her?"

"I'll see if she's home." Ashendon pulled the bell cord.

"Surely she knew I was coming. I sent you that note."

Ashendon gave an enigmatic smile. "Yes, but George dances to her own tune."

Just as the butler returned with the information that Lady Georgiana had gone out with her dog, they heard the front door open.

The first sign that she'd returned from her walk early was the wet and muddy dog that came bounding into the room. A moment later Lady Georgiana followed.

The moment she entered the room Hart knew he would need all his powers of persuasion. She was breathing hard, as if she'd been running. Her short dark hair clung in damp feathery clusters around her face. Her clothes were damp and clung to her lithe, slender body. Her hem was as muddy as her dog.

No other woman he knew would have dreamed of entering a room dressed so untidily, especially one containing a gentleman visitor, let alone a young lady expecting a marriage proposal.

Nor would most ladies inflict a damp and muddy dog on a visitor.

But her skin was pale and damp and glowed like a pearl. The dark clusters of hair framed her piquant face enchantingly. Her mouth was plum dark and endlessly enticing.

He was jerked out of his reverie by the dog. The great gray gangly creature inspected his boots, snuffed at Hart's hand, then nudged him imperiously in a clear demand.

Watching Lady Georgiana, Hart absently patted the dog's damp head. He didn't even need to bend down to do it. The dog licked his hand in return.

"Finn, come away," she ordered, and the dog padded across and flopped down at her feet.

Hart's hand was now slimy and reeked of eau de damp dog. He pulled out a handkerchief and dried it off. He supposed it was better than the animal jumping up and muddying his clothes.

Lady Georgiana addressed her uncle as if they were alone. "Burton said you wanted to see me, Cal."

"The Duke of Everingham has my permission to address you."

Her eyes turned to slits. "Oh?" It wasn't a happy kind of *oh*.

The earl rose, looking amused. "I'll leave you two alone." He left, closing the door carefully behind him.

"IT WAS JUST SO VERY UNFORTUNATE THAT EVERYONE came out of the concert at that particular moment," Hart concluded, hoping he sounded sincere. "But there it is. We have no choice, and so I offer you marriage." He'd delivered what he fancied was quite a pretty speech, balancing rueful regret at the way their private moment had been exposed, with a gentlemanly determination to protect her from the consequences.

"Well, I don't want it." She belatedly remembered her manners and added a grudging, "Thank you for the offer." Her eyes were as flinty as her uncle's. "Not that it apparently matters to you whether or not I consent. How dare you announce our betrothal to the world without asking me!"

Her nose was out of joint, Hart realized. He'd spoken too bluntly. Women wanted to be coaxed and flattered. In a soothing voice he told her the same story about the over-efficient secretary.

She cut through his explanation with brutal indifference. "I don't care. You shouldn't even have drafted such a notice before you'd spoken to me."

He tried not to show his impatience. It was all a foregone conclusion. What was wrong with her? Every woman he knew would be melting with delight at such an offer.

"I'm speaking to you now."

She made a dismissive sound. "And if you'd spoken to me in the first place, you wouldn't have been left with egg on your face."

He repressed the desire to check his face for egg. "What do you mean?"

"That I am not and never will be betrothed to you."

Hart clenched his fists. "But you must. You've been compromised—all those people who saw us. Naturally I did the gentlemanly thing." He'd calculated it all very carefully.

"*Pfft!* to your gentlemanly thing. I didn't want it in the first place."

He couldn't believe her attitude. "Don't you care about what people think?"

She shrugged. "Not much. People think all sorts of stupid things. Nothing to do with me."

"But—"

"If it's your reputation as a gentleman you're worried about, don't worry. You asked, I refused."

Hart was stunned by her indifference. He didn't give a hang about his reputation as a gentleman, but the ladies he knew were almost obsessive about theirs—especially the unmarried ones. "But the notice is in all the papers."

"You put it in, you take it out." She rose, and the dog beside her scrambled to its feet. "So, are we finished now? The rain has stopped and I want to continue walking my dog."

"No," he said curtly. "We're not finished. This thing isn't over. You don't seem to realize the consequences of your actions—"

"*My* actions? You were there too," she flashed.

"Our actions," he conceded. "You refuse me now, but I cannot think you truly understand the consequences. I will give you time to think it over."

She gave him a long, thoughtful look. "See, I was right. You can't take no for an answer. Just exactly like Lord Towsett."

Hart didn't know what he wanted most—to strangle her or to kiss her senseless. Preferably both.

HAVING BEEN BALKED OF HER PREY IN THE MORNING, Aunt Agatha returned to Ashendon House in the late afternoon. Finding Georgiana out with her dog—again!—she informed the butler that she would speak to Ashendon and his wife. She found them in the small sitting room and wasted no time in presenting her views.

"Georgiana *must* be made to understand. It is simply not acceptable that she cause such a disgraceful scandal and smear the reputation of this family."

"Lily was enmeshed in a scandal, too, but—" Emm began.

Aunt Agatha dismissed it with a wave. "That was purely gossip, spiteful gossip. Georgiana's lewd behavior, witnessed *in the flesh*—and far too much of it at that—her almost-bare legs were wrapped around the duke's waist! And witnessed by half the ton!"

Cal shrugged. "Scandal gets old quickly. The tabbies will soon move their claws on to someone else."

"Pah! You men understand nothing! And Georgiana understands less." She trained her lorgnette on Emm. "So it is up to you and me, Emmaline, to steer this family back to respectability."

Emm shook her head. "I won't be a party to forcing George to marry a man she doesn't like."

Aunt Agatha stared at her in amazement. "What has liking to do with marriage?"

Emm glanced at her husband and smiled. "Quite a lot, actually, if the marriage is to be a happy one." She held out her hand to him, and he took it and kissed it. And held on to it.

Aunt Agatha gave them a pained look. "I would appreciate it if you refrained from such vulgar middle-class behavior in my presence."

Grinning, Cal kissed Emm's hand again.

His aunt gave him a severe look. "You were irritating as a child, Calbourne, and though I occasionally have hopes for you, this is not one of those moments."

She turned back to Emm. "We *cannot* let it be known that a second Rutherford gel has let a duke—the *same* duke—slip through her fingers. The ton will start to wonder whether there is insanity in our line, and we don't want that, do we?" She looked pointedly at Emm's belly.

Emm just laughed. "I don't think we need worry about that, Aunt Agatha. After all, George has made no secret of her wish not to marry. And it's not her fault that the duke put the betrothal notice in the newspapers without consultation. I won't allow George to be forced into marriage."

"I concur," Cal said.

There was a long silence. "What is the matter with this current generation? I quite despair of the future. Letting young gels decide what is best for them—faugh! It's utter folly, mark my words."

Emm, Cal and Aunt Agatha sat in silence. There was nothing more to say.

Just as Aunt Agatha was about to rise and depart, they heard the front door open and George laughing in the hall in response to whomever had opened the door.

The clatter of claws on the floor alerted them to the arrival of Finn. He nosed open the door and trotted over to Cal. George poked her head in, saw Aunt Agatha sitting ramrod straight on the edge of her chair, pulled a face and stealthily tried to withdraw but Aunt Agatha had espied her. "Ah, Georgiana, just the gel I came to talk to."

"I need to change my clothes. I'm damp."

"It won't take a minute."

"If I stay in damp clothes, I might catch cold," said George who'd never had a cold in her life.

"I shall come upstairs with you," Aunt Agatha announced majestically and rose from her chair. "We can talk as you change. A nice cozy chat between gels."

George grimaced. *A nice cozy chat between gels?* As cozy as sitting down with a python. But her great-aunt was not to be denied. She followed George up the stairs to her bedchamber and watched critically as she changed her clothes with the assistance of Milly, the maid.

The minute Milly left the room, Aunt Agatha started on her. "I gather you are determined to repudiate the duke's offer."

"I have already declined it."

Aunt Agatha's lips thinned. "And your uncle and aunt by marriage refuse to intervene."

Her words warmed George. Dear Cal and Emm. "Good."

Aunt Agatha's eyes were like gimlets. "Then if yet another Rutherford gel is going to jilt the Duke of Everingham and cause an even worse scandal, the least you can do, Georgiana, is to explain it to the duke's mother—"

"The duke's mother? But—"

"The duchess is in extremely poor health and is mightily distressed by the way her son has been treated by the gels of this family. The least you can do is to face her in person and explain your pathetic reasoning. That way the poor lady might understand, and it will perhaps give her a little peace of mind—relieve her of the suspicion that her son has been at fault—"

"But it *is* his fault. He's the one—"

"Nonsense! He did the honorable thing and announced your betrothal. You're the one who behaved like a hussy— worse than a hussy! I saw it with my own eyes! And now you are courting even more gossip and scandal by refusing him. Any other young lady would graciously accept her fate—what am I saying? Accept her *fate*? Marriage to a handsome young duke, one of the richest men in the kingdom is not a fate, it is a *blessing*! Any gel would be thankful to be in such a position, but not you! Oh, no, not my greatniece. I am ashamed, deeply ashamed, that a relative of mine could behave so shabbily."

George gritted her teeth.

"So you must meet the duchess and explain that her son has done all he ought in this matter and is in no way at fault."

George's fingers clenched into fists. It was in all ways his fault. She'd told him she wasn't interested in marriage and the horrid beast had taken that as some kind of challenge to his horrid masculinity. And then when he'd caught her, and kissed her just outside a room full of people, at the end of a concert—who had made the first move then? Not George. And then when everyone came spilling out after the recital, catching her locked in his arms—who was it who'd announced their betrothal without even asking her? Not George. And then he'd put it in the papers! Again without asking!

So why was everyone blaming her? She hadn't wanted any of it.

To be fair, she did share some responsibility for the kissing. She hadn't exactly fought him off. And perhaps she had become a little carried away—well, a lot carried away. She'd practically climbed him like a tree!

But she knew why that was and it wasn't her fault. Nobody had warned her it could happen.

"This whole dreadful affair has quite cut up the poor duchess's peace, and her health is fragile at the best of times," Aunt Agatha continued. "If you would only talk to her, you could ease—"

"Very well, I'll talk to her," George agreed. Best to get it over with. Aunt Agatha was quite capable of going on and on and on about it all afternoon and through the night and probably for the rest of George's life.

"Excellent," Aunt Agatha said briskly. "I'll let the duchess know to expect us tomorrow at three."

"Us?"

"Of course, us. Who else would you take? That wretched animal?" Finn recognizing the reference, if not the sentiment, thumped his tail on the floor.

"No, of course not, but I thought perhaps—"

"Who? Rose and Lily have both gone to the country, Emmaline is in no fit state to accompany you anywhere, burdened as she is with the imminent arrival of The Heir. As for Dorothea"—she snorted—"no, I will accompany you and that's that. I will call for you at twenty minutes to three. Be ready."

GEORGE WOKE IN THE NIGHT, THE BEDCLOTHES FLUNG INTO twisted ropes, her nightdress scrunched up around her hips. She was hot, sweaty and restless. That dream . . . She blushed just thinking about it. She'd been kissing the duke again, her legs wrapped around his waist, only this time she was naked. And so was he . . . and his hands— No, she wouldn't think about where they'd been and what they'd done.

She slipped out of bed, pulled her nightdress down, padded to the window and pulled the curtains back. Below her Berkeley Square was deserted, the gaslights blurry golden moons shining through the drizzle.

She pressed her hot cheek against the cold glass of the windowpane. Her body was afire, and not just for anyone. For the duke.

It was like a thirst that couldn't be quenched, except by him, a hunger that only he could assuage. But would bedding him rid her of these restive, sweaty dreams, the craving for . . . for whatever it was she craved?

It was as though the desire had sprung from some outside source, a fever, an infection in her blood. And the duke was the source.

Was he also the cure?

She'd always thought she understood what passed between men and women. Even as a child she'd known how animals did it, and had supposed men and women weren't much different. It seemed odd and uncomfortable and not something she ever thought she'd want.

Emm had told her that people were different, and that the pleasures of the bed could really bring a husband and wife closer. George was skeptical, but it did seem to have worked for Emm and Cal. Cal had only married Emm because he didn't want to be bothered with Rose and Lily and her.

His attitude had certainly changed, but how much of it was because of whatever happened in the bedchamber?

Lily and Rose had talked about it too. They said it was lovely, but George had never really thought about what *lovely* meant.

She wondered now.

It didn't feel "lovely" at all; she felt raw and uncomfortable and hot and desperate. But she apparently craved it— whatever *it* was—even in her dreams. It was horribly inconvenient. She craved it—craved him and how he could make her feel—but she didn't want him. Didn't *want* to want him.

Half a dozen mind-stealing, dizzying, knee-melting kisses, and already she was having hot and steamy dreams of him. Was she addicted? How much more was there to feel?

She curled up on the window seat, pulling her nightdress over her knees and leaning against the window frame. Rain spattered in hard little pellets against the glass. Rainwater rattled down through the pipes.

She thought about the raptures Lily and Rose went into whenever they'd talked about lovemaking with their husbands—though with frustratingly little detail. Did she really want to go through life without ever experiencing that for herself?

She didn't. She wanted to feel, wanted to *know*.

She knew well the purpose of this frantic inner urge to mate—procreation. She didn't know much about babies—

only about puppies and foals and kittens and kits and chicks—and she wasn't sure she even wanted a baby.

Could she risk it? Risk falling pregnant outside of marriage?

It was very tempting, but . . . no. She'd been called a bastard often enough in her childhood to know bastardy was a dreadful thing to inflict on a child. If she were going to find out for herself what it felt like to lie with a man, it would have to be in wedlock.

But marriage to the duke? Despite the raw, ravening, uncontrollable desire that seized her whenever he touched her—oil to her flame—he was cold, cynical, autocratic and selfish.

She stared out into the night, watching the rain making ever-changing runnels down the window. Her mind and body were in turmoil.

Marriage? Giving up control of her money, placing her fate in the hands of a man—a man she didn't like? She couldn't do it. Not even to know what passion tasted like.

This rampant desire would fade—it was just a matter of waiting until the urgency passed.

Chapter Ten

❦

Where so many hours have been spent in convincing
myself that I am right, is there not some reason to fear I
may be wrong?
—JANE AUSTEN, *SENSE AND SENSIBILITY*

AUNT AGATHA'S CARRIAGE PULLED UP OUTSIDE THE DUCH-
ess's house promptly at three. George was a little surprised.
She'd expected to be taken to Everingham House, but this
house was altogether smaller—though by no means small—
and prettier.

"The duke moved his mother here when he decided to
get married," Aunt Agatha said in a disparaging tone when
George commented on it.

It would be a much more pleasant house to live in than
grim old Everingham House, George thought, but she said
nothing. She was absurdly nervous. She didn't know the
duchess—she had seen her, of course, at various events
leading up to Rose's wedding to the duke, but had never
actually spoken to her, apart from "how do you do."

It was bound to be awkward. Aunt Agatha rang the bell
and the butler instantly opened the door.

"Her grace is expecting you. She is upstairs, in her bedchamber," he intoned in a solemn voice.

In her bedchamber? George glanced at Aunt Agatha, who
showed no surprise. They followed the butler up the stairs.

He knocked on the door, then opened it, saying softly, "Lady Salter and Lady Georgiana Rutherford, your grace."

Bracing herself, George stepped into a dimly lit room. The curtains were drawn, candles were burning, and—she sniffed—was that incense? Or medicine? The atmosphere was suffocating.

The bedside table was crammed with jars and bottles and vials and strange-looking medical paraphernalia. A woman dressed in gray sat in the corner, silent and self-effacing. Some kind of attendant or nurse. She wasn't introduced.

And there were flowers, so many flowers in vases all around the room.

Aunt Agatha had said the duchess was fragile and poorly, but clearly she was a lot sicker than that.

It looked like a deathbed.

The duchess, slender and frail looking, her skin a livid pasty white, lay propped up on pillows in a vast four-poster hung with heavy brocade. Her eyes were huge, red rimmed and haunted looking. She put out a thin hand. "Lady Georgiana," she murmured weakly. "So glad . . ."

"How do you do, your grace?" George spoke softly, feeling awkward to be so healthy with this pallid husk of a woman lying before her.

The duchess sighed. "Oh, well, life is . . . uncertain," she murmured. She gave a tremulous smile, then a coughing fit took her, as if simply to speak those few words had exhausted her. The attendant hurried forward and fussed around the duchess, then a few moments later was dismissed with a feeble wave. She went back to her corner.

"Now, Georgiana, tell the duchess what you came here to say," Aunt Agatha said in a brisk voice that seemed far too loud in this otherwise hushed room.

"Oh, yes, you're going . . . to marry my son, aren't you?" The duchess gave her a wan smile.

"Um, n—"

"I wanted to meet you . . . before," the duchess continued. "In case . . ." She gestured vaguely toward the array of medicines on the bedside table.

"Your grace, I—"

"It made me so happy when I learned . . . that my son was to marry after all. That time he was left at the altar . . . So distressing." She pressed a vein-lined hand to her chest. "Your sister, wasn't it?" She gazed at George out of tragic, red-rimmed eyes.

George shriveled inside. "My aunt."

The duchess nodded. "Yes. One of the Rutherford gels . . ." She sighed again. "I've been so worried, you see, that . . . my boy will be left all alone when I . . ." She sighed. "When I go . . ." She dabbed a wisp of lace to her eyes, and when it came away, big fat tears rolled slowly down her hollow cheek.

George bit her lip. She hated it when people cried. She hardly ever cried herself, and then, only in private. When others cried, she felt mildly alarmed and quite helpless.

She glanced at Aunt Agatha, who gave an unhelpful shrug, as if to say, "It's your responsibility, you deal with it."

The duchess wheezed on. "I was so . . . distressed when dearest Agatha told me you were having . . . second thoughts—" She broke off to cough into the lacy handkerchief.

Second thoughts? George had never even had first thoughts. She'd never wanted to marry the duke. But how could she explain that to this poor lady? It seemed somehow brutal.

"For my son to be jilted twice . . . and by girls of the same family . . ."

Rose hadn't jilted him. She hadn't known Thomas was still alive. Nobody was to blame. And if the duke hadn't publicly announced their betrothal without asking . . . But who could argue with a dying mother?

"Everyone will assume that there is some ghastly flaw in my son . . ."

There was. He was arrogant and cold and high-handed, George thought. Though his kisses . . . She forced her thoughts back to the moment.

"No decent lady would want . . . to marry him then. And I have so little time left . . . to see him wed and settled."

George bit her tongue. Did this lady not understand? If the duke were cross-eyed and hunchbacked, was subject to fits and drooled he would still have women lining up to marry him just because he was rich and a duke. But it wasn't the kind of thing one could say to a dying mother.

Liquid, red-rimmed eyes fixed pleadingly on her.

George felt trapped, stifled, a bird mesmerized by a snake.

"But here you are . . . so slender and pretty and . . . charming, the very image of the girl I would have . . . picked out for my dear son. I nearly died, giving birth to him . . . did you know? I was never the same . . . afterward, but then . . . what does health matter? We mothers live only for . . . our children." She gestured and the attendant came forward with a glass of some dark liquid. The duchess sipped, coughed, then sipped again.

When she had recovered, she beckoned George closer and took her hand in a surprisingly fierce grasp. "So tell me, dearest girl . . . you will make me happy, won't you? You'll marry my son . . . and become my daughter?"

George swallowed. She wanted to fling open the curtains, let in some light and fresh air—even London air—but she was trapped, held fast by a bony grip and a pair of tragic eyes.

The duchess continued in a faint, plaintive voice. "It was always . . . my dearest wish . . . to dance at his wedding, and although that pleasure . . . has been cruelly wrested from me, you will . . . give me your promise, won't you?" She gazed beseechingly at George. "Promise me you'll . . . marry my boy. And let me go . . . in peace. Please?"

She gazed at George through those huge, haunted eyes and waited.

George bit her lip. She'd never had a mother; Mama had died when George was a baby. But she could imagine a mother's love for her child. Emm hadn't even given birth yet, but George knew she already loved her baby.

This poor lady only had one son. How dreadful to be dying in such a worried state of mind.

George thought about all her reasons for not wanting to marry the duke. He was autocratic, haughty, cynical and aloof—though not when he was kissing her.

She thought about the way he'd invaded her dreams, and how she really did want to know what it felt like to lie with a man.

Would it be so bad?

Aunt Agatha said he didn't want the usual kind of wife, that as long as she bore him children, he would let her live an independent life in the country, as she'd always planned.

If she married him, she could find out for herself what it was like to lie with a man—and rid herself of all those tantalizing, disturbing, crazy-making sensations that invaded her dreams. That made her lose all sense of herself when he kissed her. And climb him like a tree.

Her cheeks warmed. These were not the thoughts to be having in a dying woman's bedchamber.

The duchess's thin fingers gripped hers. The haggard, haunted eyes bored into her.

George writhed inside.

There were agreements to be signed before a marriage; she remembered that from Lily's marriage. Aunt Agatha had implied that they would live more or less separate lives, except when congress was necessary to conceive an heir. If he would agree to that in writing . . .

The duchess's bony grip tightened. Her eyes filled with tears. "Please, my dearest girl . . . Tell me what I need to hear. Let me go at last . . . in peace."

All through her childhood George had brought home wounded creatures—mending birds' wings, nursing orphaned fox kits, rescuing creatures caught in traps, and kittens left to drown.

It was simply not in her to crush the last hope this poor woman had. She'd been ready to resist all the other pressures that had been brought on her to marry the duke, but how could she refuse a dying woman's last wish for her beloved son?

"All right," she said heavily. "I'll marry him." She instantly felt sick and wanted to retract her statement. The duchess sank back against her pillows, her eyes closed, an otherworldly smile on her face. It was almost as if she were dead already.

"Excellent." Aunt Agatha rose. "Now come along, we've exhausted the duchess enough. She will wish to sleep now." She bustled George from the room, and before she could blink they were out in the street, climbing into the carriage.

"What's the matter with her?" George asked. "Is she really so close to—"

"It is vulgar to speculate," Aunt Agatha said brusquely. "The duchess's situation is not your concern. The sooner we settle this business of the wedding, the sooner her mind will be at rest. I'll speak to Ashendon this afternoon."

They returned to Ashendon House and Aunt Agatha, looking like the cat that had swallowed the canary, wasted no time in informing Cal and Emm that George had agreed—promised, in fact—to marry the duke after all.

Cal frowned. "Is this true, George?"

George nodded.

"You weren't forced, were you?" Emm asked worriedly.

"Because if you were—" Cal began.

George sighed. "No. I wasn't forced. I just . . . I just changed my mind."

"You're sure, then?" Cal asked. "Because once this is agreed, you won't be able to change your mind."

"She can always change her mind," Emm said serenely. "But it would look very bad. So think it over, George, dear, and be sure in your heart that this is what you want."

George swallowed. "I'm sure." She wasn't, she was filled with doubts and second thoughts, but she'd given her word to the duchess, so she wasn't going to act on them.

"So, Ashendon, you and Everingham can begin drawing up the settlements," Aunt Agatha said.

"Cal, the duke *and I* will begin drawing up the settlements," George corrected her. She still felt sick about the promise she'd made. Every part of her screamed to escape, but a promise was a promise.

And if she was going to marry the wretched duke, she would make sure she got what she wanted out of the deal.

Aunt Agatha raised her lorgnette and eyed George narrowly through it. "What nonsense! Ladies have no part in such negotiations. It would be quite unseemly."

"Perhaps," George said sweetly, "but how often have you told me I'm no lady? Seemly or not, it's my future that's being negotiated and I'm determined to have my say."

GEORGE WENT UPSTAIRS AND FLUNG HERSELF ON HER BED. Finn came padding up and nudged her gently, but she wasn't in the mood to go out, not yet. She was swamped with doubt. What had she agreed to?

Marrying the duke would put all kinds of ghastly restrictions on her. She'd have all of society watching her. Judging her. Life in a birdcage. She'd be expected to behave like a duchess, dress like a duchess, perform duchess-type duties.

How did a duchess behave, anyway? George didn't really know. She pictured some kind of an Aunt Agatha, only worse, more dignified, if that were possible. Pompous and autocratic. Not that the duke's mother was like that. But she was dying.

Downstairs she heard Cal go out on some business. She'd talk to Emm. Emm was her aunt by marriage, but their relationship was more like a maternal big sister or a friend. She was wise. And she really listened.

George found Emm reading with her feet up in the small sitting room.

Emm looked up as she entered. "That was quite an about-face you made today. You don't exactly look like a radiant bride-to-be."

George grimaced.

Emm put her book aside. "You haven't been forced into this, have you, George, darling? I know Aunt Agatha is terribly keen for you to make a splendid marriage, but if you truly don't want it, now is the time to say so."

"No, I'll go ahead with it—I've given my word now, and I won't back down, but . . ."

"But you're having second thoughts."

She nodded. "Oh, Emm, I don't know how to be a duchess. You know how I hate all that formal stuff. And I don't want to learn it."

Emm leaned forward and took her hand. "You will be the kind of duchess you decide to be. Duchesses come in all kinds of shapes and sizes and with all kinds of temperaments."

George nodded. "I know. Like the Duchess of York."

Frederica, the Duchess of York, was unhappily married to a royal prince. The duchess had retired to Oatlands, her country home, where she lived with dozens of dogs, monkeys and horses.

The thought of the Duchess of York calmed her somewhat. The duke had chosen George, and if she wasn't the kind of duchess he wanted—the kind society would expect—he'd just have to put up with the way George was. She wasn't going to change. And she'd make sure he couldn't squeeze her into a mold.

And if the Duchess of York could retire to the country and live with dozens of dogs, so could George.

"Exactly. In any case, Everingham isn't a very political kind of duke—he sits in the Lords when Parliament is sitting, and Cal says he's diligent in tending to his various ducal responsibilities, but he doesn't seem to have any political ambitions. If you think he wants you to be a grand society hostess, well"—she squeezed George's hand—"he will learn differently, but I don't think he will expect it of you."

"But what if he does? What will I do?"

Emm frowned. "George, this is not at all like you, fretting about what people expect and what people will think. Where is the girl I first met, spitting fire and brimstone, determined to forge her own way in the world? And facing problems head-on."

George bit her lip. That was true. It wasn't like her to worry over what might be. She'd lived most of her life day by day, facing whatever she had to face. It had stood her in good stead, too.

And she'd never worried about what other people thought of her—she'd always done what she thought was right and never mind the consequences.

Her brow cleared. "You're right, Emm. I am worrying about nothing. The duke put me in this position, and *he* can wear the consequences. And if he doesn't like the kind of duchess I become, that's his bad luck." She stood. "I'm going to take Finn out for a walk now. Would you like me to bring you back an ice from Gunter's?"

Emm laughed. "You know me too well. I'd love one, thanks. I just wish I could walk with you. I don't like being cooped up indoors, but I suppose at this stage, it's inevitable."

HART WAS DRESSING TO GO OUT WHEN HE RECEIVED THE note from Lord Ashendon. So, Lady Georgiana had decided to accept the betrothal, had she? And Ashendon would be obliged if he would call the following morning—with or without his man of business—to discuss the settlements.

The surge of triumph he felt on reading it surprised him. Of course he'd known her objections were for form's sake—no sane woman would turn down an offer from a duke such as he—but he had to admit to a few doubts at the time. She'd seemed so adamant in her refusal.

He adjusted his cravat, inspected his reflection in the looking glass and snorted. As bad as Lord Towsett, indeed! She was like every other female he knew—blowing hot and cold according to whim. Saying one thing while meaning another.

He had no idea what had finally caused her to accept the inevitability of their marriage, but he wasn't going to question it.

He collected his hat, gloves and cane, and headed off to his club for a quiet, convivial evening. Instead he found half the members in a fever of speculation about his betrothal: Had Lady George truly accepted? Was it really going ahead?

Who had put the notice in the newspapers? And more offensively intrusive questions upon which bets had been made.

Refusing to answer any of their questions, Hart took himself off to a gambling den where he was less well-known, where he played carelessly, his mind only half on the cards. He returned home in the wee small hours with a pocketful of winnings and a very bad mood.

"Lucky in cards, unlucky in love," one impertinent fellow had quipped.

Hart ignored him. Love was a delusion that women used to control men.

THE FOLLOWING MORNING HE CALLED ON LORD ASHENDON. The butler ushered him into the library, where he found Lord and Lady Ashendon sitting together on a sofa. Always in each other's pockets, those two. Hart couldn't understand it. Ashendon seemed like a sensible man.

Ashendon rose, and after greetings were exchanged, said to the butler, "Fetch my secretary, will you, and ask Lady George to come down please, Burton."

Hart blinked. "I thought we were to discuss settlements."

Ashendon nodded. "Yes. George wishes to take part in the discussion."

Hart frowned. "The bride? Sitting in on settlement discussions? I've never heard of such a thing."

"George is different." Ashendon turned and helped his heavily pregnant wife to rise.

Lady Ashendon paused as she passed Hart and laid a hand on his arm. "Please don't take offense, your grace," she said quietly. "Until my husband brought her into the family fold, George had little reason to trust the men in her life."

Hart stiffened at the implied criticism.

She gave him a long, thoughtful look. "You told Aunt Agatha you wanted an independent woman. In George, you have one. Do not now complain of it. George, beneath the prickly surface, is an utter darling. Whether or not you ever see that side of her will be up to you."

Hart made no response. Utter darling, was she? He'd seen no evidence of that. He had, however, experienced the wildcat in her, and that, to his bemusement, he rather liked.

Lady Georgiana entered the room with that confident leggy stride that never failed to cause his body to sit up and take notice. She was dressed in a slate-colored dress that was halfway between gray and blue. Edged with claret piping and worn under a claret-colored spencer, it was plain but stylish. Not for her the frills and flourishes most young ladies affected.

The color of her dress highlighted her eyes. The color of her spencer drew attention to her lush, ripe mouth; and the way it clung, framing her breasts . . . It was a garment meant to enhance a woman's charms, rather than keep her warm.

It more than warmed him.

Hart averted his gaze. He needed all his wits about him. Settlements were far-ranging legal agreements, and Ashendon and his niece were sure to drive a hard bargain.

George glanced at the corner where Ashendon's secretary had settled himself unobtrusively. "You didn't bring your secretary?" she asked.

"No, I don't have—" Hart broke off, remembering just in time that he was supposed to have an overeager secretary who sent notices of betrothals to newspapers. "He's occupied on another endeavor, at one of my estates."

She shrugged, seated herself and pulled out a sheet of paper. "Shall we start then? I've made a list."

For some reason, that annoyed him. He tried to tell himself that it was not unreasonable for a woman to ensure her marriage settlements were adequate, but, damn it, what did she think he was? Some kind of miserly penny-pinch? He'd been more than generous when preparing to marry Lady Rose.

Besides, settlements were men's business. She was passing from the protection of her uncle to the protection of her husband. To challenge that was to impugn his honor. He took good care of what was his.

She began. "I have an inheritance coming to me when I

turn twenty-five. I wish it to remain mine, even after marriage." She flung him a challenging look.

"I agree," he said curtly. What interest did he have in her paltry inheritance? "We will set up a trust—"

"No, I will have sole control over it. I won't have trustees telling me what I can and can't do with my own money."

Hart glanced at Ashendon, and shrugged. If that's how she wanted it . . .

Ashendon made a note. In the corner, his secretary did the same, no doubt putting it into legal language.

"You will also make me an allowance."

"Naturally." His voice was icy. Did she think he intended to keep her in penury?

She named a sum that made Hart blink. It was far too modest. Women by nature were rapacious creatures, out for all they can get. So what was she up to?

He said nothing, however, just gave Ashendon an indifferent nod. Ashendon noted it down.

"The duke will give me a house in the country— consulting with me as to the choice. The house is to be wholly mine—title and deed."

His eyes narrowed. He had a dozen country houses. What did she want a separate one for? To keep him out? To have assignations with other men?

"You already own a house," Ashendon reminded her. "Willowbank Farm."

"I want Willowbank Farm deeded to Martha Scarratt— free and clear, with her name on the title."

"But she already has the right to live there for as long as she lives," Ashendon said. "As well as an allowance to live on."

"Yes, but this way she will be a property owner and will be able to leave the place to her sister or one of her nieces or nephews. It will give her standing in the community. And the allowance is to continue for as long as she lives."

Ashendon hesitated, but his niece said urgently, "It's all I have to give—and you know what I owe her, Cal."

Hart frowned. Who was this Martha Scarratt person?

Ashendon glanced at Hart, who made a gesture that indicated his supreme indifference to the arrangement. He would make it his business to find out who the woman was and what his future wife owed her. And then he would decide what to think.

"Everingham to provide a house, with George's agreement, and Willowbank Farm to be made over to Martha Scarratt," Ashendon said and his secretary made a note. "Right, what's next on that list of yours, George?"

"Any children that result from the marriage will live with me and will not be removed from my care unless I agree."

There was a short silence, then Hart said coldly, "As long as you behave yourself, I see no problem with that." He had no knowledge of children and little interest in child-rearing. As long as he had an heir, that was all that mattered.

"Provision will be made for each child's future, when they're born."

"Naturally. As long as they're my children."

She flashed him a look of indignation. "I believe the marriage service says 'forsaking all other, keep thee only unto him, so long as ye both shall live.' I, at least, have no intention of breaking my vows."

His brow rose cynically. "If you say so."

Her eyes narrowed.

Ashendon said, "What about the duke's fidelity—don't you have anything to say about that?"

The duke's attraction was bound to blow itself out—as would hers, no doubt—and she would not, absolutely not demean herself by appearing to care what he did after that. She shrugged. "Most men are tomcats, everybody knows that."

Now it was Hart's turn to be offended. He'd planned to continue with his current way of life, which meant he would probably set himself up with a mistress once his wife took to living in the country with her dogs and horses. It was unreasonable to expect otherwise. But her attitude was insulting; if she could be faithful, so could he.

Hart waited for her next condition. She tensed and he knew this would be the big one. Women were devious—she hadn't yet made any demand that was not laughably minor. They always left the sneakiest until last.

"My horse, Sultan, is my property and will remain so."

Hart almost laughed. He hadn't expected that, but given her passion for the animal, he should have. "Will you allow the stallion to cover some of my mares?"

She considered that. "If they're of suitable quality, and Sultan likes the look of them."

"Agreed. What else?" He waited. He could tell by the tension in her body that it was something he wouldn't like.

She moistened her lips before she spoke and for a few seconds he was so focused on her mouth that he almost didn't take in what she said. Almost. "*What* did you say?"

She lifted her chin and sent him a defiant look. "I want you to promise me that there will be no hunting of foxes on any of your properties," she repeated.

"Out of the question," he snapped. Never had he heard such a ridiculous proposition. He recalled the bleeding-heart speech she'd made to him over supper at the ball the other night. "Foxes are vermin."

"They have a right to exist as much as anyone—besides, you know as well as I do that it's the chase all you men like—the hunt, the blood, the cruelty."

"Rubbish!" There was an element of truth in what she said—he did enjoy the chase—but, dammit, it was a tradition. A grand sport. And one he enjoyed.

"Whatever your reasons—or what you claim as your reasons—will you agree to cease all foxhunting on your properties?"

"I will not—and this is not the kind of subject that's appropriate when drawing up settlements."

"It is for me." She sat back in her chair and folded her arms. Her mouth compressed in a stubborn line. Hart's did much the same. There was a long tense silence.

The silence stretched, and Hart had to tamp down his growing anger. Was his marriage really going to founder over such a ridiculous condition? Was it some kind of indirect attempt to get out of it at the last minute? Foxhunting was a fine sport, and it helped rid the country of vermin. He wouldn't be blackmailed into giving it up.

After a while Ashendon coughed. "Perhaps we can reach a compromise."

Hart raised his brow.

"What if foxhunting were banned on the estate you deed to George, and one other?"

She said nothing. Her chin was braced in a stubborn line. Her folded arms tightened.

"Come on, George," Ashendon said in a coaxing voice. "Be reasonable. A man cannot be expected to give up all his pleasures."

Her eyes flashed. "Pleasures?"

"Pastimes," Ashendon corrected himself.

"I would be prepared to do that," Hart said. "And to agree that no foxhunt will be held on any of my properties while you are there—whether visiting or residing." He had a hunting box in Leicestershire, and he doubted she'd ever visit it. He'd make sure she didn't.

"There you are, George," Ashendon said. "It's a handsome compromise. What do you say?"

She considered it for a long moment, then gave a grudging nod. "Very well, as long as you know that I will continue to oppose the horrid practice in any way I see fit."

"Understood," Hart said.

"Now, is there anything else on your list?" Ashendon asked her.

"No, that's all," she said, and sat back.

He raised his brow. Her conditions had mostly been about animals. Was that all she wanted?

She started to rise from her seat. "I have some conditions of my own," Hart said. She stiffened and sat back down.

"We'll start with the allowance . . ." He named a sum that was triple the one she'd asked for. Her jaw dropped.

"I am not marrying you for money," she snapped.

He had no idea why she'd agreed to marry him, but he wasn't going to question it. "The amount you suggested is paltry," he said coldly. "I won't have my duchess scrimping and saving."

She opened her mouth to argue, but before she could speak, he continued, "I must insist on the right to conjugal visits."

"Visits?" Ashendon queried with a frown. "You're not planning to live together?"

"Naturally we shall cohabit until my duchess is with child. And after that, whenever I choose."

"I reserve the right to refuse," she said quickly.

He gave her a long look. "As long as consent is not unreasonably withheld."

Ashendon raised a brow at that, but she gave a curt nod, and he wrote it down.

"Anything else?" Ashendon asked.

"Nothing specific," Hart told him. "Take the rest of the details from the settlements we agreed on for Lady Rose. Have a copy of the final document sent to me and I'll have my lawyer look it over."

"In that case . . ." Lady Georgiana rose to leave.

"Just one last thing," Hart said.

She paused and turned toward him with narrowed eyes.

"You do intend to go through with this wedding, don't you, Lady Georgiana?"

Her gray eyes turned to chips of ice. Her hands knotted into fists, crumpling her list in one hand. "I gave you my word, didn't I?" Without waiting for his response, she swept from the room.

Ashendon blotted the document he'd made his notes on. "Doesn't do to challenge George on her word of honor, you know. As you can see, she's a mite touchy about it."

Hart snorted. "I've never met a woman yet who has any real idea of honor—it's all self-interest with them."

"Then your life is about to change." Ashendon leaned back in his chair, amusement dancing in his eyes. "I foresee interesting times ahead for you, Everingham. Very interesting times."

Chapter Eleven

❧

There is a stubbornness about me that never can bear to be frightened at the will of others. My courage always rises at every attempt to intimidate me.

—JANE AUSTEN, *PRIDE AND PREJUDICE*

AFTER THE SETTLEMENTS HAD BEEN AGREED ON AND signed by both parties, the next item to be negotiated was the date of the wedding. The duke had informed Cal he wanted it to be as soon as possible. But it was up to George and her family to make the final choice.

George wasn't sure what she wanted—in one way she'd be happy to wait for a year, but then there were those feelings, the hot, sweaty, restless, hungry-but-not-for-food feelings where she woke, enmeshed in lurid dreams of being naked in bed with the duke. A year of that would drive her mad—if indeed they lasted that long. But there was no way of telling.

She wanted them to be over and done with. Once the duke had bedded her, she was sure the disturbing sensations would go away, and she'd be able to sleep peacefully in her bed once more.

In the end they agreed on a date just over three weeks away, which gave time for the banns to be called in church. Aunt Agatha had given a flat veto to the duke's plan for a special license. "Bad enough the scandal that forced this marriage in the first place," she said. "If you rush the business through, you know what people will think. As it is, they will be counting back from the date your first child is born."

Her first child? George couldn't imagine it. She glanced across at Emm, huge now with the imminent birth of her baby. How must that feel?

"Yes," Emm said. "And we need time to order clothes. George will need a wedding dress."

"And the rest," Aunt Agatha added. "A trousseau fit for a duchess."

George didn't like the sound of that.

"I'll speak to my dressmaker, Hortense—" Aunt Agatha continued.

"No," George said. She'd met Hortense once, and hadn't liked her a bit. Toplofty, more snobbish even than Aunt Agatha, and her clothes might be very elegant but in George's opinion they were old lady clothes. "I'll get everything I need from Miss Chance." Daisy Chance was nice, and George felt comfortable with her. And Daisy had a way of making clothes that exactly suited their wearer.

When George had first come to London, she'd been still getting used to wearing dresses. The idea of ball dresses and morning dresses and carriage dresses and evening dresses and all the other kind of dresses was quite overwhelming to a girl who hadn't even owned a dress until a few months before. But Miss Chance had understood, and had even made her some special breeches that George could wear under her dresses so that she didn't feel so naked and exposed. Dresses were drafty.

Aunt Agatha sniffed. "That common little Cockney can't possibly outfit a duchess. She would have no idea where to start."

"She can practice on me, then—"

"Don't be ridic—"

"Miss Chance has done very well by all of us," Emm interjected calmly. "I see no reason why George should not continue to patronize her for her wedding dress and trousseau. So that's settled."

Aunt Agatha looked as though she'd swallowed a lemon, but she didn't argue. One didn't argue with the woman about to give birth to the Ashendon Heir.

Lord help Emm if she had a girl.

"I'll come with you to see Miss Chance, dear," Aunt Dottie offered. "I have a mind to order some garments from her too. Something a little special. We'll have fun together, won't we, George?"

George grinned. "Thanks, Aunt Dottie, that'd be lovely."

George could see Aunt Agatha was wrestling with herself. She'd rather sit in a puddle than be seen entering the House of Chance, but she also didn't want to hand over the serious business of Clothing a Future Duchess to her frivolous younger sister. Anyone who would describe such an important task as "fun" was clearly not to be trusted.

Emm settled it. "Thank you, Aunt Dottie. That will be perfect. It's a shame that Lily and Rose are both out of town at the moment. I know they'd love to go shopping with you. I wish I could go myself, but . . ." She gestured to her swollen belly and sighed. "I hope it won't be long now. I'm so sick of feeling like a caged elephant."

"Bite your tongue, Emmaline!" Aunt Agatha snapped. "Caged elephant indeed! What is a little discomfort when you have the privilege of bearing the next Heir to the House of Ashendon."

Emm gave her a dry look. Aunt Agatha had never borne a child. Easy for her to say . . . But of course, Emm would never say so.

George would, if Aunt Agatha ever spoke to her like that.

THE FOLLOWING NIGHT GEORGE ATTENDED A PARTY, HER first since the notice of her betrothal to the duke had been published. She was a little nervous, wondering what the reaction of the ton would be, and when she stepped into the room flanked by her two aunts, the sudden hush, followed by a buzz of low comment, confirmed her worst expectations.

Aunt Agatha said, "Now, Georgiana, your best behavior,

if you will. You have the Rutherford name to uphold. None of your barnyard antics here."

George gritted her teeth. Barnyard antics indeed! How she wished she had Rose and Lily with her. Or Emm.

On her other side Aunt Dottie squeezed her arm gently and murmured, "Head up, my love, and smile. The worst will soon be over."

Her hostess came bustling up. "Lady Salter, Lady Dorothea, Lady Georgiana, so delighted you could come this evening. Congratulations on your betrothal, Lady Georgiana, so clever of you to catch our dear, elusive duke."

George blinked. *Our* duke, as if she'd stolen him? And was *clever* implying she'd trapped him? She itched to point out that he'd trapped her. But she didn't. She thanked the woman politely and moved away as quickly as she could, looking for something to drink and a friendly face.

One of the young men who'd courted her came toward her, his face full of reproach. "And to think I believed you when you said you never wanted to marry. You were so adamant that you wanted to live by yourself in the country with your dogs and horses. But it was just me you didn't want to marry, wasn't it?" His voice was raw with hurt. "You had your eyes on a much grander prize."

"I'm sorry." George had no words to explain. She ached for the pain she'd caused, but there was no way to tell him that she'd been completely honest with him, and that nothing had changed, except her situation.

Nobody had shoved her into the duke's arms that evening. And nobody had made her return his kisses and climb him like a tree. That was her own fault. Or the fault of her runaway instincts.

"Well, you tricked us all, didn't you, Lady George," said another man with a bitter laugh. "More fool me for believing you meant it."

The reproaches of men who'd courted her were bad enough. Other comments were blunter and more to the point. A tightly corseted dowager congratulated her thinly, then as she turned away added in an acid aside to her friend,

"She's lucky the duke is a man of honor. In my day gels who behaved like trollops were given a good whipping and sent away in disgrace."

Another said, within George's hearing, "I suppose her uncle forced him into it. Ashendon is not a man to be taken lightly."

Several women asked her when the wedding was to be, and eyed her waistline searchingly.

But the worst were the women who congratulated her for being clever, for entrapping the duke. Their congratulations made her feel soiled, dirty.

"You sneaky thing. I've been trying to hook Everingham for the longest time. I heard how you did it. So clever, arranging to be caught like that, doing it at one of old Mrs. Gastonbury's musical evenings. Must have made the old ladies' wigs stand on end."

There was no way to explain, to put the story right. She *had* let the duke kiss her at Mrs. Gastonbury's, and so she had to bear the consequences of her foolishness.

And if people were determined to believe the betrothal was the result of some kind of devious stratagem on her part—and they were—well, she'd just have to grin and bear it.

The congratulations, the barbed compliments went on and on until she wanted to scream. But she'd agreed to marry the duke, and this was just the start of her punishment. She gritted her teeth and smiled and smiled and smiled until her jaw was aching. And then she smiled some more.

Lady Peplowe arrived with her daughter Penny, and George heaved a sigh of relief to see people she knew and liked. Lady Peplowe hugged her warmly and wished her all the very best, and such was her sincerity, George almost found herself a little bit teary.

But Penny was frankly surprised and said so. "I thought you were never going to get married, George. And I thought you really disliked the duke."

George had mumbled something about changing her mind, but inside she was squirming. She wasn't about to admit—not even to a close friend like Penny—what had really happened, how she'd more or less been forced into it, but she also wasn't going to lie and pretend she and the duke were love's young dream. It was all terribly awkward.

Penny and Lady Peplowe drifted off, and George looked around to see what time it was. When could she decently go home?

She caught sight of a clock and her heart sank. She'd been here barely forty minutes. She'd have to give it at least an hour more. Unless she pretended to have a headache. But that would be cowardly.

HART WAS PLAYING PIQUET WITH HIS FRIEND, SINC. HE'D decided to eat dinner at his club, and had run into Sinc. Afterward, with a brandy at their elbow, they'd played cards.

"Something on your mind?" Sinc asked, after having won the last three tricks.

"Hmm? No." But it wasn't true. Shortly before he'd left for his club, a note had been delivered from Lady Salter. It was a damned piece of cheek telling him—not suggesting, but virtually ordering him—to accompany Lady Georgiana to some wretched party. A party he had no interest in attending.

He'd tossed the note in the fire and gone out.

Sinc dealt the next round. And won the next two tricks. "Well, whatever it is, your mind's not on the game."

Hart sipped his brandy and considered his hand.

"Surprised you decided not to go to the Renwicks'."

Hart looked up. "Not you, as well."

"Not me what?"

"Thinking I ought to attend the Renwick party. I never attend such insipid events, you know that."

"No, s'pose not." Sinc made his discard. "Just thought . . . Oh, never mind."

"Never mind what?" Hart asked after a minute.

"I suppose you know the harpies have been getting stuck into Lady George."

Hart frowned. "What do you mean? What harpies?"

"Quite a few of 'em, from what m'sister says. Some nasty talk around. Lady George not exactly getting the benefit of the doubt."

"In what sense?"

Sinc stared at him incredulously. "You think the fine ladies of the ton will universally heap blessings on Lady George's glossy little head? After she's claimed all season to be averse to the very idea of marriage? And then she walks off with the marriage prize of the season—you. After having been caught in public with your tongue wrapped around her tonsils? Oh, yes, they purely *love* her for it."

Hart stilled. So that was what Lady Salter's note was about. "Damn!" He threw down his cards and left.

GEORGE DRAINED HER GLASS OF CHAMPAGNE AND LOOKED around for a footman. Her third glass in—she glanced at the clock—not quite an hour. She never drank more than one glass, usually. She didn't actually like champagne. Trouble was she didn't much like ratafia either. What she wouldn't give for a nice cup of tea. But she'd have to wait until she got home.

A woman hurried up to her, hands held out and a wide smile on her face. Mrs. Threadgood, the lady she'd last seen in the Peplowe conservatory.

"Good evening, Mrs. Threadgood," George said cautiously.

The woman seized George's hands in hers as if in warm congratulation, leaned forward and in a low voice said, "You don't deserve such a fine man, you little strumpet. Don't think I don't know what you were up to in that conservatory." Smiling falsely, she dug her nails into George's hands so hard that if George hadn't been wearing gloves she was sure the woman would have drawn blood.

She wrenched her hands out of the woman's grip and, temper boiling, raised her hand—and found her wrist caught from behind in a firm grip.

"Put the slap away," a deep voice murmured in her ear. The duke, drat him.

Ignoring his imprisonment of her hand she said in a clear voice, "I know what *I* was doing in that conservatory, Mrs. Threadgood. I'd spotted a rat, a big fat female one, with two friends, strumpeting on their own behalf. A rat who is now choking on her own sour grapes." She bared her teeth in a parody of a smile.

Mrs. Threadgood flushed an unlovely mottled purple. She glanced at the duke over George's shoulder, muttered something unintelligible and flounced away.

George turned to the duke and pulled her hand out of his grip. "I wish you hadn't interfered. If ever a woman deserved to be slapped . . ."

"I know. And it would have been very satisfying, I'm sure. But Lady Dorothea was looking quite wretchedly worried and so I stepped in."

George ran her hands down her dress. She was still itching to slap someone. "What are you doing here, duke? I didn't think you would come to this kind of thing."

"I wouldn't normally, but Lady Salter sent me a note telling me you were attending this party and that I owed you my support."

George was surprised. Aunt Agatha had done that? Really?

The duke continued, "And it seems she was right, if that little exchange was any indication. Tell me, what did she say to you? I only heard your response—which was brilliant, by the way."

"It doesn't matter." She could fight her own battles.

He regarded her narrowly for a moment, then shrugged. "May I fetch you a drink?"

"Yes, please." As soon as the duke left, George pulled one of her gloves off and examined the marks Mrs. Threadgood's nails had left. A series of red crescent indentations marked the back of her hand. She rubbed it. The wretched woman had claws.

The duke returned with a footman bearing a tray with a variety of drinks. "Did that woman do that to you? Let me see."

He reached for her hand, but George pulled it away. "No, it's nothing." She pulled her long satin evening glove back on and selected a glass of lemonade from the footman's tray. They stood, sipping their drinks, observing the people at the party.

"Are you enjoying yourself?" the duke asked after a minute.

She gave him an incredulous look, then snorted. "Oh, yes, I couldn't think of a more delightful way to spend an evening."

He grimaced. "Like that, eh? So Lady Salter was correct."

George shrugged. "She occasionally is."

"Was that woman—La Threadgood—typical?"

"About average. The consensus seems to be that I have entrapped you into marriage. Some resent it; others are congratulating me on my 'cleverness.'"

She directed an accusing look at him and seemed to expect him to say something.

"I see." Hart could see she was angry, but there was nothing he could say to her that would mitigate the gossip. "I thought you didn't care what society thinks."

It was the wrong thing to say. She turned her head sharply. "Why would you think that?"

"In the conservatory that time—with Mrs. Threadgood and her friends—you said as much."

"Oh, them—they only thought I was odd. I don't care about that kind of thing. A lot of people think I'm odd." She made a careless gesture. "I suppose I am."

"Then how is this any different?"

"Because this time they're calling me dishonest, saying I've been deceitful and devious and hypocritical and immoral. It's insulting."

He didn't say anything, so she added, "Don't you see? They're accusing me of entrapping you, of catching myself a rich duke by devious means. Accusing *me*."

"I see."

She rolled her eyes.

He frowned. "But you know you haven't done any of those things, so what does it matter?"

She eyed him with exasperation. "It must be so nice to exist on your rarefied mountaintop, looking down at the rest of the world from your superior position, untouched by what people say about you."

"People talk about me all the time," he said coolly. "I have learned to ignore it."

She bared her teeth at him. "Well, I'm still learning. And I don't really mind if people talk about true things about me—it's the lies that make me angry."

He could see that. She was in an invidious position—and his actions had put her there. So it was up to him to do something about it. "There is no point trying to argue against ill-natured gossip—the harder you oppose it, the more it will confirm in people's minds that it must be true."

She sighed. "I know. I just have to be patient and hope the gossips move on to some other scandal. But I hate waiting! I just want to hit people."

His gray eyes glinted. "I would not advise it."

She narrowed her eyes at him. "I particularly feel like hitting people who stay unnaturally calm, especially people who got me into this horrid position in the first place." She flexed a gloved hand and said reflectively, "I've never hit a duke before."

"Possibly it is a treat in store for you in the future. In the meantime, let us demonstrate to the ignorant that we are in this together." He presented his arm, and, with a cautious look she slipped her hand into the crook of his arm.

He led her forward a few steps, then paused and looked down at her. "And you're not odd. You're an original."

He led her in a slow stroll around the room. He greeted people, sometimes with just a nod, and sometimes he stopped to chat with the more influential members of society in attendance, presenting her as his betrothed each time.

George remained fairly silent, speaking only when spoken to. She kept a pleasant expression on her face, but underneath she was still seething. Naturally the compliments and congratulations held no barbs—hidden or blatant—this time around.

She wasn't sure whether she was relieved to have the slings and arrows stop, or even angrier at the hypocrisy that would happily attack her but pour the butter boat over him for the same thing.

Not that many people actually addressed her; she was merely the appendage on the duke's arm. Was that to be her future? she wondered. Not if she could help it.

All the time they circulated, she was horribly aware of the warmth of the duke's arm under her palm, his strength. The faint, distinctive scent of his shaving cologne teased her senses, making her want to lean closer and inhale him. *Inhale him?* She caught herself just in time.

It was still happening, she thought gloomily. When would this wretched state come to an end?

After an hour, Aunt Agatha glided up and indicated that it was time to leave. George was never more thankful of anything in her life. The duke escorted them to the carriage, bowed over her hand and then strolled off into the night. George watched him go. It was so unfair. Men had so much more freedom.

GEORGE AND AUNT DOTTIE WENT SHOPPING FOR A WEDding dress the next morning. Aunt Dottie was particularly eager to go. She'd heard about the House of Chance from some of her friends, and in particular from an old crony, Beatrice, Lady Davenham, who ran a kind of literary society. Lily often attended it when she was in London, and after Aunt Dottie's first visit, she'd become a regular attendee. As was, surprisingly, the dressmaker, Miss Daisy Chance.

As expected, Aunt Agatha declined to accompany them on the excursion, saying in her lofty way that she quite washed her hands of them and would take no responsibility for Georgiana's final outfit.

"Why should you?" George asked her. "You're not the one getting married."

With a sniff Aunt Agatha swept regally out.

Aunt Dottie giggled. "She wouldn't want to take responsibility for what I'm planning to buy either."

"What are you getting?" Emm asked curiously.

"Bea Davenham showed me the most delightfully naughty nightdresses and bed-jackets that Miss Chance made for her. Did you know Miss Chance and her husband and little daughter live with Bea—they're some kind of family connection, I believe. Anyway, I want some of those nightdresses, and a couple of bed-jackets—so pretty they are."

Emm smiled. "They are indeed. I have several. One of my former students sent me the most beautiful nightdress from Miss Chance for my wedding. That's how we met her, in fact. She was the only dressmaker we knew in London."

"Except for Hortense," said George, pulling a face. "And we didn't like her at all."

Miss Chance was most enthusiastic about the plans for a wedding dress for George. She drew out a sheaf of designs she'd sketched when she'd first seen the betrothal announcement in the newspaper.

"Something simple, like you usually like, Lady George, only I wasn't sure if you'd prefer something light, or something a bit heavier in a rich fabric—we're gettin' into summer, and you don't want to be hot. Then again, knowin' London weather, it might be freezin'.

"And what jewelry will you be wantin' to wear? Pearls is the usual thing for brides. Would you want pearls sewn onto the bodice, like this one"—she showed George a design—"or something like this?" She pulled out another sketch. "Or do you want embroidery—because, if so, we'll need to decide pretty quick so that my girls can get started on it. Three weeks ain't very long, you know."

Everything was in white or cream, which George was heartily sick of. And she'd rejected out of hand the idea that she would wear silver tissue over white satin, which Princess Charlotte had worn to her wedding, poor lady.

But Aunt Agatha had stated, and Emm and Aunt Dottie agreed, that it was vital that she marry in white, given the rumors and gossip. George comforted herself with the reflection that after this she'd never have to wear white again.

Miss Chance then left George with a pile of designs to examine at her leisure while she took Aunt Dottie to an-

other room where she had a display of the kinds of night-
wear that would gladden Aunt Dottie's heart.

George leafed through the various sketches, discarded
the more elaborate designs and quickly narrowed the choice
down to two of the simplest designs. No frills, no lace, no
pearls.

But which of the two? The hail-spotted white muslin
with the tiny puffed sleeves? Or the one in cream silk with
piping around the hem?

Her inability to decide annoyed her. What did it matter
what she wore? This was not a dress to celebrate in. She
should simply toss a coin to decide.

But for some reason she couldn't make herself do it.

"Why don't you take them home for Lady Ashendon to
see," Miss Chance suggested, finding George still trying to
decide. "As long as you don't want lots of embroidery or
beading or pearls sewn on—and I can see you don't—we
have plenty of time to get it made."

"Oh, lovely idea," Aunt Dottie said immediately. "Poor
Emm is feeling so out of everything with this confinement
of hers. I'm sure she would love to see these designs."

So that was that. Miss Chance placed the sheaf of designs in an elegant folio and handed it to George, while
Aunt Dottie hugged to her bosom a fat squishy parcel, tied
with ribbon. "She had some already made up that were a
perfect fit for me," she confided to George in an excited
whisper. "I've ordered some more."

"Oh, but, Aunt Dottie," George began. Miss Chance had
a peculiar rule, that her customers had to pay for their clothes
before taking them home. She claimed that toffs were bad at
paying bills. But before George could explain, Aunt Dottie
pulled a wad of banknotes from her reticule.

"It's all right, my dear, Bea warned me about it. I find it
refreshingly straightforward. I'm forever forgetting to pay
bills."

They left, promising to come back in a day or two with
a final decision.

Chapter Twelve

> I have frequently detected myself in such kind of mistakes... in a total misapprehension of character at some point or other: fancying people so much more gay or grave, or ingenious or stupid than they really are, and I can hardly tell why, or in what the deception originated. Sometimes one is guided... by what other people say of them, without giving oneself time to deliberate and judge.
>
> —JANE AUSTEN, *SENSE AND SENSIBILITY*

THE BARBED COMMENTS CONTINUED TO FLY. IT SEEMED there was no way George could escape them, except by hiding at home all day and night or by having the duke at her side, and she wasn't going to resort to either stratagem.

But each day her temper was sorely tried.

She and Aunt Dottie went to the Pantheon Bazaar to shop for stockings and other bits and pieces. Waiting in line to pay for their purchases, George heard a woman behind them saying, "That's the jade who snared the Duke of Everingham in her web."

"Take no notice, my love," Aunt Dottie said in a crisp, audible voice. "The woman is ignorant as well as ill-bred."

Another woman elbowed George as she passed, hissing, "Jezebel!"

George gritted her teeth and held on to her temper.

In the park, people who used to smile at her now eyed her thoughtfully and failed to meet her gaze. She didn't receive the cut direct from anyone, but it wasn't pleasant.

Wherever she went, whispers followed her. She had entrapped the duke. She was a hypocrite, a liar, a shameless hussy who'd taken advantage of an honorable man. She was carrying his child.

George got more and more furious.

She went to Hatchards to buy a book for Emm, who was feeling housebound, and two ladies on the other side of the bookshelves were talking. George could see them through the shelves.

"There she is, the one who seduced the Duke of Everingham and got him to agree to marry her."

"Not as pretty as the first one he was going to marry, is she?"

"I suppose that's why she had to seduce him."

To the discomfiture of the ladies George pulled out a couple of books, and through the gap in the shelves bared her teeth in a smile. "Shocking isn't it, ladies? I'm not nearly as pretty as Rose. Obviously I had to do *something*!"

She bought the book for Emm and sailed out, angrily aware that she should never have lost her temper and that behind her a fresh buzz of gossip was brewing.

"I know it must be infuriating, George, dear, but gossip grows stale quite quickly, as long as it is not fed. You must try to rise above it," Emm said when George confided in her. "And for heaven's sake, don't hit anyone, tempting as it might be."

But it was the duke George wanted to hit.

"Tedious as it may be," Aunt Agatha said, "you must realize that the rumors are merely a reflection of your triumph."

"Triumph?" George repeated incredulously.

"They are gnashing their teeth with jealousy," Aunt Agatha said loftily. "You have what they could not achieve."

I have what I never did want. But she didn't say it aloud.

IT WAS A WARM AFTERNOON AND THE DUKE HAD INVITED George for a drive through the park at the fashionable hour. Since she knew that he disliked the slow pace and the constant greeting and gossip sharing that was the park at that time of day, she realized his purpose was to present them to the ton as a couple yet again.

He arrived on time, driving a very smart curricle pulled by a magnificent pair of matched bays. A liveried groom was seated behind.

Leaving a mournful Finn behind, she allowed the duke to assist her into the curricle; she could have climbed up easily if it weren't for these wretched skirts.

They said very little as he negotiated the busy London traffic; horse and carts and wagons and barrow-boys and piemen and urchins and dogs, all hurrying in different directions. But once through the gates of Hyde Park it seemed somehow calmer, even though it was crowded in a different way, with elegant ladies twirling their parasols, gentlemen with canes as well as fine carriages stopping to take people up for a short time and put them down again.

It took nearly twenty minutes to pass through the first hundred yards, what with everyone wanting to congratulate George and quiz the duke on finally being caught—ha ha.

"Lady George, you clever creature. Fancy you being the one to lead our elusive duke to the altar."

"And all the time we thought you meant it when you said you never wanted to marry."

"Still waters run deep, eh?"

"How does it feel to be caught in parson's mousetrap once more, your grace?"

By the time the crowd had thinned out a little, George was ready to spit. She was fed up with the insincere compliments, the veiled accusations of her having trapped the duke into marriage, the indirect—and some quite blunt—accusations of hypocrisy.

The idea that *he* was the one who'd been caught, and that *she'd* done the catching, infuriated her.

She glanced at the duke to see if he felt the same, but as usual, his face was like a graven mask; she could read nothing, no emotion on it.

"Shall we take this path?" he asked, and without waiting

for her response, turned the curricle down a less used pathway, away from the fashionable press. They drove in silence for a while, and George gradually calmed, lulled by the golden afternoon and the breeze in the trees and the quiet. There were only a few pedestrians here and there, and one or two people on horseback, who nodded but didn't stop for conversation.

"I'm taking you to Venice for the honeymoon," he said after a while.

"What? No." She turned to him. "I mean, it's a nice idea, but I can't leave Emm until she's had the baby."

"I've made all the arrangements." When she didn't respond, he added, "Why do you need to be there? You're not a midwife, are you?"

"No, of course I'm not, but I'm not leaving her anyway."

"Why, what can you do?"

"I don't know. Be there."

"For heaven's sake," he said, exasperated. "Your uncle is besotted with his wife. She will have the finest medical attention available."

"Princess Charlotte also had the 'finest medical attention' in the kingdom, and look at what happened to her, poor lady." Princess Charlotte had died in childbirth, surrounded by the most highly regarded physicians in the land. Of course the finger-pointing and blame happened afterward, but George didn't know or care who was at fault—she wasn't going to leave Emm until she was safely delivered of her baby. "So you can go to Venice if you want; I'm staying here."

"Don't be ridiculous."

"In any case," she added, "should you be thinking of traveling out of the country? What about your mother?"

"What about her? She'll get along perfectly well without me, I assure you. In fact, the less my mother and I see of each other, the happier we are."

She stared at him in disbelief. To speak so about his dying mother. She was deeply shocked. "You really are heartless, aren't you?"

He shrugged. "Hence the sobriquet the ton has bestowed on me."

She shook her head. "I don't know how you can even think of leaving your mother in her condition."

There was a short silence. "What condition would that be?"

George couldn't believe her ears. "Surely you know. She's dying."

He gave her a sharp look. "What makes you think so?"

"I saw her just the other day. She looked terrible. I got the impression she had just days to live."

His eyes narrowed. His hands tightened on the reins. "You met my mother? How? Where?"

"At her home, of course. Aunt Agatha took me to see her. She's clearly not fit even to leave her bed."

His face hardened; his eyes blazed cold and fierce. He said in a clipped voice, "So, you visited her, and talked with her. Can I assume it was the day you changed your mind and decided to marry me after all? The day before I came to arrange the settlements?"

"Yes, but— What are you— Watch out!"

Pedestrians scattered as the duke pulled his horses around in a circle and drove rapidly back the way they'd come. George clung to the side of the curricle. "What on earth do you think you're doing?"

"Taking you to see my mother."

"Now? But why?"

He didn't answer. With a grim expression he wove swiftly through the London traffic. George would have admired his skill with the reins had she not been so bemused by his overreaction to the idea that she'd met his mother. What was so bad about that?

It was only natural that a mother would want to meet her son's intended.

Or did he not know of his mother's grave illness? Had she broken a confidence? Nobody had mentioned it was to be kept from him.

"Hold 'em," he instructed his groom as they pulled up in

front of the duchess's house. The lad jumped down and ran to hold the horses. The duke swung George down, took her hand in a firm grasp and towed her up the steps to the front door.

"What are you doing?" She pulled to release her hand but his grip only tightened.

He yanked hard on the bellpull and a bell jangled loudly inside the house.

The butler opened the door. "Your grace, I—"

"Upstairs, is she?"

"Yes, your grace, in her dressing r—"

The duke pushed past him and, keeping George's hand firmly in his grasp, took to the stairs. She tried to pull back. "What are we doing here? You can't go into her dressing room unannounced!" But he kept going and as he didn't release her, she had no option but to go with him.

He flung open a door. "Ah, there you are, Mother." With a curt gesture he ushered George into the room. Two elegantly dressed young gentlemen immediately jumped to their feet. They bowed, but George had no eyes for them.

The duke ignored the men as well. In an icy voice he said, "You've met Lady Georgiana Rutherford, I gather, Mother."

The duchess turned toward them, showing no self-consciousness. "Yes, of course. How do you do, Lady Georgiana?"

George forgot to respond. She stared at the duke's mother, stunned.

The duchess was seated, fully dressed, in front of a large round looking glass where she had clearly been making the final touches to her toilette. Her skin glowed, her cheeks were delicately tinged with color. She was dressed to go out, in an elegant, rose-pink silk ball gown, a lacy shawl draped over her almost bare shoulders, darker pink satin slippers on her feet. A magnificent diamond set graced her throat, ears and wrist. On the dressing table before her lay a pair of long white satin gloves and a painted ivory fan.

She was the picture of health.

The two gentlemen, also in the most formal of dress,

were, it seemed, her escorts for the evening. They were about the duke's age.

George didn't know what to say. "But you're looking so well, your grace. I thought . . ."

"It was a miracle," the duchess said composedly. "Snatched back from the brink of the grave, I was." She smiled at the two gentlemen, who made sympathetic noises.

The duke said in a hard voice, "You've had a lot of miracles in your time, haven't you, Mother?"

The duchess was oblivious of her son's sarcasm. "I have been blessed," she admitted modestly.

He turned to George. "Seen enough? Right then, goodbye, Mother." And he towed George from the room.

She followed him blindly, her brain whirling. Without a word he helped her into the curricle, took the reins and drove away.

After a while, she gathered her thoughts enough to speak. "You mean her illness was—"

"Faked."

"I thought she was dying."

"Yes, she's good at that." He gave her a grim, sideways glance. "She's had a lot of practice. Was it the full scene—candles, incense, all the medicines, the lavish use of cosmetics, the onion in the handkerchief?"

"The onion in—?"

"Helps the tears along."

He sounded so matter-of-fact—furious, but matter-of-fact—that George was stunned. "Does she often do this kind of thing?"

"From time to time. It's her way of controlling people. I didn't begin to see through it until I was fourteen or fifteen." He paused to negotiate a narrow passage between a wagon and a street barrow. "My father never saw through it at all. He danced to her tune all his life." His voice was bitter. "Of course, she pulls the deathbed scene only when there's something she really wants. The rest of the time it's some imaginary ailment, or simply her 'nerves.' We are all slaves to Mama's nerves." It sounded like a quotation.

They reached Berkeley Square and he pulled over, on the far side of the square from Cal and Emm's house. He snapped his fingers and his groom jumped down and ran to the horses' heads.

He dropped the reins and turned to her. "So that's how she got you to agree to marry me?" His voice was grim.

George nodded.

"And that's what caused your change of heart?"

"Yes. My aunt Agatha must have been in on it as well. She took me there. She must have known. She's known your mother for years."

"Probably."

There was a short silence. The breeze picked up, sending the leaves of the plane trees rustling. The sun was low in the sky and she shivered, feeling suddenly cold. Without a word, he bent and pulled a soft rug from a compartment beneath his seat and wrapped it around her. He was still deep in thought, a frown on his face, a grim, faraway look in his eyes.

"I must apologize for my mother's deception," he said at last in a cold, clipped voice. "And since she's the reason you agreed to marry me, I suppose I must release you from your promise."

George was stunned. It was the last thing she would have expected from him after all the trouble he'd gone through to ensure their betrothal. Perhaps there was a streak of honor in him after all.

She smoothed her gloves over her fingers, giving herself time to think of what to say. "You're more like your mother than you think," she said at last.

"What?" His brows snapped together. "I'm *nothing* like my mother."

"You are, you know. She staged a dramatic scene to trick me into giving a deathbed promise and make me agree to marry you. Whereas you"—she met his gaze calmly—"you staged a seduction scene in the very place and at the very time when you were guaranteed to have dozens of witnesses—just before the supper interval at Mrs. Gastonbury's *soirée musicale*."

He whitened. His lips compressed.

"And then," she continued, "you sent off the notice of betrothal to the newspapers in order to force my hand. There was no overeager secretary, was there?" It was a guess on her part, but he didn't deny it.

He shook his head. "But I—"

"You trapped me in exactly the same way as your mother did, placing me in a position where I had no choice. Oh, your tactics were different, but you and your mother had exactly the same intention—to force me to do what you wanted, regardless of my own wishes."

He stared at her, stunned by her accusation. "I never thought—"

"No, I'm sure you didn't. You just saw something you wanted and did what you had to to get it."

He opened his mouth, then shut it. A pulse beat in his jaw.

"You could have wooed me, courted me, like any other man might have—"

"But you were adamant you didn't ever want to marry."

She tilted her head. "And there it is again, you see? You thought you knew what I wanted but it wasn't what you wanted, so you just trampled over my feelings, my opinions, my wants in order to get your way. What I wanted didn't matter to you at all. Just like your mother."

He stared at her. He was white around the mouth. Her words had shocked him to the core, she could see.

Good. He needed shocking.

She pushed the rug aside and prepared to get down from the curricle.

"I'll drive you—"

"No, I'll walk across the square." Unaided, she jumped lithely down from the curricle. He followed her.

"I will put a notice in the newspapers, canceling our betrothal." His voice was heavy but sincere. "I'm sorry. I didn't think—I didn't realize—" He broke off and shook his head. "I have no excuse for my behavior. I'm truly sorry."

George looked up at him. She'd never liked him so much

as at this moment, when she was about to be free of him. "No, don't do that," she heard herself saying. "Call on me tomorrow and I'll tell you of my decision."

The cynical look returned to his eyes. "Toying with me, are you? Making me wait? Well, I suppose I deserve it."

Anger sparked. "Don't *ever* accuse me of that. I'm not the one who deals in strategies and playacting and lies. What I say, I mean. Please yourself then—call on me tomorrow or send a notice to the papers, I don't care!" And she stormed off across the park.

Hart drove home in such deep shock that when his horses pulled up in front of his house, he looked around, blinking, having no idea how he'd driven from Berkeley Square to his house. He tossed the reins to his groom and went inside, deep in thought.

He had deliberately distanced himself from his mother over the years, ever since he'd first realized that the various illnesses and disabilities and megrims she suffered from were devices she used to trick people into doing what they wanted.

Her dishonesty disgusted him. He had prided himself that he was nothing like her. And now . . . Georgiana Rutherford's words echoed around and around in his brain.

You're more like your mother than you think.

And she'd proved it to him. He *had* gone out of his way to try to force her into marrying him. He'd been—now he came to reflect on it—quite proud of trapping her, in fact.

Ever since that first kiss at her family's ball he'd made up his mind to marry her. She was everything he wanted; independent, attractive, wellborn, a girl with a sense of her own future, who would not be looking to him to fulfill all her needs, a woman who would not hang off his sleeve day in, day out.

He'd kissed her, just as an experiment, to see whether she might suit him, to check whether she had an antipathy to men or not. Not that it really mattered to him; sexual preference had little to do with marriage and the procreation of heirs.

But that kiss . . . It had set off a, a conflagration inside him. He'd almost lost all sense of himself. Never had he experienced such a reaction to a simple kiss.

His body had hungered for her ever since.

She'd felt it too, he knew by the way she'd reacted. He'd made up his mind, then and there.

You're more like your mother than you think.

She was right. Knowing her stated aversion to marriage, he'd set out to entrap her, coolly and deliberately. He hadn't even thought about the rights or wrongs of it. He was a hunter. Always had been. He'd even thought himself quite clever.

He sat down at his desk and drew out a sheet of paper.

Lady Georgiana had held out against seduction; she'd stood firm against family and society pressure. She had said, over and over, quite openly, that she wanted never to marry, that she wanted to live her life in peace in the country, raising dogs and horses.

She'd only buckled when—no, *because* he and his mother between them—and damn it for a truth that sickened him—had trapped her.

And society had blamed her for it.

He would write to the newspapers and withdraw the betrothal announcement. He picked up the pen, dipped it in the inkwell and stared at the blank page. They'd blame her for that too. Men didn't withdraw from betrothals—it was too dishonorable. A gentleman's word was his bond. Only women could withdraw.

But if the betrothal were cancelled she'd be labeled a jilt. And worse.

He put the pen down and pushed the paper aside. Damn it all, what was he going to do?

GEORGE WAS GLAD OF THE SHORT WALK ACROSS THE PARK. She needed the air and the exercise to clear her head. The afternoon sunlight dappled the grass, filtering through the leaves of the plane trees overhead, throwing long shadows.

Tiny daisies were scattered across the lawn, like stars in a green firmament.

The duke had offered to release her from their betrothal.

It was the last thing she'd expected of him. She hadn't even thought it was a possibility when she'd accused him of being just like his mother.

What an appalling creature his mother must be, to lie so easily and often. She hadn't so much as blushed or batted an eye when her deception was exposed.

The duke had grown up living with that kind of behavior. It explained quite a lot.

His acceptance of her accusations had surprised her. He hadn't argued, hadn't made excuses or tried to bluster his way out of it, taking refuge in anger. He'd taken it on the chin, like a man—and he'd apologized.

A man who could accept honest criticism. A man who could apologize. How rare was that?

And he'd offered to release her, which had really taken her by surprise. After all the trouble he'd taken to trap her in the first place. So the apology must be sincere.

She'd told him to wait, to ask her tomorrow. Why? She was desperate to be released . . . wasn't she?

The breeze picked up, rustling the leaves overhead. She shivered, and picked up her pace, almost running the last few yards before she crossed the street and sounded the knocker of Ashendon House.

It was a few minutes before anyone answered and when the door opened, it was by a very distracted-looking butler. "What is it, Burton?"

"It's her ladyship. She's started."

"Started? What— Oh! You mean the baby's coming?"

He nodded, and without waiting for any more, she hitched up her skirts and ran up the stairs, taking them two at a time. She found Cal on the landing outside the bedchamber he shared with Emm, pacing back and forth like a caged lion.

"Cal, what's happening?"

He turned an agonized face toward her. "She's in there."

He jerked his head. "The doctor's been and gone. He says there's nothing to worry about. He brought a midwife, and she's in there with Emm's maid and Aunt Agatha."

"I'm going in." George tried the door, but it wouldn't open.

"Locked," Cal said grimly. "They won't let me in either."

She nodded. Men weren't usually allowed to attend their wives' confinements. But she could go in, surely. She knocked on the door. There was no answer, so she knocked again, louder.

The door opened a crack and Aunt Agatha looked out. Her face was pale and she looked rattled but determined. "Go away," she said, addressing both of them. "Childbirth takes time, and there's nothing you can do."

"Can I come in?" George asked. "I can help."

Aunt Agatha snorted. "You'd only be in the way. Besides, childbed is no place for an unmarried gel."

"But—"

Aunt Agatha shut the door. They heard the key turn in the lock.

"But—" George stared at the closed door. She hadn't ever attended a human birth, but she'd helped deliver puppies and foals; and once she'd come across a cow in labor and had helped a farmer deliver the calf that was turned the wrong way around. She turned to Cal and started to say something, but Aunt Dottie appeared.

"It's no use, my love. Aggie won't be budged. She insists that only married women—and servants—attend dear Emm, says it's not fitting for men and unmarried gels to witness." She snorted. "I might not be married, but it's a long time since I was a gel."

"But she's never had a baby herself, has she?"

"No, but she puts a lot of store in a wedding ring, does Aggie." She linked her arm through Cal's. "Now come along, dear boy—it won't do anyone any good to wait here, wearing holes in the carpet. Come downstairs and pour us all a drink."

But Cal wouldn't budge. "I'm not leaving her. I might not be allowed in there—Aunt Agatha says my presence

will only upset Emm, and I suppose that could be right—
but I'll be damned if I leave her. I'm going to be right here
in case she needs me."

Aunt Dottie then arranged for chairs to be brought up,
and a small table, cards and some wine. "No, don't argue,
dear boy, you won't help Emm any by fretting. Sit down
and let us play a relaxing game of cards while we wait."

But Cal couldn't concentrate—he was focused on every
little noise coming from inside the bedchamber, so Aunt
Dottie played patience, while Cal paced.

George used some of the time to write to Rose and to
Lily and Edward, informing them that Emm's labor had
started. She stared at what she'd written, then screwed up
the letters. Rose and Lily were too far away to come in time
for the birth. Such news would only cause them to worry;
better to wait until she had some real news. She prayed it
would be good news.

After an hour or so, Finn needed to go outside, so George
took him for the fastest walk ever, and raced back . . . to find
the situation unchanged.

Darkness fell and the gas lamps were lit.

Some time later a footman arrived, summoned by a bell
in the bedroom. Emm's maid, Milly, opened the door and
asked him to bring up a can of hot water and some fresh
towels. They fell on her with questions and she did her best
to soothe them.

"It's going just fine. M'lady is doing well. Babies can
take a long time to come, especially first babies. My sister
was just the same with her first, and the midwife says
everything is going just as it should. She'd send for the doctor if she was worried. Truly, there's nothing to worry about,
sir." Milly had been with Emm since before her marriage
and was very protective, so her assurance was somewhat
comforting. Somewhat.

The footman returned with the hot water and a maid
carrying a stack of towels, and then, with an apologetic
look, Milly withdrew, shutting the door behind her.

An hour later Burton brought up a plate of sandwiches, but only Finn and Aunt Dottie ate any. Time crawled past.

Then a scream shattered the silence. Cal leapt to his feet, swearing, and pounded on the door. There was another scream, and he pounded harder.

Then there came a wavering, high-pitched wail that grew in strength.

Cal stilled, and turned a white face to George and Aunt Dottie. "Is that . . . ?"

"A baby, yes."

He turned back and pounded on the door again. Aunt Agatha yanked it open. "You have a son. The Ashendon Heir has been born."

"How is Emm?" He tried to push past her, but she stopped him.

"Your wife is tired, naturally, but perfectly well. We are just tidying things up. You may come in and see her when she is ready to be seen." She gave him a searching look. "Did you hear me, Ashendon, you have a son, a healthy baby boy. An heir."

Cal nodded distractedly. "How long before I can see her?"

"As long as it takes." And she shut the door in his face.

Cal turned away, staggered to a chair and collapsed into it. He pulled out a handkerchief and wiped his face. "Thank God, thank God." And then a few minutes later. "Never again."

Aunt Dottie laughed. "Men, always so dramatic. Now, since Emmaline is well and you have a healthy baby boy, I think we should celebrate, yes?" She rang for Burton and ordered champagne.

In a short while the door was opened and Cal was admitted. George and Aunt Dottie waited impatiently.

A short time later Aunt Agatha opened the door again. "You may both come in for a few minutes only. Emmaline is naturally very tired, but she has done very well, very well indeed. A healthy baby boy. The Ashendon Heir."

They entered, and found Cal sitting on the bed beside

Emm, his arm around her, her head resting on his chest and a white bundle in her arms. She looked exhausted but strangely serene.

"How are you?" George whispered. She didn't know why she was whispering, but it somehow seemed appropriate. She glanced at the white bundle. All she could see was a tuft of dark hair.

Emm smiled. "We're both well. Tired, but"—she glanced up at Cal—"very happy."

His arm tightened around her.

"Have you decided on his name?" Aunt Dottie asked.

Emm glanced at Call and nodded. She smoothed her hand gently over the tuft of hair. "Meet Bertrand Calbourne George Rutherford." The bundle stirred and made a little murmuring noise.

"George?" George repeated. "You mean—?"

"Yes, named after you. Well, you're going to be his god-mother, aren't you?" Emm said, smiling. Cal nodded.

George couldn't say a thing. There was a lump in her throat, and tears blurred her eyes. She nodded. A baby, named after her . . .

"Now that's enough," Aunt Agatha said crisply. "Emmaline and the baby need to sleep. Off you go." She started to shoo them all out like chickens, but Cal refused to budge.

"Thank you, Aunt Agatha," he said firmly. "I shall see to my family now."

"You surely aren't—"

"Yes, thank you for your help, Aunt Agatha," Emm said softly, "but I'd like to be alone now with my husband and our baby."

"Come along, Aggie," Aunt Dottie said to her sister. "There is champagne waiting downstairs. A new Ashendon heir has been born and we need to celebrate his safe arrival."

Aunt Agatha blinked, hesitated, then nodded, and they all filed out of the room.

Chapter Thirteen

❧

What one means one day, you know, one may not mean the
next. Circumstances change, opinions alter.
—JANE AUSTEN, *NORTHANGER ABBEY*

THE FOLLOWING MORNING, GEORGE AND CAL WENT RIDING
as usual. They didn't talk much. They rarely did, but this time
they were both lost in their own thoughts. Cal was probably
still thinking about the baby, George thought, but she didn't
ask. They were both still a bit stunned—particularly Cal.

They rode hard and fast and she felt the better for releas-
ing the tension and thought Cal probably did as well.

After breakfast, which Cal took upstairs with his wife
and baby, he headed out on some business. Aunt Dottie was
still asleep. George, feeling strangely restless, filled in
some time by writing letters to Rose and Lily telling them
only that Emm had safely been delivered of a healthy baby
boy. She wondered when they would come to London—
certainly for her wedding but perhaps sooner, to see the
baby.

She missed them. Strange how after years of living by
herself, with only Martha and Finn for company, she now
missed having a family around her. She left the letters on
the hall table for Cal to frank and a footman to post.

She hesitated, then went upstairs and knocked softly on Emm's door—not loud enough to wake her, but if she was awake . . .

Emm's maid, Milly, opened the door. "Hush, she's asleep," she whispered.

"I won't wake her. I just want to see the baby," George whispered back.

Milly nodded, and George tiptoed in. Emm was sleeping peacefully in the big bed she shared with Cal. Beside her stood a high cradle made of carved and turned rosewood. In it lay a small white bundle.

George peered in. She'd never had much to do with babies, never seen one so young as this close up.

Bertrand Calbourne George Rutherford, Lord Bertrand, heir to the Earl of Ashendon. Such a big name for a little creature. More of him was visible this time. He was as ugly as a new-hatched baby bird, bald, with a fluff of dark hair sticking up like a crest. His face was red, crumpled and squashed looking, his eyes a dark blue. They stared at her fuzzily, as if trying to focus, to make sense of the big, strange creature looking down at him.

"Hello, baby," she whispered. "Baby Bertie. I'm your cousin, George." A cousin. She'd never had a cousin before, and the idea caught at her throat. And he was named partly after her. This strange little baby bird was family.

A tiny pink fist emerged from the white wrappings and waved aimlessly around. George stared at it fascinated. Five miniature pink perfect fingernails. The baby opened his fist and waved a fat little starfish hand at her.

"You should stay tucked in," she whispered, and with some vague idea that babies needed to be warmly wrapped all the time, she tucked his waving hand back in. Her hand looked so big against the tiny perfect hand.

"Ohh." A soft little hand closed around a finger and held on tight.

She couldn't move. She stood staring down at him, this tiny bundle of humanity, so new and fragile, clinging to her finger with such determination and strength. A swell of emotion rose in her, and for a moment she thought she might cry.

A movement behind her caused her to look around. It was Emm, sleepily sitting up.

"I'm sorry, I didn't mean to wake—" George began.

"I was only dozing," Emm assured her. She looked into the cradle and her face softened.

"He's holding on to my finger," George said, which was a stupid thing to say because it was obvious. "I went to tuck his little hand back in."

Emm laughed softly. "I'll have to learn to swaddle him better, because every time I do it, he always manages to wriggle at least one hand out." The two of them gazed in silence at the little bundle of determination.

"Well, what do you think of my son?" Emm said at last.

George looked down at the ugly little baby bird so firmly attached to her finger and nodded. "He's beautiful," she said. And she meant it.

The little face screwed up and grew redder. A wail came from him, then another a little louder.

"What did I do?" George said anxiously. He was still gripping her finger.

Emm laughed softly. "Nothing. He's just hungry, that's all. Pass him over, will you, George." She sat up in bed, and Milly hastened to arrange pillows behind her.

George stared at the baby. "What, me? What if I . . ." What if she dropped him?

Emm, smiling, just held out her hands. George took a deep breath and lifted the angry little bundle from the cradle. He was so tiny and light, but the noise that he could produce—he was yelling by now. She passed him to Emm, who had opened the front of her nightdress.

George blinked, not quite sure where to look. "You're going to feed him?"

Emm smiled and held the baby to her breast. The sudden silence was shocking, broken only by the sound of vigorous sucking.

"I thought . . ."

"You thought I'd have a wet nurse?"

"Yes. Aunt Agatha said . . ." Aunt Agatha had been very firm about it.

"It's not at all fashionable, I know, but I asked the midwife and she said she thought it was better for both mother and baby if I feed him, at least for a while. She said if I don't want to continue, she'd find me a good and reliable wet nurse. But"—Emm gazed tenderly down at her infant son so energetically suckling—"for most of my adult life I never imagined I'd even have a baby, and now I do, I don't want to miss out on anything. I won't hand Bertie here over for some other woman to feed, not at the beginning, anyway."

George had fed orphaned baby lambs, and a litter of kits once, but had never given any thought to the feeding of babies. It seemed very . . . personal. "What does it feel like?"

"The sensation is . . . indescribable," Emm said after a while. "A little strange but very, very right." After a while she gently lifted the baby off her nipple, and just as he began to wail, she swapped him to the other breast and he was abruptly silent, except for contented little feeding noises.

Emm looked so serene, so happy, so . . . right.

As both Emm and the baby grew sleepier, George left them to it. Deep in thought she closed the door quietly behind her. Finn, who Milly had kept firmly excluded from the baby's room, padded up behind George and gave her a pointed nudge.

"All right, boy, we'll go for a walk." She grabbed a lead and headed for the front door.

The bell jangled as she was bounding down the last few steps. Burton opened the door, glanced back at George and said, "Yes, your grace, Lady Georgiana is at home."

George skidded to a halt. The duke. She'd forgotten all about him.

HART HAD PASSED A RESTLESS NIGHT. LADY GEORGIANA'S accusation, that he was as bad, as scheming and contriving as his mother, had cut deep. He'd been angry at first, and his initial reaction had been to reject it totally—she was talking nonsense; he was an honorable man.

All his adult life he'd prided himself on not being like his mother, on being so much better than she. He'd always seen himself as an honorable man, too honorable to stoop to her low stratagems.

But Georgiana Rutherford had seen right through him and put her finger squarely on the truth: he was not so different from his mother as he thought.

The realization flayed him. Shamed him.

A line from a speech he'd once been made to memorize kept echoing in his mind. *For Brutus is an honorable man.*

Now he stood on her doorstep, waiting to see whether she'd reject him or not. He deserved to be rejected, he knew, but . . .

All night he'd tossed and turned, self-disgust, shame and uncertainty warring within him—none of which he'd ever experienced in his life. It was deeply unsettling.

But through the confusion, through the turmoil of his thoughts, one thought grew stronger and clearer: he wanted Lady Georgiana.

Logic told him he could find women more beautiful than she, more assured, more sophisticated, more tractable, more suited to be a duchess—and a damned lot less trouble.

But he *wanted* her. More than that, he wanted *her*.

Not one woman in a million—no man either—would have had the courage to confront him about his scheming behavior. Especially since it would be so strongly to her disadvantage.

Though he wasn't sure she'd see it that way.

He cleared his throat. "Lady Georgiana."

"Your grace." She stared at Hart as if he'd dropped from the sky. Her dog pulled forward to sniff his boots, his tail wagging gently. Did she not expect to see him again?

"I said I would call this morning." Though it hadn't been a firm arrangement. What had she said before she marched away? *Call on me tomorrow or send a notice to the papers,*

I don't care! Had she expected him to simply cancel the betrothal and inform the papers? If she had, she surely couldn't
have thought of the consequences to herself.

She shrugged. "Sorry, I forgot."

"You *forgot*?" He couldn't believe it. How could she forget something as important as whether or not their very
public betrothal was to be canceled?

"Emm—my aunt—had the baby last night."

"Oh. I see. Er, congratulations. Is . . ." He groped to recall what people usually said in this situation. "Was it a boy
or a girl?" An heir was the thing.

She gave him a cool look. "My aunt is recovering nicely,
thank you, and the baby is a healthy boy." She glanced
down at her dog. "I was just going to take Finn for a short
walk. Can you wait?"

Hart glanced down at the dog. "I will accompany you.
We can talk on the way."

She nodded and they crossed the road and entered the
park. "It's just a short walk," she repeated. "We've already
ridden this morning and he had a good run then."

They strolled along, making desultory conversation—
the weather, the approach of summer, dogs—while the dog
followed up fascinating smells. Passers-by eyed them curiously. Hart could see the speculation in their eyes. Impertinence. He gave a cool nod to those he knew, sufficient to
be polite but with a clear intention not to engage in conversation.

Lady George didn't look at anyone; she kept her gaze on
her dog. Was she reluctant to be seen with him? Was that
what she was going to tell him? That she wanted to be released? Or was it a simple—and understandable—reluctance
to face any more gossips?

Hart was in a fever of impatience. He wanted to get to
the point of his visit, but it was impossible to have any kind
of significant conversation while they waited for a dog to
finish christening trees.

Lady Georgiana seemed in a world of her own, thinking
deeply about something—was she deciding whether or not

to marry him, or was it something else? Did he even figure in her thoughts? He couldn't tell.

He'd thought of nothing else but her all night. She'd forgotten he was coming.

It was a lowering reflection.

Finally they returned to Ashendon House. Lady Georgiana led him to the drawing room, ordering tea on the way in. The dog came too.

Hart tamped down on his impatience while the butler brought in tea and cakes and a dish of what looked like rusks. Lady Georgiana poured it out, handed him his cup and held out a plate of small iced cakes.

"No, thank you." He set his cup on a side table, untouched.

"Would you prefer biscuits? Cook baked some ginger nuts yesterd—"

"Nothing to eat, thank you. Lady Georgiana, have you given our situation any thought?"

She fed her dog a rusk. He waited, his temper rising.

"I have given it some thought, yes," she said eventually.

"Because you do realize that if we break off the betrothal, you will be the one to be blamed. You have already endured unpleasantness from some of the harpies in the ton, and this will likely be even worse. You will be called a jilt. Or worse."

She gave him a thoughtful look. "No, I didn't even consider it."

That surprised him. "Well, it's true, and before you make any hasty decision—"

"I will honor our betrothal."

"—you should at least talk to your—" His brows snapped together. "*What* did you say?"

"I said, I will honor our betrothal."

"You will?" The degree of relief he felt at her words shocked him. To cover his reaction he picked up his tea cup and took a gulp of tea. It was hot and scalded his mouth but he swallowed the pain. He stared at her for a long moment. "Why?"

He could have bitten back the word as soon as he'd uttered it. What did it matter why she'd agreed to continue the betrothal? What sort of a fool was he to stir up the argument again? All that mattered was that she was still going to marry him.

That she'd agreed—finally—to be his. Freely agreed. Of her own free will.

"Why?" she repeated. She seemed to ponder the question a while, then she shrugged. "I suppose I'm more used to the idea now. I always knew that you'd deliberately tried to entrap me, and even now that I know your mother obtained my promise on a false premise . . . I have said publicly that I will marry you, and I won't go back on that. Besides . . ."

He waited. "Besides?" he prompted after a minute.

She lifted her chin, looking a little self-conscious. "I've decided I want a baby."

LATER THAT DAY, GEORGE AND AUNT DOTTIE WENT BACK to the House of Chance to finalize the order for her wedding dress. They'd shown the designs to Emm, and because Aunt Agatha haunted Ashendon House these days—supervising the care and feeding of The Heir—rather, railing against Emm's feeding him—to no effect—Aunt Agatha also gave her very decided opinion.

George didn't really care which of the designs she chose, but in the end—surprisingly—they all liked the plainer one, to be made in cream silk with piping. George liked its simplicity, Emm said it was both elegant and charming, Aunt Dottie said she'd look like a queen in it, while Aunt Agatha gave it as her opinion that she supposed it would be dignified enough for the bride of a duke. So that was that.

The carriage pulled up outside the House of Chance, and, as George helped Aunt Dottie to alight, a couple of ladies strolled along, eyeing her as they passed. She could only hear snatches of their conversation, but she had no doubt of their subject.

". . . she's a bastard, I heard . . . I wonder he allowed himself to be caught . . ."

". . . outrageous . . . lewd behavior . . . entrapped . . ."

"Ignorant and ill-bred people," Aunt Agatha said loudly. "Ignorant and ill-bred."

George set her teeth and went into the shop.

Two more ladies were inside. As George entered, they exchanged glances and rose to their feet. One muttered, "This place will take anyone."

The other said loudly, "There's nothing here that any *lady* could possibly want." The two women left.

George looked at Miss Chance in dismay. Was she driving customers away? The House of Chance was a relatively new business, she knew.

Miss Chance caught her look and laughed. "Don't give 'em a thought, Lady George. The world is full of small-minded petty bitches—forgive the language, Lady Dorothea—and I learned young never to take notice of 'em."

"Quite right, my dear, quite right," Aunt Dottie said briskly. "I have observed an astonishing lack of conduct in ladies of the ton these days. No upbringing at all. Their nannies should have been dismissed without a character—their charges certainly exhibit none. Now, George, my dear, show Miss Chance the design we chose."

Miss Chance approved their choice, checked George's measurements—they never changed—and took them through to a back room where a new shipment from China had just come in. It was an Aladdin's cave of gorgeously colored silks and satins, embroidered fabrics and ready-made sequined and jeweled motifs of exquisite and intricate design. Miss Chance's husband ran a large international trading company, and she had first choice of their goods.

They oohed and aahed over the glorious fabrics, and Miss Chance showed them the silk she recommended for George's wedding dress. It was cream silk, fine and luxurious, but heavy enough to drape beautifully.

Aunt Dottie also took collection of a gorgeous new nightdress in delicate peach silk, all ruffles and lace, practically transparent, with a bed-jacket to match. She held the nightie up against her body and posed. "Not suitable for an old lady at all, is it, George, my love?"

George didn't know what to say. Aunt Agatha would have a fit.

Aunt Dottie giggled. "It's perfect, Miss Chance, just perfect. Wrap it up—I'll take it with me now."

The decisions all made, they left. The carriage was waiting and the footman hurried to let down the steps. A small group of ladies was walking toward them. They lowered their voices as they approached, but George could see from the malicious glances that they were talking about her. She clenched her jaw and waited while Aunt Dottie handed her precious parcel up to the footman.

". . . scandal that a catch like the duke should be caught by a strumpet of no background."

"Certainly one of no morals."

"Do strumpets have morals? I don't think so." Tittering, they flounced past George with smug looks and superior smiles.

She gritted her teeth. That. Was. It. She'd had enough.

"Now, George," Aunt Dottie said warningly.

She gave her aunt a brittle glittering smile. "It's all right, Aunt Dottie—just realized I forgot something. In Miss Chance's. Back in a minute."

She dived back into the House of Chance. Its proprietor looked up in surprise. "What is it, Lady George? Forgot something?"

"Changed my mind." She grabbed Miss Chance's hand and towed her into the back room. She glanced around and pointed. "I want my dress in that fabric."

Miss Chance frowned. "For your weddin' dress, you mean?"

"Yes. That."

Miss Chance gave her a searching look. "You sure now? Time is tight and if you change your mind . . ."

"I won't change my mind." She nodded at Miss Chance and hurried back to the carriage.

"What did you forget?" Aunt Dottie asked as the carriage moved off.

"Nothing much. A small detail I wanted included."

"What detail?"

George shook her head. "It's a surprise."

A FEW DAYS LATER, GEORGE CAME DOWNSTAIRS AFTER her regular morning visit to Emm and the baby. Mother and baby had both drifted off to sleep, and she was considering how to pass the rest of the morning. She was sick of shopping—she failed to see why she needed so many more things just because she was getting married. Besides, shopping wasn't as much fun without Lily and Rose to encourage and advise her. Aunt Dottie thought everything was lovely and Aunt Agatha thought nothing George liked would do for a duchess.

Lily and Rose would be coming to London soon, returning for her wedding—and, of course, to meet baby Bertie. George couldn't wait. Maybe she'd write to them. She was heading for the library, when the sound of voices coming from the front entry hall distracted her. It was too early for anyone to be paying morning calls—and in any case it was too soon after Emm's confinement for her to be receiving callers.

The voices increased in volume. One was male, the voice low and indistinguishable, the other sounded very much like Aunt Dottie—an increasingly agitated Aunt Dottie. George hurried to investigate.

"Give them to me. I must leave at once!" Aunt Dottie was protesting. "Every minute counts." She was dancing up and down with impatience.

The butler, Burton, was holding a small portmanteau and a bandbox back behind him, out of the old-lady's reach. What on earth was going on? Bits of garments poked messily out beneath the lids. No servant would have packed like that; Aunt Dottie must have done it herself, which was unheard of.

"Surely you should consult Lord Ashendon bef— Oh, there you are, Lady Georgiana," said Burton in relief. "I was just explaining to Lady Dorothea—"

"He won't give me my things, George," Aunt Dottie said distressfully. "And I must leave." She was almost in tears. George had never seen her so upset.

"Aunt Dottie, what's wrong?"

"I am needed at home. I need to leave right this minute." She turned back to the butler. "Did the boy at least order the yellow bounder as I told him to?"

"Yes, m'lady, but—" He gave George an agonized look, a clear plea for assistance.

"Aunt Dottie, what on earth is the matter?"

"I told you—I need to go home, right this minute. Or as soon as the wretched post chaise gets here."

"But why are you leaving, Aunt Dottie? Has someone upset you?"

"A letter came for her this morning, from Bath," Burton explained. "Whatever it said has upset her. She sent the new footman to order a post chaise, but he didn't clear it with me, and I didn't realize—"

"The silly man wants me to wait until Cal gets back. But I don't need Cal's permission to do anything, and I haven't got *time*," Aunt Dottie wailed. "I have to go to Bath *now*!"

Obviously George wasn't going to get any sense out of Aunt Dottie while she was in this state. "Let's have a cup of tea and some cake, and you can tell me all about it," George suggested in a soothing voice.

"*Tea?*" Aunt Dottie said in a voice of loathing. "*Cake?* I am talking life or death and you offer me tea and cake?"

Just then they heard the sound of a carriage pulling up outside. "Is that for me?" Aunt Dottie pushed past Burton and wrenched open the front door. "Yes, yes, it is. A lovely shiny yellow bounder. Now give me my baggage, Burton, or I'll go without it."

The butler said in a low voice to George, "You can't let the old lady travel all the way to Bath on her own, Lady George. Not in a hired carriage."

"Who are you calling an old lady?" Aunt Dottie demanded. She jumped and made a grab for the bandbox, pulled it from his despairing grasp and hurried down the steps, calling to the postboy to help her.

"Lady George, you have to stop her."

"How? I can't very well wrestle her to the ground or lock her up," George said. "She's determined to leave at once and—oh, lord! Wait, Aunt Dottie," she called out. "I'll come with you. Give me two minutes." To Burton she said, "Send a footman to hold that postilion. The state she's in, I don't trust her not to leave without me."

Burton made a strangled sound of protest, but he snapped his fingers and sent a footman running. "You can't mean it, Lady George. Go all the way to Bath without any preparation?"

She turned a hunted look on him. "There's no other choice. Cal isn't here, and I don't want to distress Emm—she's still recovering from the baby—so what else is there to do? As you said, Aunt Dottie can't go all that way on her own, and even if we sent a maid or footman with her, can you see her listening to a servant in this state? Now quickly, give me a pencil and paper—I'll leave a note for Cal and you can explain it in more detail."

Burton handed her some notepaper and a pencil. "But you don't have any luggage, m'lady."

George scrawled a hurried explanation. "I don't care about luggage. Send some after me if you want, or I'll buy or borrow something. I don't know what's got her so distressed, so I have no idea how long I'll be away." She thrust the note at him. "Give that to my uncle when he gets in and tell him what's happened."

Finn, with a dog's instinct for any change in routine, trotted up behind her, pressed against her legs and gave her a meaningful, where-are-we-going look. She glanced at the post chaise. It was too small to fit two people and a large, hairy dog.

She clipped his lead on, scratched him affectionately behind the ears. Murmuring apologies to Finn, she handed the lead to Burton. "Don't let him follow the coach—because he will if you give him the slightest opportunity."

Burton snapped his fingers to summon a footman and passed him the lead. "Give the animal a meaty bone and lock him in the garden. Don't let him out of your sight." Dragging against his lead, Finn was led reluctantly away as if to his execution.

George felt ridiculously sad to be leaving her dog behind. They'd never been separated before. "You will take good care of him while I'm away, won't you, Burton?"

"Of course, m'lady. Now, do you have any money? I doubt Lady Dorothea has even thought of it."

"No. Oh, curses! What will I do without—"

"Here." Burton unlocked a drawer and pulled out a small wad of banknotes. "That should cover you both until you get to Bath."

"Burton, you're a treasure. I could kiss you!" She grabbed the notes and, wishing she was still in her riding breeches which had sensible things like pockets, stuffed the notes into her bodice, grabbed Aunt Dottie's portmanteau, ran to the post chaise and climbed in.

"Now *move*, postboy," Aunt Dottie shouted. "*Spring 'em!*"

George sat back, waiting in silence while the postilion skillfully steered them through the ever-shifting tangle of London traffic. Aunt Dottie was clearly too anxious for conversation. She sat, leaning forward on the edge of her seat, her hands pressed against the glass window that stretched across the front of the carriage. "Faster, faster, faster!" she urged the postboy. Not that he could hear her from his position on the back of the left-side horse, thank goodness.

It might have been better to hire four horses, instead of two, but Aunt Dottie was in no state to think of that, and clearly the young footman didn't know to order four. Good. George had never had to hire a post chaise before—never even traveled in one—but she'd heard they were expensive, and four horses and two postilions would be even more expensive. She pulled out the money Burton had given her, and surreptitiously counted it before tucking it back inside her bodice. She'd come away without even a reticule.

Finally the city fell behind them. They'd passed through Kensington, the traffic had lessened, the road was smooth and well-made and the carriage bowled along at a smart clip. They couldn't keep that up for long, George knew, but it served to relax Aunt Dottie somewhat. She sat back against the leather squabs and heaved a sigh.

George took the old lady's hand. "Now, Aunt Dottie, tell me, what's all this about?"

Aunt Dottie gave her a puzzled look. "Didn't I tell you, dear? Logan is dreadfully ill."

"Logan? Your butler?" All this, because her butler was sick?

"My Logan, yes. Cook wrote to say he was ill, running a terrible fever. They'd had the doctor to him, but she thought it best if I come." Her mouth wobbled. Her eyes filled. "You know why people want you to come when someone is terribly ill, don't you? Because they think . . . because they expect . . ." She burst into tears.

George put her arms around the old lady and let her sob into her shoulder. Her mind was whirling. She knew Logan had worked for Aunt Dottie for years, but this was an over-reaction, surely.

And then she thought, what if it were Martha who was ill, possibly dying, maybe even already dead. Martha, who had been like a mother to her. Would not George race to be at her bedside?

She rubbed Aunt Dottie's back in a slow, soothing rhythm and, once the sobs had quietened, Aunt Dottie curled into the corner of the seat and closed her eyes. Poor thing, she must be exhausted by all the worry and the emotional storm. George pulled a rug out from a compartment and tucked it around the old lady, and soon she was asleep.

The journey stretched before her. Wishing she'd brought a book, George put her feet up against the front of the carriage and watched the countryside slip by. Aunt Dottie slept on. It was only when they stopped to change horses that she woke, and urged that they get moving again with all speed. Once they were back on the road, she dozed off again.

George wished she could do the same. Alas, she was not built to sleep in a rattling, bouncing carriage. At every posting station she got out and stretched her legs while the postilion changed horses. Sometimes she purchased food or drink, and at others she had to convince Aunt Dottie that making a call of nature would not hold them up. Not that there was a choice.

"WHERE ARE WE?" THE VOICE STARTLED HER. AUNT DOTtie was sitting up, yawning, but wide awake. She peered out of the window, rubbing the mist away with her glove.

"I'm not sure. I was miles away, not taking much notice of where we are, I'm afraid."

Aunt Dottie nodded. She seemed calmer now. Perhaps because of the weeping storm and the sleep, or perhaps it was simply that they were on their way and there was nothing else to be done except wait to arrive.

George opened her mouth, then closed it. Would it upset Aunt Dottie to talk about Logan or not? She didn't want to stir up her distress once more. Then again it might help pass the time if they talked.

Aunt Dottie took the decision from her. "I suppose you're wondering. All this fuss for a butler."

George nodded cautiously.

"You know, of course, that he's not just a butler, that he's much more to me than that, don't you?"

George didn't know what to say. She did think he was just a butler; he was clearly the kind of butler who was almost one of the family. "Like Martha was more to me than just a cook or housekeeper?"

Aunt Dottie gave a tremulous smile and shook her head. "Not quite the same." She snuggled back into her corner seat, pulled the rug around her and settled down to tell her story. "I've known Logan since I was a young girl. He was one of my father's grooms. I remember the day he first started work—I was almost fifteen. I'm talking about Ashendon Court—that was my home back then, of course."

She gave a fluttery, reminiscent sigh. "So young and tall and handsome he was—he's only three years older than I am, but three years seems an age when you're not quite fifteen and he's already turned eighteen."

She smiled mistily. "Of course I fell in love with him. What girl wouldn't? I wasn't mad about horses back then—I rode, of course, but it wasn't a passion with me, not like it is with you, dear. But once Logan started work, oh, my, yes, I positively haunted the stables. Papa was so pleased to think I was finally taking an interest in his horses. But of course my fascination was entirely with Logan."

Fifteen? George gave her a troubled look. At that age, girls could be very vulnerable to the attentions of handsome older men. Especially gently raised girls, who were kept so ignorant of their own bodies and how easy it was to get carried away. And girls who were due to inherit fortunes were a temptation for men who worked with their hands.

Emm, she knew, had been ruined in her youth by a handsome scoundrel of a groom. She'd lost everything—or thought she had, for years. Until Cal offered her a convenient marriage.

And as a girl, George herself had developed a very painful attachment for a young man only a few years older. He wasn't a groom; he was worse—a gentleman. So-called. He'd been neither gentle nor honorable . . .

"Fifteen is very young," she began.

Aunt Dottie laughed. "I know. But in that I think Rose and I are alike. She says she knew Thomas was the man for her, even though she was only sixteen, and I knew Logan was the man for me." She laughed again. "The problem was that Logan didn't agree. He's terribly straitlaced, you know. It was years before he would let me kiss him properly, and even then he refused to let it go any further. I had to have two whole seasons before we so much as kissed. Such a waste of time—though those London balls were lovely. I did have a lot of fun in my seasons, and several very flattering offers, but of course I wasn't interested. I'd already found my Logan."

"But you didn't marry him."

"Oh, heavens no, we couldn't let on that there was anything between us. Papa—your grandfather, dear—would have had poor Logan horsewhipped and thrown off the estate, or even bundled onto a ship and forced to emigrate. Or worse. And me married off by force to some horrid old duke—there were several who were interested." She pulled a face. "Old goats.

"You didn't know your grandfather, but he wasn't a nice man. Very proud and autocratic and horridly strict—you cannot imagine. No interest in his daughters or what they wanted. Our only duty was to marry well and produce heirs for their husbands. You can see how that attitude shaped poor Aggie—she married well, but heirs?" She shook her head. "Still, you can see a little of my father in her, can't you? The pride and arrogance and inflexibility, and she still thinks that's all girls are for."

George nodded. She wasn't sure she'd ever forgive Aunt Agatha for the part—the several parts she'd played in arranging George's own wedding. She might have accepted her betrothal now, but that didn't justify Aunt Agatha's deception.

Aunt Dottie continued, "My brother, Alfred, once he inherited the title, was even worse. He was such a high stickler that even your father—his heir—avoided him wherever possible. And by his standards, he *indulged* Henry. Mind you, Henry was always lazy and selfish and irresponsible, even as a boy."

George sat drinking this up. She knew so little about her family. She'd never met her father, Henry, who'd abandoned her and her mother shortly after their forced wedding. And she knew very little about her grandfather, Aunt Dottie and Aunt Agatha's brother, Alfred, who was Cal and Rose and Lily's father. And what she knew wasn't very nice.

"When Alfred remarried, he allowed his second wife to more or less edge poor Cal out of the family—he was still just a boy, sixteen or so—but was never really welcome at Ashendon after that. The army became Cal's home."

And when Alfred's second wife had died, George thought, he'd done much the same thing with Rose and Lily, taking his two recently bereaved daughters away from everything they knew and dumping them into an exclusive seminary for girls.

Aunt Dottie sighed. "Alfred was never a good father. He had the same attitude to girls as our father had. The way he treated poor Lily after he'd discovered her little problem." She shook her head. "My brother only ever did two good things in his life, and one of them was to let me buy a little house in Bath and live there with a companion—once he'd been convinced I had an aversion to marriage." She gave a mischievous half smile. "I did, but only to his kind of cold-blooded marriage. Not to men, and especially not to Logan."

She stared out of the window for a long moment and her mouth quivered. "Oh, Logan. What if . . . ? I couldn't bear . . ." She wiped a tear away. "No, I must be brave. He *will* be all right. He *will*."

George waited for her to add, *I have one of my feelings about it.* Aunt Dottie's *feelings* were famous. But she didn't say it, which was a worry.

"What was the other good thing your brother did?" George prompted gently. The reminiscences seemed to be doing her good. And, besides, they were fascinating.

"What? Oh, sending Rose and Lily to a seminary in Bath. His reasons were vile—he couldn't be bothered with girls, and he found poor little Lily an embarrassment—but it meant I could see a lot of the girls." Her face softened. "They've been like daughters to me." She glanced at George and patted her on the arm. "As are you, dear child, even though your very existence was unknown to us for so long."

She sighed. "The Rutherford men have a great deal to answer for—all so selfish and so arrogant. All except for dear Cal—I wonder how he turned out so different? Protective and responsible and loving. Did his mother play Alfred false, I wonder?"

George opened her mouth to object, but Aunt Dottie shook her head. "I suppose not. All you have to do is look at the family portraits, and you'll see his likeness looking back at you from a dozen frames. Yours too, my dear—anyone can see at a glance you're a true Rutherford. But Cal is kind—which is not a male Rutherford trait. Interesting, isn't it? I wonder who little Bertie will take after . . ."

Before George could suggest that with Emm and Cal as parents, young Bertie couldn't go wrong, the carriage pulled into an inn yard, the wheels rattling loudly over the cobbles. Darkness had fallen. Ostlers ran out. The postilion dismounted and walked a little stiffly toward them.

Aunt Dottie peered out into the lowering gloom. "What is it, postboy? Why are we stopping?"

He opened the carriage door. "We'll stop the night here, ladies."

"No, no!" Aunt Dottie's face crumpled worriedly. "We must go on."

He gestured at the sky. "No moon tonight, and even if there was, see that there fog gatherin' in the hollows? It's good and thick and it's only going to get worse. Can't drive on a moonless night in the fog, m'lady. Too dangerous."

"Light some lanterns then." Aunt Dottie's voice rose with incipient panic. "We *have to* go on."

The postboy—he was about forty and no boy—shook his head. "Sorry, m'lady, but I won't do it."

"I'll pay you extra to go on." She clutched her reticule, and George wondered if it was a bluff. Aunt Dottie never usually carried money.

He hesitated, and shifted uncomfortably, but shook his head. "Not worth me life, ma'am, nor yours." He glanced at George, a silent plea for her support. "Best stay the night, m'lady, safe and warm in the inn—it's a good place, clean and honest—and we'll go on first thing in the morning."

George slid an arm around her. "He's right, Aunt Dottie.

You wouldn't do Logan any good if you had an accident on the way. We'll leave first thing in the morning, at dawn."

"Dawn." Aunt Dottie's eyes filled with tears. "You know that's when people . . . you know. Just before the dawn . . ."

George squeezed her gently. There was nothing to say to that. "Come along, Aunt Dottie."

All the fight drained from the old lady. All the hope too, George could see. She seemed to have aged ten years in the last day. The last ten minutes.

Traveling and reminiscing had kept the demons of worry at bay for a time, but they were back now in full measure.

A good night's sleep—if such a thing could be had in this situation—would make the old lady feel better. Stronger, anyway. As long as . . . as long as Logan survived the night. He was no longer a young man . . .

"The sun will rise around five. We can be on the road by then, and be in Bath before noon." She glanced at the postboy, who nodded.

"And in the meantime we pray," Aunt Dottie whispered.

Chapter Fourteen

But there are some situations of the human mind in which
good sense has very little power...
—JANE AUSTEN, *NORTHANGER ABBEY*

HART GREETED HIS HOST AND HOSTESS, LORD AND LADY
Filmore, ignoring the hush that accompanied his arrival,
the low speculative murmur. He swept the room with an icy
glance. Beneath it, eyes dropped, gazes slid sideways. His
lip curled.

The previous week Lady Salter had sent him a list of all
of Georgiana's engagements in the lead up to the wedding.
The sooner he was married, the sooner this going-to-parties
nonsense would be over, and people would move on to
some other source of gossip.

He wouldn't even be in London. He and his bride would
be on their way to Venice.

He glanced around the room. Where was she? He could
see Lady Salter in an alcove talking to some of her cronies.
No sign of Georgiana or the plump little aunt. He strolled
into the next room. Not there, either.

He glanced into the card rooms. He didn't think she was
fond of cards, but he still didn't know her very well. She
wasn't there. He frowned.

The Filmore house had no garden, just a small terrace

and courtyard, but it was drizzling, and nobody would be outside. So where was she? The ladies' withdrawing room?

He accepted a glass of wine, sipped it—a very inferior vintage—and set it on a nearby table. He waited. Ladies came and went, but none of them was Georgiana. He sought her aunt.

"Lady Salter, did you not inform me that Lady Georgiana would attend this—"

"Oh, yes, duke," she said hastily. "I'm so sorry, I should have sent a note around. My niece is, ah, indisposed this evening. I do apologize."

"Nothing serious, I hope."

"No, no, just the—the headache." She seemed a little flustered. It was unlike her.

"I see." Hart made a few polite inquiries about Lady Ashendon and the baby, then took his leave. A wasted evening, he thought as he headed out into the night. But he was glad to escape the party. Inane conversation, inferior wine and nobody there he cared two pins about.

THE YELLOW BOUNDER RATTLED INTO BATH JUST BEFORE noon and pulled up outside Aunt Dottie's house. She almost fell from the carriage in her haste to get down, but George caught her in time. They were both exhausted. Aunt Dottie had been restless and anxious the entire time. She'd barely eaten a mouthful of the very good dinner the landlady had provided, and though they'd gone to bed straight after dinner, the old lady had barely slept a wink—she'd jumped out of bed a dozen times through the night, peering out of the window into the darkness and wondering aloud how much longer it would be until the dawn. And since George and she had shared a room, George hadn't slept much either.

Aunt Dottie hurried up the front steps and rang the doorbell.

The jangling of the bell echoed within. They waited.

Aunt Dottie choked off a sob. "Logan always opens the door for me. *Always*."

Not knowing what to say, George rubbed her arm in a comforting manner. Eventually light footsteps came running. The door opened and Betty, Aunt Dottie's maidservant, opened the door. Normally neat and trim, she looked bone weary. Her hair was a mess and her face was stained with drying tears. "Oh, m'lady, I'm—"

"Nooo!" Aunt Dottie wailed, clutching the doorjamb.

"No, no," Betty said hurriedly. "He's alive. The fever broke in the early hours of this morning. Mr. Logan is out of danger."

"He's alive?"

Betty nodded. "He's upstairs in his bed, m'lady, sleeping peaceful as a baby. He—"

But Aunt Dottie was gone, puffing up the stairs as fast as her short legs could carry her. George followed. To her surprise, instead of the servants' rooms, on the upper floor, Aunt Dottie went straight to her own bedchamber.

George knew Aunt Dottie's bedchamber. George, Rose and Lily had lived with Aunt Dottie in the weeks leading up to Cal's marriage to Emm. But the old lady went through her bedchamber, directly into her dressing room and opened a door George had never noticed.

It led to a small chamber containing a large bed, and in that bed lay Logan, sound asleep. Aunt Dottie gazed at him, tears rolling down her face, and smoothed his silvery hair back from his brow.

"You're sure the doctor said he'd be all right?" she whispered.

"Yes'm, he left not an hour ago," Betty whispered from the other doorway that led to the servants' stairs. "He says Mr. Logan is to sleep as much as possible and that when he wakes he's to be given soup and a little bread. Nothing heavy."

"Soup? He hates soup."

Betty smiled. "Cook is making chicken soup now. Smells lovely, it does."

Aunt Dottie glanced around. "Is there only you and Cook here?"

Betty wrinkled her nose. "The new girl didn't want to

stay, not with fever in the house. She would have it that Mr. Logan had scarlet fever, but the doctor said that was non-sense."

Aunt Dottie frowned. "So who has been looking after Logan?"

"Mostly me, ma'am. Me and Cook and my cousin Sue who came in some days to give us a hand, after that silly maidservant left." That explained Betty's frazzled appear-ance. The poor woman must be exhausted.

There was a short silence. "Thank you, my dear." Aunt Dottie took Betty's work-worn hands in hers and kissed her on the cheek. "I am . . . you have no idea how grateful—"

"Ah, 'tis nothing, ma'am," Betty said gruffly. "You and Mr. Logan been good to me and Cook. There ain't nothing we wouldn't do for either of you."

"It's not nothing and I shall think of some way to express my thanks to you all later." Aunt Dottie pushed her maid toward the door. "You can help me now, Betty, by putting yourself to bed and getting some much-needed sleep—no, don't argue. The rings under your eyes tell their own tale. I am here to care for Mr. Logan now."

Betty went reluctantly and the old lady gave a gusty sigh. "I am blessed in my servants. Now, unhook me, George, dear." She presented her back to George.

"Here?" She glanced at Logan, sleeping in the bed.

"Yes, of course here. Where else?" Slightly bemused, George helped the old lady remove first the dress, then her stays, petticoat, shoes and stockings until she was down to just her chemise which, to George's relief, stayed on. Aunt Dottie was the old-fashioned type who wore no drawers.

Then Aunt Dottie slipped into the bed beside Logan. He stirred. "That you, Dot?"

She kissed him. "Yes, love. I'm here now."

His arm wrapped around her. "Missed you."

"I missed you too, my darling. What a fright you gave me, but you're through the worst of it, thank God. Now, back to sleep, love. Sleep and get well again." She snuggled her head on the old man's chest, closed her eyes and, under

George's fascinated eye, the elderly couple drifted off to sleep.

George was ever so slightly shocked. It was one thing to know that Aunt Dottie and her groom had fallen in love all those years ago. That wasn't so surprising. And even after Aunt Dottie had told her how they'd even talked about marriage and babies, it still hadn't occurred to her that it was anything but a story of the long-distant past. She'd assumed that they'd stayed together out of friendship and loyalty. And habit.

But that they were lovers—still. She hadn't really taken it in.

They were old. Did they still . . . ?

She recalled the pretty—and revealing—nightdresses and bed-jackets Aunt Dottie had purchased from Miss Chance. George's face warmed just thinking about it. Obviously they still . . .

All the time George had lived in this house she'd never had any idea that there was any more to Aunt Dottie and Logan's friendship than, well, friendship. Of the mistress and servant kind. Though, come to think of it, Logan had made a point of calling Aunt Dottie "my mistress" and sometimes "my dear mistress." With an odd little smile.

She found herself grinning. The sneaky old thing.

She was certain Rose and Lily had no idea—if they'd known, they would surely have said something. Aunt Dottie had made no secret of the fact that she'd known Logan since she was fifteen. It was clear she was fond of him. And he was clearly devoted to her and took excellent care of her.

But the idea that there was anything more to it had never occurred to George. Or, apparently, to anyone else. All these years . . .

Who was it who said that Aunt Dottie could never keep a secret?

She turned and found Betty watching from the doorway. "Innit sweet?" Betty whispered. "Such a fond old couple they are. I hope I end up like that one day."

The thought had never occurred to George. What would

it be like to be loved like that? Together for fifty years or more, and still to be a loving couple. She swallowed. She was marrying the duke. She was never likely to find out.

She tiptoed from the room and closed the door quietly behind her.

AUNT DOTTIE SLEPT AWAY THE AFTERNOON AND ONLY appeared later in the evening, wanting soup for Logan who she reported as feeling not only better but hungry. After feeding him the soup she joined George for a quick supper.

"How is he, Aunt Dottie?"

Aunt Dottie beamed. "He's asleep now, but he was grumbling about needing proper food, not soup—isn't that wonderful?—so manlike, and it shows how much better he's feeling—but he drank the whole bowl right down—and it stayed down. Cook's chicken soup is as good as any doctor's potion."

They both went up to bed early, Aunt Dottie because she needed to keep checking on Logan, and George because she was tired and because there was nothing else to do. She'd read all the books in Aunt Dottie's small library last year, and had no patience with playing patience. She didn't embroider or knit or tat, and there was no dog to walk or play with.

She hoped they were remembering to feed Finn, and then decided that, given his thespian talents, he was probably more in danger of being overfed.

OVER THE NEXT FEW EVENINGS HART DILIGENTLY AT-tended the events on the list Lady Salter had sent him, but found no sign of Lady Georgiana at any of them. It was very annoying; Lady Salter had been most pointed about sending him the details of the social events his betrothed was scheduled to attend, yet she couldn't be bothered apprising him of any changes. Nor did Lady Salter turn up herself.

A bare minimum of politeness obliged Hart to stay at least half an hour at each event, making mindless chitchat until he could escape. They were the kind of insipid events he most loathed, and by the time he left the third one he was fuming.

Sinc thought it hilarious. "You're famous for failing to turn up to events to which you've been invited. Now the boot's on the other foot. Sauce for the goose, eh?"

"Must you witter on, spouting clichés," Hart told him.

"If the cliché fits . . ."

But beneath his bad temper, Hart was starting to get worried. Clearly whatever was keeping her away was more than a headache.

He called at Ashendon House the next morning and met the Earl of Ashendon himself coming down the front steps. Hart stopped him, saying bluntly, "I've come to inquire after Lady Georgiana."

"She's not here." Ashendon's curricle was waiting, his groom holding the horses.

"She's not ill, is she?"

"George?" Ashendon snorted. "Girl's never been ill a day in her life. No, she's gone haring off to Bath."

"To *Bath*?"

Ashendon nodded. "She and my aunt. No idea why. Got some maggot in their heads about something and just headed off without explaining a thing—you know how women get." He climbed into the curricle.

"When do you expect her back?"

"No idea. Girl's got a mind of her own. But don't worry, she usually comes home eventually. Good day, Everingham." He gave Hart a brisk nod and moved off at a smart trot.

Hart stared after him. What the devil did he mean "She usually comes home eventually"? Was he suggesting that Georgiana made a habit of running off without notice? It certainly sounded like it. But why had she "hared off" in the first place? And why Bath?

Dammit, Ashendon ought to exert better control of his

niece. He didn't even seem to know—or care—why she'd run off.

Hart cared, rather a lot. Was it something he'd said or done? Or hadn't said? Or failed to do? Had he not taken into sufficient account the way she felt about the sly and malicious comments that had come her way since the betrothal was announced?

Had she decided to flee? To abandon him?

The thought curdled in his stomach. Dammit, no. She would learn that Hart was not the careless protector her uncle was. Georgiana had given him her promise, and Hart would damned well make sure she kept it.

GEORGE SLEPT BADLY, HER DREAMS HAUNTED BY A DARK, saturnine face with chips of ice for eyes and a mouth that for most of the time seemed so severe and yet could cause such . . . turmoil in her. He was such a contradiction. Ice over fire.

She didn't understand him, she was sure—well, almost sure—that she didn't like him. Though that time he'd turned up at the Renwick party and walked her around the room, in a silent challenge to the malicious rumors about her . . .

She didn't need his protection; she could handle the toxic tarts of the ton—even hampered as she was by the promise Emm had drawn from her not to hit anyone.

But it was . . . nice that he'd troubled to turn up and stand by her. It was his fault she was in the situation in the first place, so it was fitting that he had, but he hadn't needed to. He'd been tactful about it too. For him. In his cold, autocratic duke-ish way.

How was it that a man that was so wrong for her on so many levels could nevertheless visit such wretchedly carnal dreams on her? Amorous dreams that left her hot and panting in the night. Even now, when he was far away in London, he still managed to affect her. She had no more self-control around him than a . . . a cat.

When would this period of unwanted arousal—of fervid, sensual, *mindless*, impossible heat—end? And why had nobody ever warned her about it?

She wanted her mind back. She wanted the dreams to end. She wanted the torture to stop.

She would have to ask Aunt Dottie.

She tackled her that afternoon. Logan was sleeping again and Aunt Dottie had come down for tea and cakes.

George took a deep breath. "Aunt Dottie."

"Yes, dear." She picked up a cream-laden cake and took a large bite.

"How long does a woman's season last?"

"The season?" Aunt Dottie responded when she'd swallowed. "There's no set dates, really. It's tied in part to when Parliament is sitting—"

"No, not *the* season, a *woman's* season."

Aunt Dottie tilted her head curiously. "A woman's season, dear? I'm not sure what you mean. Unless you're worried about being left on the shelf, which I've always thought a ridiculous analogy. And besides, you're going to wed that handsome duke, and I do think—"

"No, I mean a woman's own personal season. When she goes into . . . into *heat*." Her cheeks warmed.

Aunt Dottie choked on her cake. When she'd finished coughing and taken a good mouthful of tea, she said carefully, "In heat, dear? You mean like dogs and horses?"

"Yes, and cats—exactly. I suppose there's a different term for it with people, but I've never heard it used. People are so secretive about things to do with, with congress and procreation. It's ridiculous that girls are kept so ignorant."

"But why do you ask, my love?" Her expression was warm and sympathetic.

George's face burned. "Because, with the . . . with the duke, I can't seem to help myself. I don't want to, to *desire* him, but I can't seem to help myself. The moment he touches me . . . And I don't even think I *like* him, but . . ." She gave Aunt Dottie a tragic look. "I climb him like a tree."

Aunt Dottie laughed. "Darling girl, don't worry your head about it; feeling like that is perfectly normal."

"Is it?" She thought about it a moment. "But I don't want to feel that way. I need to know when my season will be over. When can I go back to being normal again?"

"I can't tell you that, my love."

"But—"

"Because there isn't any such thing as a woman's season. I can see why you might think so, of course, but we're not like dogs or horses."

"Or cats?"

"No. There is no 'in season' or 'out of season' for women, but . . ." She paused.

"But what?" George said hopefully.

"With the right man, my love, a woman is always in season."

George was horrified. "Always?"

"Always," Aunt Dottie said firmly. "That's how it is with Logan and me. And always has been."

"Since you were fifteen?"

Aunt Dottie chuckled. "Well *I* was ready at fifteen, but Logan insisted on keeping us pure—well, pure-ish—until I turned twenty-one."

"But you kissed him before that?"

"Oh, heavens, yes, once I'd had my two seasons—my London seasons, that is—we kissed and kissed and kissed. And how well I remember wanting to climb *him* like a tree—but he would allow nothing more than kisses. And a little cuddling. The dear boy wanted me to be sure. Noble, but so frustrating."

"And now you still . . . um?"

Aunt Dottie laughed. "Oh, yes, we still very much um. Not as often as when we were young, but it gets better with age. Like fine wine."

George couldn't imagine that terrible out-of-control desperation being anything like fine wine. Though she supposed it might be a bit like being drunk on brandy. Drunk on the duke. Yes, she could see how that could happen.

"You've never regretted not marrying?"

"Not for a minute."

"You didn't want children?"

"Oh, yes, I wanted them, and so did Logan. And we had an agreement; if ever I found myself with child, we'd get married and go and live in America. Sadly it never happened."

"Why America?"

"Darling girl, we could never live comfortably in England as a married couple. My people would never accept Logan—could you imagine your aunt Agatha sitting down to dinner with him?"

George tried to imagine it, and wrinkled her nose. "Not unless it was to eat him alive."

Aunt Dottie laughed. "I can't imagine who would be more uncomfortable—Aggie or Logan, or the others sharing the table. And his folk would never be comfortable with me. Logan couldn't bear the thought of my losing all my friends and the society I was used to, and he had no interest in mixing with them anyway. He knew that in America it would be difficult, but possible—things don't seem so rigid over there, and nobody would know who we were, anyway." She spread her hands. "But I never did conceive a child and so the question never arose. And we've lived a very happy life together without the outside world gossiping about us and judging us."

"Really, nobody knows?" George could hardly believe it.

Aunt Dottie gave a mischievous giggle. "A few people might suspect—your uncle Cal has given me a few dark looks when I forget myself and call Logan 'dear,' but I doubt he has any real notion of the true state of affairs. Our servants live out for the most part, and those few who don't—well, whatever they know or suspect, they've all been wonderfully loyal and discreet. So you see, my love, it's been a most delicious secret."

"And that's why it doesn't bother you when Aunt Agatha calls you a failed spinster?"

Aunt Dottie laughed. "Exactly. Every time she says it, I have a secret little chuckle to myself." Her soft face sobered. "Poor Aggie, she's been married three times but has never really been loved. It's natural that she gets a little bitter at times. But she means well, and will do anything to support the family."

"As long as it's what she wants," George said darkly.

"Yes, Aggie usually gets her way in the end." Aunt Dottie leaned forward and hugged George. "But not always, my love. Not always." She dusted crumbs off her fingers. "Now, I must go back upstairs. Are you clear about this 'season' business?"

"You're sure it won't go away?"

"Oh, it might, of course. With some people the heat of desire fades after a short time. The honeymoon period, they call it."

"Oh." George brightened.

"But for the lucky ones, like Logan and me, and your uncle and Emm, it only ripens. It's a blessing for a lifetime." She rose and smiled down at George. "I think Lily and Rose have it with their husbands, and I suspect you and your duke might be lucky that way too. I have one of my *feelings.*"

George mustered a weak smile. A lifetime of being in heat for the duke? Being like putty in his hands? She couldn't bear it.

LOGAN WAS MAKING A GOOD RECOVERY AND GEORGE DE-cided to return to London the following day. Aunt Dottie would stay in Bath until Logan was fully recovered, but she assured George that she'd be back in time for her wedding. "I wouldn't miss it for the world," she said.

George set out the next day, taking Betty's niece Sue with her. It had occurred to her that she'd need a maid of her own once she was married, and thought Sue might be a possibility—a nice, comfortable ordinary girl, rather than the kind of intimidating dresser that some people—for instance Aunt Agatha—had. She would see how well they traveled together.

Sue, when asked, jumped at the chance to visit London. It was, she confessed, her heart's desire; she'd never traveled more than ten miles past Bath.

They'd made good time and spent the first night in a comfortable inn. Sue's first time in an inn—she even found the truckle bed brought in for her in George's room exciting. They continued their journey after a good, early breakfast. The traffic was sparse, the weather was fine and they were making good time. George was gazing dreamily out of the window, thinking over what Aunt Dottie had told her, when a coach-and-four traveling in the opposite direction suddenly veered into the middle of the road.

The postilion's shouts alerted George to the problem. The coach-and-four bore down on them. The postilion yelled, the coachman bellowed at him to pull over, Sue screamed and George held her breath helplessly and braced herself for the inevitable crash.

It didn't come. At the last minute the coach-and-four pulled smoothly to one side and stopped. The postilion steered his horses onto the grass verge opposite, and dismounted. He stalked toward the coach, yelling furious abuse and waving his whip in a threatening manner.

George leapt down from the post chaise, determined to give the carriage driver a piece of her mind and to prevent a fight from breaking out. Though seeing that the carriage driver had not left his perch, there was not much danger of actual violence.

The carriage door swung open and a tall dark gentleman stepped down. "Lady Georgiana," he greeted her smoothly.

"You!" She confronted the duke furiously. "You almost crashed into us! Is your driver drunk?"

"Not in the least. He judged things to an inch." He strolled forward and murmured a mild apology to her fulminating postilion and slipped something into his palm. The postilion, much to George's fury, stopped fulminating, pocketed the bribe and with a "No 'arm done, gov'nor, pleasure doin' business with you," sauntered back to his horses.

The duke turned back to George and said, calm as you

please, "As soon as I realized it was you in that yellow bounder I told my driver to stop you. So he did."

George could hardly believe her ears. "You mean you deliberately forced us off the road? We might have been killed."

"I hardly think so. Jeffries knows his business. He's been with me for years. Besides, both vehicles were traveling at a trot. There was no question of a collision."

She glared at him. "What are you doing here, anyway?"

He raised a sardonic brow. "Looking for you, of course."

"Looking for me? Why?"

A few drops of rain spattered down. He glanced at the sky. "It's going to rain. Send your maid back to Bath. We'll continue this conversation in my carriage."

She bristled. "Send her back?"

"She's not needed now."

"You mean I should travel with you, alone?"

"We're betrothed, are we not? In ten days' time we'll be married." It started to spit. "Get into my carriage. I'll speak to the maid and pay off the postilion."

"No. My maid, my postilion—I'll do it." Furious with his high-handedness George stalked back to the post chaise, spoke to Sue and the postilion, then returned and climbed into the duke's carriage.

Chapter Fifteen

❦

Which of all my important nothings shall I tell you first?
—JANE AUSTEN, LETTER TO CASSANDRA, 1808

HART WAS PLEASED WITH HER OBEDIENCE. HE WOULDN'T have been too surprised if she'd climbed back into the post chaise and driven off. He gave his coachman a signal and the carriage moved off with a slight jerk, turning around to head back to London.

Georgiana sat opposite him, her arms folded and her chin raised. She was still angry, then. So be it. "Well then, duke? What's this all about?"

She never addressed him by name, he noticed. Perhaps that would change after the wedding. "You left London without notice, without informing me, for no reason I could fathom."

She gave a careless shrug. "There wasn't time. It was an emergency. I didn't even have time to explain to my aunt and uncle—I had to leave them a hasty note."

Her apparent indifference annoyed him. "You should have consulted me. Sought my permission. We are betrothed. At the very least you should have consulted me about your plans . . . And your reasons for leaving in such a hurry."

"Permission?" Her eyes kindled. "This! This is why I

never wanted to get married. This . . . this *right* that men seem to think they have to control every aspect of a woman's life! Or else leave them and their children to sink or swim as best they can. Never anything in between."

Hart hung on to his temper by a thread. What the devil did children have to do with it? Or swimming. "What is it precisely you object to, madam? Is it—"

"Don't 'madam' me!"

He ignored her. "Is it not my right to be kept informed of my affianced wife's whereabouts? Our wedding is in ten days' time and you—you disappear without explanation."

"So?" She flung her hands up in outrage.

"You belong to me, and don't you forget it."

She made a vehement gesture. "No! I don't belong to you or anyone else. I belong to myself. I am yours only as long as I choose! I am not your—your possession. Or your chattel. The only thing that holds me is my promise to you."

He clenched his jaw. She damn well did belong to him— or she would once they were married. But he knew better than to remind her of it.

She must have read something in his expression, because she stormed on. "I go away for a few days to accompany my elderly great-aunt because she had an urgent need to return home, and you come storming after me as if I'd run off with—with some rake!"

"I did nothing of the sort," he said stiffly. It was exactly what he'd done.

She stared at him a moment. Her eyes narrowed. "Good grief—that's it, isn't it? You thought I was planning to jilt you. Even though I had given you my word I would marry you—my word!—you didn't trust me to keep my promise."

"Nonsense." It was exactly what he'd thought.

"Then why did you come chasing after me, breathing fire and brimstone and sending my maid away?"

"What has the maid got to do with it?"

"She's not your maid."

"She's not yours, either."

"No, but my great-aunt sent her to accompany me. You had no right to order her around."

Hart didn't give a snap of his fingers for the maid. He glanced past Georgiana, out of the back window and saw the yellow post chaise following with the maid still in it. He swore under his breath. "And so she's coming anyway. Do you ever do as you're told?"

"Not if I don't agree with it. Sue was so excited to be coming to London—she's never been much past Bath—and I'm not going to disappoint her at this late stage."

"And what about disappointing me?" Not that he was disappointed—more like furious. And strangely relieved that she hadn't been planning to jilt him. And frustrated.

She snorted. "Is it possible to disappoint someone who is so cynical he thinks the worst of everyone? In any case, I'm not going to disappoint her just because you don't have the courtesy to ask me what *I* want."

He didn't think the worst of everyone. Just most people. "You, Lady Indignation, didn't even have the courtesy to inform *me* you were going out of town."

"I told you, there wasn't time. It was an emergency. Besides, what business is it of yours where I go and what I do? We're not married yet."

"I was worried, dammit!"

"Worried? I was with my great-aunt. Why on earth would you be worried?"

"Because that other great-aunt of yours was weaseling around my questions, that's why. It was obvious she was hiding something." Something shady.

"Weaseling? Aunt Agatha?"

"First, you weren't at the Filmore party because, according to her, you had the headache. Then you missed the Compton ball because you were indisposed. And then you weren't at Almack's on Wednesday because—"

"*Almack's?*" Her jaw dropped. "You went to Almack's? But you *never* go to Almack's."

"Don't change the subject," he said curtly. His appearance at Almack's, knee breeches and all, at the ludicrously early hour that was required, had caused an annoying ripple of reaction. Sinc had been beside himself with glee. *How the mighty have fallen.*

The memory fueled his irritation. "Your great-aunt claimed you had a megrim. Hah! I'll wager you've never had a megrim in your life! You forget, I know all about the shams and pretenses women assume to get their way."

Her breath hissed in. *"Pretenses?* I don't make pretenses! And don't you dare suggest I do. *I'm* not your mother."

He didn't even blink at the insult. "Then why would Lady Salter make all those excuses, if not to hide something untoward?"

"I don't know. I didn't ask her to. I never even spoke to her before Aunt Dottie and I left. There wasn't time."

"And when I called at Ashendon House to inquire about your welfare—because I was worried and thought you might be ill—Ashendon was just leaving, and all he said was that you'd run off to Bath without any explanation."

"He knew I was with Aunt Dottie."

"He also implied that you make a habit of disappearing without explanation, but that eventually you came back."

She made a dismissive gesture. "Pooh, that was years ago. Well, more than a year anyway."

"So what was I to think?"

Her eyes sparked chips of anger. "There could be any number of reasons, but you chose not to give me the benefit of the doubt. You chose to assume that I'd run off with another man, or to another man."

He couldn't deny it. Though he wasn't going to admit it and give her more ammunition.

Her eyes narrowed. "You did think it, didn't you? Even though I agreed to remain betrothed to you. Even though I gave you my word. Which you obviously don't believe in."

He couldn't deny that either, but he said in a conciliating tone, "But I must, must I not, because you claim you don't break your promises."

It apparently wasn't conciliating enough. She bared her teeth at him. "There is a first time for everything."

"What if you have a child?" And where had that question come from? He needed an heir, of course, but . . . It was her duty to him that was the issue. Surely.

"Then of course I will belong to them," she said as if he'd asked a particularly stupid question.

At that, the tension in him began to abate. Yes, he couldn't see her leaving a child to the uncertain care of servants. She'd probably be as fiercely protective as a mother bear . . .

They each looked out of their respective windows. Several miles passed in silence. She gave a cross snort and said as if to herself, "As if I would run off with a rake." A moment later she added in a low mutter that he was sure he wasn't meant to catch, "I wouldn't touch another man with a barge pole. It's bad enough with you."

A hollow opened up in his stomach. "What do you mean? What's 'bad enough'?"

There was a long silence. Color rose in her cheeks, and just when he was sure she wasn't going to answer, she said in a low voice, "This . . . these feelings."

"Feelings?" He held his breath, waiting for her response.

"Sensations, then," she muttered unwillingly. She'd turned a glorious wild rose color.

His breath came rushing back. His anger dissolved. He moved to sit beside her. "What sort of sensations?" he almost purred.

She glared at him and crossed her arms defensively. "You know perfectly well what I'm talking about."

"You mean this?" He stroked a finger along her arm, almost but not quite touching the soft swell of her breast. "Or this?" He trailed the back of his hand down her cheek.

"Stop it!" She moistened her lips, unaware of how seductive he found it.

"You like my attentions, don't you?"

She pressed her lips together and looked out the window. Refusing to answer him because then she would have to tell him the truth. Because she always did.

Because she always did . . . Something unraveled inside him.

A woman who refused to lie. A woman he could trust. Could he believe it? If it were true, what a gift she would be.

Time would tell whether she was making a fool of him or telling the unvarnished truth. In the meantime, there were these *sensations* to explore.

"Georgiana—"

She tossed her head. "I don't answer to that."

He was not going to call her George. It was an offense to her deep femininity. She didn't act particularly lady-like, and she might crop her hair and assume boyish mannerisms—that glorious walk of hers—and she might ride like a boy—better than most boys, in fact—but the way she kissed . . . He took a deep breath. The female in her called to the male in him with a power he'd never before experienced.

She could never be a George to him. George was a fat German king, not an elegant, leggy, entrancing firebrand.

Why did she affect boyish mannerisms? He was curious as to how that had happened.

"What if I called you Georgie?"

She wrinkled her nose. "No."

"Georgette? Georgia? Georgiarella?"

She snorted with reluctant humor. "I told you, it's George or nothing."

"George, then, since you insist." He supposed he could get used to it. Not that she gave him a choice.

"I do."

He lowered his voice. "Well then, George . . ." He slipped his arm along the back of the seat.

She eyed him suspiciously. "What?"

"We haven't finished discussing these sensations of yours."

"There's nothing to disc—" She broke off as he slid a finger beneath her collar and caressed the nape of her neck. She shivered and arched against his hand like a cat.

"Stop it," she muttered. Without very much conviction.

"Don't you like it?" He stroked her again.

Her response was silence. Glorious, golden silence. Because she refused to lie to him. He moved his fingers to the tender skin behind her ear, and caressed her lightly. "Such pretty ears."

She gave a kind of shrug, as if rejecting his compliment—she wasn't comfortable with compliments, he'd noticed that before—but she didn't move away. He bent and sucked on her earlobe.

She jumped. "What are you doing?"

"What do you think?" He ran his tongue around the delicate whorls of her ears. She shivered against him and hunched her shoulder up, pulling back a little.

"That's very . . ."

"Very what?" he purred. "Pleasant? Agreeable? Delightful? Tantalizing?"

She gave him a baleful look. "Strange."

He laughed softly and continued caressing her nape and the tender skin behind her ear. "But you like it, don't you, George?" There was, he decided, a delightful contrast between the very down-to-earth masculine name and the deeply feminine response he was getting.

She stared at him, her eyes wide, her pupils velvety dark. She opened her mouth, seemed about to say something, then closed it. Her gaze slid over his face like an invisible touch. She stared at his mouth, met his gaze, then returned to his mouth.

It was an invitation he could hardly resist. But he forced himself to. He wanted her to come to him.

She bit down on her plump lower lip and he almost moaned. A faint shudder rippled through her. She turned her head away and looked resolutely through the window.

"What's the matter? Changed your mind?"

"About what?" As an attempt to sound airily unconcerned, it fell sadly flat. She was aroused. Her nipples thrust hard against the smooth fabric of her bodice, making themselves known through who knew how many layers. He resisted the temptation to stroke the hard little nubbins.

"You know you want me," he said.

She continued staring out the window. "Do I indeed?" Trying to sound indifferent.

He ran his thumb across her lower lip and she jumped as if scalded. "Stop that."

"Why?"

George tried to think of some way to explain. She wanted and she didn't want. She was determined not to let him see the effect he had on her. "Because—*mmmff*," she ended as he planted his mouth on hers.

It had its usual effect; she lost all awareness, except the feel and the taste and the intoxication he created whenever he kissed her.

His hands moved to her breasts and she felt hot threads of sensation vibrating through her with each caress . . .

And then—deliverance! The carriage pulled over to change horses.

While the ostlers hastened to swap teams, George gathered her scrambled senses and pushed him away. "Stop it. This, this kissing and such is a problem for me."

Hart frowned. "What kind of problem? You can't tell me you dislike my attentions; it's very clear you do."

"I know. But I feel . . . I feel manipulated, somehow. You can turn me into a puddle, you know you can, and I'm helpless to resist. But I don't like it."

Hart stared at her. She likes it but she doesn't like it? What kind of twisted female logic was that? Or was it some kind of ploy to keep him dangling? Drive him mad with frustration and wanting? He said in a hard voice, "I don't understand."

She gave him a troubled look. "All this"—she made a vague, frustrated gesture—"is just bodily sensations."

"As is natural between a man and a woman. And your point would be?"

"You desire my body"—she blushed—"and I desire yours, but really, we know very little about each other."

"So? We're getting married. We have years in which to learn."

She nodded. "Yes, but . . ." She bit her lip.

Hart closed his eyes briefly and tried to conceal his impatience.

"The thing is, when you touch me, the sensations are"— her blush deepened—"they affect me strongly, but I also think that you would behave much the same with any suitable woman."

"I wouldn't." He'd chosen her out of all the women in London. Did she not understand that? Did she think that he'd compromised her by accident?

"But you know so little about me—it's really my body, not me you're making love to." She glanced at him and added, "That might sound a little foolish, but it's how I feel."

It sounded a lot foolish to Hart, but if that's what she felt, well, you couldn't argue with a woman's feelings, no matter how illogical they were.

"What do you expect me to do?" he asked in an expressionless voice.

"I want *us* to get to know each other better." She emphasized the *us*.

Hart stared unseeing out of the window. The carriage swayed and bounced along. The horses' hooves sounded briskly, rhythmically on the hard surface of the turnpike road. Getting to know each other. The whole thing was ridiculous. In a short few days they'd be married. Nobody knew their spouse before marriage. And some not even afterward . . .

He heaved a sigh and turned back to her. "Very well, let us start, then. Earlier you said you would belong to your children—you said 'them,' plural. You intend to have more than one child, then?"

She nodded. "God willing." She glanced out at the passing scenery for a moment, then added, "It is lonely being an only child. I would like my children to have brothers and sisters."

He watched her watching the scenery—or pretending to. The thought crossed his mind that her apparent indifference was often a disguise, masking some deeper sentiment. "You were an only child."

She nodded.

"Did you not have friends?"

She shook her head. "Mostly my friends were animals—my dog, my horse, wild creatures. We lived a good distance from the village, and the local children . . ." She sent him a straight glance. "It was believed by the villagers that I was some lord's by-blow, and children raised by ignorant parents are not kind to unwanted bastards."

He frowned. "But you weren't a bastard."

She hunched a shoulder, feigning indifference. "Truth or gossip—which do you think is tastier? People didn't exactly ask to see my mother's marriage lines. It's easier—and more interesting—to believe the worst."

Hart thought about the rumors about her that had circulated after their betrothal was announced. Was that why she'd handled the nastiness so well? She'd grown up with it.

"What about school? Surely you found some kindred spirits there."

"I never went to school."

"Never?" That was a surprise. He'd assumed she'd attended the same exclusive girls' seminary that her sist—no, her aunts—had. He never remembered that Lady Rose and Lady Lily were her aunts—they behaved more like sisters.

She shook her head. "There was a small village school, but you can imagine how welcome I would have been there—and in any case the teacher was a drunkard and a bully and hardly anyone attended. And there was no money to send me to a better school."

"So, a governess then?" He knew she was literate, and from various references and responses she'd made, she seemed quite well educated.

"A governess?" She gave an ironic huff. "Those creatures who have the strange desire to be paid for their efforts? No, there was no money for that either. Martha—my nursemaid, and later my cook and housekeeper—taught me my letters and to do basic sums. And I had the remnants of my grandfather's library—his books weren't entailed—as well as some poetry books and novels my grandmother left."

"Entailed?" He frowned. "I thought your mother's side of the family were yeomen farmers."

"They were. Doesn't mean my grandfather wanted anything left to a useless female."

"Useless female?"

She made another one of those shrugs. "The whole time he was alive, my grandfather never let an opportunity pass to remind me that if I'd had the good sense to be born a boy I would not only have inherited the family farm but that my father would have acknowledged me and that I would have had the upbringing and all the benefits of being his heir." She snorted. "But a girl? A girl was useless."

She gave a humorless chuckle. "If he'd ever learned my father was the son and heir of an earl—he knew he was the son of a rich man, but not which rich man—and that I would have been an earl now, had I had the good sense to be born a boy, my grandfather would probably have, I don't know, exploded."

"Believe me, as a boy you would have been nothing extraordinary. As a girl now—"

She grimaced. "I know, I'm a freak, an eccentric."

Did she have no idea how very appealing she was? "Not in the least. A little eccentric, possibly, but the aristocracy rather values its eccentrics. Say rather that you are a *personality.*"

She laughed then with genuine humor. "Trying to butter me up, duke?"

"No, I doubt it would work anyway. You're not very good at accepting compliments, are you?" And now he'd learned more of her story, he could see why. Brought up to think she was useless?

She looked uncomfortable.

"If I told you I find you refreshing, enticing and quite entrancingly beautiful, you wouldn't believe me, would you?"

"Of course not."

"Then I won't tell you. I'll just have to think it."

She gave him a doubtful look, unable to decide if he was serious or not. She probably thought he was mocking her. He'd never met anyone with more of a sense of herself, yet at the same time, so lacking in vanity. Though now he knew a little more about her upbringing, it was starting to make sense.

"Tell me about this Martha."

Her brows knotted in surprise. "Martha? You want to know about Martha?"

"You're giving her a farm, I'd like to know why."

"Not a farm, just a house and the small bit of land surrounding it. It's still called Willowbank Farm, but it's not a farm."

His arm lay across the back of the seat. Unthinkingly he began stroking her nape again.

She jumped. "Stop that. It's—it's distracting."

"Distracting? I'm not distracted," he lied. Having her so close, soft and relaxed, that velvety nape just inches from his fingertips—it was pure enticement. But she was all look but don't touch.

"You're distracting *me*."

"Oh, you. You dislike it when I do this, do you?" He stroked her nape again.

She shivered and hunched her shoulders as if to dislodge his hand. "I said, it's distracting." So, she didn't dislike it, she just found it distracting.

He hid a smile. "Good." Her transparent honesty, her unwillingness to lie, even on such a subject—especially on such a subject—delighted him. The number of women he'd known who'd claimed his every touch, his every move was ecstasy, even as they feigned pleasure . . . And here was his prickly little George, wishing to pretend otherwise but unable to lie.

She turned her head indignantly. "Good?"

"As long as you don't *dislike* it . . . Now, tell me about Martha."

"Not until you remove your hand."

He moved it down to her arm and started to stroke the silky skin in the inside of her elbow.

"Stop that. Put your hands in your lap," she ordered.

He placed his hands in his lap. "So, Martha?"

Her expression softened. "Martha is a dear. She was the closest thing I had to a mother, growing up. She began as my nursemaid, and later became my cook and housekeeper. But she was always more than that. She taught me my manners, taught me my letters, taught me everything—did her best to make me a lady, even though I resisted all the way. But unsatisfactory though I was, she never stopped loving me. Even when the money ran out and there was nothing for food, let alone wages, she stayed with me."

"No money for food?"

She shrugged. "I don't know why the allowance from my father stopped—it was long before he died—but it did. Perhaps he thought I was old enough to support myself—I was sixteen. We had no way of contacting him, but we managed. We grew vegetables and there were eggs, and of course I hunted."

"Hunted? But I thought you objected to—"

"I object to hunting foxes for sport. Hunting rabbits and hares for the pot is different. It was a necessity."

So this "useless girl" had staved off starvation by hunting to keep herself and her servant alive. Her father deserved a thrashing. Pity he was dead; Hart would have liked to deliver the thrashing himself.

A thought occurred to him. "If you were so short of money, how did you acquire that stallion of yours?"

She dimpled, and said in a suspiciously airy voice, "I had rich neighbors, and some of them were, let us say, careless with their horses."

"You *stole* that horse?"

"No!" Her expression was part guilt, part glee. "Not exactly. My grandfather left one good mare—a beautiful Arabian called Juno—originally bought for my mother, so the mare was mine. She was a lovely creature, getting on in years but still able to bear progeny. She came into season at the very same time the rich and careless guest of one of my neighbors left his stallion out in the paddock while he went off with friends . . ."

"You put your mare in with the stallion?"

She wrinkled her nose. "Not exactly. But I did put her in the next paddock and let nature take its course. The stallion jumped the fence, of course. I returned him to his paddock afterward, and nobody knew what had taken place. But as I'd hoped, he got a colt on Juno. Sultan was her last foal." She slid him a glance that was part guilt, part triumph. "I know it wasn't very ethical, but you should have seen how carelessly this fellow treated his horse. And he had the worst seat I've ever seen. He didn't deserve such a fine animal."

Hart shrugged. He had no issue with a stallion jumping a fence to reach a mare in season. He knew exactly how that stallion felt.

"So when you were so hard up, why didn't you sell Sultan? You could have sold the animal for a good sum." Her answer should have surprised him, but it didn't.

"Sell Sultan? I couldn't. When he was born, I helped deliver him—Juno had a difficult birth—and I raised him and trained him. He's family."

Of course he was. Dog, stallion, elderly servant—Lady Georgiana Rutherford's family. Until the last year, apparently, when she'd discovered her real family . . .

"Now it's my turn," she said.

Hart frowned. "Turn for what?" He knew perfectly well what.

"To ask you about your life."

"There's nothing to tell. Childhood spent at Everingham Abbey, my family seat; then school, Harrow, followed by Cambridge; and you know the rest."

She gave him a stern look. "I don't know the rest—and as a life story, that was pathetic. I gave you details, stories, people. Tell me what you did as a child, who you cared about, what you learned."

"There's nothing to tell. It was all very conventional, very dull. Oh, look. London. We're almost there."

She peered out the window. The carriage had just reached the top of a slight hill and the city of London was spread out in the distance. For a few moments she gazed at the view, picking out the features, no doubt. But then she turned back to him. "There's still plenty of time to tell me about your childhood. Or school—tell me about your schooling. Did you enjoy it or did you hate it?"

"Neither. I did what I had to."

She made a frustrated sound. "You are a terrible story-teller! And you're not playing fair."

He shrugged. "You're the one who wanted to play 'let's get to know each other.'" He loathed stirring up the past.

"Yes. Each other." She folded her arms, fixed him with a look that was heavy with expectation and waited.

"Very well, then, I met my best friend, Sinc—Johnny Sinclair—on the first day of school. We've been friends ever since."

She waited, and when it was clear he didn't intend to say any more, she made a huffing sound and turned back to the view out of the window.

They passed the last few miles in silence. She was annoyed with him, and he understood why, but it wasn't going to make him open his budget about things better left in the past. All this cozy exchange of stories, it wasn't for him.

And it wasn't necessary for marriage. A man and wife met in the bedroom and that was all that was required—at least in the kind of marriage he intended to have.

"HE WAS HOPELESS, EMM. AS TALKATIVE AS A . . . A POST. He dug so much out of me—and I tried to be honest with him and shared. And it wasn't easy. But when it was his turn, he told me nothing—nothing personal at any rate. He just pokered up and looked down his nose and shared precisely nothing. Except that he'd met his friend, Mr. Sinclair, at school. Which everyone knows anyway."

George squirmed now at the shameful things she'd revealed about herself; her loneliness growing up, the scorn of the villagers—he had experienced for himself the attitude of the local gentry toward her—the fact that she and Martha had been so poor they almost starved, the unethical acquisition of Sultan. She wished she could take it all back, but it was too late now.

They were in Emm's bedchamber. Emm had finished feeding baby Bertie, and now held him against her shoulder, rubbing his back. "Do I take it that you no longer detest the duke?"

"I want to strangle him."

Emm laughed. "That's not quite the same thing. I occasionally want to strangle Cal, but I love him dearly all the same."

George pondered the question. She'd definitely softened toward the duke. A bit. His kisses drove her wild, but that wasn't it. She mightn't be in season like a mare or a cat—though she was still sure that *something* was going on—but liking, respect or love had nothing to do with physical desire—she knew that much. Men were like stallions, only on two legs. They'd jump a fence for a filly they fancied.

She'd been angry that he'd come chasing down to Bath after her but . . . though jealousy was unattractive, it at least showed he cared, even if he didn't trust her. And with a mother like his . . .

Actually, that was when she'd started to soften toward him first, when he realized how his mother had deceived and manipulated her. He could have left it, not exposed the lie—it would have made it easier for him—but he hadn't. He realized she'd given her promise based on a false premise and he'd taken her to see for herself what his mother had done.

And then he'd offered to release her. Despite all his efforts to entrap her. He'd played fair, shown her a side of him she hadn't suspected—an honorable streak.

And then, when she'd told him he was just like his mother, just as ruthlessly manipulative—well, he had every right to be furious with her. She wouldn't have been surprised if he'd denied it, and refused to give her opinion any credence at all.

But he hadn't. He'd listened, he'd thought about it. And he'd taken it on the chin—and later he'd apologized.

That was probably the moment she'd looked at him, really looked at him, past the haughty manner and the cold arrogance, and glimpsed the possibility of another man.

The baby belched loudly, startling George. She didn't

think such a tiny thing could make such a sound. "What a clever boy you are," Emm murmured as she placed him on his back on the bed beside her. He lay quietly among the pillows, staring intently at the world around him with bright, dark blue eyes. He waved a little hand and George slipped a finger in it, smiling as he gripped her firmly.

"Just because a convenient marriage is arranged," Emm said, "it doesn't mean that's how it will continue."

George said nothing. She played with the baby's hand. She'd seen plenty of marriages where the husband and wife might as well be strangers, for all the concern they showed for each other.

Emm continued, "When I married your uncle, there was no talk of love—it was a purely practical arrangement. He wanted someone to take care of—and control—you three girls, and I, I wanted security, a home and the chance of having a child of my own."

George looked up. "But you're in love with Cal, aren't you? And he with you?"

Emm smiled. "Oh, yes, but that came afterward. And that's what I want you to think about. Try to keep your mind open about the duke. I know you think he's arrogant and cold and—"

"He is." But George knew now that wasn't all he was.

"Yes, but think back to how Cal was when you first met him. Was he not arrogant, bossy, infuriating?"

"He most certainly was."

"So what changed? Did Cal change? Or did you?"

George thought about it. Cal was still pretty arrogant, and very bossy at times—only not with Emm. He'd been downright hostile toward Rose's long-lost husband . . . until he decided that Thomas was all right. That Thomas could be trusted.

He was being protective of Rose, and she couldn't really fault him for that.

As for how he treated George, they'd started off badly when he more or less kidnapped her, but now she thought about it, he'd softened quite a bit toward her, and in fact had championed her on a number of occasions, particularly with Aunt Agatha.

"You've begun to let the duke get to know you—that's a good start. And if he's reluctant to open up himself, persist, but gently," Emm said. "Some men find it very difficult to reveal the softer side of themselves, to let themselves be vulnerable."

"Vulnerable?" George couldn't imagine the duke being the slightest bit vulnerable to anyone or anything. He only wanted her to feel vulnerable.

"Vulnerable to love. Cal was as tightly bound up against letting himself love as any man could be. He didn't have an easy time as a young boy, losing his mother and being rejected by his father's second wife. And then there were his years in the army, where a man has to arm himself against the softer emotions simply to survive. He was out of the habit of even thinking about love. It simply never occurred to him. And if you recall, it took the rather drastic action of someone shooting me to shock Cal into the realization that he loved me." She smiled. "I, of course, knew a long time before that that I loved him. But even so, it was a nerve-racking realization."

"Nerve-racking? For you?"

"Oh, yes. After years as a spinster, never expecting to love or be loved, to marry or to have a child, I had to open myself to the frightening possibility of love. And with that came the equally terrifying possibility of rejection. And of making a fool of myself, and earning my husband's scorn—he'd made an intensely practical marriage, recall, not a love match."

George was silent. She hadn't really thought of it like that. It had seemed inevitable to her that Emm and Cal should be in love; but now, looking back, and in the light of Emm's explanation, she could see that it wasn't so simple.

And that she had more in common with Emm than she realized.

Emm leaned forward and smoothed a stray curl back from George's face. "Men aren't the only people who find it hard to open up to someone else."

George grimaced. "You mean me, I suppose."

"I mean all of us. Love takes a leap of faith. It's an act of courage."

Her words hung in the air. Little Bertie gave a half-hearted wail, and his mother picked him up and began to wrap him in his soft baby blanket. "You have a lot of love to give, George, dear. You give it unstintingly to those closest to you—Rose, Lily, Cal and me, your Martha, Finn, and"—she kissed the baby—"to little Bertie here. You're a loving person, and loyal to the backbone."

George felt her cheeks heating. She never knew how to take compliments. And talking about emotions made her uncomfortable. "What's the 'but'?"

"No 'but,' I'm just reminding you that you are a prize to be won."

George didn't feel like much of a prize—nobody had ever thought of her as a prize—but Emm's words warmed her.

"And the duke has gone to a lot of trouble to win you."

"Win me? He *trapped* me."

"Perhaps, in his mind, it's the same thing."

George scowled. It wasn't the same thing at all. But he'd offered to release her and for some stupid reason she didn't fully understand yet—midsummer madness?—she'd agreed to honor the betrothal.

"And you have always had a particular soft spot for wounded creatures. Think about that when you look at your duke."

"The duke? A wounded creature? Don't make me laugh."

"You've met his mother, haven't you?"

George stilled.

Emm added, "We are all wounded creatures in one way or another—Cal, me, Rose, Thomas, Lily, Edward, the aunts and you—yes, you, dear George. The duke has his points of vulnerability, as we all do, and manlike, he'll do his best to conceal them from the world—and you. So think about it."

George tried to think of the duke as a wounded creature, but failed. He was a predator. One who took more than he gave. Wasn't he?

Chapter Sixteen

❧

There are very few of us who have heart enough to be really
in love without encouragement.
—JANE AUSTEN, *PRIDE AND PREJUDICE*

GEORGE WAS HAVING THE FINAL FITTING OF HER WEDDING
dress. It was spectacular, but she had to admit she had an
occasional qualm about wearing it, now that first angry im-
pulse had passed.

Miss Chance pinned the last tiny alteration in place,
stepped back and eyed her critically. "I must admit, Lady
George, I had me doubts when you first chose this fabric,
but you were right. It's stunnin'."

Stunning? In what sense? George wondered as she
gazed at her image in the looking glass. Shocking or beautiful? She'd chosen it to be shocking, but she had to admit
the color did suit her.

She'd chosen it to shock, to defy all those harridans
who'd twitted her about entrapment and implied she was a
money-grubbing, title-snatching, hypocritical strumpet.

And to remind the duke who'd entrapped whom.

"I'll finish off those last little bits and send it around this
afternoon," Miss Chance said. "Now, your maid knows
what to do with it?"

Sue nodded eagerly. Miss Chance's assistants had given her thorough instructions about how to care for a silk dress.

George was pleased she'd taken only Sue with her to the dressmaker. Lily and Rose and their husbands were on their way to London, and she didn't want them—didn't want anyone—to see the dress until her wedding day.

The day finished with a visit from Aunt Agatha. George almost refused to see her—she was still angry about the way Aunt Agatha had helped the duke's mother to deceive her. But she was about to get married; it was time to put past grudges behind her. Aunt Agatha, meddling old woman that she was, was still family. And according to Aunt Dottie, she meant well.

"I have some words of advice regarding your marriage," Aunt Agatha announced. George sighed, sat down and pretended to listen.

"Men are animals," Aunt Agatha declared. "They will lie down with females of all kinds—young, old, pretty, plain, aristocratic or plebeian—it makes little difference to them. But the act is not in any way important to them—and should not be to their wives. It's merely an itch they have to scratch."

George kept a polite expression on her face. An itch to scratch indeed.

The old lady continued, "Ladies, on the other hand, have a tendency to read more into the significance of the act, ascribing meaning and emotions to it that simply don't exist." She peered at George to make sure she understood. "So, protect your heart, Georgiana, protect your heart." She gave a brisk nod and departed, leaving George staring after her.

Was that what Aunt Agatha had learned from three marriages? All George's irritation with the imperious old lady drained away. It was rather sad when you thought about it. But it was clear she meant her advice kindly.

Protect your heart indeed. George sniffed. Her heart was in no danger from the duke.

* * *

"WHY DIDN'T YOU TELL US?" ROSE DEMANDED THE MIN-
ute she and Lily were alone with George. They'd arrived in
the early afternoon, spent an hour with Emm and the baby
and then had gone for a walk in Hyde Park at the fashionable hour and very cleverly returned shortly after Aunt Agatha left.

They had also, it seemed to George, caught up with all
the gossip they'd missed by being away in the country the
last few weeks. In one little walk in the park.

"Tell you what? You knew I was betrothed—I wrote to
you both."

"About the gossip," Rose said.

"Letter?" Lily rolled her eyes. "Edward read mine to
me—the whole half dozen lines:

> *"Dear Lily and Edward,*
>
> *"I hope you're both well. We are all well here. Emm has
> had the baby and he is very sweet. And they are both
> healthy and strong. Aunt Agatha is in alt. Aunt Dottie
> is in Bath. You probably saw the notice in the papers
> and were surprised, but it's true. I am betrothed to the
> Duke of Everingham. It wasn't what I wanted, but I'm
> committed to it now. But it's all right, he's giving me my
> own house.*
>
> *Love from George and Finn and Sultan."*

"Much the same as the one you sent me," Rose said.

George shrugged. "You know I'm not much of a letter
writer."

"Not much? It was appalling!"

"Why? The spelling was all right, wasn't it?"

"The spelling was fine, it was the, the infuriation of it!"
said Rose.

"The frustration," Lily added.

"The complete, utterly provoking lack of information!" Rose finished.

"But I told you about everything—the baby, the aunts, and my betrothal. What else is there?"

Rose rolled her eyes. "Detail, that's what's missing. You've always been hopeless at gossip."

"I hate gossip."

Rose smacked her lightly. "This is not gossip, silly. It's about you! Now, sit down and tell us all about it, from the beginning. I've ordered tea and cakes and a footman is taking care of Finn, so don't think you'll wriggle out of it. Now tell us, how, how, *how* did you become betrothed to the Duke of Everingham? I thought you despised him."

"I did." George settled down to tell the tale. Truth to tell, she had no desire to wriggle out of talking about it. Rose and Lily were a sympathetic and attentive audience and it was a relief to be able to talk to people her own age. Emm and Aunt Dottie were lovely, and had helped her sort through her confused thoughts and feelings, but Rose was refreshingly blunt and Lily was wonderfully sympathetic.

Burton brought in a tray with a large pot of tea and a plate of mouthwatering cakes and dainty biscuits. Lily poured, and, while they ate and drank, George told them how the duke had singled her out at Rose and Thomas's ball—Rose, of course, had had so much going on herself that she hadn't noticed.

Lily had. "So that's why you were asking about kissing," she said with a smirk. "I knew it."

George described how the duke had entrapped her, compromising her on the landing at old Mrs. Gastonbury's *soirée musicale*. She didn't exactly tell them she'd been caught with her dress hitched up and her legs wrapped around him—just that they'd been caught kissing. And that there and then, the duke had announced their betrothal to everyone at the Gastonbury party. And how the very next morning there was a notice of it in the papers—announcing it to the world!—and he hadn't even asked her!

"What a sneaky beast." Rose eyed George thoughtfully.

"He was never like that with me. He was always quite cool and formal. It's almost as if . . ." She pursed her lips, considering.

When George told them about how Aunt Agatha had conspired with the Duchess of Everingham to trick her into making what she thought was a deathbed promise, Rose hissed with outrage.

"I never did like that woman," she said. "All the time I was betrothed to her son she was—I don't know how to describe it—always very sweet to me but with a kind of poisonous undertone."

"I know exactly what you mean," George said. "Sounding as sweet as honey, but you know there's something rotten beneath. Took me a while to realize it."

Rose nodded. "She's going to make a frightful mother-in-law."

George wasn't so sure. If the duke adored his mother, it would be ghastly, but he didn't. He was very aware of her selfish, manipulative nature. And when it counted, he had stepped in, very much on George's side.

"And of course the duke must have known what she—" Lily began.

"No, he didn't," George said quickly. "In fact, as soon as he realized what had happened, how his mother had tricked me, he insisted on exposing the lie, and . . ." She bit her lip.

"And what?" Rose asked impatiently after a moment.

"He offered to release me from the betrothal."

There was a moment's shocked silence.

"He offered to release you?" Lily looked puzzled. "But you're still betrothed—aren't you?"

Rose exchanged a knowing glance with her sister. "Yes, George, why is that?"

"Ohhhh," Lily said on a long note of discovery. "You *like* the duke, George."

"I do not," George said emphatically. "He's arrogant, high-handed and bossy. He thinks he knows what's best for everyone, and he does what he wants and everyone else has to jump to his command."

Lily gave her a considering look. "That's quite a list. What do you think, Rose?"

Rose said archly, "Methinks the lady doth protest too much."

George continued, "He's selfish and closed-up"—she tried to think of more grievances she had against the duke—"and he's possessive. When he thought I'd run away to Bath—I'd gone with Aunt Dottie—he came chasing after me and ordered me into his own carriage—even though I was already on my way back to London."

"He thought you'd run away?" Rose echoed.

"Yes, with a rake."

"Which rake? Do you even know any rakes?" Rose asked. George ignored her.

Lily said thoughtfully, "Possessive? I rather like the thought of possessive."

"You can have it, then," George retorted. She was feeling oddly defensive. "I don't like it. It makes me feel . . . I don't know, trapped." Though that wasn't quite the word. "I need to be free."

"And yet when he offered you your freedom, you chose to remain betrothed," Lily pointed out. "Why was that?"

"Yes, George, dear," Rose cooed. "Why was that?"

George pondered the question. Truth to tell, she still wasn't quite sure why she'd allowed the betrothal to stand when she'd been offered a clear way out. She gave an awkward shrug and wished she'd never begun this conversation. It was taking her into uncomfortable depths.

"I suppose I was used to it by then. I didn't want to make a fuss."

Rose burst out laughing. "Not want to make a fuss? You? You'll have to do better than that, George, dearest. This is us, recall? We know you."

"All right, then," she said grumpily, "I decided I want a baby."

"Well, of course you do. We all do, especially after seeing Emm's darling little boy. Isn't little Bertie just adorable?" Lily gushed. "Those big bright eyes."

"No, it doesn't wash," Rose said. "If it was just the matter of a baby, George could have chosen any one of the perfectly nice—and easy to control—men who've been mooning after her all season. It doesn't explain why she stayed betrothed to the duke—seeing she 'dislikes' him so much. Or claims to."

"There's the kissing," Lily suggested. "Remember, when he kisses her, her knees turn to jelly."

"How do you—? They do not!" George protested.

"At your ball, remember?" Lily reminded Rose. "Afterward she asked us about kissing and knees dissolving." George felt her cheeks heating. Lily might have difficulty reading, but she had an excellent memory. Drat it.

"Oh, yes, that's right," Rose said. "And then he kissed her again at Mrs. Gastonbury's soirée and she completely lost track of where she was."

"I did not!"

Rose arched an eyebrow. "So you knew all those people were coming out onto the landing, heading for supper? And you kept kissing him anyway?"

"No. I didn't realize—"

"In other words, it was such a splendiferous kiss you lost all sense of where you were," Rose concluded triumphantly. "So, one, she wants a baby, and two, she likes his kisses." She numbered them off on her fingers. "What else?"

"Nothing else," George mumbled, her face hot.

"Oh, yes, three, you didn't like to make a fuss," Rose agreed ironically, marking off a third finger. "You, who's never worried about a fuss in your life. A most compelling case, m'lud. Now on the other hand, one, he's clearly gone out of his way to entrap you—"

"Against my will!"

Rose waved a dismissive hand. "Pooh! He gave you the option of leaving and you didn't take it. So one, he really wants you; two, he kisses like a dream—and you know, all the time he was betrothed to me he kissed like a . . . like a fish."

"A *fish*?" George sat up, outraged. "He does *not* kiss like a fish!"

"See?" Rose winked at Lily. "Number three, she defends the glory of his kisses." She laughed at George's expression and added, "Seriously, he kissed me a couple of times, George, and . . . nothing. And that seemed to please him. Pleased us both, actually, neither of us wanting any emotion in a marriage—or so I thought at the time. It seems he's changed his mind about that too."

"Another one on the duke's side," Lily said. "Since the betrothal, he's been attending parties with her—and you know he never used to. He never did with Rose, either. Penny Peplowe said he even went to Almack's looking for George, and when she wasn't there he stormed out."

"Almack's?" Rose said, impressed. "He hates Almack's."

"Possessive," George muttered. Though she'd been quite impressed herself when he'd told her.

Lily continued, "Penny said he only began going to parties after people started saying nasty things about you entrapping him."

George nodded. That was true. And she couldn't help but be touched by it.

"So, five, he's protective."

"Yes. But love isn't a nice neat set of numbers that add up." Rose flicked her fingers out as if getting rid of her lists. "Apart from her knees dissolving when the duke kisses her, the biggest clue is that when George was offered her freedom, she refused it. And she can't explain why. But whoever said that love had to make sense? So what I think is—"

George narrowed her eyes. She didn't want Rose to say another word.

"Our dear, loyal, prickly, independent, I-don't-need-anyone—I'm-perfectly-all-right-on-my-own—"

"As long as she has dogs and horses," Lily interjected.

"—yes, our darling I-don't-need-anyone—I'm-perfectly-all-right-on-my-own-with-my-animals George is finally, at long last, in love."

"I am not!" George mumbled. How could they possibly think that? She hadn't told them anything nice about the duke, and there were actually a few nice aspects.

"All the signs are there, George, dearest," Lily said warmly. "I'm so happy for you."

George squirmed.

"George is in love, George is in love," Rose crooned in a singsong voice.

"Oh, stop it." George rose to her feet. "You're both talking a lot of nonsense. I need to take Finn for a walk." She put two fingers in her mouth and let out a shrill whistle. Finn bounded up and slid to a halt on the polished floor. "Come on, boy."

A moment later she slammed the front door behind her.

She pounded along the footpath. Her head was in a whirl. Rose and Lily were wrong. She wasn't in love with the duke. She couldn't be.

They were certain she was in love only because they were in love with their husbands. It wasn't the same for her. The duke was no Edward or Thomas. They were warm, kind, loving men. The duke was . . . an icicle.

Except when he kissed her.

Blast and botheration! Why couldn't she just go back to the way it was before? Before he'd noticed her. Before she'd noticed him. Before he'd kissed her. Life had been so much simpler then, so much more enjoyable. She'd known what she wanted and exactly how to get it. Now . . .

Now she didn't know anything. Why hadn't she taken her freedom when the duke offered it? Rose was right. It wasn't just because baby Bertie had made her realize she wanted a baby of her own. She pulled her hat off and rubbed her head, as if somehow she could make sense of it all.

Whoever said that love had to make sense?

It wasn't love—was it? She knew who she loved—her dog, her horse, Martha, her family . . .

But it wasn't the same. She wasn't afire to kiss any of them. The duke was like a fever in her blood.

Aunt Dottie had said that for some people that fever faded after the honeymoon. George wasn't sure whether the thought of that was a comfort . . . or a worry.

A comfort, she told herself firmly, because if this was love, it was confusing and uncomfortable and she didn't want a bar of it. She picked up a stick for Finn and threw it as far as she could.

IT WAS THE NIGHT BEFORE THE WEDDING. HART, MUCH against his inclination, had allowed Sinc to drag him out for a few convivial drinks with some friends. "Not natural for a bridegroom to pass the night before sober and alone," Sinc insisted. "You need drinks and company to chase the nerves away."

"I'm not nervous in the least," Hart lied.

"Not worried about the wagers, then?" Percy, one of the friends said.

"*Wagers?*" Hart repeated in a steely voice.

"Nothing, no wagers," Sinc said hurriedly. "Old Percy's three sheets to the wind—silly fool doesn't know what he's saying."

"No, I'm not," Percy said indignantly. "There's a dozen different wagers on the wedding not going ahead."

"Shut up, Perce!" Sinc hissed.

But though Percy might not be three sheets to the wind, he was drunk enough not to take a hint. "You know yourself, Sinc, that the money's on a second Rutherford girl jilting the poor fellow. Lady George not the sort to make a duchess. No ambition in her. Swore she'd never marry, and I for one, believed her. Anyway, I saw you lay a bet myself, so what are you pokering up and pulling faces at me about?"

Sinc groaned.

"If that's what you think, you have wasted your money," Hart said coldly. He rose and opened the French doors to the balcony, hoping some cool night air might calm his temper. After a while Sinc followed him out.

"Did you bet on my wedding?" Hart asked him.

Sinc pulled a rueful face. "You know me, Hart, can't resist a good bet."

"And what did you bet on?"

"That she won't let you down, of course. A straight arrow if ever there was one, Lady George." He stared at Hart. "You didn't imagine I'd bet against you, did you?"

Hart relaxed a little. He hoped Sinc was right, but doubts continued to plague him. He still didn't understand why she'd decided to go ahead with the marriage. She'd fought so hard against it at first, but then, when he'd offered her her freedom, she didn't take it. Why?

Every other woman who'd ever shown interest in him hadn't been able to look past his title, his fortune and his estate. What was she getting out of this marriage? She wasn't ambitious, she didn't care about titles or his fortune—she'd made that abundantly clear in the settlement discussions.

And yet, despite her lack of interest in his position and assets, she truly did seem to see *him*—Hart, not the duke. She saw him, but she didn't seem to like him very much. They quarreled almost every time they met. So why would she marry him? For a baby? She could get that from any man.

He stared into the golden depths of his glass, then drained it. These were not thoughts to calm a nervous bridegroom. He could think of no good reason why she'd be at the church in the morning. All he had to cling to, like a man in danger of drowning, was that she'd given him her word. And she hadn't let him down yet.

He knew why he'd chosen her. He wanted her, wanted in a way that he didn't care to examine too closely. It was enough that he desired her and that she was independent enough not to be the sort of wife who would cling and want to live in his pocket.

He went inside. There was no point in going round and round and round with the same unanswerable questions. It was simple: either she'd turn up at the church tomorrow or she wouldn't.

He held out his glass for a refill.

Chapter Seventeen

She is loveliness itself.
—JANE AUSTEN, *EMMA*

GEORGE STOOD IN FRONT OF HER LOOKING GLASS, CON-
templating her reflection while her maid, Sue, fluttered
around her, making a few last-minute adjustments. "Lordy,
m'lady, I never seen a bride dressed so bright before. My
sister wore her best Sunday-go-to-church dress for her wedding, and it was a lovely bright blue, but this—"

"It's a new fashion," George said.

"You don't say. I was thinking maybe you'd wear silver
tissue like the poor late princess, but I suppose people think
it's a bit of a sad fashion now." Sue tweaked the skirt to
adjust the fall. "In the country if a girl wore red to her wedding, well, people would talk . . ."

People would talk in London too, George thought. That
was the point. They'd called her a hussy, a jezebel, a strumpet, and today she would flip it back in their smug, hypocritical faces. She'd show them she didn't give the snap of
her fingers for their stupid opinions.

Besides, white made her look sallow.

"Fetch me the black silk domino from the wardrobe,
would you?"

"Domino, miss?"

"A black silk cloak thing with a hood."

Sue looked horrified. "You're not going to wear black to your wedding, are you, m'lady?"

George laughed. "No, just to the church. It's a bit chilly outside—that breeze—but I'll take it off before I get out of the carriage." Really the domino was to stop any potential argument from her family. Who knew what aunts, especially skinny old busybodies, might still be lurking about.

A knock sounded on the door. "His lordship is waiting downstairs, Lady George," Burton called. "The carriage has arrived."

"Coming." Sue settled the domino around her and George pulled it close so that not an inch of dress was visible.

Right, this was it. She was off to marry the duke. An hour from now she'd be his duchess. Or not.

She hurried down the stairs. Cal was pacing back and forth in the hallway. "Cutting it fine, George. Emm and the ladies have gone ahead—" He broke off, staring at her. "Good God! What the devil are you up to? You're not wearing black to your wedding, George. Not even you—"

"Of course I'm not wearing black. It's chilly outside, that's all."

His frown didn't shift. "There are any number of cloaks in this house that are better suited to a wedding."

"I didn't have time to find one, and anyway I'll take it off before I get out of the carriage. Now, come on, I don't want to be late."

Cal glanced at the clock in the hallway. "Hell, no." He hurried her into the carriage, oblivious of the various servants who'd gathered in the hallway to wish her well.

George waved to them as the carriage set off. Cal sat opposite her, his arms folded and his face grim. "What kind of mischief are you up to, young George—and don't give me that innocent look. I know mischief when I see it."

"Mischief?" She grinned.

"You won't be able to play your tricks on the duke, you know. He's a very serious fellow."

She quirked her lips and gave a careless shrug.

"Every man is a bundle of nerves on his wedding day," Cal continued, "and Everingham will be more on edge than most, given what happened with Rose."

"He's the one who forced this wedding on me," she said lightly.

"He tried," Cal agreed. "But you weren't forced. You agreed of your own free will."

She had. And truth to tell she was ridiculously nervous. The closer to the church they got, the more her courage seemed likely to drain away. But she was determined to start as she meant to go on.

The carriage pulled up in Hanover Square at the foot of the steps leading up to St. George's church. George took a deep breath and shrugged the domino off. With a whisper of silk, it pooled softly around her.

Cal, who had exited first to help her down, turned to assist her and froze. "Good God, George, what the hell do you think you're wearing?"

She tossed her head. "It's a new fashion."

He snorted in patent disbelief and shook his head. "Everingham has no idea what he's taken on, does he?"

He assisted her from the carriage. A small hopeful crowd had gathered; a society wedding was always of interest to the *hoi polloi*, and grooms were known to share the largesse on happy occasions. People stared at George and made audible comments: "Red for a wedding?" "Never heard of such a thing." "Looks a right jezebel, she does."

Rose and Lily hurried forward, looking shocked and dismayed. "George, what on earth—"

Too late now. George hurried up the steps. "Now I know why you refused our help dressing," Rose muttered as she and Lily arranged the skirt into graceful folds. "You look gorgeous—but you have to know what a stir it's going to cause. What on earth were you thinking, George?" Rose was thinking about the duke's last wedding, which had ended in disaster. She probably still felt a bit guilty about that. Well, that wasn't George's problem.

Lily just looked at her and shook her head. "I hope the duke won't be too angry."

"I'm here, aren't I?" George said. "Come on, Cal, let's get this over with."

"Says the blushing bride," Cal said sardonically.

"Oh, she's not blushing," Rose pointed out dryly. "It's just the reflection of that dress."

THE CHURCH WAS COLD. HIGH SUMMER AND YET THE chill sank into Hart's bones. His cravat was too tight. He ran his finger around it, hoping to loosen it. It didn't help.

His stomach felt hollow. Had he eaten? He couldn't remember.

The bishop, in his magnificently embroidered crimson and gold robes, moved around the altar. It was the same fellow who'd presided over the debacle that had been Hart's last wedding. The man's frequent darting glances at Hart showed he remembered.

Hart was just as restless. He took a deep breath and eased a finger once more between his throat and his collar.

"For goodness' sake, if you fiddle with that one more time, you'll ruin the so beautiful arrangement of your cravat," Sinc said. "Stop worrying. She'll be here soon enough."

"I know that. I'm not the least bit worried," Hart said stiffly. He'd pushed her into this marriage. Would she panic at the last minute and bolt? "She'll be here," he said, as much to reassure himself as Sinc.

Sinc laughed softly. "Can't fool me. You're as nervous as a cat on a sinking ship. Understandable, given what happened last t—"

"I. Am. Not. Nervous," Hart said in a low, vehement voice.

"Of course you're not," his friend said in a tone that was intended to be soothing but instead made Hart want to throttle him. "If it helps, I made another bet on her."

Hart turned wrathfully toward him. "You *what*?"

Sinc held up his hands peaceably. "Don't look at me like

that—I only bet that she'd turn up on time. Just thought that you'd want to know how much faith I have in her."

It was not done to strangle your best man before the wedding, Hart reminded himself. He took a few deep breaths, forcing himself back to an appearance of calm before saying coldly, "If you ever—I mean *ever*!—make a public bet on my wife again, so help me, Sinc, friend or not, I won't be responsible for my actions."

"No, no, of course, not. Don't know what got into me. Sorry, Hart. Meant no disrespect, just can't seem to help m—"

The organ sounded an emphatic chord. The congregation hushed. Slowly Hart turned toward the entrance . . .

She stepped through the doorway and paused at the head of the aisle. There was an audible gasp, followed by a ripple of murmurs and whispers.

Hart's mother gave a loud moan and swooned dramatically over the nearest man. Only he and her companion reacted, the companion fluttering forward with smelling salts.

Hart ignored it. He only had eyes for his bride. She stood motionless, a pale, slender sprite wrapped in flaming scarlet. No demure pastel or ivory bride this. The dress screamed defiance, flamboyance and a warning. It was utterly outrageous.

It clung to her upper body like a second skin, every slight curve faithfully outlined until it flared out at her hips. Her small breasts were framed by the scooped neckline, like a delectable dish to be served.

He would taste that dish very soon.

She stood straight, her head flung back as if daring him—or anyone—to criticize.

The congregation stared and muttered and whispered and looked to him for a reaction. Hart didn't move. She would come to him.

Sinc leaned forward and murmured, "Told you she'd lead you a merry dance."

And what a dance it would be, Hart thought. She was glorious. Magnificent. Unique. And she was his.

The music swelled and, one hand on her uncle's arm, she strode down the aisle with that long leggy gait that purely drove him wild. Her eyes were locked on his. Here I am, she was saying. I belong to myself. Marry me if you dare.

Hart dared, all right. He couldn't wait.

She came to the end of the aisle. Ashendon removed her hand from his arm and offered it to Hart. Every eye was on them. Everyone was waiting to see what Hart would do.

Her skin, so pale and perfect in the dim light of the church, was like a pearl. Her lips were rich, dark and moist; her eyes met his with a mix of defiance and uncertainty.

Slowly Hart pulled off her scarlet satin glove and stuffed it in his pocket. Her hand was cold. Her fingers were trembling. So, she was not as certain as she appeared. His bold, contrary girl . . .

He raised her hand and kissed it formally, ostentatiously—there was a ripple of comment in the congregation. Then, his eyes locked with hers, he turned her hand over and placed a warm kiss in the center of her cold palm.

The whispers turned to a furious buzzing.

The bishop cleared his throat portentously. Hands clasped, they turned to face him. "Dearly beloved . . ." The bishop's rich, fruity tones washed over them.

Hart barely took in the words. He waited, her cold hand still trembling in his grasp. Her tension seemed to be rising. His, now she was here and things were underway, was dropping. He just had to get past the speak-now-or-forever-hold-your-peace part. Ah, here it came. He braced himself.

"Therefore if any man can show any just cause, why they may not lawfully be joined together, let him now speak, or else hereafter for ever hold his peace," the bishop intoned.

There was a long, endless pause. The bishop scanned the congregation. Hart was aware of people looking around the church, as if hoping for someone to leap out from the shadows and forbid the wedding. Again. He stood stiffly and waited.

But nobody spoke. The service continued. Hart felt his tension draining away. It was going to be all right.

His bride, however, seemed to be getting more tense by the minute. He slid a sideways glance at her. She was pale, rigid, staring straight ahead. Her fingers shook. He squeezed them gently in reassurance, but she didn't shift her gaze.

The bishop listed the promises they would make to each other. "I will," Hart said in a clear voice. His bride mumbled something unintelligible. The bishop frowned, and glanced at Hart. Hart nodded to him to continue.

Then came the vows.

In a clear, firm voice, Hart repeated, "I, Redmond Jasper Hartley, take thee Georgiana Mary Rutherford, to my wedded wife, to have and to hold from this day forward, for better for worse, for richer for poorer, in sickness and in health, to love and to cherish, till death us do part, according to God's holy ordinance; and thereto I plight thee my troth."

Then it was Georgiana's turn. She repeated her vows in a low, almost inaudible voice. "I, Georgiana Mary Rutherford, take thee Redmond Jasper Hartley to my wedded husband, to have and to hold from this day forward, for better for worse, for richer for poorer, in sickness and in health, to rub, cherish, and to *olé*, till death us do part, according to God's holy ordinance; and thereto I give thee my troth."

Hart frowned. Had he heard her aright? *To rub, cherish, and to* olé?

He looked at her. She stared straight ahead, unmoving, her gaze fixed on the stained glass window above the altar.

The bishop hesitated, frowned and gave Hart a hard questioning look. From his expression he wasn't sure he'd heard her correctly. He wasn't a young bishop; likely he was a bit deaf.

"Continue," Hart said.

And so the ceremony rolled on until "Those whom God hath joined together let no man put asunder." They signed the registry and Hart quietly released a long sigh of relief. The bishop had a lot more to say, and there were more prayers, but Hart took very little notice. It was done. She was his.

As they came out of the church, the duke dug in his pockets and produced several handfuls of coins, which he flung over the heads of the crowd of onlookers. While they scrambled for the money, he helped George into the waiting carriage and they drove away.

He leaned back against the leather seat and eyed her quizzically. "So, rub, cherish, and *olé*, eh?"

George braced herself for the argument. At least he hadn't reacted in the church, though she had half expected it. "I only said that because—"

"I know. Because you weren't prepared to make a promise you weren't sure you could honor."

She blinked. "Yes. That's right." He'd understood. Without any need for explanation or justification on her part. She could happily promise to cherish him, but love? When she wasn't sure whether she loved him or not? You couldn't order love.

As for promising to obey him, that was never in question.

He nodded. "Thought so. Just one question. What does *olé* mean?"

"*Olé?* I believe Spanish bullfighters say it to bulls."

"So . . I'm a bull, am I?" There was a glint in his eyes that she didn't trust.

"No, it's just a word expressing excitement." It was the only word she could think of that rhymed with *obey*. And *rub* rhymed with *love*. Sort of.

"You're excited?"

She said in a dampening tone, "Not particularly."

"Then I'll have to work a little harder, won't I?" He glanced at her and added, "Not here, of course. Later."

"*Olé* is more of a celebratory thing," she said firmly. She wasn't going to think about later. That would come soon enough. She didn't know whether she was looking forward to discovering what it was all about—or dreading it.

"I see. So you've promised to rub, cherish and celebrate me. Sounds delightful."

She eyed him cautiously. He couldn't possibly be accepting her alteration of the sacred wedding vows so calmly, could he?

She'd braced herself for a quarrel. But if he wasn't going

to argue, she had no complaint. Quite the contrary. But she did feel a little deflated.

His gaze ran over her slowly, like a warm caress. "And that dress . . ." Her mouth dried. Her skin felt suddenly hot and tight.

"Y-yes?" Her voice cracked. She swallowed. How could a look affect her as potently as a touch?

"It's stunning. You look glorious."

Glorious? "You don't mind the color?"

"I gather it was in the nature of a statement." For whom, he didn't specify.

Dumbfounded by his calm acceptance—and his understanding of her reasons—and distracted by the confusion of her feelings—she just nodded.

"The color suits you wonderfully. Much better than those whites and pastels you usually wear."

"I hate wearing white, but Aunt Agatha insisted." She mimicked the old lady's dry pedantic tone. "Do not argue with me, Georgiana. All young unmarried gels—decent, highborn gels, I mean—wear white."

He laughed. "I can imagine it." He actually laughed. She'd never heard him laugh before. Who was this man?

She'd almost bolted at the church door, not because she had second thoughts about marrying him but because she didn't want him to think the dress was aimed at him.

Her anger with him had drained away long ago. The duke wasn't responsible for all the nasty gossip. He might have caused it—some of it; she was also responsible. But though the spite and vitriol had been directed solely at her, he had stepped up to support her.

But she'd ordered the dress in a fury, and even afterward, she'd wanted to make a stand. And so she had. And had been prepared for the backlash.

His face as she'd walked down the aisle—she'd never forget the expression. That light in his eyes. And that moment when he'd kissed her hand—in front of the entire disapproving congregation. And then placed that kiss in the center of her palm.

Her heart had given a great big thump then and cracked wide open. It had taken all her self-control not to cry.

He'd understood, he'd actually understood what she'd been trying to say. And he'd given society the clear message that he would support her, even honor her.

She'd given him every chance to reject her and he hadn't. Instead, he'd made a push to understand her. How rare was that? It was as if the duke saw who she really was—not simply Aunt Agatha's conveniently unmarried great-niece, an earl's daughter, but George, plain and simple, with all her many faults. And accepted her.

Married her.

The carriage turned a corner and for the first time George noticed where they were. "Where are we going?"

"To my house."

"But what about the wedding breakfast?" It was to be held at Ashendon House. The servants and Emm had been working for days to arrange it all.

"We have time," he said tranquilly.

Time for what? she wondered. Was this what he meant by "later"? But she wasn't game to ask; it seemed she'd used up all her boldness for the moment. And the duke had—apparently—taken it all in stride.

Butterflies danced in her stomach. Was he taking her inside to consummate the marriage? To make sure of her? Now? In the daylight? Before the wedding breakfast?

Her palms were damp.

The carriage pulled up outside Everingham House and the front door opened. The duke ushered her inside. The hallway was filled with people: his servants, she realized, waiting to congratulate the happy couple. George's next few minutes were filled with a confusing series of introductions and congratulations. She would never remember all of them, but their warmth and welcome were unmistakable.

She felt a sudden prickling of tears. She hadn't expected this at all.

The duke held up his hand and there was instant silence. "My duchess and I thank you for your warm wishes," he said. "Will you join us in a toast? Champagne for everyone, Fleming." And with no delay at all, champagne corks popped and fizzing glasses were passed around—even to the young girl who George thought was the scullery maid. The butler, Fleming, made a short speech and then proposed a toast to the happy couple. Everyone drank, then, as if at a pre-arranged signal, the entire staff melted away, and George and the duke were left alone.

"I hope you don't mind," he said. "I've given the servants the night off. More private that way."

The butterflies returned to her stomach. "Not at all," she managed.

He held out his hand. "Shall we go upstairs?"

George swallowed. He really was going to do it, consummate the marriage—now. They'd be late to the wedding breakfast and everyone would know what they'd been doing. But they were married; she had no option but to go with him.

He led her upstairs, to a room that was obviously his bedchamber. The faint scent of his cologne hung in the air. The furniture was heavy and dark. In the center of the room sat a huge carved wooden bed, hung with rich dark red fabric. It would take place there, then.

"Take a seat and wait here," he said. "Don't look so worried, I won't be long." He went through into a small room off his bedchamber.

Take a seat? There was no seat, only the enormous bed. She waited. What was he doing? Getting undressed? Should she get undressed too?

After a while—it felt like an age to George but the clock on the mantel said only five minutes had passed—the duke returned—fully dressed—with a flat box in his hand. He handed it to her. It was covered with faded velvet.

Cautiously she opened it. And stared.

"My grandmother's rubies. A little old-fashioned, perhaps—"

"No, they're beautiful."

"I thought they might suit you. She too was noted for her restrained elegance."

Restrained elegance? Was that how he saw her? The compliment warmed her. George didn't feel either restrained or elegant, but perhaps she could aspire to that—in her dress, at least.

The jewels glowed even in the dim light of the bedchamber. The rubies were large, and the setting was finely wrought gold, but the necklace itself gave the impression of delicacy. It really was lovely. And very expensive.

"I had them cleaned last week. There's a ring, a bracelet, a brooch, earrings and a tiara, but you won't need the tiara yet." The necklace glittered in his long strong fingers as he lifted it out of the box and held it up against the light, and then next to her dress. "Yes, the exact right shade. I thought it might be. Turn around."

He turned her away from him. She could see their reflection in the long cheval mirror. She looked pale and nervous; he looked dark and severely handsome as he bent his head, frowning over the catch of the necklace. Her husband . . .

She took several deep breaths and tried to will some color into her cheeks.

The necklace felt heavy and cold around her neck, but his fingers were warm as they brushed across her skin. With his hands resting on her shoulders, he met her gaze in the looking glass. "Perfect," he breathed, then bent and pressed a warm kiss on the sensitive skin of her nape.

A shiver of heat rippled through her and without conscious volition her eyelids fluttered closed and she leaned back into his body.

After a moment he moved back and, feeling a little embarrassed, she remembered to open her eyes and look at the necklace in the mirror. It was a perfect match for the dress.

"Earrings?" He handed her a dainty pair of ruby earrings and she put them in, then turned her head back and forth, examining them in the looking glass. "They're lovely." She didn't often wear earrings—she'd only had her ears pierced when she came to London—but these were pretty.

"Now these." He clasped the bracelet around her wrist, then slid the ring onto her finger, next to her bright gold wedding ring. The ring was unusual, a square-cut ruby, the setting the same intricate gold design. He stood back to examine the overall effect. "What do you think? Not too old-fashioned?"

The earrings danced as she shook her head. "No, they're beautiful. Antique, rather than old-fashioned. Thank you, d—" She broke off. She couldn't keep calling him duke. "What should I call you? Redmond, as your mother does, or would you prefer me to call you Everingham? Or Hart, like your friend Mr. Sinclair does?"

He considered it. "My mother calls me Redmond, but I've never liked the name. But I don't mind what you call me."

She grinned. "Ooh, dangerous suggestion. That leaves the choice wide open." She thought about the rubies that were his grandmother's. "What did your grandmother call you?"

"Redmond." He wrinkled his nose.

"Then I think I'll call you Hart, as your friends do. Thank you, Hart. And I am honored and delighted to be wearing your grandmother's beautiful jewels." She stepped forward, raised herself on her toes and kissed him lightly on the cheek.

He looked down at her, an odd, intense look in his eyes. "No, it's I who should thank you." His voice was husky. Then seeing the question in her eyes, he added, "For marrying me." He drew her slowly toward him.

Cupping her cheek in one hand he kissed her mouth, a mere brush of skin against skin, the barest whisper of a kiss, but sensation shivered through her, a delicate spiral of pure heat. She leaned in closer, wanting more, and slipped her hands around his waist.

He pulled her hard against him, wrapping his arms around her and tightening his hold so they stood chest to chest, stomach to stomach, thigh to thigh. And mouth to mouth.

His mouth was warm, demanding and she opened to him. The taste of him flooded her senses, potent as brandy.

Moving as one, they moved back toward the bed, kissing. His kisses robbed her of all thought. The backs of her knees hit the edge of the bed and she sank onto the mattress.

He released her and stepped back. Confused, still dazed, she blinked up at him.

His smile was rueful. "I know, but we have a wedding breakfast to attend." His chest was heaving as though he'd run a mile.

"Oh." She couldn't keep the disappointment from her voice. "I thought . . ."

"We have all night for that." His voice was deep, rich as thick dark chocolate with the promise of the night to come.

Gathering her shredded composure, she managed to stand. With shaking hands she tidied her hair in the looking glass, straightened her dress, then turned to go. And met his intense, heated, approving gaze. There was a world of dark promise in that look.

She blushed as red as her dress and the rubies around her neck.

Chapter Eighteen

❦

Her heart did whisper that he had done it for her.
—JANE AUSTEN, *PRIDE AND PREJUDICE*

THEY WERE THE LAST TO ARRIVE AT THE WEDDING BREAK-fast, and George was surprised to see that the guests' reactions were less about the bride and groom's lateness, or even the color of her dress, and all about the ruby set she was now wearing.

Aunt Agatha marched up to her saying, "I cannot believe the spectacle you made of yourself—of us all—" She broke off, her eyes bulging, then produced her lorgnette and took a closer look.

"The famous Hartley parure! How did *you* get that?"

"How do you think?" George retorted, insulted by her great-aunt's tone. "The duke gave it to me."

Aunt Agatha glanced at the duke, who was talking to some other guests. "It's a disgrace! To give it to you, after your outrageous appearance at the church."

"Why shouldn't he give his bride jewels?" Emm asked. "I think it's a lovely gesture and the rubies go perfectly with George's dress."

Aunt Agatha eyed the dress and winced. "The less said

about that wretched dress the better—you know, of course, what everyone has been saying."

"The duke didn't seem to mind it, Aunt Agatha, and really, isn't that all that matters?" Emm said mildly. "It's unconventional, certainly, but the color suits her."

"I don't give tuppence for what everyone is saying, Aunt Agatha," George told the old lady. "It's mostly hot air, spite and envy, and for all I care the gossips can choke on it." She smiled. "And the duke told me he *liked* my dress."

"*Pfft!* What choice did he have?"

George touched the jewels at her throat. "He didn't have to give me these jewels either, but he did." She realized now why he'd given them to her before the wedding breakfast—so that all the guests would see and know that she had his approval and support. She was deeply touched by the thoughtfulness—and loyalty—of the gesture.

The duke was turning out to be rather different from the man she thought she knew.

Aunt Agatha glanced at the rubies and pursed her lips. "He should never have done so. His mother should have had them years ago—I know she asked for them often enough. They're priceless, a treasured family heirloom, but the old duchess always refused to hand them over. Claimed they weren't part of the entail and so she could choose who to give them to." She shook her head. "But to give them to you, and after your disgraceful appearance at the church. Truly outrageous."

Aunt Dottie bustled forward and gave George a warm hug. "You look stunning, dear girl—and oh! I see you're wearing the famous Hartley parure. The old dowager duchess would have approved, I know."

"And how would *you* know, Dorothea?" her sister said in an acid voice.

Aunt Dottie gave George a mischievous wink. "I know she despised her daughter-in-law, Aggie, dear. And our darling George is going to make her grandson very happy, so of course she would have loved her and wanted her to wear her jewels—especially as they suit her so well."

George glanced at the duke on the other side of the room, talking to several men she didn't know. Would she make him happy? She had no idea. Would he make her happy? She had even less of an idea.

THEY REACHED EVERINGHAM HOUSE JUST AS EVENING was falling. Hart considered carrying her over the threshold, but then decided she'd probably hate it. Besides, there was nobody to open the door; he'd given the servants the night off.

She'd been very quiet on the way, hadn't said a word.

The house was in darkness, except for a soft glow coming from inside the front entrance hall. He pulled out his key and opened the door. His butler, Fleming, had left a candle lamp burning on the hall table.

Not for the first time Hart wished he'd overruled his mother on the subject of gas lighting. It was brighter in the street outside than it was in his house.

"When you redecorate, we'll get gas lighting installed," he told his bride as he lit another candle lamp.

"When *I* redecorate?" She grimaced. "Rose or Lily are the ones for that kind of thing. I have no interest in wallpaper and suchlike. I grew up in a run-down old farmhouse and never saw anything wrong with it."

"Never mind; there are people we can hire." He picked up a lamp and passed the other to her. "I was really thinking about the light. My mother preferred candlelight to gaslight."

She nodded. "More flattering to aging skin, I expect. I don't mind candles though." She glanced around. "Where are we going?"

"Upstairs." Where else? They'd eaten and drunk their fill at the wedding breakfast and she'd delayed leaving far beyond the usual time for a bridal couple to depart. She'd even wanted to change into her everyday clothes and take her dog for a walk, until her uncle had volunteered to take care of the dog himself, leaving her with no more excuses.

She was nervous—he'd watched it coming on all through the afternoon. She hadn't been at all anxious when they'd been here earlier; she'd been eager for him then. But now bridal nerves had set in.

She gave a jerky nod, gathered the skirt of her glorious dress up in one hand, and started up the stairs, the lamp held high. The candlelight shimmered in the folds of the rich fabric and danced in the rubies at her ears.

She paused on the landing. "Where do I sleep?"

He gestured to the open door. "*We* sleep in my room, of course. In my bed." Oh, yes, she was nervous, all right.

She hung back, loitering on the landing. "You married me for my horse," she said, striving for lightness, "so maybe you should sleep with Sultan." Her skin was almost colorless in the soft light.

He laughed softly, caught her by the hand and drew her slowly against him. "I don't think so."

She stiffened, and then pulled away. What the devil was the matter? She'd been afire for him before the wedding breakfast. What had changed?

Bridal nerves, he decided. "I'll light some more candles." He set hers on a side table, then entered his bedroom and used his candle to light a dozen or so of the candles that his staff had set around the room. Lanterns would throw a better light, but he had a vague notion that a nervous bride might be more comfortable in candlelight.

He'd turned, having expected her to follow him inside. Instead she had remained on the landing. He went to her, and was surprised when she took a step back.

"Before . . . before I go in there, I need to warn you." She bit her lip, looking troubled.

He stiffened. "Warn me? About what?"

She took a deep breath and said in a rush, "I might not be a virgin."

"*What?*"

"I said, I might not be a virgin." She hesitated, then added, "I remember you saying once to Rose, *Virginity is a requirement for any bride of mine*."

He stared at her dumbfounded. Why had she waited until after the wedding to share this interesting fact with him? It was a little late now to be confessing the sins of her past. Not that it would have made any difference to him. "What do you mean you 'might not be'? Either you are or you aren't."

She scowled. "It's ridiculous anyway, requiring brides to be virgins. You're not a virgin, so why should I be?"

He said through gritted teeth, "Are you or are you not?"

"It's only so that men can make sure any children of a marriage are theirs, but there's no way to ensure that, except the woman's own personal honor."

"A woman's honor?"

"Yes, a bride can be a virgin on her wedding night but betray her husband with a groom or a footman or another gentleman shortly afterward—and who can be sure of the father? Not even the woman, sometimes. Unless she's a person of honor."

"Are you?"

Her eyes flashed with indignation. "I shouldn't have to tell you that. If I weren't a woman of honor, I never would have married you."

"I know that. I meant, are you a virgin?"

"Oh." There was a short silence. "I don't know."

"How can you not know?"

She flushed. "People say—well, Martha used to say, and she wasn't the only one—that if a girl rode a horse bareback—and astride—she would, um, not be a virgin. That it would um, rupture the, um, maidenhead." She looked away, her cheeks flaming, lips pressed together. She swallowed convulsively, then turned to face him. "I used to ride bareback and astride all the time. So . . ."

Relief rushed through him. So she wasn't about to confess some sordid past. Candlelight flickered and danced across her profile. She looked young and uncertain and vulnerable. And sweet and brave and true.

He took her hand in his. "It doesn't matter."

She hesitated. "You don't mind?"

"Not at all. Whether or not you are physically a virgin now, it will make no difference to our future."

"Are you sure? Because if I'm not, I don't want you throwing it up in my face whenever we quarrel."

He arched a brow. "Will we quarrel?"

"We're bound to."

"I see. Well, as long as we make it up in bed, I'll accept that. And whatever the outcome, I promise I won't throw your virginity or lack of it in your face. In fact, I'm already bored with the subject. Can we go to bed now?"

She nodded and allowed him to lead her into his bedroom.

George glanced around the duke's bedchamber. His servants had obviously prepared it. In the soft candlelight, everything gleamed with care and attention. As she'd observed earlier in the day, it was a very masculine room, with heavy carved furniture and curtains and bedcovers of rich dark red brocade, but now vases of flowers sat on the mantelpiece and on top of a chest of drawers. The delicate fragrance of the flowers mingled with the sharp, clean tang of beeswax. The furniture had been newly polished.

His enormous bed seemed bigger than ever. The heavy brocade coverlet was turned back invitingly, revealing fresh white sheets and pillows.

"Your staff has made a special effort." She was pleased to hear she sounded almost normal, despite the butterflies thundering around her stomach.

He glanced around vaguely. "Have they? I hadn't noticed. Oh, yes, flowers." He pulled off his cravat and tossed it aside, then turned back to her. "Would you like me to act as your maid?"

Her *maid*? She gave him a blank stare.

He smiled. "I meant, do you need my help unfastening your gown? There being no one else in the house."

"*Erghmh.*" Her mouth had gone completely dry.

Taking that as assent, he gently turned her around and began to undo her dress.

He stood close, so close she was aware of every point on

her body where his body brushed against hers. She closed her eyes briefly and inhaled the scent of him. The spicy tang of his cologne and the scent of sun-dried sheets mingled with the fragrance of beeswax and flowers, but pleasant though they were, the scent that drew her, enticed her, aroused her was the warm, darkly enticing man scent of his body. Aroma of desire.

She stood stiffly while he slowly unhooked her, his breath warm on her neck. By the time he'd undone half a dozen of the hooks that ran down the back of her dress she'd had enough. "No, stop!" She turned around.

"Why? What's the matter?"

"You need to kiss me first." It came out a little high, almost squeaky. "I'm ridiculously nervous and I don't know why, because it's not that I don't want to do this—I do, I really do—but I'm just, I don't know, stupidly skittish and I know I have no reason to be, but if you kiss me, I'm sure it will be better, because when you kiss me—" She stopped abruptly.

"Yes? When I kiss you . . . ?" His voice was deep, knowing.

She smacked him lightly on the arm. "Oh, don't look so smug. You know perfectly well what I'm trying to say."

"I do indeed," and he kissed her.

This time there was no hesitation, no light brushing of mouth against mouth, no teasing of the lips. It was neither gentle nor tentative—a bold possession—and her blood sang as she opened to him. The dark, familiar male taste of him flooded her senses.

This, this is what she craved. It was as if there was some deep ravening hunger in her that needed to be fed, and only he could feed it.

She pressed herself against him, twining her fingers in his hair, pulling him closer, all doubts, all hesitation gone. He pulled her hard against him, deepening the kiss, drawing a response from her she hadn't known was possible.

She ran her palms along his jaw, enjoying the faint abrasion of his bristles, and all the time kissing and being

kissed, not knowing where she began and he ended. Intoxication.

The edge of the bed pressed against the back of her legs
and she let herself sink onto the thick mattress. She needed
him closer. She hooked a leg around him.

"Easy there," he murmured. "Almost there."

Almost where? She opened her eyes to ask him, and felt
a cold draft on her upper body.

"Sit up a moment," he said.

She sat up and her dress fell down around her hips. "You
unhooked me while we were kissing?" She wasn't sure
whether she approved. She hadn't been able to think of a
single thing while he was kissing her, but he apparently had
been able to unhook a dress and kiss her senseless.

"Lift up," he said, and when she did, he slipped the dress
out from under her. "I'm very fond of that dress, don't want
to ruin it." He draped it carefully over the rail on the end of
the bed. "Now, where were we?" He turned back to her and
sighed. "I suppose your stays are laced."

She nodded, impatient to have him back in her arms, but
quite enjoying his frustration.

His eyes devoured her. "Pink silk drawers, George?
Very dashing."

She blushed a little. They were presents from Rose and
Lily—along with a couple of even more dashing nightdresses.
"I always wear drawers. It's too drafty the old-fashioned
way."

"I was rather fond of the old naked-under-the-skirt fashion, but I won't complain. This is like unwrapping a most
enticing parcel."

"I'm not a parcel," George said.

"I know you're not: you're a gift." He turned her around
and began to unlace her stays, kissing down her spine as his
fingers flew to release her. Then she felt a tugging, and he
swore. "Blast!"

He turned her to face him. "I can't undo it. The wretched
thing is knotted." He bent and kissed her breasts. "Let's
try—aha!" He reached into the stays with his long clever

fingers, drew out the busk and tossed it aside. "Now . . ." He peeled the top of her stays down, taking her chemise with it, baring her breasts to the air.

"So pretty." He cupped them in his hands, and she shivered with the sensation. He teased the nipples with his thumbs, and she closed her eyes as tiny shudders began deep within her body. He laved one breast with his tongue, then placed his mouth over it and sucked. George almost came off the bed as a shaft of pleasure/pain speared through her.

His mouth and hands roved over her, the shudders grew stronger and stronger and she vaguely realized that her body was no longer under her control. Some ancient, irresistible force had taken over. Her legs trembled and fell apart and following some vague instinct, she lifted them to wrap them around his waist.

"One moment; first we need to get rid of—there." He pulled off her drawers and tossed them aside, then, to her shock, he buried his face in the fur between her legs and inhaled.

"I'm sorry, George. I can't wait any longer." His mouth came back to devour hers; she felt a warm, blunt object pushing at her entrance and then a sharp pain. She gasped, suddenly drawn back to awareness. Her body felt stretched, full, as if she might burst.

He checked for a moment and eased out of her, though not all the way. He slipped his hand between her thighs and stroked her with his fingers, and after a moment the shivers started again.

"Better?"

She managed a nod, and wriggled a little. It felt better, so she wriggled again. He groaned. "Lord, George, don't— I can't—" With an apologetic grimace he surged into her, and thrust again and again.

And suddenly her body found the rhythm and she moved with him. It felt right, this thing she had been craving for so long. He reached a climax and with a loud groan shuddered into her and collapsed.

They lay there, the duke lying on top of her, breathing heavily, for what seemed like a long time. George lay quietly, savoring the whole extraordinary experience, and quite enjoying the feeling of his weight pressing her into the mattress. Eventually he eased himself out of her and raised himself up on one elbow.

"I'm sorry, George. I should have— I lost control."

"You lost control?" She wasn't sure what that meant. Everything had happened more or less as she'd imagined it would. She just hadn't imagined the rawness of it, the power, the almost animalistic instinct that had taken over her body, moving and reacting without conscious volition. Though it made sense to her. Humans were animals too, she'd always maintained.

He nodded. "I should have waited, should have made it better for you. I have no excuse. You drive me wild with desire. I've been aching for you ever since that first kiss."

Wild with desire? For her? Then she wasn't the only one who'd been feeling tense and a little out of control? Had he also had wild, erotic dreams?

Pleased, she reached up and stroked his cheek. "It's all right."

"It's not." He kissed her again, caressed her half-exposed breast, then groaned. "I didn't even let you get fully undressed, and as for me . . ." He was almost fully dressed. Apart from removing his cravat, he'd unfastened the fall of his breeches and pushed them down over his backside, but that was all.

"Well, we can certainly do something about that." George sat up and reached for the buttons on his waistcoat.

"I can do it," he said and started to undo them himself.

She slapped his hands away. "You got to unwrap your parcel, this is mine." She swiftly denuded him of coat and waistcoat, pulled his shirt over his head, removed his shoes and stockings and pulled his breeches and drawers off. In minutes he was naked.

She stared at him, breathless. She'd seen men without

shirts before, and viewed paintings and marble statues of naked men, but never a flesh-and-blood naked man. He was fascinating, beautiful. Strong and sculptured.

And his manhood. She'd expected something much smaller after seeing the paintings and statues.

At first he didn't seem to mind her inspection of him, but after a few minutes he stood up. "You're still half dressed," he pointed out, and bent to remove her shoes and stockings. "As for this—" He walked into his dressing room and came out with a small knife. "I'm going to remove those wretched stays." He did so. The stays fell away and he pulled off her chemise.

His eyes devoured her. "You are the most beautiful . . ." He pulled her against him, and kissed her deeply, then flipped back the bedclothes and lifted her in. He got in beside her and pulled up the bedclothes.

He surely wasn't going to sleep, was he?

George flipped back the bedclothes. "I'm not finished looking at you," she informed him. She stroked his chest, fingering the tiny flat male nipples and wondering if they were as sensitive as her nipples had proved to be. She experimented and when he shivered and arched slightly under her hand, she smiled. Sauce for the goose . . .

She slipped her hand lower, caressing his flat, hard stomach in slow, tantalizing circles.

"Ah, so you begin to honor your wedding vows."

"What?" She frowned at him, puzzled. "My wedding vows?"

"Tsk-tsk, forgotten them already? You promised to rub, cherish and *olé* me." He lay back, like a big lazy cat. "Where do you propose to rub next?"

Chapter Nineteen

❧

**If I could but know *his* heart, everything
would become easy.**
—JANE AUSTEN, *SENSE AND SENSIBILITY*

GEORGE WOKE AT DAWN. SHE HADN'T HAD MUCH SLEEP—
they'd spent half the night exploring each other's bodies—
but she was in the habit of waking early.

She lay in bed, reflecting on the last few days. She was
married. It still didn't feel real, even though her body told
her she was well and truly married. She was a little bit sore,
but her body also felt looser and very satisfied.

She lay watching the dawn appear behind the curtains,
and listened to the duke's rhythmic breathing. His hand lay
loosely splayed on her belly, warm and oddly heavy. Was
this how she'd awaken in future, in a big richly furnished
bed with her naked husband beside her?

No, of course not. She recalled the agreements they'd
made. There would be a honeymoon and then she would
live in her own house and he would make conjugal visits to
ensure she gave him an heir.

The thought was strangely depressing, even though it
had been exactly what she'd wanted before. She hadn't
known him then.

She still didn't really know him, but she didn't feel the

same about him as she had. It wasn't just the marriage con-
summation, either, though that had engendered a certain
intimacy, a feeling of closeness between them.

It wasn't just a physical connection she felt, though.

Even before the wedding night, the way he'd behaved
toward her since the betrothal became real, his reaction to
his discovery of his mother's deception, the unspoken but
public support he'd given her, his reaction in church to her
scarlet dress, the rubies—there was more to him than she'd
ever imagined.

Her bladder urged her out of bed. She found what she
needed through his dressing room exit, and on the way back,
feeling self-conscious to be walking around stark naked, she
borrowed a richly masculine embroidered silk robe that was
hanging on a hook. On her return she found him awake.
"Morning." She felt herself blushing.

"Good morning," he murmured. "You look very fetch-
ing in that robe. How do you feel?"

"Fine. Very . . . relaxed." She stood uncertainly, his robe
clutched around her, her bare toes digging into the deep
luxurious pile of his Persian carpet.

He got out of bed, and apparently quite unembarrassed
by his nakedness or the semi-aroused state of his manhood,
he kissed her briefly, then headed for the dressing room. He
returned a short time later, belting a tie around another
robe. "You've woken very early. I didn't let you sleep much
last night—you don't want to sleep in?"

She shook her head. He pulled the curtains open, and
the morning sun streamed in.

"I don't sleep in very often," she explained. "We—my
family and I—usually go for an early ride, especially in
summer." She wondered if they were riding out now.

His green-gray eyes glinted. "I would show you another
kind of dawn ride, except I suspect you're a bit sore."

Her sleepy body leapt to life at his words. She swallowed, and said diffidently, hoping she didn't sound too
eager. "I'm not really."

He took two strides toward her and slipped his hands

between the folds of her robe. His warm hands caressed her, slipping down over her hips, cupping her buttocks, then sliding up her body in slow tantalizing sweeps coming to rest just beneath her breasts. "Are you sure? Because you were indeed a virgin, and—"

"I'm fine. So if you want to . . . I don't mind." Not mind? She was already aroused.

He cupped her breasts and swept his thumbs over her hardened nipples. She gasped and arched toward him. Slipping her own hands under his robe, she reached down to grasp him.

He pulled back. "No, don't touch me. Not yet. This time is for you." He walked her backward and pushed her gently onto the bed. He flipped the robe open and sighed. "You are so lovely."

In response, she pulled his robe off him and ran her hands over his magnificent shoulders. He was beautiful too, though if she told him that he'd probably think she was trying to flatter him. He was too used to flattery. The knowledge inhibited her.

He ravished her with mouth and hands, exploring her body, licking, kissing, nibbling, surprising and exciting her with small nips—like a stallion did with a mare, only more gentle. Her body was afire.

His mouth closed over her breast, laving and sucking at her nipple and she gasped with pleasure as hot spears of sensation spiraled through her. Vaguely she realized his hand was between her legs. His fingers moved in slow, tantalizing, rhythmic circles, and she wriggled and thrust her body against them, trembling and shuddering, her legs shaking. Not long now, she thought.

She ached for him to enter her. He was hard and erect and ready, but every time she reached for him, he stopped her with his hands. "Not yet."

The tension spiraled higher. She was frantic with need. "Now, Hart, now!"

He pushed her legs apart, and she waited for him to enter her, but instead she felt his hot breath, there. He parted her with his fingers and—oh, God!—he was licking and nibbling and sucking and . . .

She couldn't . . . she couldn't . . . She was going to . . .

She gripped his hair and screamed. And shattered around him in an explosion of ecstasy . . .

She might have slept for a while, she wasn't sure, though someone had covered her up. But when she finally gathered her scattered senses enough to think, only two thoughts came to mind. The first was that it was no wonder that Lily and Rose often arrived late for their morning ride. She stretched luxuriously. If this was married life, she liked it very much.

The second thought came a few moments later: he hadn't entered her at all.

She sat up. He was lying on his side, his head propped on his elbow, contemplating her. "Did you like that?"

She couldn't keep the smile from her face. "Yes, but—"

"But? After all that, there is a *but*?" he said, pretending indignation.

She laughed. "You know there isn't. But you didn't . . . um." She blushed.

"I didn't 'um' because I 'ummed' several times last night, whereas you hadn't 'ummed' at all. It will get better with practice, and we will both 'umm' together, but in the meantime, you needed to find out what 'umming' was all about." He leaned forward and kissed her nose and got out of bed. "Now, I'm off to bathe and shave, and you, my duchess, will have a bath. I've ordered hot water to be brought up in twenty minutes."

George lay back against the pillows. Then her eyes flew open. "The servants are back?"

"Of course. We need bathing and shaving water and breakfast, don't we? And your luggage and maidservant will have arrived. I told her not to come until this morning."

George looked at him in dismay. "But if the servants were here this morning"—she pressed her hands against cheeks grown suddenly hot—"they will have *heard*." She distinctly remembered someone screaming, and it wasn't the duke. Her face was hot with embarrassment.

His expression was half smug, half amused. "Then they'd better get used to it." He picked up his robe and, naked, walked from the room.

AT BREAKFAST THE BUTLER BROUGHT IN THE MORNING mail. The duke glanced through it quickly, sorting it into piles, then frowned over one particular letter. "Blast. I was hoping we could set off on our honeymoon today." He glanced at the letter again and then up at her. "I'm afraid Venice will have to wait."

She didn't mind that at all. The only time she'd ever been on a boat, she'd been horribly seasick. "Why, what's the matter?"

"There's a child—my ward, my late cousin's son—and he's disappeared."

"A child? How old is he?"

"Seven. He was orphaned last year and his father left him and the estate in my hands. I'm to be trustee until the boy turns twenty-one."

"When did he go missing? Do they have any idea of what might have happened?"

He glanced at the letter. "He was first missed three days ago. They suspect kidnapping, but no ransom note has been received."

"Three days? And they've only just notified you?"

He rolled his eyes. "It will no doubt turn out to be a storm in a teacup, but I'll have to go there—the boy is my responsibility."

A storm in a teacup? "Aren't you worried about him?"

"The boy is probably playing a trick on the servants and is hiding somewhere."

"For three days? What if he's unhappy and has run away?"

He gave her a blank look. "Why would he run away? He

has everything he needs. More to the point, where would he go? Lakeside Cottage is a few miles the other side of Quainton in Bucks. There is nowhere to run to." He shook his head. "My guess is he'll be hiding. I did much the same when I was a boy."

"For three days?"

He nodded. "Yes. You can please yourself what you do while I'm gone—stay here in Everingham House—you might want to talk to Rose and Lily about redecorating it. Or you could return to your uncle's house, or visit one of your aunts. Whatever you like."

"Wait in London?" Be set aside like a parcel until he was ready to collect her again? She could imagine the gossip that would arise from that—the duke, abandoning his bride the morning after the wedding. As for redecorating the house . . . "I'm going with you."

He frowned. "Are you sure? It'll probably be quite dull."

"I don't mind."

"I'll have to leave straightaway. I'd planned to ride. It's a solid day's ride from here."

"Oh, dear, and I'm so awkward on horseback," she said dryly.

He gave a huff of amusement. "I was thinking of the rain." He gestured to the window, where rain had just begun to spatter against the glass. "So much for the morning sun."

She shrugged. "I won't catch cold from a little rain."

"Probably not, nevertheless, if you're coming, we'll take the traveling chaise. It won't take much longer, and if we need to, we'll hire mounts in Quainton." He tossed his napkin aside and rose from the table. "How long will it take you to be ready?"

"Half an hour."

He gave her a skeptical look. "Most women would take two hours at the very least."

"I'm not most women."

His slow smile warmed her. "Indeed you're not."

* * *

THE CARRIAGE LEFT EXACTLY THIRTY-ONE MINUTES LATER. The extra minute was for Finn, as George's maid, Sue, had brought him with her, and George couldn't leave him alone in a strange house. "Besides, it'll be good to have his company," she told Hart as Finn clambered into the carriage and sprawled across his feet.

"I'm sure it will," he responded with unexceptional politeness and a distinct lack of enthusiasm. He eyed Finn and added in a severe tone, "And you'd better not have gorged on leftovers from the wedding breakfast, my lad, or you'll be riding on the roof." Finn wagged his tail.

As they drove out of London, George asked Hart how he had come to be the guardian of a small boy and trustee of his estates.

"I've no idea. The boy's father is a distant cousin, and the first I heard of these arrangements was after he'd died. He certainly didn't ask me. I suppose he assumed that as head of the family it was my duty." He sounded irritated.

"Didn't you want the responsibility?"

"It's not the responsibility so much as the mess my cousin left things in. He was a hopeless gambler—and I use the word 'hopeless' advisedly. Despite his losses, he couldn't break the habit. In the ten short years since he inherited, he managed to run a decent estate into the ground, leaving his son with nothing but debts to inherit."

It was that last that was responsible for the suppressed anger in his voice, George thought. Leaving the boy's inheritance in a mess.

"Do you gamble?" A lot of men did, she knew. And some women.

"Rarely. Sometimes I do when I'm playing cards, and I bet on my horses when I race them. When I do gamble, I generally win." He glanced at her. "You don't need to worry about me—I never gamble more than I can afford."

"Horses? I didn't know you raced horses."

He nodded. "Are you interes— Foolish question. Of course you are. The next time I have a horse running I'll take you to the races."

He was being remarkably kind. And surprisingly open, George thought. Was that because they were married? Or was it because of the intimacy established through their activities in bed?

She'd always been unsettlingly aware of him, but since their wedding night, that awareness had sharpened. It was as though her skin had become extra sensitive, and every touch, even the brush of his sleeve against her skin, sent a small reverberation through her. The same went for his scent, the clean tang of his shaving soap, the cologne he used, the smell of freshly washed and ironed linen—he was fastidious—and beneath it all the dark, musky man-smell of *him*.

He stretched out his legs, crossing his boots at the ankle, and she was intensely aware of the muscled thighs beneath the snugly fitted buckskins.

He cracked his knuckles and a shiver ran through her as she recalled the way he'd stroked her nipples with those same knuckles.

She forced her gaze elsewhere and tried to focus on the conversation. "What happened to the boy's mother?"

"Died giving birth to him."

"And there was no other family he could go to?"

"No."

Poor little boy. George knew what it felt like to grow up having no family—none that she knew of at the time, anyway, thanks to her father keeping her existence a secret. She was eighteen before she knew she had a family—one who actually wanted her.

"Couldn't he—I didn't catch his name—couldn't the boy live with you?"

"Phillip? With me? In London? The city is no place for a child. Besides, I know nothing about children. No, I moved the boy to one of his father's minor properties that I gather had been quite overlooked in his scramble to sell all he could. I'm in the process of reorganizing the main estate and one other that was stripped of all valuables and mort-gaged to the hilt. If all goes as planned, by the time the boy is of age, he should have a substantial inheritance."

She nodded. To repair the damage Phillip's father had done was admirable, of course, but to move a small boy to a new place, when he'd just lost his father . . .

Silence fell. He gazed out the window, tapping his fingers impatiently, drumming a soft tattoo on the seat leather. He was restless—he probably would have preferred to ride and feel more active. George watched the long, strong fingers and thought about the unexpected sensations they had coaxed from her. A warm ripple of remembrance clenched her insides. He seemed to know her body better than she did.

"Why did you move Phillip away from all that was fa-miliar to him?"

He frowned. "I didn't—at least that wasn't why I moved him. He should be away at school by now, but according to his tutor he's delicate, and academically he's not yet ready for school, so this place is temporary. Besides, the boy's home brings in far more in rental than the small house he's in now."

"But he's a small grieving boy."

He looked at her, surprised. "I did it for the best. I'm doing all I can to ensure that by the time the boy reaches his majority, he won't inherit his father's massive debt. I moved him out of his family home because it's a large house at the center of a huge estate—an estate that ought to be prosperous but instead is in debt. I've put in a new man-ager, made a raft of changes and innovations and rented out the house to a wealthy cit who has a fancy to live like a gentleman. And, yes, he wanted to buy it, but I'm deter-mined to save it for the boy."

She nodded. "I can see that, but what about Phillip?"

"What about him? I'm doing this for him."

"He'd just lost his father."

He shrugged. "I don't suppose the boy knew his father any better than I did. Neither of my parents spent much time at Everingham Abbey, where I grew up. My mother loathes the country and only ever went there on sufferance. And, of course, my father indulged her."

So both his parents had been more or less strangers to him, George thought.

He continued, "As far as I know Phillip's father spent most of the time in London gambling hells or at country house parties. Besides, at that age, servants are the most important thing in a child's life. But he was too old for a nanny, so I hired a tutor who would prepare him for school."

"So he had nobody familiar?"

"What does that matter? As I said, he'll be starting school as soon as his health improves, and there will be nobody familiar at school. I didn't know a soul when I started there."

"How old were you?"

"Seven."

She was horrified. "Seven? But you were still a baby."

He snorted. "Tell any seven-year-old boy he's still a baby and he'll hate you for it. I managed."

"Did you like it?"

He thought for a minute. "Does anyone like school at first? I got used to it, eventually. Once I'd made a few friends there, things were a lot better." He glanced at her. "Some of those friends are still my friends today—Sinc, for instance. Johnny Sinclair. We met on the first day, but it took us a while to take to each other. Sinc has a knack for making friends easily." He grimaced. "I don't."

She could understand that. She was beginning to understand why he was so reserved and cold seeming. He'd grown up not being able to trust the people he should have been able to believe in, and he'd been raised by servants. Not by someone like Martha, who had loved George for herself and had stayed on even though there was no money, but by people who cared for a small boy only because they were paid to.

"You said you'd hidden away for several days when you were a child. Why did you do it?"

"A puppy. I was only found because he barked and gave us away."

"A puppy?"

"I'd cadged a puppy from a nearby farm and hid with him in the attic."

"Why?" Why would he have to hide?

"Mother didn't like dogs, so I wasn't allowed to have one."

But he'd said that his mother rarely visited him in the country. What sort of people wouldn't allow a lonely small boy to have a dog? A dog was the best companion in the world.

"What happened to the puppy?"

He glanced away and said in a flat voice, "He was taken away."

The pup was probably destroyed. George stared out of her window and thought evil thoughts about the duke's mother, and sad thoughts about a lonely small boy and a doomed puppy. It wasn't exactly the privileged upbringing she'd imagined. She changed the subject. "When did you inherit the title?"

"The dukedom? My father died when I was nineteen, but I've always been titled. I was born a marquis."

That would be a barrier from the start, she thought. There would be boys who would be jealous and want to bring him down for his imagined superiority. And some boys would toadeat him, wishing to be friends with a titled boy. Few of them would see who he was, himself—by all accounts a shy and lonely boy.

And as he grew older, women would be added to the mix, wanting him for what he could bring them, not for who he actually was. And all most people would see was his position and his titles and his assumed advantages.

As she had at first. Seeing only the arrogant-seeming, self-contained man.

She thought about the time five years before, when he'd knocked her off her horse, after she'd disrupted the hunt. She'd mentioned it to Martha at the time, and Martha had made inquiries. He'd been staying with Michael Stretton. Of course.

Martha had been scathing. *Those Strettons invited the duke, hoping to snare him for one of their daughters.* She'd snorted. *That lot think so much of themselves, a duke in the family would be just what they think they'd deserve. I don't know exactly what happened, but by all accounts the duke really fell out with his friend and stormed off in a temper.*

"I heard you left Michael Stretton with a broken nose," she said.

He frowned. "What made you think of that? It was years ago."

She shrugged. "Did you? Break his nose, I mean."

He glanced away. "I didn't wait to see the result, but it was a good solid punch, so it wouldn't surprise me. Serve him right for—for what he did. I don't like being lied to."

Because Michael Stretton had sent the duke to punish her for ruining the hunt? And lied to him, suggesting she was male? She recalled the duke's horror when he realized he'd roughly dragged a girl off her horse.

He'd broken his friend's nose for her. It shouldn't have pleased her, but it did. Immensely.

"Thank you."

"For breaking Michael Stretton's nose?" He gave a quizzical half smile. "You didn't like him?"

"No." But she wasn't going to explain. There was no need to tell him of her embarrassing infatuation with Michael Stretton when she was a green girl, how she'd thought him the handsomest boy in the world, the best rider.

She'd watched him from afar, adoring him from a distance, expecting nothing from him, knowing she was well out of his class in all the ways that counted. They'd never even talked.

And then came the night of his twenty-first birthday. His family held a ball. Hidden in a tree, George had watched through the long ballroom windows as he'd danced with all the prettiest girls in the district. She wasn't even jealous— perhaps a tiny bit envious, but more wistful, really. And admiring.

And then he'd come outside with a friend to smoke a cigarillo, standing below her tree. And the way he'd talked about some of those girls—girls she knew were decent, virtuous girls—had shocked her. She must have dislodged a twig or something, because his friend had looked up and said, "I say, there's a girl up there in your tree, Stretton."

George had frozen, mortified.

And then Michael Stretton said, "I know. She follows me everywhere, the dirty little slut. She's too scrawny to screw yet, but her day will come."

George's infatuation had shriveled and died on the spot. And when a year later he'd come sniffing around, presumably deciding she was no longer so scrawny, she'd rejected him emphatically.

Later, when he discovered she was the one disrupting the hunt, his anger had become personal. And vindictive.

So the thought that the duke had been responsible for Michael Stretton's broken nose delighted her.

"It wasn't the first time Stretton had crossed your path, then?"

"No. He and his friends often tried to run me to earth, threatening to give me a thrashing. And worse." There was a grim look in her eyes as she added, "They almost had me one time, but the dear old squire came roaring up, waving his whip and threatening to horsewhip the lot of them for treating a lady so." She smiled reminiscently. "A lady. I was in breeches and boots with mud on my face and hands, but the old squire, he was a gentleman." She grinned. "Michael and his friends ran like frightened little rabbits."

He took her hand in his and squeezed. "Sounds like the squire was a good man." She made no move to pull her hand away.

"He was, and a force of nature to boot. For all that Michael and his friends thought themselves so much better born than the squire, the old man was a true gentleman— something that they could never be. He didn't leave it there, either; he visited each of their parents and told them what he'd seen, and what he promised if he caught them at it again. His threats worked too. They never bothered me again."

Instead Stretton had tried to get Hart to do his dirty work. Hart wished now that he'd given Stretton a good thrashing, instead of just a broken nose. His hand tightened around hers.

She smiled, a mixture of triumph and smugness. "That nose never healed properly, you know. It's permanently crooked. And Michael was always so vain about his good looks. So thank you." She leaned over and kissed him. Her lips were sweet and soft.

"Now that's an idea," he said and pulled her across his lap. He pulled up her skirt and discovered something interesting. "Going old-fashioned today, are we? I like it."

She pushed his hands away. "In the carriage?" she said sounding shocked. "We can't do that here."

"Why not? We're married." He cupped her chin and added, "If you don't want to umm, George, just say so."

"It's not that." She looked away, blushing rosily. "But people might see."

He followed her gaze out of the window. "You're right," he said as if much struck. "There's all those sheep, for a start. And cows too. We wouldn't want to shock them, would we?" He reached past her and drew the curtains on her side of the coach, and then did the same for those on his side. He closed the back curtain as well. "There now, that's better, isn't it? There's nothing worse than a shocked sheep or a blushing bovine."

"Cows don't blush," she said, trying not to smile.

"No, but you do, George, don't you?" he murmured.

"You can't possibly see—I mean, it's too dark. I can't see." She was jumpy, a little embarrassed but he knew if she really didn't want this, she'd have no hesitation in stopping him. She was modest, that's all. The thought did not displease him.

He placed a finger under her chin, and turned her face toward him. "Then just feel." And he lowered his mouth to hers.

* * *

AFTERWARD, SHE FELL ASLEEP AND SLOWLY TIPPED OVER against him. Hart lifted his arm and drew her against his chest, tucking a rug around her. He gazed down at her sleeping face and stroked a lock of silky dark hair back from her face. What the hell had he got himself into?

He hadn't meant to make love to her again, not so soon. He'd always prided himself on his control. But with George . . . He shook his head. Apparently he was insatiable.

The carriage slowed as it labored up a hill. It was getting colder. One handed, trying not to disturb her, Hart pulled out a travel rug from a side pocket and tucked it around her.

It wasn't meant to be like this. He hadn't planned to have . . . *feelings*. It was supposed to be a convenient marriage—his own convenience at that. He'd wanted a woman who attracted him and wouldn't be a hardship to bed, a woman who wouldn't hang off his coat sleeve all the time, who would and could live independently. And who would give him an heir.

Theoretically his wife was all those things. Except for these . . . *feelings*.

The warm weight of her rested against his chest.

He'd imagined his planned convenient marriage as a cheese sandwich kind of thing. Bland, and would do a satisfactory job.

Instead he'd ended up with a luscious trifle. And with every taste he only wanted more.

He glanced down at the crescent of lashes lying dark against her skin, the tumbled curls, the soft, responsive mouth.

It would be all right, he told himself. He could manage this . . . this whatever it was. Control, that was the thing. Self-discipline. He had a job to do with this missing boy. That should distract him.

After an hour, she stirred and sat up. "I've been asleep," she said in surprise. "I never sleep in carriages."

"You haven't exactly had a lot of sleep in the last few

days," Hart said, and then because his mind—and body—went straight to the reason why she'd had so little sleep, he pulled out a portable chess set. He was fond of chess, and often whiled away a journey playing one hand against the other.

He held up the chess set. "Do you play?"

"No."

"Then I'll teach you."

An hour later, with much laughter, it was agreed that there were two kinds of chess players; one who thought several moves ahead and always had a long-range plan, and the other who reacted in the moment and wasn't at all interested in thinking ahead for possibilities.

"There is a third kind," she said after he'd shared this insight with her. "Or possibly it is a subset of the second kind—the chess player who never thinks ahead except to decide that she has absolutely no interest in chess."

He laughed. "What about cards?" So they played cards the rest of the way.

Chapter Twenty

<figure>❦</figure>

Prepare yourself for something dreadful.
—JANE AUSTEN, *PRIDE AND PREJUDICE*

LAKESIDE COTTAGE WAS A FEW MILES BEYOND THE VIL-
lage of Quainton. It was late afternoon as they drove up the
graveled drive The house was much bigger than George
had expected; it wasn't anything she'd call a cottage. Dukes
had a different standard of cottageness, it seemed.

It was a large brick, double-story building with several
chimneys and a line of dormer windows set into the attic.
To one side stood several substantial outbuildings, one of
which George presumed would be the stables.

The house stood in a large—she wouldn't call it a garden
so much as a plain expanse of lawn. There were no flowers
or shrubs or trees, and to her eyes it looked quite bare.
George preferred a proper garden, with trees and flowers.
But it was well maintained, all very neat and tidy with a
high, well-clipped hedge on three sides.

Finn leapt down first and went off to sniff for rabbits and
other intruders and claim his territory. George paused in
the doorway of the carriage and scanned the surrounding
area visible over the top of the hedge. It was quite an iso-

lated location, with only a few scattered cottages in the distance—her kind of cottage, not the duke's. A small lake lay a short distance away, fringed on one side with willows.

She could see what Hart meant by *Where would Phillip go?*

A groom came around from the side of the house and a middle-aged couple emerged from the front door and hurried down the steps.

"Your grace?" the woman said. "Oh, we're so glad you've come. We don't know what to do. I'm sorry, so sorry—" She broke off, sobbing.

"There's news?" Hart asked sharply. By his tone of voice he feared the worst.

"Nope," the man said. "Bin no sight nor sound of the lad at all." He went around to the back of the carriage to help unload the luggage. Finn sniffed him interestedly.

"No ransom demand received yet?" Hart asked.

The woman—who turned out to be Mrs. Harris, the housekeeper—shook her head. "Nothing of that sort at all, your grace."

Wiping her face with her apron Mrs. Harris led them inside. Hart asked to speak to the tutor, but he was out searching for Phillip. Apparently he'd gone out searching every day since Phillip went missing.

Hart then assembled all the servants in the sitting room and questioned them closely about the last time they'd seen Phillip and where they thought he might be. Had they searched the house and outbuildings thoroughly? Even the attics? The cellars?

Yes, of course, but there was no sign of him.

Had anything upsetting or out-of-the-way occurred before he went missing?

No, everything had been quite normal. Which made it all so very worrying.

George sat, watching and listening and trying to understand what had happened. They all seemed quite distressed about Phillip, and every single one of the servants stressed over and over, what a good, quiet, well-behaved little boy Phillip was.

George distrusted "good, quiet and well-behaved." In her opinion, it wasn't a natural state for a small boy.

Hart then instituted a search of his own and, aided by George and the servants, he personally examined every nook and cranny of the big house and every corner of the outbuildings.

George was most unimpressed with the stables. Oh, they were clean and well-kept, but there was only an elderly horse and a gig. Where was the pony for Phillip? A growing boy needed a horse. Apart from Finn, there were no dogs to be seen either.

"Well, that's that," Hart said when the search was concluded. He sent the servants back to their duties. "No sign of him. He can't be hiding."

"You don't know that yet," George said. "You've only searched the buildings."

Seeing his confusion, she explained. "He could be hiding beneath a haystack, or in the hedgerows—there are all kinds of nooks outside where people can hide. In all weathers." She smiled at his amazement. "Finn and I will look for them in the morning."

"How do you know to look in these kinds of places?"

"You had a big house with attics and storerooms and hidden closets. I didn't. Where do you think I disappeared to when I needed to be alone?"

"Alone?" He raised a brow.

"With my dog, of course, and sometimes my horse, though Sultan wasn't as easy to hide."

He looked shocked. "By yourself, outside? In all weathers?"

She gave a huff of amusement. "I'm no delicate flower, you know."

"I'm beginning to see that. And appreciate it."

George felt a warm glow inside. To be appreciated for knowing how to hide in hedgerows and haystacks—it was the last thing she would have expected from the duke.

A short time later the tutor, Jephcott, bustled in, looking flustered and spouting apologies and excuses for his absence when they arrived. A fastidiously dressed man in his late middle years, he became visibly distressed when Hart began to question him, clearly fearing to be blamed for the boy's disappearance.

"I *assure* you, your grace, that I took the *greatest* of care of the boy. Phillip is a delicate little fellow, prone to catch every illness that's going around, but he means well, and works hard and does his best to please. I cannot *imagine* what dreadful thing caused him to disappear. I *promise* you, he was only out of my sight for a *bare* few minutes."

"What time did you first notice he was gone?" Hart asked.

Jephcott frowned in pained recollection. "I can't be sure. It was late afternoon—before teatime certainly. He'd finished his Latin declensions, and I gave him an hour or two free time to play. But I was watching him from the terrace."

Dozing on the terrace, more like, George thought.

"Where did you think he went?"

"To the lake—he likes to dangle a fishing line in. He never catches anything, of course."

"Could he have fallen in?"

"It was the *first* thing I thought of, but we checked and there was *no* sign that he'd been there. His fishing rods were undisturbed and the small rowing boat he occasionally takes out was moored as usual—of course he's not allowed to fish or take the boat out alone, and he's a *very* responsible and obedient boy."

George was feeling more and more sorry for the child. To be so responsible and obedient at not quite seven years old. It wasn't natural. She wasn't sure what Latin declensions were, but they sounded horrid. And with no proper garden, no horse and no dog, what was there for a small boy to do?

Hart dismissed the tutor and sent for drinks to be brought in, brandy for himself and a sherry for George.

"I'll investigate that lake first thing in the morning." Hart's face was very grim. "That fellow is not the right kind of tutor for a small boy. I should have interviewed him myself for the position. His references were excellent, but now I've met him, I can see he's too old and fussy for a young boy."

George was a little shocked that he'd appointed the tutor sight unseen, but she knew now that Hart's first priority had been the reorganization of and restoration of the estate Phillip was to inherit, which at the time was a much bigger problem—and who was to say that was wrong? But Hart was clearly blaming himself for whatever had happened to Phillip.

"It's not your fault," she began.

Hart cut her off with a sharp gesture. "The boy is *my* responsibility."

Dinner was served then, and a very quiet meal it was too. They went up to bed. George wore one of the lovely night-dresses from Miss Chance, but to her surprise, Hart barely seemed to notice. He pulled on a nightshirt and climbed into bed without a word.

She slipped in beside him. "We have to think positively," she said softly.

He grunted and rolled over, his back to her. Obviously there was to be no lovemaking tonight. He was too worried about Phillip.

"Good night, Hart." She lay down and closed her eyes, then turned and slipped her arms around him.

He rolled over to face her, his eyes somber in the shadows. "I'm sorry, I just can't help thinking about that little boy."

"I know. Me too." She smoothed his forehead. "Just get some sleep and let us hope that things look better in the morning."

He kissed her, and curved himself around her, holding her in his arms until at long last they both fell asleep.

THE NEXT MORNING THE NEWS WAS EVEN WORSE. MRS. Harris brought it in with the breakfast. She stood there,

waiting in the doorway, looking worried until Hart beckoned her in. "What is it, Mrs. Harris?"

She bobbed an anxious curtsey. "Begging your pardon,
your graces, but one of the daily girls says she heard that
another little boy has gone missing, a local lad, Danny
Glover."

"What? Two small boys missing?"

Mrs. Harris grimaced. "It's just gossip at this stage, your
grace, but I thought you'd want to know."

Hart nodded. He surely did.

Jephcott followed her into the breakfast room. "But it's
not the same thing, your grace, it can't be. This Danny
Glover is just a poor boy, rough and ignorant—there's no
question of a ransom for such as he." He shook his head,
perplexed. "Not that a ransom note has come for Phillip
yet, but I'm sure it will. It must."

Hart pushed his breakfast aside. "How long has that boy
been missing?"

Mrs. Harris twisted her apron in fretful hands. "Nobody's sure—he's the kind of lad that runs wild. His parents don't show much interest in him. Possibly two or three
days."

Jephcott said soothingly, "This cannot be anything to do
with Phillip, your grace. Count on it, that other boy will
have just run off somewhere, as such boys are wont to do."
But not, according to him, a boy like Phillip.

One boy from a wealthy family might be taken for ransom, but a second boy of the same age, and from a poor
family? That could not be coincidence.

Hart rose from the table. He wasn't going to say anything at this stage—they were all worried enough. "I'll
check the lake first, then I'll speak to the parents of this
Danny Glover."

"I'll come with you," George said.

Hart turned to the housekeeper. "Send for the groom, if
you please. I want him to hire some horses for her grace
and me to ride. The best available."

As they walked to the lake, accompanied by the tutor

and a manservant, and with Finn lolloping on ahead, George took Hart's arm and said in a low voice, "Do you think we might be dealing with the kind of man who preys on small boys?"

He glanced at her. Trust his wife to voice the unthinkable, the very thing he'd been considering but hadn't said aloud for fear of upsetting the ladies.

"It's possible. But let's check the lake first. It's just as possible that two small boys could get into trouble together."

"Let us hope so." She hugged his arm as they walked along, and it occurred to him he didn't have to moderate his pace for her. Those long, lovely legs . . .

They found the lake and, as reported, the fishing gear and the little dinghy looked neat and undisturbed. Hart and George walked all around the lake, examining the mud at the lake's edge, but the only marks were the tracks of birds and of one large, exuberant wolfhound. There were no small human footprints.

When they returned to the house, they found two horses waiting for them, decent enough hacks but nothing special, George said. And then she laughed. "Have you noticed the saddles, Hart?"

It took him a moment to realize that there was no side-saddle for his wife. "Dammit, they should have known—"

"It's all right, I have my breeches and my divided skirt upstairs," George assured him. "And I'm not particularly fond of sidesaddles, so this suits me better." And she ran up the stairs to change.

DANNY GLOVER'S PARENTS LIVED IN A COTTAGE A COUPLE of miles away. It was part of a small farm where cattle and sheep grazed together. Hens scattered as Hart and George approached on horseback, and from the smell, there was a pigsty nearby.

A woman answered the door. Not wanting the fuss that would no doubt accompany an unexpected call by a duke and duchess, Hart introduced himself as merely Hartley, guardian of Phillip Wooldridge of Lakeside Cottage. Mrs. Glover immediately turned to a small boy about five years old, saying, "Peter, run and fetch your da'. Tell him gentry come calling." The boy ran off. He was clean and neatly dressed; he didn't look like the brother of a "rough, ignorant, wild boy."

Mrs. Glover hesitated, then nervously invited them in. She ushered them into a painfully neat parlor, saying her husband wouldn't be long. "Better he talk to you." She then left them to wait, a breach of country hospitality that surprised them.

"Perhaps she'd feel more comfortable talking to you," Hart murmured.

George shook her head. "I don't think she's shy. Maybe her husband doesn't like her talking to strangers. I wouldn't want to get her into trouble. Let's see what he says first."

They didn't have long to wait. Glover arrived about ten minutes later, a heavy, thickset man. He entered, wiping his hands. "Well, what's this about, then?"

Hart came straight to the point. "We heard a rumor that your son Danny is missing."

"So?" Glover said indifferently. "What business is it of yourn?"

A little taken aback, Hart explained that his ward, Phillip, was also missing.

Glover shrugged. "Nothing to do with me."

"How can you say that?" George burst out. "Danny is your son."

Glover's expression showed he didn't approve of being questioned by a woman. He said to Hart, "I'm not the boy's father, just his stepfather by a wife who died a few years back. Danny's not my blood, not my responsibility."

Hart hung on to his temper. "When did you first notice Danny was missing?"

Glover shrugged. "Coupla days. Give or take."

George said, "Do you know where he might have gone? His friends, for instance? Would he know Phillip?"

Glover gave her a sour look. "He'd better not. Danny's

got no friends. This is a working farm—he has work to do. There's no time for gadding about with friends, especially not with the sons of the gentry. Now is that all? I got more work than ever now that he's run off." He rose.

"Run off?" Hart said. "Where would he go?"

Glover lifted an indifferent shoulder. "No idea, lazy little bastard."

"Is Danny's natural father alive?" George asked. It was a good question, Hart thought. With a stepfather like this, an unhappy boy might look for a better alternative.

Glover's answer was a contemptuous snort.

Hart said, "Does Danny know who his natural father is? Do you?"

It was an impertinent question. Glover gave him a long, hard look. Hart met his gaze squarely, making it clear he was not moving until he had the answers he needed. Glover's lip curled. "She were a housemaid got with child by one of the gentry, over east." He waved a hand in that direction. "He offered this farm to any man willing to marry her. So I married her to give her bastard a name."

"Surely it was to get yourself a farm," George pointed out sweetly.

He scowled at her. "And then the stupid cow up and died and left me with her whelp to raise." He hitched up his breeches and added belligerently, "I got me a proper wife now, and children of my own, so if that young cur has run off and gotten hisself into trouble, he's no get of mine and I wash my hands of him."

"You realize he's the second young boy who's disappeared in the last week," Hart said.

The man shrugged. George's hands bunched into fists. Hart reached out and took one of her fists in his hand. If anyone was going to punch this swine, it would be him, not George. Though he understood and shared her anger.

George ignored him. "Danny might be dead. Murdered. Don't you care?"

"No business of mine if he is. Not my blood, not my son." And without even saying good-bye, he walked out.

George jumped to her feet. "Horrible, horrible, *horrible* man! I'm going to talk to his wife. She might know something that could help us."

But when George found the wife, she just gave them a scared look, glanced out at where her husband had gone and shook her head. Three well-scrubbed small children clustered shyly around her, hiding behind her skirts.

Hart and George left, disgusted. "Why, why, why do perfectly decent women marry ghastly men like that!" George said in a low, furious voice. "He obviously had no respect for his first wife—he just wanted the farm—and look how he's treated Danny, who was his means to *get* the wretched property! And now he's terrorizing a second woman. Men like that shouldn't be allowed to marry. I hope he chokes on his stinking farm!"

Hart was a little taken aback by her vehemence.

She continued, "Men should never be allowed have children if all they do is palm them off on someone else and ignore them. Poor little unwanted boy."

Which boy was she talking about? Danny or Phillip? But she wasn't just talking about the boys. There was personal history in that rant. Her own father had abandoned her before birth, he recalled.

They rode for a time in silence.

"I wonder who Danny's real father is," she said after a while. "Does he know how his son has been neglected? Would he care?"

"That farm was a substantial dowry," Hart said. "On that alone, we could assume he thought he was making good provision for the girl and his child."

She glanced at the duke. "Do you have any—"

"No. And if I did, they'd be well cared for. But I haven't."

"If we do find Danny alive, we should try to find out who his father is," she said. "Would that be possible, do you think?"

"First we have to find Phillip," he said heavily.

"I know." She rode closer and reached out for his hand,

and they rode on like that, hand in hand. It was strangely comforting. He hadn't realized how much he'd pinned his hopes on Danny being a key to finding Phillip. He'd been convinced he'd find the two boys together, up to their ears in mischief and afraid to come home.

But learning of Danny's home situation had changed all that. Danny had good reason to run away. Phillip had not.

The specter of a man preying on small boys loomed larger in his mind.

They continued searching and questioning neighbors in the area for the rest of the day. There were a few vague sightings, though people were uncertain as to which boy they might have seen. A boy was a boy, apparently and they all looked the same.

Tired and dejected, they returned to Lakeside Cottage as evening was falling.

They were met at the front door by the housekeeper, in great distress. With tears running down her face she babbled on about carpets. "Oh, your grace, something terrible, I'm so sorry. It was the carpets you see, we only take them up once a week to beat and today's the day, only when we took up the mat at the front entrance there it was, underneath. Someone must have shoved it under the door, but instead it went under the mat and nobody knew, nobody knew. It might have been there for days, and goodness knows what those villains thought when they didn't get any reply—and, oh, what if they hurt him, poor little lad? And all because of the carpet."

Hart unraveled the torrent of words. "What went under the mat, Mrs. Harris?"

"The letter—the ransom note, of course! It was addressed to Mr. Jephcott, so of course he opened it."

"What? Where is this ransom note?"

Jephcott, having heard the commotion in the hall, came hurrying down the stairs brandishing an envelope. "Here it is, your grace, I have it." He handed it to Hart who scanned the note inside.

Bring £5,000 to the bridge by the old mill and leave it under the broken stone just before dusk. Or the boy dies.

There was no date, no way of telling when the note had been written. And nobody knew how long it had been under the mat.

Hart glanced at the sky. "It's almost dusk now, but—"

"Come on." George was already running for the stables.

They rode to the old bridge, taking Stanley, the groom, as a guide. They found the broken stone, but of course there was no other sign of anything or anyone. They searched the old mill, but going by the thickness of the dust and cobwebs that covered the place, nobody had been there for years.

"Any other likely buildings nearby?" Hart asked the groom. Stanley suggested a couple of run-down and abandoned buildings, and even though full dark had fallen, there was enough moonlight to enable them to find those buildings, and ascertain that they too were uninhabited.

They returned to Lakeside Cottage even more dejected than before. Had the delay in discovering the ransom note caused the death of young Phillip?

"All we can hope for," Hart said to George as they prepared for bed that night, "is that the gossip that spread the news of young Danny's disappearance will also reach the kidnappers and let them know that their ransom note has only just been found."

"Are you going to pay it?"

"At this stage," Hart said heavily, "with the ransom demand having gone astray for an unknown length of time, I don't think I can afford not to. Their patience must be almost at an end. I won't antagonize them any more by delaying. Of course, we still have tomorrow during the day to track them down, but if we haven't discovered anything by nightfall, I'll leave the ransom there."

"Can you get that much money in time?"

"Before I left I arranged a large sum of money to be

transferred from my London bank to a local branch. I'll ride over and withdraw the ransom sum tomorrow morning."

He didn't say so, but George realized he must be going to pay the ransom out of his own pocket. Phillip's father had left nothing but debts. He was a good man, her husband.

She knew he wouldn't be interested in making love that night—they were both too tense from all the revelations of the day. Leaving aside the flimsy seductive nightdress that Lily and Rose had given her, she donned a plain cotton one, her mind whirling with depressingly unanswerable questions.

"Does the fact that we received a ransom note for Phillip augur well for the fate of young Danny?" she wondered aloud. "I mean, they wouldn't murder one boy and ransom another, would they? It doesn't make sense."

"We don't even know if Phillip is alive," Hart said heavily. "For all we know, that ransom note has lain under that blasted mat for nearly a week. I can't imagine kidnappers waiting indefinitely with no response to their demand. They'd most likely cut their losses and move on."

He sounded so weary and dispirited, so full of self-blame and despondency, she hurried across and wrapped her arms around him. She knew what he meant by "cut their losses"— it meant they'd kill Phillip. There was nothing she could say to comfort or reassure him; there was no comfort to be had from words.

He held her hard against him, saying nothing. She could feel his heartbeat under her ear, and ached for him. She could not comfort him with words, but there were other forms of comfort. She slipped her hand beneath his drawers, and caressed him lightly. "Come, let us go to bed." He hardened immediately against her palm.

"Yes." He kissed her, and she tasted despair and brandy and need.

They made love then with quiet desperation, seeking solace and oblivion. But Hart did not neglect her. For the first time ever, as he came to his climax, she shattered around him in hers.

And they slept.

* * *

HART COLLECTED THE MONEY THE NEXT MORNING AND left the ransom in place late that afternoon, well before dusk. "I can't risk not paying," he told George. "The money doesn't matter. There's no chance to investigate or negotiate. I don't want to antagonize them any more with any further delay."

The following morning George and Finn rode with him to the drop-off point. Hart dismounted and lifted away the broken stone—and swore. He turned to George with agonized eyes.

"What is it?" George called.

"The money is still here." There was no sign that anyone had been by—and no sign of Phillip.

Tears sprang to George's eyes. "Oh, Hart, I'm so sorry." George slipped off her horse and ran to embrace him. "You did all you could."

But Hart wasn't to be comforted. They had found the ransom note too late and Phillip had paid the price. All they could hope for was that the kidnappers had released him, but as Hart said, that was unlikely. The boy would be able to identify them.

They rode back in gloomy silence. As they passed the lake, Finn veered off investigating something. George ignored him at first, but when she whistled and he made no move to return to them, she became curious. "I'll just see what he's up to," she told her husband apologetically. "It's probably something disgusting and he'll want to roll in it. I need to stop him. I won't be a moment."

Hart made an indifferent gesture, waving her to go.

George rode to the edge of the lake, and when she dismounted she found Finn snuffing interestedly at a small shoe. Something caught in her throat. A few feet away lay another shoe. They were small, well-made leather shoes, about the size a seven-year-old would wear.

"Hart, I think you should see this," she called.

Hart rode over. He examined the shoes and swore under

his breath. "No village cobbler made these," he said heavily. "They can only be Phillip's."

They turned to look out over the lake. "What's that?" George said. Before Hart could react, she'd waded into the shallows and pulled up a sopping pair of nankeen breeches. Again they were boy-sized, and quality made by a professional tailor. Silently she passed them to Hart.

The shoes and breeches told a terrible tale.

Poor little boy. They must have thrown him in the lake; he was probably tied up. Or already dead. Though why they'd divested him of his shoes and breeches, she shuddered to imagine.

Gazing over the deceptively placid surface of the lake, she noticed a stream of bubbles rising to the surface near a clump of reeds. "Look, Hart, bubbles!" Without hesitation she dived in.

"No, don't—" Hart yelled, but she was already underwater.

He waited, anxiety rising. More bubbles rose, but there was no sign of George. He dived in after her, and found her caught underwater, fighting a snag that had caught her divided skirt and trapped her.

In a surge of fear and rage he ripped it free and they bobbed to the surface, George coughing and spluttering.

"Nobody there," she managed between coughs. She was filthy and dripping with lake weed.

He wanted to shake her. He pounded her on the back, scolding her fiercely. "You damned little fool, what the hell did you think you were doing, risking yourself like that? It's madness!"

"M'all right," she gasped and vomited up a gush of brown lake water.

"You are damned well not all right!" He stood over her furiously, helplessly, and when she'd finally stopped vomiting water, he lifted her into his arms and marched toward his horse.

"I can walk." She struggled weakly to get down.

"Shut up," he said savagely. "One more word or argument and I—I'll throttle you." She laughed weakly. He placed her carefully on the horse, and swung up behind her.

"I thought . . . the shoes, the breeches—"

"I know what you thought." He wanted to shake her and at the same time cradle her next to his heart and never let her go. Bad enough that he'd lost Phillip, but the thought of losing her . . .

"He's dead, isn't he?" she said.

Hart nodded. After a while he said, "The lake will have to be dragged."

She leaned into him then, her face pressed to his throat, and he realized she was weeping silently.

He carried her into the house, and called for hot water and a bath. "And then it's bed for you," he told her severely.

Chapter Twenty-one

❧

Seldom, very seldom, does complete truth belong to any
human disclosure; seldom can it happen that something is
not a little disguised or a little mistaken.

—JANE AUSTEN, *EMMA*

HART DECIDED TO RETURN THE MONEY TO THE BANK AND
leave George to take a nap. He didn't want such a large sum
of money lying around. On the way he passed the Glover
farm, and wondered whether there was any news of Danny.
Would there be two small bodies found when they dragged
the lake? He decided not to stop. If he had to speak to
Glover once more, and listen to the man deny any interest
in his stepson, he'd probably kill him.

Then he saw a small figure, lurking in the bushes near
the house. It was a boy, but not the boy, Peter, he'd seen
there before. This boy was taller. Hart rode closer. Good
God! It was Phillip!

"Phillip!" he cried. "Phillip!"

To his amazement, the boy backed warily away.

Did the boy not recognize him? He had, after all only
met him once. "Phillip, it's Everingham, your guardian."

Phillip started to run. Hart followed him. The boy darted
in and out of the bushes. Hart followed. It was uncomfortably like chasing a fox.

"Phillip, it's all right," Hart called. "You're not in trouble, I promise." But the boy took no notice. "Look at me when I'm talking to you, boy!" Hart roared in his best scary-duke voice. The boy hesitated and glanced back, giving Hart just enough opportunity to bend from the saddle and scoop the child up.

He yelled and kicked and struggled—what the hell was the matter with him? "I'm your guardian, you little idiot. Stop fighting. I'm not going to hurt you." But Phillip kept struggling.

Hart clamped the boy facedown across his saddle, like a hunting prize, and headed for Lakeside Cottage. All the way back he tried to get Phillip to talk to him, but all he got was stubborn resistance.

His relief at finding Phillip alive was tempered by frustration. The poor little chap was obviously badly traumatized. Lord knew what dreadful things his captors had put him through. Still, it was irritating to be welcomed like a kidnapper instead of a rescuer. But Hart had him safe now; he would be all right eventually. Children, they said, were resilient.

GEORGE'S BATH HAD REFRESHED HER. SHE HAD NO INTEREST in a nap, and since her husband had not come to bed with her, she was feeling restless. She watched him ride off, visibly despondent, to return the money. His failure to protect Phillip had shaken him to the core. She'd offered to go with him, but he'd scowled and ordered her again to take a nap, reminding her that she'd nearly drowned and needed to recover.

George wasn't so feeble. And it seemed to her that he was more shaken by her near drowning than she was.

She decided to go for a ride, shake the misery out and take Finn for a run. And perhaps see if she could find any sign of the other missing boy, Danny. Phillip's death was devastating, but Danny's fate would have nothing to do with kidnappers. His appalling home situation had moved her deeply. If there were any chance he might be alive . . .

Children were so precious. They needed to be nurtured and protected and loved, and at the same time encouraged to explore and develop their confidence. She would make sure her own children were not left to servants to raise, and, for the convenience of those servants, turned into obedient, responsible little adults before their time.

She avoided the depressing sight of the lake. It would be dragged tomorrow—Hart had gathered some willing locals.

Finn bounded ahead, sniffing and exploring, the plume of his tail waving like a happy banner. She smiled, watching him. She ought to get Hart a dog; dogs weren't only good company, they never failed to cheer her up.

As she was watching, he dived into a clump of bushes. A rabbit? A hare? She waited, hoping it wasn't a fox. But nothing, no animal came bursting out. Finn wasn't the watch-and-wait kind of dog—if it didn't run, he wasn't interested. So what was he doing?

She called him, but he didn't emerge. She called him again, and she heard a yip and a rustle, so he was in there. She dismounted and went to investigate. There was a kind of tunnel leading into the thicket where he and possibly other creatures had forced their way in. Bending double she entered.

And found Finn sitting with a small boy, a boy whose arms were wrapped around her dog. A boy about seven years old.

"Danny?" she said cautiously.

The child turned a dirty, suspicious face toward her. He peered out at her from behind Finn. "Who are you?"

"I'm George."

"No, you're not, you're a girl."

She laughed. "Yes, I'm a girl called Geor—" She broke off, suddenly realizing he'd spoken with quite a cultured accent. "But you're not Danny, are you?" Her voice broke as she said, "You're Phillip."

He glowered at her, neither confirming or denying it. But she was certain now. This was Phillip. She said gently, "It's all right, Phillip, I'm a friend. I'm married to the Duke of Everingham."

He frowned. "My guardian?" he said doubtfully.

Relief and gladness rushed through her. Phillip was alive, but still frightened and suspicious—and no wonder. She spoke in a calm, friendly voice. "We've been looking everywhere for you, Phillip. Are you all right?"

He hesitated. "There were bad men. Kidnappers."

"I know. But they've gone now."

His arms tightened around Finn. "Are you sure?"

She nodded. "Your guardian paid the ransom, but nobody collected it. They must have left. Did they let you go?"

He gave a funny secretive smile. "Not on purpose."

"You mean you escaped? That was clever of you—and very brave." She could hear her horse, grazing placidly outside Phillip's hiding place. "How about you come home with me now—back to Lakeside Cottage, I mean. I'm sure you must be hungry. Mrs. Harris will want to make you the biggest dinner with all your favorite things."

The mention of Mrs. Harris seemed to convince him to trust her. He followed her out of the thicket, and stopped dead when he saw the horse. "On a horse?" He gave her a troubled glance. "I can't ride."

"Don't worry, you'll be with me. I won't let you fall off. And later, if you want to, the duke and I will teach you to ride. Would you like that?"

He nodded. She mounted, then leaned down and held her hand out. "Take my hand, and when I say three, you jump as high as you can. I'll swing you up in front of me. One, two, three." And Phillip jumped.

Joy singing in her heart, George rode back to Lakeside Cottage, Phillip sitting up proudly in front of her. What a lovely surprise this was going to be for Hart.

As they neared the house, she saw him coming over the brow of the hill from the other direction, something bundled over the saddle in front of him. "There's the duke," she told Phillip. "What a fine surprise we're going to give him."

Both horses rounded the hedge at the same time and came to a halt. "Good God," Hart exclaimed. The bundle in front of Hart wriggled and, with Hart's aid, sat up.

They stared, unable to believe their eyes. On the saddle in front of each adult sat a small grubby urchin. George looked from one to the other and back. Small grubby *identical* urchins.

"Phillip?" Hart exclaimed.

"Danny?" said George.

"Danny," cried Phillip joyfully.

"Phil," Hart's urchin responded.

George and Hart stared at each other, then Hart shook his head. "We'll get to the bottom of this eventually, I'm sure—"

"But first, food and baths all round," George finished for him.

"WE WERE PLAYING A TRICK ON MR. JEPHCOTT," PHILLIP explained between mouthfuls as the two boys plowed through a mountain of food. Mrs. Harris had cooked up a storm, but she'd insisted on baths before dinner.

"We swapped clothes," Danny said. "He never even noticed. He doesn't even know which one of us is which."

"Has he gone?" Phillip asked.

That was a point. "I don't know," Hart said slowly. "I haven't seen him today at all."

"Me neither," George said. "In fact, I haven't seen him since yesterday."

Hart glanced at Mrs. Harris who was hovering maternally over the boys, and gave her a silent signal. She nodded and hurried out.

"So we were both dressed in the same kind of clothes— makin' him see double, you see—and I was all ready to cross the lawn—he was snoozing in the sun as usual—when someone grabbed me and shoved a bag over me head," Danny said. "I tried to yell, but they shoved a rag in me mouth, and tied me up and threw me into some kind of cart and took off with me."

"I saw it happen," Phillip said, "so of course I followed."

Hart frowned. "You didn't call for help?"

The two boys exchanged glances. "No," Phillip said. He was holding something back.

"Good thing too," Danny said, shoving a whole potato in his mouth. When he'd swallowed it, he added, "Wouldn'ta made any difference anyway."

"Why not?"

Again the two boys exchanged glances. "Are you sure Mr. Jephcott's not here anymore?"

"Mrs. Harris has gone to check," George assured him. "We'll know in a few moments. So go on—what happened next? I want to know how you escaped—I presume it was Danny who escaped?"

"Yes, I followed them," Phillip said, "and I saw where they took him. It was a little tumbledown shed over the back beyond the mill."

"So then what did you do?"

Again the boys hesitated, but at that moment, Mrs. Harris returned. "Jephcott's gone," she announced breathlessly. "All his things are gone too—he's made a clean sweep. One of the maids said she saw him creeping off yesterday morning—would you believe it? Without a word to anyone."

Phillip gave a satisfied nod. "I was all ready to go for help and tell people what I'd seen and where Danny was—"

"—and then he seen old Jephcott comin' right up to the shed where they had me trussed up like a Christmas goose—" Danny continued.

"Yes, and he knocked and then walked right in," Phillip said indignantly. "And half an hour later he came out again—"

"—and left me in there with those rotten bast—"

"Bad men, he means," Phillip interrupted hurriedly, with an apologetic glance at George. "So then I wondered, if Mr. Jephcott was in league with the kidnappers, who else might be involved?" He glanced at the housekeeper. "I'm sorry, Mrs. Harris. I didn't know who to trust."

"Never you mind, Master Phillip," she assured him warmly. "It weren't none of us. We've all been worried sick about you. That wicked man. I never liked him, you know.

None of us did. He thought himself so superior with his Latin and his Greek."

"I'm sorry to be suspicious," Phillip continued. "And for hiding. I didn't want anyone to find out that Danny wasn't me, because . . ." He hesitated.

Danny said bluntly, "Because he knew me old man wouldn't cough up a farthing for my sake."

"Yes, and then Danny would be in danger," Phillip said. "And he was my responsibility."

Hart nodded in approval. "You did the right thing."

"So how did you escape, Danny?" George asked.

Phillip grinned. "I stole a couple of bottles of brandy from the cellar. I know where the key is kept and I sneaked in one night. I left them near the shed, and when the men got drunk, I let Danny out."

"Clever boy!" George congratulated him.

"But what about your shoes and the breeches in the lake?" Hart asked after a moment.

Danny looked embarrassed. "Them shoes were too tight—my feet are bigger than Phil's, and after wearing them for near on a week, I was well rid of them."

"And the breeches?"

Shame filled Danny's eyes. He looked down and mumbled something inaudible. Phillip leaned forward and whispered in Hart's ear, "The bad men didn't always let him relieve himself in time. The breeches were soiled, so we threw them away. Danny stole back some of his old clothes."

Hart hoped he'd been able to keep his thoughts from his face. The swine, to shame a boy so, through sheer laziness. And then he had to steal back his own clothes.

"Well, all I can say is that you boys have behaved admirably—with courage, intelligence and good sense," Hart told them. "I'm very proud of you both."

The boys swelled visibly. "I was wondering . . ." Phillip began. "Danny doesn't really want to go back—"

"To that horrid man?" George interrupted, "I should think not! He will live with us, of course."

The duke, Phillip and Danny all stared at her.

"With *us*?" Hart queried gently.

"Naturally." Avoiding his eyes, she forged on. "We're not going to leave Phillip by himself in the country again, even though Mrs. Harris has been wonderful, and certainly Danny cannot go back to live with that vile creature who calls himself a stepfather. No, you boys will live with the duke and me. And Finn."

"Here?" Phillip asked carefully.

"No, I cannot believe it would be pleasant to remain in the place where you were almost kidnapped, and I don't imagine Danny will want to live close to his stepfather."

"No fear," Danny said. Phillip's eyes were wide.

"So that's settled. You're both coming to live with us at . . ." She finally met his eyes. "At the duke's place?"

"Yes, at my place," Hart said. The dazzling smile she gave him left him breathless.

THEY REPORTED THE KIDNAPPING TO THE LOCAL AUTHOR-ities, and Hart wrote off to engage a runner from Bow Street to track down Jephcott and his accomplices.

"His references were genuine," he told George, "but clearly the man was fed up with tutoring small boys and wanted to set himself up for a comfortable retirement."

That night in bed, after making love, George asked Hart if he minded her declaration that the boys would go with them. It had been a spur-of-the moment decision, and she didn't regret it for a second, but she was aware that she'd given him no choice.

"No, of course not," he assured her. "I wouldn't have expected anything else of you. The boys will be much bet-ter off living with you."

With *you*, she noted. Not with *us*.

It was a sobering reminder.

Two days later, they all removed to Everingham Abbey. As they arrived, staff spilled out of the front door and lined up to greet the duke. More than twenty people, all standing starched and straight; they were a daunting sight until George noticed the warm and genuine smiles that greeted the duke. He spoke to each one of them and introduced her to each by name.

He was loved here, she could see. But by his demeanor, she wasn't sure he knew it.

The two boys, once they'd recovered from the sheer size and awe-inspiring atmosphere of the ancient pile, took the duke's invitation to explore the place for themselves to heart.

They took to their new location with gusto, finding enough fascinating nooks and crannies indoors to delight and entertain young boys in wet weather, and a sprawling garden, a bubbling stream and a nearby forest to explore by sunshine.

George, too, was enthralled by its ancient archways and worn stone steps; the rich paneling; artwork in every room, amassed over multiple generations; the new sections grafted on to the old; the modern kitchen and the luxurious room set aside just for bathing.

It was a fascinating mix of eras and styles and she loved its eccentricity. Hart, when he showed her around the house, was apologetic about its sprawling inconvenience and the rabbit warren of hallways and corridors, especially in the old sections, but she could tell his diffidence masked a powerful love of this place.

The master bedroom was huge and a little intimidating, but once she'd passed the night with Hart, making love in the big old, extremely comfortable bed, she was reconciled to the heavy draperies and the general air of consequence. Once more the duke invited her to redecorate, but she wasn't up to that yet.

Besides, she had to remember that this wasn't to be her house; in the marriage settlements they'd agreed on, she was to get a house of her own. The thought weighed on her.

Danny, with an eye to future treats, ingratiated himself with the kitchen staff first, while Phillip introduced himself to the stable inhabitants. Every morning he raised some comment about life in the stables, indirectly and very politely reminding George of her offer to teach him how to ride. While after every meal, skinny little Danny gave the staff lavish compliments about the food.

It amused Hart. "Those boys will do well in life," he said to George after breakfast one day. "They know what they want and, each in his own way, goes after it; the subtle and the blatant."

On the second day George sent for her horse, Sultan, who she'd missed. Though the duke already had some lovely horses in his stables, none were suitable for small boys, so they took the boys off to a nearby farm and selected two well-mannered ponies suitable for boys just learning to ride. And when she heard about a litter of springer spaniel puppies in the neighborhood, she took the boys to choose a puppy each.

THE FOLLOWING MONTH WAS LIKE NOTHING THE DUKE had ever experienced. It wasn't at all how he'd imagined his honeymoon. Faint visions of gondolas and canals faded before the brisk domesticity of life at Everingham Abbey.

The arrival of two small energetic boys and one slender, energetic bride had livened up the old house considerably. It wasn't what he was used to, but he had to admit he enjoyed the change.

George had very decided ideas on how they would all spend their time. It was to be a holiday, she insisted. A holiday, not a honeymoon.

Acknowledging that Hart needed to deal with his correspondence and see to the supervision of the various estates he was responsible for, she graciously allowed him the mornings for that. The rest of the day—and the nights, she said with a sultry look—were hers.

Hart had no quarrel with that. Their lovemaking was . . . He had no words to describe it. Richer. Deeper. Moving him in ways he'd never dreamed possible.

Phillip, having discovered an interest in the pianoforte, was taking music lessons in the mornings, while George herself gave Danny his first lessons in reading, writing and arithmetic. The plan was for him to be caught up to Phillip by the time they would both go to school. Together, she told Hart firmly. When they were twelve or so.

After luncheon, the activities were all outdoors, making the most of the good weather. George and Hart were teaching the boys to ride—and to care for their own ponies. At first Danny had objected to having to groom and muck out his pony, thinking he was somehow being demeaned, but Hart had raised a brow and said coolly, "A gentleman cares for his animals first. There are times when a groom will care for your horse, but you must first know how to do it yourself—properly." After that, Danny had fallen to the work with a will.

Hart had never taught anyone to ride and he was surprised how proud he felt at each boy's progress. Phillip was careful and precise in following instructions, Danny was eager and occasionally reckless, but both boys were doing well.

And once the boys had taken possession of their puppies, they competed to have the best-trained dogs. As for Finn, he was at first dubious about the roly-poly little creatures who seemed to adore him and follow him around, but within the week he'd resigned himself to their attentions, even to letting them chew on his ears and feet and tail and clamber over his body. Until he'd had enough, and rose and with great dignity stalked away.

It was late summer. The weather was glorious, and they taught the boys to swim, the boys and Hart dressed in just their drawers, and George in drawers and a chemise. The boys were young enough not to notice how the garment clung, molding to her every slender curve, but Hart couldn't take his eyes off her. His body reacted predictably, but with the boys present, he had no option but to stand waist deep in the cold water and think of unexciting things. And wait until evening came and he could take her to bed at last.

Some days they rode out without the boys. They would swim, and picnic, and make love in the grass. He'd never made love in the open before. Neither had she. But it was glorious—as long as he remembered to take a rug.

Time flew. Venice faded completely from his mind.

"They're gaining so much confidence—have you noticed?" George said to him one afternoon as they watched the boys putting their ponies through their paces. "Phillip has been almost naughty several times."

Hart gave her an incredulous glance. "You're happy that he's becoming naughty?"

"Of course. It's healthy in a small boy. He was so painfully well-behaved and responsible before."

Hart frowned. "You say 'responsible and well-behaved' as if they're bad things."

She grinned, understanding. "In an adult, responsibility is admirable—even necessary—but in a small child it's . . . it's unnatural. Poor little Phillip is afraid of making mistakes—even small, insignificant ones. But how can anyone learn if they don't try things and make the occasional mistake?"

"Then I suppose you're positively delighted with Danny," he said sardonically.

She laughed. "Danny is making progress too. He's not nearly so prickly and he's really only rebellious if he's uncertain or on edge—haven't you noticed? But he learns from Phillip—the respect and care both boys have for each other is wonderful—and they both look up to you enormously, Danny especially. He is starting to model himself on you, you realize."

"Model himself on *me*?" Hart watched the scruffy urchin urging his pony over low jumps with loud yells more suitable to a savage. He could see no evidence of any modeling. "I hardly think so."

"It's true," she said tranquilly. "Both boys admire you tremendously. And they're both making wonderful progress." She raised her voice. "Oh, well done, Danny. Now you, Phillip."

Hart watched her calling encouragement to the two orphaned boys. If they were making progress it was because of her. Both boys adored her. To them she was some magical combination of mother, sister, mentor and playfellow.

And Hart? He was purely dazzled by her.

Family life. He'd experienced nothing like it in his life. She hadn't grown up in a family either, so how did she know how to do this? Make four very disparate people, including two very different children, happy? But somehow she did.

He'd only married to get an heir, and he'd chosen Georgiana Rutherford because the very sight of her swamped him with desire. And because she was independent and self-sufficient and wouldn't be a drain on his time.

But she was so much more than he'd expected.

"By the way, I've discovered who Danny's father is," he told her quietly.

Her head whipped around. "Who?"

"Take a guess." They'd speculated about it in bed often enough, but there was no proof.

"Phillip's father?"

He nodded. "I discovered the evidence in the estate record. Lakeside Cottage was only part of one of my cousin's minor estates. He sold it off piecemeal, a chunk at a time to pay his gambling debts, retaining only the main house by the end. I suppose it would have been the next to go if he hadn't died. There is a note in the estate records, just over seven years ago, noting a tenant's cottage and small farm acreage to be transferred to the use of Judith Glover and her child."

"Danny and his mother."

He nodded. "Of course I had no idea of this when I sent Phillip to live at Lakeside Cottage." He glanced at the boys racing each other around the paddock, whooping and laughing. Half brothers. "A mistake that ended well, I suppose."

He lowered his voice. "The interesting thing was the phrasing of the document. The cottage and farm were transferred 'to the use of Judith Glover and her child *for their lifetime.*'"

"But Judith's dead. And Danny's no longer there."

He nodded. "I had the document checked over by my

legal man, and I have every right to throw that brute Glover off the property."

She clapped her hands. "Oh, that would be wonderf—" She broke off. "But what about that poor downtrodden woman and those little children? I can't see Glover putting himself out to support them if he was put off the farm. He's the type to look after himself first, and abandon them to their own devices."

Hart smiled. He knew she'd react like this. "I've been giving that some thought. The farm is Danny's by right, and though he doesn't want to live there now, it would be to his advantage to own some property in the future. I can transfer the property permanently into his name, and rent it out to the Glovers."

She nodded. "I suppose that's the sensible thing to do. I just wish . . . But there are the children to think of. And though the man is a brute, I've never heard Danny say anything bad about the woman."

Nor much good, Hart thought, but he supposed the woman was too downtrodden to withstand her husband's orders. "I could offer them tenancy of the farm, but only in Mrs. Glover's name. Then, technically at least, she would be in charge."

Her eyes lit up. "What a marvelous suggestion, Hart. Horrible Glover will then have to defer—at least in theory— to his wife, and if he leaves, she'll still have the security of a home." She sobered. "But I think you should talk about it privately with Mrs. Glover before you do anything. Just in case Glover reacts badly and takes it out on her."

He nodded. "Good idea. You can come with me. She'll probably feel more comfortable talking to a woman. But I'll tell the boys about their relationship at teatime. I think they'll be thrilled to find they're half brothers. I'll discuss the question of the farm with Danny too. He's young, but he's shrewd."

Chapter Twenty-two

❧

You pierce my soul. I am half agony, half hope… I have loved none but you.
—JANE AUSTEN, *PERSUASION*

A MONTH. THEY'D BEEN MARRIED A MONTH ALREADY. George found it hard to believe. In some ways it felt like they'd been married forever; in another it felt just a short time, the time had flown so swiftly.

It wasn't quite an anniversary, but she thought it deserved a little celebration.

After all, she had promised to rub, cherish and *olé* him. There had been quite a lot of rubbing—she grinned to herself—and the cherishing had been lovely too. Now it was time for some celebrating.

She woke early and chivvied him out of bed for a dawn ride—and not the kind he wanted. "On horseback," she said, and he'd groaned and turned over. And then, grumbling, got out of bed.

It was a perfect late summer morning and the ride was glorious. On returning home, she went upstairs for a quick bath, and he went into the library where his mail awaited him.

Joining him at the breakfast table, she noticed he looked rather grim. "Is anything the matter?" she asked.

He nodded. "I have to return to London. I can't stay down here any longer. I have important things to deal with and I can't attend to them from here."

"You're leaving?"

He nodded. "In the morning." He barely looked at her, just frowned at the documents on his right. He rarely brought correspondence to the breakfast table.

A cold lump formed in her belly. "Tomorrow?"

He glanced up. "Yes. I'm sorry if you don't like it, but this little sojourn, delightful as it has been, must come to an end."

The lump hardened, and something was blocking her throat. "What about the boys?"

"What about the boys?" But it wasn't really a question. His blank look confirmed that as far as he was concerned the boys were her business.

George's porridge congealed slowly in the bowl. He was saying it was over. The honeymoon—the honey month— was over. And he was returning to his life in London, and she was going on—to what?

And the terrible thing was, this had been her idea. She was the one who in the settlements had specified a house of her own, a house in the country, separate from the duke. She hadn't done anything about looking for a house yet.

"Can we stay here for a while? The boys and I?"

His brows snapped together. "Here? You want to stay here?"

She nodded. "I don't have a house of my own yet. I suppose we could go to my uncle's place, Ashendon Court, for a while, if you don't like us staying here."

He stared at her for a long moment, his expression unreadable. "No, stay here as long as you like," he said coldly and returned to his correspondence.

"If you'll excuse me," George blurted, "I have things to do." She hurried from the room and made for the privacy of her bedchamber—only she didn't have a bedroom of her own. There was no privacy here. Everything in it evoked his presence.

Those wretched settlements. She'd thought back then that it was how she wanted things, but now she'd changed. She'd done what she'd thought impossible—fallen in love with the duke. But she wasn't going to go back on her promises.

He said he'd want conjugal visits. She would respect that—and if she dreamed about him every night, well, wouldn't that be almost as good as having him in her bed?

No. She knew the difference now. And it wasn't just his lovemaking she'd miss.

Or the look in his eyes when he was thinking about taking her to bed. Or the way his voice would deepen and turn to warm, dark chocolate. And melt her from the inside out.

It was also the low-murmured conversations they had in the dark, about nothing much, just the day's events and stray thoughts and plans. He listened, really listened.

And she'd miss waking up in the night and feeling his big warm body lying spooned around her on chilly nights, or sprawled in relaxed abandon just a fingertip away. And the scent of him, not just his cologne, or his fresh-pressed linen, but the intoxicating man smell of him, like nobody else, unique and himself.

The duke. Others saw his pride, his arrogance, his cold control—the man she'd imagined he was when she first met him. But now she knew the real man beneath the stern facade, the man who cold-bloodedly entrapped her and proceeded to seduce her—and not just in the bedchamber.

He was a man who took his responsibilities seriously, who valued honor and honesty, who would put off a much desired honeymoon in Venice to search for a small lost boy he hardly knew. And then take in that boy and his illegitimate half brother as his own responsibilities. And teach them how to be men.

A man who would take a half-wild, prickly, suspicious, difficult, contrary, lanky, flat-chested, boyish female, put up with her wild starts and even try to understand them—and then marry her and cherish her as nobody ever in her life had cherished her.

She dashed the tears from her eyes. She would *not* become a watering pot. All his life, his mother had tried to manipulate him with emotion. George would not do the same. She would honor the agreement she'd so foolishly made. Calmly, reasonably and without fuss.

And if he wanted her out of his way, living in the country as they'd agreed, while he did whatever he did in London—and she would not even mind if he wanted to see those dreadful women who pursued him so shamelessly—well, yes, she did mind, she wanted to wring their scrawny, bejeweled necks!—but she would try not to show it. She would try to be dignified, as a duchess should. At least while he was watching.

She would remain in the country with the boys. It wouldn't be a hardship—she loved the countryside.

And if she missed him, as she would—terribly—well, who was it who'd made that stupid condition in the first place? What was that saying? *Be careful what you wish for.*

This was what he'd wanted, what they'd agreed to, after all. And though it would half kill her to let him go, she would do it. Because she loved him, and wanted him to have everything he wanted. And she refused to be a millstone around his neck.

They made love several times that night, and it was wonderful and terrible, bittersweet and achingly moving. They didn't talk much. George had no words; she was afraid if she tried to say anything, it would all spill out in a terrible emotional flood, and she'd be no better than his mother, trying to make him stay when he wanted to leave.

And he was never terribly chatty in bed.

But, oh, every touch, every caress . . . She did her best to save them up in her mind, to keep for later and revisit when he was gone, but each time he took her to the edge . . . and over . . . and her awareness splintered into glorious rainbow-colored shards.

HART'S BAGS WERE PACKED, AND THE CARRIAGE WAS WAIT-ing. They'd made love at dawn, and it had left him feeling empty, completely shattered.

But she, she seemed calm and organized and dignified. She'd arranged food and drink for the journey, as if he were a child being sent off to school. The boys, solemn and serious and looking unhappy and bewildered, shook his hand like little men, and then she sent them back inside.

He was gutted by the ease with which she was preparing to wave him off, out of her life. But he had no leg to stand on. He was the blasted fool who'd signed the blasted settlement documents agreeing to her blasted conditions.

He hated those conditions now.

But he'd trapped her into marriage in the first place, and he owed it to her now to give her the freedom she desired. At least he'd insisted on conjugal visits. But, oh, how would he ever bear long months without her? Or weeks. And not just in bed.

He'd always believed he was a naturally solitary fellow. She'd changed all that.

She'd even taught him to enjoy the company of two rambunctious little boys.

George was the sun around who they all rotated, the source of all warmth and life.

But Hart had always prided himself on his control and he wasn't about to crumble now and make a fool of himself. And entrap her into the kind of marriage she had explained quite clearly that she didn't want.

He kissed her good-bye, and if it was a little desperate and needy and he could hardly make himself let go of her, well, that couldn't be helped. It was nothing to what he really felt.

He climbed into the carriage, took a deep breath and rapped on the roof. With a jerk the carriage set off. Hart didn't look out the window. He hated good-byes, didn't want to see her standing there, waving, her lovely gray eyes bright with unshed tears . . .

Bright with unshed tears?

Unshed tears?

He rapped loudly on the roof of the carriage, and without waiting for it to stop he threw open the door and jumped down.

George took a few steps toward him. "Did you forget something?"

He took a deep breath. "Yes. You."

She stared at him, her expression unreadable.

"I don't want to leave you, George. I don't want us to live in separate rooms, let alone separate houses or separate towns." He took another deep breath, and forced the words out that had been stuck in his throat for so long. "I want us to stay together, in sickness and in health, as long as we both shall live."

"You do?" she whispered.

"I do. I love you, George—oof!" He staggered back, battling for balance as he hung on to his wife, who had run at him full pelt and hurled herself bodily into his arms. She wrapped her legs around his waist and clung to him, kissing him frantically, plastering his face with kisses. "Oh, I love you, Hart, I love you so much, I know you didn't want love but—"

"Who said I didn't want love?"

She pulled back a little. "You did."

"I can't have been such an idiot."

She gave him a misty smile. "You were. We both were. I didn't want marriage and now I can't imagine life without you." She kissed him again and he thought his heart would burst.

With George still wrapped around him, planting small kisses on every available piece of skin, he carried her inside and marched straight up the stairs to their bedroom.

They made love again, and afterward, shared the thoughts and feelings they'd bottled up so long, too careful, too respectful of what they imagined the other had wanted.

"When you said you had to go to London, I thought you meant that was the end—you said, you actually *said* it was the end of our delightful sojourn. What else was I to think?"

"Not that. I'm a clod, a stupid, unaware clod. I do need to go to London, but all I meant was that it was the end of our time here. Our time, not my time. I'd assumed we would all go to London together. But when you asked to stay behind . . ."

He hauled her close and said into her hair, "I felt like I'd been kicked."

She stroked his neck tenderly. "Why didn't you say anything?"

"I trapped you into marriage in the first place. I wasn't going to force you to stay with me, just because I . . ."

"Because you . . ?"

"Because I was madly, deeply, thoroughly and permanently in love with you."

"Oh, that's lovely." Her eyes glittered with tears and she kissed him again. "I've known for ages that I love you, but I didn't want to be like your mother and use emotion to manipulate you. I would rather die than force you to stay when you didn't want to."

He laughed. "Anyone less like my mother, I couldn't imagine."

After a while, she murmured, "It's exactly a month since we were married. I'd planned to *olé* you."

He moved suggestively against her. "Oh, I feel very *oléd*."

She laughed. "They turned out to be rather good wedding vows, don't you think?"

"I doubt the bishop would agree, but I'm perfectly satisfied. More than satisfied." He kissed her again. "O*lé!*"

Epilogue

*You are invited to a ball to celebrate the marriage of
the Duke and Duchess of Everingham
at Everingham House
in London.*

GEORGE WAS FINDING IT WAS EASIER TO BE A DUCHESS than she'd feared. She had only to express a wish, and it was done. The duke had an army of servants eager to provide their new mistress with whatever she wanted.

The Everingham House ballroom glittered and gleamed. Decorated in green, cream and silver, with ferns, pale orchids and other white flowers from the duke's own conservatories, and silver-painted branches tied with scarlet ribbons, the air was fragrant with the scent of flowers and the tang of beeswax.

George took one last look at her reflection and nodded. Tonight, at Hart's request, she was dressed in scarlet again, a new ball dress, and the rubies he'd given her on her wedding day.

Her heart was so full. She was happier than she'd ever dreamed was possible. She had a big sprawling family she loved and who loved her, a smaller instant family of boys, dogs and horses—Sultan had been bred to several of the duke's mares. And, best of all, she was married to a tall, stern, arrogant, beautiful man who adored her, and demonstrated it daily—and nightly—in so many ways.

And the blessings kept coming.

Earlier in the week, baby Bertie had been christened, with George and Hart as his godparents. And then, immediately afterward, in a move that surprised many, young Danny Glover was also christened—and with the same godparents.

"The lad has never been christened, and it will do him no harm to be known as godson to the Duke and Duchess of Everingham," Hart had told George when he planned it. She'd hugged him. It was a generous and thoughtful move on his part. The connection would do much to ameliorate the disadvantage of Danny's birth.

Her coldhearted duke; she'd been so wrong about him.

And now there was to be a grand ball.

"You look stunning," Hart said from the doorway. "Ready?"

Arm in arm, they walked downstairs, to where their family and closest friends had gathered for dinner before the ball. They were all there, everyone who'd ever mattered to her—even Martha looking proud and stylish in her new bronze silk bombazine dress. Heaven knew how Hart had persuaded her to come to London, but he had.

At George's request, they entered the dining room informally and seated themselves around the table however they wished. This was just for family and friends. Champagne was poured, and Hart was about to give the signal for the food to be brought in when George tapped him on the arm, then rose to her feet.

"I know it's not done, but we are all family here, and I want to make a speech," she said. Aunt Agatha lifted her lorgnette and pursed her lips.

"I want to propose a toast," George continued. "To my darling Martha, who raised me from an infant and was the closest thing to a mother I ever had, loving and long-suffering and patient." She turned a mock severe glance at Phillip and Danny, who had been allowed to attend their first grown-up dinner and were sitting in their best clothes, trying not to fidget. "Boys, you are *not* to ask Martha about anything I did when I was a girl." The boys turned speculative gazes on Martha, who was simultaneously wiping her eyes and chuckling.

"To Cal, who brought me kicking and yelling—literally—into the Rutherford family and made me a lady—yes, I know, Aunt Agatha, only in the technical sense, but it was the first I knew I had a title."

Everyone laughed.

"Cal, you have also been loving and long-suffering and even *almost* patient at times."

Everyone laughed again.

"To Emm, who became part mother, part sister, beloved friend and mentor. You might not have succeeded in making me into a lady but you showed me what a true lady was." Cal who, unfashionably, was sitting beside his wife, kissed Emm's hand.

"To my sisters of the heart, my aunts, Lily and Rose, who were the first real friends I ever had. And to their husbands, Edward and Thomas, my brothers-in-law of the heart."

"To Aunt Dottie, full of love and wisdom and who is the living embodiment of how to live a happy life." Her smile took in Logan, who'd traveled to London with Aunt Dottie and was hovering behind her chair, acting as her own personal waiter.

"To Aunt Agatha, who also tried to make me into a proper lady, and whose auntly interference accidentally resulted in my happiness—but don't do it again! Interfere, I mean."

There was more laughter at that. Aunt Agatha frowned, then gave a tight little smile and preened a little.

"To my grandfathers of the heart, dear Lord Galbraith and Sir Humphrey." George smiled at Edward's grandfather and at Emm's father, Sir Humphrey Westwood, who wasn't really all that close—he was something of a hermit—but she couldn't leave the poor old fellow out.

George turned to the duke's mother. "To my new mama-in-law, who taught me . . ." She paused mischievously. The duke's mother tensed. ". . . to look beneath the surface. And who I hope will forgive me for making her into a *dowager* duchess." The duke's mother grimaced slightly, then pasted a false smile on her face.

She would remarry quickly to be rid of the aging title "dowager," Hart had told George earlier. Apparently it was a sure thing. Sinc had a bet on it.

George smiled at Sir Lionel and Lady Peplowe and their daughter Penny, who had Thomas's friend, Mr. Oliver Yelland, on one side and Mr. Sinclair on the other. "And to my dear friends. What a gift friendship is. Thank you."

"Finally I want to welcome the next generation, little Bertie, my godson, and Phillip and Danny, the two newest members of the family. And"—she gave Rose a misty smile—"to the babies yet to come."

She raised her glass. "For most of my life I never knew what it was like to have a family—or friends, really, except for animals—and now"—her voice broke and she had to choke out the last words—"now I am rich in both family and friends—all of you who are here tonight." Her eyes filled. "Oh, drat it. Hart?" She put out her hand, and her husband placed his handkerchief in it.

There was a scattering of laughter and a few more handkerchiefs produced to wipe eyes.

The duke rose to his feet. "To complete the toast on my wife's behalf, when I first proposed marriage—"

"You never did, actually," she muttered sotto voce, and he laughed and caught her hand in his.

"—I didn't know much about families, but my beloved wife has taught me that family is created not just through marriage and by the joining of bloodlines. A family—a true family—can also be built through acceptance, trust and, most importantly, through the power of love. So, a toast: To my wife, to our friends and family, and to the power of love."

"To my husband," George added. "And to the power of love."

They all raised their glasses. "To the power of love."

*   *   *

THE BALL WAS GOING BEAUTIFULLY AND EVERYTHING WAS perfect. George had just popped out the back to let Finn and the puppies out. In a few minutes, her husband would come looking for her for the supper dance, a waltz. And later they had plans to meet in the library and reenact their first kiss.

She was coming back in through the servants' entrance when a movement caught her eye. Out in the deserted kitchen courtyard, Aunt Dottie and Logan were dancing to the music from the ballroom. George watched, smiling, as they twirled together in dance steps all their own, but graceful and full of joy.

"What are you doing in here, George? Hart is looking for you for the supper dan— Oh, my goodness!" Rose broke off, staring.

"Is that Aunt Dottie *and Logan*?" Lily peered over Rose's shoulder.

The music ended, and Rose and Lily gasped as Logan twirled Aunt Dottie around, one last time, then drew her close and kissed her. Aunt Dottie's arms twined around his neck and she kissed him back, as passionate as any girl.

Her words came back to George. *With the right man, my love, a woman is always in season.* George understood what she meant now.

"Aunt Dottie *and Logan*?" Lily exclaimed again.

"Hush!" George whispered urgently. "It's a secret. And if you tell a soul, it will ruin everything."

"But how long has this been going on?" Rose asked.

George smiled. "Since Aunt Dottie was fifteen and Logan was eighteen."

"That long?" Lily exclaimed. "But that's—"

"Forever," George said softly. "She says it will be that way for each of us too. She has—"

"One of her *feelings*," they all chorused. Linking arms, the three young ladies tiptoed back to the ballroom, to where their husbands were waiting.

ABOUT THE AUTHOR

Anne Gracie is the award-winning author of the Chance Sisters Romances, which include *The Summer Bride*, *The Spring Bride*, *The Winter Bride* and *The Autumn Bride*, and the Marriage of Convenience Romance series, including *Marry in Scandal*, *Marry in Haste* and *Marry in Secret*. She spent her childhood and youth on the move. The roving life taught her that humor and love are universal languages and that favorite books can take you home, wherever you are. Anne started her first novel while backpacking solo around the world, writing by hand in notebooks. Since then, her books have been translated into more than eighteen languages and include Japanese manga editions (which she thinks is very cool) and audio editions. In addition to writing, Anne promotes adult literacy, flings balls for her dog, enjoys her tangled garden and keeps bees. Visit her online at annegracie.com. You can also subscribe to her newsletter.

Ready to find
your next great read?

Let us help.

Visit prh.com/nextread

Penguin
Random
House